WITHDRAWN

"What part of 'mage' did you not understand?" asked Briar.

He reached into the sling on the ground next to him. Taking out a seed ball, he flipped it to the edge of the firelight closest to the road. It burst, immediately sinking roots into the ground. The vines shot up and out, sprouting long thorns as they grew. By the time they stopped, they were three feet tall, with thick stems forming large curls around one another. Even in the flickering firelight, Parahan could see the four-inch thorns.

Fascinated, Parahan walked toward the plant. "You could kill a man with that," he said, his voice cracking.

"We don't keep them for toys," Briar replied.

BATTLE MAGIC

TAMORA PIERCE

SCHOLASTIC INC.

Copyright © 2013 by Tamora Pierce
www.tamorapierce.com

This book was originally published in hardcover by Scholastic Press in 2013.

All rights reserved. Published by Scholastic Inc., *Publishers since 1920*. SCHOLASTIC and associated logos are trademarks and/or registered trademarks of Scholastic Inc.

The publisher does not have any control over and does not assume any responsibility for author or third-party websites or their content.

ISBN 978-0-439-84298-3

10 9 8 7 6 5 4 3 2 1   15 16 17 18 19

Printed in the U.S.A.   40
First printing 2015

The text type was set in Sabon MT.

Book design by Christopher Stengel

To the veterans:

Family and not,

Friends and not,

Past, present, future,

Because William Tecumseh Sherman was right

And war is all hell.

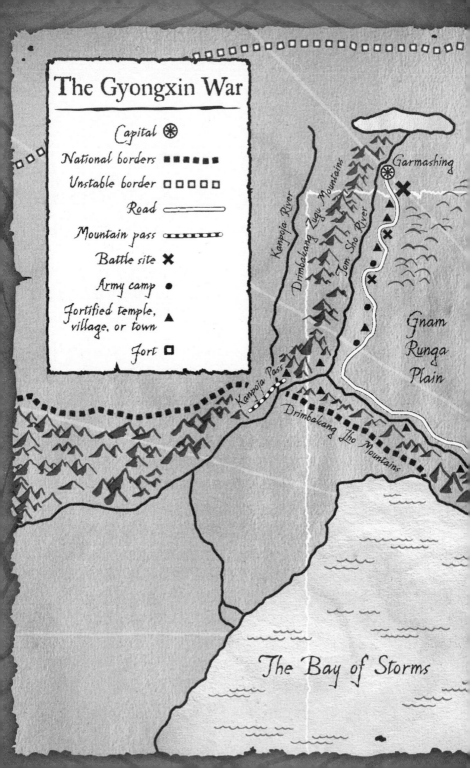

The Gyongxin War

Capital ⊛

National borders ▰▰▰▰▰

Unstable border ▢▢▢▢▢

Road ═══════

Mountain pass ⬭⬭⬭⬭⬭

Battle site ✖

Army camp ●

Fortified temple, village, or town ▲

Fort ▢

Kanpoia River

Drimbakang Zugu Mountains

Jom Sho River

Garmashing

Gnam Runga Plain

Kanpoia Pass

Drimbakang Iho Mountains

The Bay of Storms

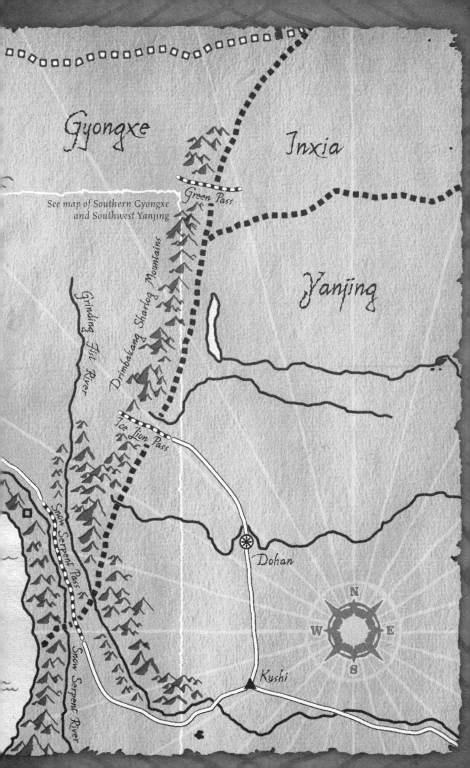

Gyongxe

Inxia

Green Pass

See map of Southern Gyongxe
and Southwest Yanjing

Yanjing

Drimbakang Sharlog Mountains

Grinding Fist River

Ice Lion Pass

Snow Serpent Pass

Dohan

N
W   E
S

Snow Serpent River

Kushi

BATTLE MAGIC

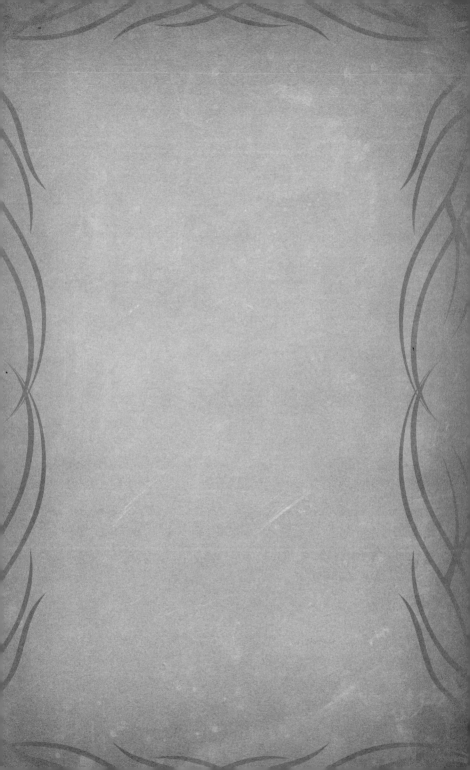

CHAPTER
ONE

Two boy-men sat on the river's eastern bank, where an open-fronted tent gave them shelter from the chilly spring wind. It whistled down the canyon, making the banners around them snap.

Briar Moss was the older of the two, sixteen and a fully accredited mage of the Living Circle school in Emelan. He was the foreigner, his skin a light shade of bronze, his nose long and thin, his eyes a startling gray-green in this land of brown-eyed easterners. He wore a green silk quilted tunic patterned with light green willow leaves, gold-brown quilted breeches, and the calf-high soft boots that were popular in the mountains. He sat cross-legged on cushions with a traveling desk on his lap, but his eyes were fixed just now on the events across the river.

There five shamans from the Skipping Mountain Goat Tribe stood before a sheer rock face on the cliff opposite Briar and his companion. Crouched near to the shamans were two horn players, a drummer, and three players of singing bowls. The musicians sounded their instruments. Briar would not call what they produced "music." The shamans — three men and two women in dark brown homespun robes — shuffled, turned, and hopped, ringing the small cymbals that were fixed to their hands. As they did, Briar started to feel a quiver under his rump. The longer the shamans danced, the more pronounced the quiver grew.

"What are they *doing*?" he asked the boy who sat nearby. "Aren't you worried?"

The God-King looked up from his own desk. The ruler of Gyongxe was an eleven-year-old boy with the ruddy bronze skin, long brown eyes, and short, wide nose of his people. He was dressed even more simply than the shamans in an undyed, black-bordered long-sleeved tunic, undyed quilted breeches, and black boots. Like most Gyongxin boys and girls, he wore his shiny black hair cut very short, with one exception. From the moment he had been chosen as God-King, he had grown the hair at the crown of his head long. He wore it in a braid, strung with rings of precious metals or semiprecious stones, each a symbol of the eleven gods he served. He also wore eleven earrings, six in one ear, and five in the other, made of the same materials.

"Why should I be worried? I told you what they're doing," the God-King reminded Briar. "They're calling a statue for their temple out of the cliff. It does involve a little bit of shaking."

Briar looked at the ink in the dish by his side. It quivered, too. "What if the cliff falls on us?" he demanded. "How do you know they're doing it right?"

The God-King chuckled. "They always do it right. That's

why there's more than one dancer, so if one gets a step wrong, the others correct for it. People have been getting statues from Gyongxe's stone for generations, Briar. They haven't pulled the cliffs down yet." He nodded to a waiting messenger and held up a hand for that young woman's scroll.

Briar scowled at the river, then at the dancing shamans. "This kind of religion is too odd for me," he muttered to himself.

He looked at the group of people near the shamans, trying to spot his student, Evvy. There she was with some of the local stone mages and the warriors who had escorted the shamans. Evvy was standing far too close to the cliff for Briar's liking. Suddenly he grinned. First Dedicate Dokyi, head of Gyongxe's Living Circle temple and a stone mage himself, wound a big fist in Evvy's tunic and gently towed her back from the cliff. Ever since Briar and his companions had arrived in Garmashing between blizzards four months ago, the busy First Dedicate had made time in his day to instruct Evvy. That morning he had told Briar that he, too, wanted to see how the shamans worked — it was very different from the way the scholar-mages did their magic — and so it would be his pleasure also to keep an eye on Evvy.

Briar was grateful. Evvy had frustrated the few other Earth dedicates they had met who specialized in stone magic. Like Dokyi, they worked their magic with charts, books, and spoken words, letting the magic they were born with pass through stones that responded. Evvy, like Briar and Briar's mentor Dedicate Rosethorn, drew her magic directly from the outside world. Stones gave Evvy her power, just as plants gave their magic to Briar and Rosethorn. Dokyi at least had spent years with the sha-mans and in other lands. He could adjust to a mage who worked

3

in a different way. He could show Evvy the books, charms, and spells of stone magic that could strengthen what she did. He could also sense when she tried to experiment on her own and stop her before things got out of hand. His special stones helped him with that.

"Should I make Evvy come here?" Briar asked the God-King, who was reading his message scroll.

"Hmm?" The younger boy looked up and grinned. "Let her stay. Dokyi can handle her. Ah, they make progress."

If "progress" meant "more noise," Briar agreed. Small rocks and sand fell down the cliff face, though nothing appeared to land on the shamans, musicians, or other mages who waited there. Briar suspected that Evvy was sending the stones away from the people, particularly when he saw one large rock arc away from the cliff to drop in the river.

Needing something to occupy his hands, Briar picked up one of a number of stones that Evvy had left with him before she had crossed the river with Dokyi. She was always collecting bits of rock and handing them to him or Rosethorn while she gathered more. Before they moved on there would be a painful session at which she would have to choose the pieces she could not do without and those she would have to abandon.

After nearly two years in Evvy's company, Briar knew limestone when he held it. The surprise lay in the image embedded deep in its surface: a curved section of leaf much like a fern. Interestingly, it was unlike any fern that Briar knew — and after five years of Rosethorn's teaching, he knew many. He stared at the cliff across the river, not really noticing the twenty-foot-tall rectangular crack that was writing itself into the rock face.

As he would if the fossil were a living plant, Briar reached for it with his magic, only to find nothing. The limestone held an image, but no remainder of the plant that had left it. Briar glared at it and reached for another piece of stone. It was unmarked, but the third rock he examined gripped a fossil much like a sardine.

"This is a sea fish," Briar muttered. Life near the docks from early childhood had taught him the look of salt- and freshwater fish, flesh and bone.

"Eons ago all the Gyongxin flatland was a sea," murmured the God-King. Slowly he straightened. His pen fell from his hand. "Then the Drimbakang mountain gods were born. They shoved their molten bodies up against the shore and dragged the Realms of the Sun with them." He said it as if chanting an ancient tale, half awake, half sleeping.

Briar tried not to shiver. It felt as if every hair on his body were standing.

The God-King continued in that unearthly voice. "Higher they drove the shores and the sea. Greater they grew, the youngest gods, clawing at the sky, rising toward the Sun and the Moon and the Stars. When they could grow no more, when they stood taller than any other mountain gods, the sea drained away between them, seeking its ocean mother. The immense shoreline forests of palm, cactus, and fern withered. Only firs, spruces, larches, junipers, and hemlocks thrive here, and rarely on the open plateau. Here the gods see everything. Gyongxe has nowhere to hide from the gods of this world." He slumped. Briar was almost afraid to breathe until the younger boy blinked and straightened. Rubbing the back of his neck he looked at Briar sheepishly. "Did I go off? They never give me any warning, you know. I've told them and told them that it frightens people when they grab me, but gods and spirits don't really understand fear."

"Do they do that to you often?" Briar whispered, goose bumps rippling all across his skin.

"Often enough. The land is crowded with them, what with one thing and another, and I can never tell when one of them will work through me."

A large crash split the air. The God-King jumped to his feet with a whoop. "There we go!" he cried as if he had just won a wager.

Briar remembered what had brought them to this cold ledge on a chilly morning. Setting aside the boy's tale to ponder later, he looked across the river.

Rock tumbled from a rectangular hole at least twenty feet high in the cliff's face, cascading around a solid shape at its center. The shamans continued to dance and the musicians to play as they backed toward the place where Evvy and the other observers stood. Briar whistled in silent admiration: He knew *he* couldn't dance and walk backward, yet the shamans and their musical helpers never faltered. Only Evvy moved, walking forward around the line of shamans. Dokyi lunged to grab her again and missed. Evvy took a place on the riverbank, in front of whatever was going on in the cliff, and held out her hands.

Briar fought to stand, spilling the tray of ink. He ignored it, but he could not ignore it when the God-King grabbed one of his arms.

"Stop," the younger boy ordered in a voice that froze Briar where he stood. "She will be *fine*. Watch."

He released Briar, who instantly found he could move again. Rather than continue to try to reach his student, Briar waited.

He wasn't quite sure if Evvy made any noise. The racket caused by the grinding, collapsing wall of rocks drowned out any other sound except, of course, for the God-King's voice. Briar wondered if Evvy might not be chanting a spell, though. He knew she was working her magic, because the tumbling rock split on either side of the opening it made, like curtains before a window. That was pure Evvy. Neat piles of broken stone grew from the falling rock on either side of the rectangular gap in the cliff. At its heart stood a pair of embracing, human-like, stone skeletons. As the heaped boulders and chips in front of them shifted to either side, the twenty-foot-tall skeletons walked out of the cliff.

Evvy wavered. She was trying to do too much at once. Worried, Briar stepped up to the edge where the tent was pitched, then halted again. Dokyi had reached the girl. He stood next to Evvy, writing signs on the air as he worked spells of his own. She straightened, able to control the falling stone again with Dokyi's help.

The skeletons, which had paused when she seemed about to fall over, resumed their walk away from the cliff. One of the two skulls looked curiously at Evvy and Dokyi while the other scanned the riverside behind them, the gap in the cliff, and then the shamans and their musicians. An arm from that skeleton reached around to tap the skull that had cocked its head as it stared at Evvy. When that skull turned to glare at the other, the tapping hand pointed to the shamans. Both skeletons lumbered toward the dancers.

Briar looked at the God-King. "What are they for, the statues? I don't think you said."

The God-King squinted at the dancing skeletons. "Such things are a promise from this realm to those who build their temples here. They are our blessing on the temples, and a sign of our protection. They tell invaders that the temple is guarded by the gods of Gyongxe as well as the gods of the temple where the statues stand."

Seemingly unafraid and without missing a step, the dancers and musicians continued to back up, dancing or playing as they went. The warriors mounted horses to form a half circle around them. Other members of their group that handled the wagon they had brought helped the musicians into it. As smoothly as if they often traveled this way, the warriors and wagon set off in the lead, their half circle ending with the dancers just inside. The two skeletons, arms around each other's stone spine waist, came last of all.

Dokyi turned to Evvy and bent until they were face-to-face. He grabbed her by the ears and pressed his forehead to hers. Briar wasn't sure if he was trying to scold Evvy or just knock two rock heads together. Thinking that he ought to intervene before Evvy said or did something rude, he turned to excuse himself to the God-King. The boy was scowling at the message he had just received.

"You don't look very happy," Briar said.

"I have not heard from the king of Inxia." That was the realm to the northeast, a country that stood between Gyongxe and the Yanjing empire. "I often do by now. Our mages who deal in conversations at a distance have not heard from his mages in several months. No horse messengers have come through the Green Pass, either."

"It *is* only the third month of the year," Briar reminded him. "It's probably frozen solid."

The God-King gave him an absentminded smile. "The Green Pass is in hill country, beyond the mountains of the Drimbakang Sharlog. Usually it is open by this time, though the weather has been very harsh in the hills this year." He stopped speaking as he stared off into the distance.

Briar waited longer than he would have waited for anyone else to resume talking. When he was sure the God-King had simply forgotten what he'd begun to explain, Briar asked, "So what has this Inxia fellow to do with how well you'll sleep tonight?" He could tell the God-King was worried.

"All three kingdoms north of Yanjing have been fighting the empire for the last five years," the God-King explained. "Since Inxia is our closest neighbor, we have sent mages and soldiers to their assistance for four of those years. We should have heard what they will need for this year's fighting by now."

Briar nodded. Now he understood. "Because if Inxia falls, Gyongxe is next."

"I would like to think not," the younger boy replied, but he did not sound convinced. "We have very little to interest the Emperor Weishu. Except the gods and spirits, who are closer here than anywhere else in the world, and you can't pay soldiers with those. There are the temple treasures, but surely Weishu's mages do not believe they can take the curses from temple goods. We do spread word that there are curses on anything stolen from the temples of Gyongxe, and we cannot remove them." The God-King sighed. "I would feel better if I knew the Yanjingyi armies were denting their teeth on my neighbors again this year."

A surge of pity raced through Briar's heart at the expression on the God-King's face. That's not the look any boy his age ought to wear, thought Briar. I'd even feel sorry for a man of twice my years in his shoes.

It was at moments like these that Briar understood why the gods of Gyongxe had told their priests to choose this boy to rule over the many different tribes, villages, cities, faiths, and temples of Gyongxe. There was something great inside the God-King; something larger than Briar was. He wouldn't have spent a day in the God-King's skin for all the pretty girls between there and home.

"Briar, did you see it?" While they had talked politics and war, the rest of the statue-raising party had crossed the river bridge to join the God-King's group. Evvy raced over to the tent. The pockets of her orange wool tunic sagged with what Briar knew were more stone fragments. "You aren't even looking!"

"We watched the statue raising," the God-King told her. "I've seen such things before, you know. Briar was impressed."

"I was," Briar assured the girl.

Evvy stopped at the open doorway and bowed to the God-King, then braced her hands on her knees while she struggled to catch her breath. They had been in high mountain country for nearly two years, but Evvy and Briar would struggle with the thin air if they tried to run. Rosethorn had trouble breathing all of the time. Although their entire journey had been Rosethorn's idea, she had been forced to spend much of it resting. She had chosen to work on the spring gardens instead of taking the awkward journey down the cliff into the river canyon with Briar and Evvy that morning. Briar looked forward to getting back to lowlands again, so his Rosethorn could breathe more easily.

"Could you see what *I* did?" Evvy demanded. "I kept the scrap rock from falling on anyone!" She grabbed the pack she had left with Briar and emptied her stones into it. "Do you know it's going to take them at least ten *days* to walk back to their home temple? They only had the five shamans who could do the spell, so there's no one to keep the magic going at night. If they aren't dancing, the statues won't move. They're going to be awfully tired — the shamans, not the statues. I offered to clean up the loose rock, but Dokyi said the Drimbakang Zugu have their own way of dealing with it. What does that mean?" She gathered the stones she'd left with Briar and stowed them in her pack as well.

Evumeimei Dingzai was a skinny former slave who never missed a meal if she could help it. She was five feet tall with a strong Yanjingyi face: wide cheekbones, sharp chin, and long black eyes. Briar liked to tease her that she'd smacked her face into a door once, since her nose was flat at the tip. Her hands and nails showed scars and scratches from two years of hard work as a stone mage and a lifetime as a cat owner. He had found her scraping for a living in a slum. Although her magic was different from his, he had learned that he would not give her up to a teacher of her own power who would be unkind to her.

The God-King stood and moved off the giant pillow where he and Briar had spent the morning. "Wait a moment, Evumeimei."

Evvy scowled. From the very beginning the God-King had treated her as a beloved sister. She had soon lost any shyness she could be expected to feel in his presence. "You always tell me to wait. I'll have you know I am older than you —"

"I am the two hundred and ninety-eighth God-King in a straight line of choice from the first God-King," he replied as he did whenever she brought up their difference in age. "You will have to be as old as —"

The stone beneath Briar's feet had begun to shake. He sat hurriedly and pulled at Evvy's arm. She signaled for the God-King to join them. Everyone outside was sitting as well.

Briar heard the kind of grinding noise that brought landslides to mind. Looking across the river, he felt his stomach roll. He clapped his hands over his mouth to keep his very good breakfast where it was supposed to be. Stones that had fallen, gravel that had dropped off a cliff, dust that had settled after the skeletons had gone for their walk belonged on the ground. All of these things had no business rising into the air in front of the gap in the cliff. None of them should be entering that gap, nor should any of the boulders on the riverbank or the stones between the water and the cliff be rolling to it and climbing over one another in their eagerness to fill in the hole left by the skeleton statues. Now more stones rattled down the slopes of the mountain that stood behind the cliff. They hesitated only briefly on the edge of the drop, then rolled over. In a maneuver that left Briar feeling as if he had been inhaling strange smokes, the new stones fell not straight down, but in a curve, dropping into the hole where the rocks from below had still left gaps. Now, except for a few openings, the rectangular space that had provided the statues was filled.

"Who did that?" Evvy cried. "Is that what Dedicate Dokyi meant when he said the mountains would clean up the loose rock?"

"That is what he meant," the God-King said, getting to his feet. "And I am glad the work is finished. I don't like to leave before the cleaning-up is done. There have been accidents in the past." He went to the edge of the rock slab and held his hands out palm up. Tilting back his head, he opened his mouth. Sounds came out, spoken in something other than the *tiyon* language that he'd used all morning with Briar and Evvy, the common tongue of the east. These words rolled along the canyon, grating on Briar's bones. He pulled his tunic over his ears, willing to do nearly anything to make them stop. Evvy rose, her face alight, and listened until the God-King lowered his hands.

Briar uncovered one ear. Normal sounds were returning to the canyon. He cleared his throat and got up. "What was that about?" he asked the God-King.

"I was thanking the canyon," the younger boy replied. "The shamans did it, of course, but the little gods appreciate it when I say something, too."

Evvy was slowly coming back to herself, her joy being replaced by her usual liveliness. Dedicate Dokyi found her as they waited for the servants to gather their tent and the cushions. He was a gnarled and sun-wrinkled man in his fifties, with dark eyes buried under heavy lids. His wide-lipped mouth, like his eyes, was framed by laugh lines. His knotted legs and muscled arms showed he was no stranger to hard work and plenty of it. Even his brown dedicate's habit didn't soften the hard shape of his body.

"Nicely done back there earlier, Evvy," he said, tweaking her nose. "I don't suppose you could teach me how you made the stones overhead fall backward into the opening?"

Evvy reached out with her hands, opened and closed them,

then shook her head with regret. "I asked them to go that way," she explained.

Dokyi looked at Briar. "She asked them. I see them as tools to be set in place along the frame of a spell pattern, and your student treats them as partners in the work."

Briar, who asked plants to do things, smiled at the older man. At least Dokyi wasn't hostile about the way in which Evvy worked, unlike many of the mages they had encountered in their travels.

A pigeon caught their attention as it swooped to and fro, trying to fly past them into the tent. Briar spotted the small tube bound to one of the bird's legs and moved Evvy out of the way so the bird could fly to a landing on the God-King's shoulder.

Servants rushed to complete the packing of the tent, as if the pigeon were a signal. Dokyi walked over to take the bird so the God-King could undo the ties around the delicate strip of paper. Once he had it, the God-King reached one hand into a pocket and brought out a selection of dried berries and seed. Dokyi took that and fed the bird as the boy read the message.

"What is it?" Evvy demanded. The silence had stretched too long for her liking.

Briar gripped one of her ears between his thumb and forefinger, giving that organ a gentle twist that promised to get harder if she did not behave. "Didn't me and Rosethorn have that little talk with you about 'affairs of state' and you sticking your neb where it oughtn't to go?" he asked in Imperial, the language they had taught Evvy to use. "You don't go around asking kings about their messages!" The thought of Evvy being so impertinent to Duke Vedris, back home in Emelan, made Briar shiver. Vedris was a good old fellow for the most part, but when he got on his dignity, he could freeze someone's hair off. And Evvy was more fragile than she acted.

"It seems that although the Green Pass is not open and we cannot get word to or from Inxia, the great emperor of Yanjing is more than capable of sending messengers through Ice Lion Pass," the God-King said. The look on his face was quite strange. "This, though my weather mages tell me that Ice Lion will not be open for at least two months. A messenger from the emperor waits in my audience chamber bearing letters for me and for Rosethorn."

The imperial messenger was sleek and elegant, dressed in three overlapping silk robes, each heavily embroidered. Briar's fingers itched for an eastern-style ink brush and a pad of paper sheets, knowing that his foster-sisters would never forgive him if he couldn't describe imperial fashions and decoration perfectly. He wondered what such plain dressers as Dokyi and Rosethorn made of the messenger's yellow, green, and black garments, or of the black silk cap with wings that were stiffened to stick out straight on either side of the man's head. It was impossible to tell from their faces, which were as blank as any stone. Dokyi wore the plain brown habit of the Earth temple here in the east, with the black border of the initiate, or mage. Briar was relieved to see that Rosethorn had cleaned up from her morning's work with plants. She wore a clean habit in the Earth green of the western Living Circle temple, also with the initiate's black border. Her short, dark red hair was still wet. Months spent indoors had kept her skin the ivory shade she preferred, while she held summer suns and wrinkles at bay with a large selection of creams she made herself. Her large brown eyes missed nothing, ever. That was why

Briar kept Evvy half hidden in back of him now. She ought to have been stone like the rest of the people in the room, but instead he felt her shake with silent giggles. If he had to guess the source of her merriment, it was the messenger's hat. It did look silly, but Briar could control himself.

"Rosethorn's watching," he whispered out of the corner of his mouth. "Do you want to spend another week washing our clothes yourself?"

That calmed Evvy down. She respected Rosethorn like no one else, not even her first teacher and friend, Briar.

As if she knew she was being discussed, Rosethorn moved until she stood next to them. Dokyi came with her.

The Gyongxin guards stood at attention. Two of their number struck a pair of large brass gongs, while one of the rotating number of priests from Gyongxe's many temples cried, "The God-King is here!"

Together with some residents of Gyongxe and a handful of other visitors, Rosethorn, Briar, and Evvy bowed low. The boy ruler walked briskly into the room through a side entrance and climbed the steps to the backless pile of cushions that served the God-King as a throne. There he sat, lotus fashion, propping an elbow on one knee, and looked at the Yanjingyi group. As soon as he was settled, his advisers ran up the steps to stand on either side of the throne. Dokyi remained with Rosethorn and the two young people, a gesture Briar appreciated.

The moment they took their places, one of the Yanjingyi group, a barrel-chested man in black silk trimmed with yellow satin, stepped forward. He began to speak in a deep, thundering voice that boomed in the huge throne room. Briar didn't recognize the language. He glanced back at Evvy, who looked as confused as he felt. Briar didn't check Rosethorn's face. He doubted that this was a language she knew, since he actually understood more languages than she did.

"It's the language of the imperial court in Yanjing," Dokyi said in a voice that went no farther than the four of them. "It's as old as the imperial line, that's what they say. If they caught anyone not a noble or not of the imperial household speaking it, that person would die the death of ten thousand cuts."

Briar looked down so no one could see the face he made. He tried to remember if he'd ever heard of anyone dying for a language before.

The herald stopped speaking. At the sound of rustling cloth, Briar looked up again. Everyone in the imperial party, led by the chief messenger, had knelt on the floor. Now, in unison, they placed their hands on the floor, leaned down, and touched their heads to the cold tiles. They straightened, then repeated the head-touching exercise seven more times. Finally everyone but the messenger halted, their heads against the floor. The messenger straightened and began to speak to the God-King. He did not stand, and the language he used sounded much like that spoken by the herald.

Evvy could stand it no longer. Speaking quietly, she told Briar in Chammuri, "Only eight bowings and touchings! They insulted him! They give the emperor *nine* bowings and touchings!" Chammuri was the language she had spoken when they first met. She was taking a chance on it being unknown to anyone from Yanjing. Traveling messengers might know Imperial, which was spoken over many western lands.

"Maybe they think they were complimenting him, giving him almost as many as their own master," Briar murmured in the same language. "Now hush."

"Your accent is a delight to the ear, and your facility with words a pleasure to any listener," the God-King told the messenger in *tiyon*. "You will forgive me if I ask you to favor us with what I do not doubt is equal mastery of *tiyon*. My guests, whom you seek, have never been granted the opportunity to study the golden phrases of the imperial speech, nor will they have the years it takes to master it as you have done." Briar noticed that he said nothing about his own obvious mastery of the Yanjingyi language.

The messenger bowed first to the God-King, and then, half turning, to Rosethorn. "Forgive this unworthy servant of a great and glorious master," he said in perfect *tiyon*. "If offense was given, I offer my life to blot it out."

"A bit extreme, don't you think?" Briar heard Rosethorn murmur to Dokyi. Briar turned his snort of laughter into a cough. By the time he had gotten himself under control the messenger was making a flowery speech in *tiyon* to the God-King, passing on greetings from the emperor in the east. Briar ignored the fellow, who added half bows and gestures as he talked, to look at Rosethorn. The corner of her naturally red mouth was tucked deeper than usual, a sign that Briar knew meant she was contemptuous of the messenger's overwrought manners. At least she had not crossed her arms, the signal that trouble was brewing behind her brown eyes.

Evvy nudged Briar with a bony elbow. She had noticed the tucked corner of Rosethorn's mouth, too, even if she hadn't heard her comment.

The messenger got to his feet as gracefully as a dancer. Once he was upright, he reached into one wide sleeve and produced two scrolls, each bound with gold streamers and secured with what looked like green jade buckles. He touched them both to his forehead, then offered one to the God-King.

Does he think the God-King is going to run down the steps to get it? Briar wondered.

If the messenger did, he was disappointed. One of the generals who had been in residence in the palace all winter walked slowly down to the messenger to accept the scroll for the God-King. Only when the general had worked several spells over it without result did he let the boy ruler have the message.

Once the God-King was reading his scroll, the messenger turned until he faced Dokyi and Rosethorn. "Is this unworthy one correct?" the messenger asked. "Has this one the honor to address the First Dedicate and Dedicate Initiate of the First Temple of the Living Circle, and Dedicate Initiate Rosethorn of Winding Circle temple?"

"I am Dokyi," the older man said without bowing. "This is Rosethorn."

The messenger bowed slightly and offered the other scroll. "Then I am honored to present my master's invitation to Dedicate Initiate Rosethorn and her companions," he said. His dark eyes flicked over Briar and Evvy. He bowed, very slightly, but there was still respect in his voice as he said in *tiyon*, "Am I mistaken? Have I also the honor to stand before *Nanshur* Briar Moss and his student, Evumeimei Dingzai?" *Nanshur* was the *tiyon* word for mage.

Briar was impressed in spite of himself. Few adults gave him his proper title, refusing to believe that someone his age had achieved a mage's certification and power. He returned the bow and nudged Evvy with his foot until she did the same. Since he had been at the courts of royalty and the houses of nobles enough by now to navigate their mazes of manners, Briar said politely in *tiyon*, "May I have the blessing of one's own name, so that I may thank one's ancestors for the pleasure of a son with such grace and perception?"

"I can't believe you just said that," Evvy muttered.

Briar burned to give her a proper scolding. Instead he kept his face pleasant and watched the messenger. If the man heard Evvy, he showed no sign of it, but bowed a little more deeply to Briar. Were the movements all measured out for him? It made Briar wonder if he had a measuring stick at home, and if he practiced bowing to each particular notch on it so he would know just how far to bow to a lord, or a mage, or someone who had paid him a compliment.

"Forgive this humble messenger, gracious *nanshur*, but when this humble servant of the emperor, great is his name, Son of all the Gods, Master of Lions, speaks in the voice of so great and puissant a master, his own pathetic name and being is obliterated. Only the name of the mighty Emperor Weishu Maorin Guangong Zhian, sixth of the Long Dynasty, remains." The courier cocked his head slightly, his black eyes glittering with more than a little touch of mischief.

"And if we wanted to ask how was the weather in the passes, would we say, 'Excuse me, you?'" Evvy wanted to know. "How could the emperor in his distant palace know the weather in the mountains?"

Briar wouldn't call the swift look that the courier shot Evvy a glare. Distaste, perhaps. The man found a smile — a tiny one — to plaster on his face. That was what he offered to Evvy. "But it was the Eagle of the Heavens, the Leveler of Mountains, who arranged our easy journey through the Ice Lion Pass," he said coolly. "Such is his eagerness to meet Dedicate Initiate Rosethorn, *Nanshur* Briar Moss, and even the student of such acclaimed magic workers that our dread master banished the storms and split the snows in Ice Lion Pass to allow this unworthy messenger to bring the gracious imperial invitation to you."

Rosethorn finally looked up from the scroll, her brown eyes shining. "It — this is amazing." She looked at Dokyi, first, then the God-King. "I had told you that our plans were to travel through Yanjing with a Trader caravan when the passes cleared, then sail home from Hanjian. Our hope — my hope, and Briar's — was to visit as many gardens and gardeners along the way. I never thought . . . I didn't expect . . ." She took a breath and let it out. "Briar, the emperor has invited us to visit the Winter Palace in Dohan. He is offering to show us his gardens there himself."

"You are also invited to be guests, all three of you, at the celebration of the Son of the Gods' fiftieth birthday," the messenger said. "It is the rarest of honors. There will be lords of Yanjing who will be gnashing their teeth with vexation that they have not been included."

"The gardens at the imperial palace in Dohan," Rosethorn whispered, running her fingers over the raised gold letters on the scroll of invitation. Her perfectly arched eyebrows snapped together in a worried frown. To the God-King she said, "Will you be offended if we leave soon? Because you've been so good to us, and I really don't want to offend you."

Briar looked at the God-King. Did he dare say no, given his concerns of that morning? He had not sounded as if he looked forward to any kind of conflict with the great emperor of Yanjing.

The God-King smiled at Rosethorn. "Keep you from the most famous gardens in our part of the world? I would not be so cruel. You have given us four glorious months of your company. I am only sorry to lose you as I would have been if you had left us according to your original plan, in six weeks." To the messenger he said, "I do hope you will let them have two days to pack and let us say our farewells."

The messenger faced the God-King, knelt once more, and touched his forehead to the floor. Those who had come with him had not budged from their positions in all that time. "My glorious master has ordered his humble servant to give all obedience to the God-King of Gyongxe," he replied.

"I suppose that means yes," Briar heard Rosethorn murmur to Dokyi now that the messenger wasn't looking at her.

Briar let a sigh of relief escape him. She was her usual mocking, hardheaded self. It was understandable that she would be excited by the chance to see the emperor's famous, *personal*, gardens, but after the God-King's remarks and all of the rumors and stories about the emperor that Briar had heard over the last four months, Briar wanted Rosethorn at her most hardheaded. With Rosethorn and Evvy both to look after, Briar wanted all of the good sense he could find, buy, or steal.

OUTSIDE THE WALLS OF DOHAN
WINTER CAPITAL OF THE YANJING EMPIRE
FIVE WEEKS LATER, THE SECOND WEEK OF SEED MOON

Evumeimei Dingzai was very unhappy. First of all, she was hot. Once they had come down from the heights of the Drimbakang Sharlog, they had found themselves in wet, sunny lands that were already warm despite it barely being spring. Today was even warmer than usual. To add to her discomfort, she and Rosethorn were traveling in the most elegant of palanquins, on their way to the first part of Emperor Weishu's birthday celebration. Bearers carried them along one of the many roads of the Winter Palace, a skull-thumping "honor" Evvy would have happily done without. The curtains of the palanquin were drawn, they had been told by their servant-guardians, to keep the emperor's favored guests from being stared at by the vulgar, and to keep dust from their clothes. It meant they bounced along in an airless silk-wrapped box.

Only the thought of Rosethorn's grip on her ear if she voiced her feelings kept her silent. Surely even Rosethorn could understand how a girl in three layers of silk robes, with her hair oiled, braided, and secured by jeweled pins, might want to say something, even if she only muttered it. Still, Rosethorn so often held strange views about the behavior she expected of her traveling companions that it was really better for Evvy to keep any complaints behind her teeth. That was, at least, if she wanted her ear to stay in its normal position on her head.

It wasn't fair, Evvy wanted to say. Court etiquette only required Rosethorn, a dedicate of an established religion, to wear garments like those she wore in service to her gods. Of course, the emperor required that those garments be silk: a white shift and the pine-green habit worn by Earth dedicates of the western Living Circle. Rosethorn wore no collar. Evvy had three, all of which framed more of Evvy's bare skin than she thought was right. She tried to tug a layer over her upper chest and failed.

"Stop fussing," Rosethorn ordered. She lay back against the cushions, waving a fan to cool herself. "The clothes will be easier to wear if you forget you're wearing them. You don't see Briar tugging and squirming."

"I don't see Briar," Evvy grumbled, trying to slouch. "*He* got to ride a horse."

"If we wore clothes suitable to horseback riding, I'm sure we would have been allowed to do the same."

The palanquin tilted suddenly; Evvy tumbled among the cushions. The slaves who carried the chair with its box-like compartment were climbing. Evvy wriggled back to a sitting position and risked a peek through the curtains. "Stairs," she told Rosethorn. "Big flat stone ones, like in that old temple back on the Sea of Grass." She let her magic drip down into the polished surfaces below their palanquin. The stone steps were old, quiet, and sleepy. She had woken them up to ask them questions. "There's dips worn into them by people coming and going, but they say they don't mind." She let the ancient voices roll through her bones. "They say humans tell them they are white marble from Sishan. They've been here for more wet seasons than they can count, if they could count." She leaned back, letting the curtains shut. "They're going back to sleep." She sighed, feeling better. Carefully she smoothed one of her sleeves, then confessed in a tiny voice, "I wouldn't fuss so, only I'm scared."

"I had noticed," Rosethorn said quietly. "We are guests, Evvy. The emperor made promises to the God-King and First Dedicate Dokyi that we would be safe. We have to trust that he's telling the truth. We *have* heard how much pride he takes in his gardens. From his letter to me, he believes I am a gardener of great renown. He wants to show off. Perhaps he would even like me to do a little work with some plants of his."

Evvy bit her lip. Until she was four, her parents had taught her that the emperor could do anything he wished. When she lived in her burrow in the rock in Chammur, the old Yanjingyi woman Qinling had told her stories of home. In them, the emperor had figured as being one step below the gods. Evvy had survived on her own for years by avoiding powerful people. This trip to the imperial court went against every survival instinct she possessed.

Their palanquin bearers slowed to a stop, but when Evvy tried to get out, a frowning eunuch appeared in the opening of her curtain. He shook a finger at her and closed the curtain with a yank.

"We're *hot*!" Evvy snapped in Chammuri, vexed.

Rosethorn slapped her arm lightly. *"Manners,"* she warned. "We aren't in Gyongxe."

"I can't *breathe*," Evvy whined. She felt cramped and suffocated in this cushion-stuffed silk box.

Suddenly someone thrust a tray with two bowl-like cups through the curtains. Rosethorn frowned, then chose a bowl. Evvy took the other. It was chilly on the outside. There was no spoon, so the contents must be drinkable. She took the tiniest of sips. The taste was as refreshing as cold water, but with a slight, unfamiliar, fruit-like taste that cleared her head. She drank eagerly.

"Very nice," Rosethorn said appreciatively when they had returned their bowls to the tray and the patient arm. Both tray and arm pulled away. "It's coconut water — I showed you coconuts in the market last week. You see, Evvy, there are benefits to this."

Evvy stared at her. "Yanjing has hungry ghosts that eat the insides of people and take their skins. Is that what happened to you? Is that why you're all calm?" Then she noticed the beautifully carved supports around them. Rosethorn had run a hand over the wood once they were inside, telling her what it was called, though Evvy hadn't listened. She was attentive now. The frame over Rosethorn's shoulder had sprouted a couple of leafy twigs. Shame twisted inside Evvy's belly. While she had fussed, Rosethorn had been so tense that the wood of the palanquin had grown saplings to console her, despite its layers of polish.

Evvy smiled at Rosethorn. "The drink was very nice," she said agreeably.

Rosethorn raised her brows. "That was too polite. What is the matter with you? Are you unwell?"

"I just don't mean to be a burden to you," Evvy explained as the palanquin surged into motion once more.

Immediately Rosethorn set the inside of her wrist against Evvy's forehead. "No, you're not running a fever," she said. "Where did you get this 'burden' notion?"

The palanquin moved into the shade and halted again. This time eunuchs on both sides opened the curtains. They offered silk-clad arms so the emperor's guests could climb out of their luxurious box.

Once they were on their feet, imperial waiting-women rushed forward to straighten Evvy's layers and even Rosethorn's habit. They backed away when Rosethorn glared at them — or had they seen the tiny saplings that also sprouted on the outside of the palanquin's box? Evvy wasn't sure. She held still, determined to be good for once and not give Rosethorn anything to worry about. Instead she looked at the ceiling while the women tidied her robes and hair.

There was a ceiling because they had been brought inside a huge stone building. The rafters were dark, gilded wood hung with huge paper lanterns. Evvy was grateful that the lanterns weren't lit. It was fairly cool in here, except for the occasional drift of warm air from outside.

An insistent thumb called her away from her thoughts on weather and rafters. A maid was pushing on her chin while another waited with a pot of red lip paint.

"I'm too young for that," Evvy said flatly in *tiyon*. What she wanted to say was that the court women with their single drop of red on each upper and lower lip looked stupid, but Rosethorn wouldn't like that. "Take that red stuff away."

"Evvy," Rosethorn said, warning dripping from her voice.

"I let them put the white stuff and the rouge on my face because you told me to," Evvy said. *If anyone within earshot speaks Chammuri, it serves them right for eavesdropping,* she thought fiercely. "I look like a tumbler in a show. I will not let them give me the drop of blood." The maids at their guest pavilion had told them that was the name for the current style in lip paint.

Both she and Rosethorn turned when they heard the scrape of a chain on the floor. "But all the ladies who must make their kowtow to his imperial majesty wear the drop of blood and the lily face," the stranger said. He had stopped next to the newly arrived Briar, as if for contrast.

Briar was a slender youth, handsome and smiling in his own set of green, peach, and ivory-colored robes. He did not wear the stiffened black silk cap of a *nanshur* or a noble, leaving his short, glossy black hair uncovered. The newcomer also had very short black hair. He wore only a white garment like very loose, draped breeches that ended at his knees. He was a darker bronze than Briar, heavy with muscle, and scarred as a warrior was scarred. His wrists and ankles were secured by gold shackles and connected by lengths of heavy gold chain. His wrist shackles were chained to a throat collar, also gold.

He saw the direction that Evvy's eyes had taken and raised his wrists a little, tightening the chains that led from throat to arms to feet. "No, I'm the only one required to wear these," he said, a wry twist on his mouth. "It makes it difficult for me to run away."

He bowed deeply and saluted first Rosethorn, then Evvy, then Briar by touching his fingers to his brawny chest, then to his lips, and last to his forehead. "I am Parahan, the latest imperial amusement. Just now I am ordered to bring you into the presence."

"I am —" Rosethorn began.

"Rosethorn," Parahan interrupted. "Though I have trouble believing that so beautiful a rose has any thorns at all."

"You have no idea," Briar murmured as he fell in step with Evvy behind Parahan and Rosethorn as they walked out into the open.

The big captive led them to a small cluster of three chairs at the foot of a stone dais. Evvy saw now that they stood at the top of a short pyramid. Its point had been lopped off to make a platform. Briar dug a sharp elbow into Evvy's side and nodded in the direction of the throne. The emperor was looking at them. Hurriedly Evvy joined Briar and Rosethorn in a deep bow. Parahan managed to kneel without his chains getting in the way. Like the emperor's messengers in Garmashing, he touched his hands and forehead to the stones.

The emperor only nodded casually to them. Then he turned his attention to what lay before them all. They did the same as Parahan got to his feet.

The view spread out below the pyramid left all three of the newcomers silent and staring. Before them horsemen rode in complex patterns, fighting mock combats with long spears and swords, shooting at targets, and racing down grassy strips set on either side of the sprawling field. Periodically, at the rear of the performing troops, something would boom. In the distance, earth would explode into the air and fall.

"What was that?" Evvy cried the first time it happened.

"Boom-dust," Briar muttered in Imperial. His hands were clenched into fists on the arms of his chair. He still had nightmares of the time pirates had attacked his and Rosethorn's home with the brand-new weapon, maiming and killing many.

Parahan sat cross-legged on the stones between Rosethorn and Briar. "I don't know your name for it," he said in *tiyon*, half turning to look up at Briar. "Here it's called *zayao*. And I think they have the right to call it whatever they want, since they invented it." His gaze sharpened as he took more notice of Briar's hands and the movement under his skin. "Raiya be kind, what happened to you?"

Briar sighed and stretched out one hand so Parahan could have a closer look. "I was trying out a little tattoo," he explained. "Something with vegetable dyes I made up myself — I'm a green mage. I applied it with one of my foster-sisters' needles."

"She's a stitch witch," Evvy said cheerfully. She never tired of the story. She spent so much of her time feeling stupid around Briar that it was very comforting to know he could be stupid, too.

"She is more than a stitch witch," Rosethorn corrected. "She is a thread mage. He borrowed the needles she uses in her magic."

"It wasn't like she has one set for sewing and one for magic," Briar protested. "Her sewing *is* her magic. *Anyway*," he told Parahan, after glaring at Rosethorn, "it should have worked. Only the flowers I put on my hands weren't just pictures after all."

"They grow," Evvy explained. "They bloom and move around and die and grow some more. And they're growing up along his arms. I think it's *splendid*."

"Hmm," Parahan said. "May I?"

Briar let the man turn his hands over and inspect them. Parahan saw deep pockmarks in Briar's palms, reminders of a determined thorny vine that had not wanted to release the boy when he was younger. The man noted that the flowers and leaves grew under Briar's fingernails. When he lifted Briar's hand to let the silk robes slide back, he even saw that the colorful plants continued up the young man's arms, moving and opening leaves or new blossoms and sending out new stems as he watched.

Finally he said cautiously, "I find it very interesting that a young fellow would want to put flowers on his hands. Might you have been trying to cover over something, oh, between your thumb and forefinger, perhaps?"

Evvy covered her giggles with both hands. This friendly stranger had guessed Briar's secret. Before he had been a mage, Briar was a thief and jailbird, with two arrests to his discredit — and two jailhouse X tattoos, one on the web between the thumb and forefinger of each hand. He'd been arrested a third time, about to go to hard labor for life, when a mage had seen the magic in Briar and brought him to Rosethorn.

Briar glanced at the throne and its occupant. Neither the emperor nor his immediate court was within earshot. "I'm reformed, practically," Briar said quietly, his voice very dry. "And I do so much more damage as a *nanshur* than I did as a thief."

Parahan released him with a sigh. "I am only envious," he confessed. "Had I been a mage of your skills, instead of a spoiled warrior prince, I might have stopped my uncle from selling me to the emperor. You *were* wondering about my attire." He shook his wrists, making his chains jingle.

This interested Rosethorn. "Your *uncle* sold you?"

Parahan grinned, displaying strong white teeth. "You should pity him. I know he would much rather have killed me so he would be sure to inherit my father's throne someday. Sadly my uncle did not dare to do so." Parahan looked out over the field. The horsemen were forming in brigades to either side of the great field. "In Kombanpur — where I come from, one of the Realms of the Sun — it is very bad luck to kill a twin. I have the good fortune to be one such, with my sister Soudamini. Actually I am not certain if my uncle believes in bad luck in general, or if he simply knows what would happen if Souda learned I was dead by his hand." He winked one large brown eye at Evvy. "I'm the easy-going one. Souda is the battle cat."

Anything else they might have discussed was drowned out as musicians came forward to strike drums, blow horns, and hammer large gongs. The explosions stopped; those who had set them off cleared away. In the distance Evvy could see a line of color. Slowly it grew larger and larger still, until she realized that she was look-ing at line after line of armored soldiers, flanked by officers and flag bearers. After them came teams of camels pulling catapults and companies of archers.

Spaced between companies of foot soldiers, archers, and the teams that worked with each catapult and its ammunition were men and women on horseback. Many of them wore the long black silk robe and cap of a *nanshur*. Evvy did not need the ward-robe to identify the role played by the new arrivals. To her ambient magic, the power of these people blazed from around their necks and wrists. They had to be wearing some kind of spell-worked stones as jewelry. If they embroidered occult signs or threaded their stones on cotton or linen, they would be just as obvious to Rosethorn and Briar.

None of them spoke as the army marched, and marched, and marched, its members coming all the way up to the foot of the imperial pavilion. When at last the drums, gongs, and horns fell silent and there was no more movement on the ground, the army stretched as far as Evvy could see. Her skin was crawling with goose bumps. She had never seen such a large force in her life.

The officers yelled something, and the warriors shouted in *tiyon*. Three times they repeated it, making Evvy's ears ring. It took her a moment to realize they had cried out, "Long live the emperor!"

When they stopped, the emperor left his throne and walked down to the foot of the dais, where those soldiers who were fairly close could see him. Two black-clad mages moved forward to stand each at one of his elbows. Then he raised his hands and began to speak.

Stones at the mages' necks blazed. The emperor's voice rolled across the field like thunder. He praised their strength; he praised their obedience to him and to the gods of Gyongxe. He promised his warriors battles and honor and tales to tell their grandchildren. Last of all he cried, "Death to the enemies of Yanjing!"

All of the people who stood before him — even the riders had dismounted by then — dropped to their hands and knees. Nine times in utter silence they touched their foreheads to the ground. The last time they remained in that position.

"I am really starting to hate that ceremony," Briar muttered softly in Imperial.

The emperor and his mages walked away around the far side of the dais. Other mages and nobles streamed off the dais after him.

"Are we supposed to follow?" Rosethorn asked Parahan.

"I have been placed in charge of escorting you to the Hall of Imperial Greetings," the big man explained. "We're waiting for the crowd to ease. Then we can go."

"Why didn't he greet us here?" Evvy wanted to know.

"I would imagine because he wanted you to admire one of his armies," Parahan replied blandly. "He likes to show them off to visitors."

For a long moment no one said anything at all. Evvy was wondering if she was the only one left breathless by Parahan's words when Rosethorn said, "This is just *one* of his armies?"

"Oh, yes," Parahan said quietly. "Specifically it is the one for Center Yanjing. I have also seen the armies for North Yanjing and South Yanjing. South is much larger. I am told North was much larger, before he decided to fight three of his neighbors at once."

"Why does he show you all his armies?" Briar asked.

Parahan shook his head. "Oh, it's nothing to do with me. He likes to show them off to everyone. He reminds his friends that he is a dread enemy, and he gets word to his enemies that it would be better if they surrendered."

"And his guests?" Rosethorn asked. "Our home in Emelan is neither friend nor enemy. Why show them to us?"

Parahan replied, "So you will tell those you meet what you have seen."

CHAPTER

THREE

THE HALL OF IMPERIAL GREETINGS
THE WINTER PALACE
DOHAN IN YANJING

They were not presented immediately. Parahan escorted them to their guest pavilion, where a Yanjingyi meal waited for them. Before they could eat, however, the maids who waited on them removed what Briar had mockingly called their "army-viewing clothes." These were replaced with loose robes so they could eat without fear of spoiling any silks or linens.

Rosethorn wasn't sure what made her happier, the cooler garments or the food. She had been afraid she would have to face the official presentation with no more in her belly than coconut water. Now, as she settled on crossed legs before the low table, she realized that Parahan meant to stand back with the dining room servants. "Join us, please," she said. "I won't be able to touch a bite if you loom over us."

The servants twittered, shocked that their guests would ask a captive to eat with them but once Rosethorn caught their eyes, they fell silent. Parahan didn't need to be invited twice. Immediately he sat on his heels next to Briar and helped himself to pulse-bean soup, roast goose, cherries preserved in honey, and baked lamb. Rosethorn had only taken a few mouthfuls before she noticed that the servants were all too willing to give Evvy rolled fried cakes, sugared jujube berries, and numerous other sweets while they ignored Parahan.

If the emperor's people were going to insist on serving his guests, as they had done since the newcomers' arrival from Gyongxe, Rosethorn decided she might as well take advantage of it. She looked at the servants and raised a single eyebrow. They were so well trained that they froze instantly. Once she had their attention, she looked at Parahan — since he had not been supplied with eating sticks, he was using his fingers — then looked at the servants again. Immediately one of them brought a finger bowl so the big man could wash his hands. Another placed a fresh pair of eating sticks in a proper stone holder before him. A third maid waited for him to indicate his choices for a second helping. Parahan blinked up at her, then began to point. Satisfied, Rosethorn whisked three small dishes of sweets away from Evvy and showed her own server that Evvy could have twice-cooked fish, water-reed shoots, and sliced turnips in sauce. If she let the child eat according to her own taste, Evvy's teeth would rot out, mage or no. Evvy glared at her new meal, her lower lip thrust out. Rosethorn ignored her. The girl would eat, or not.

Briar at least was minding his manners and pointing out his choices to the maids. They had almost started an incident on their arrival when Rosethorn had tried to insist that they would serve themselves. It had taken the august Mistress of the Guest Pavilions herself to explain that things were done in a certain way when one was a guest of the emperor, and to do them any other way was to get one's servants' heads cut off. After that Rosethorn had ground her teeth and borne it. As a dedicate, she was far more accustomed to being the servant, or at the very least, to doing her part of the chores. Being waited on itched in all of the places where her vows had become part of her.

With Parahan and Evvy properly attended to, she picked at her own roast goose. Her appetite had shrunk since their arrival at the Winter Palace. So many things here had a deadly result for the servants, not the guests. She couldn't even go for a walk in the gardens. Seeing the gardens would have soothed her, but the servants were supposed to keep her from doing so until she, Briar, and Evvy had been officially presented to Emperor Weishu. How many ceremonies would they have to endure before she could see the emperor's famed gardens? His lily ponds alone were renowned as far west as Emelan.

Parahan had gotten Evvy to talk about her magic. Not only was she chattering away but she was eating her vegetables. Briar caught Rosethorn's eye and winked, making her smile. Bless him, too, she thought. She hadn't thought how much she would come to depend on Briar's support when they had set out on this very long journey. He had taken complete charge of Evvy in Gyongxe, when it was such a struggle for her to breathe. Rosethorn had tried to thank him for it once. He had only kissed her on the forehead and told her not to be silly. It made her feel both grateful and weak, and she hated to feel weak. Only the knowledge that he was her boy, and they had passed beyond what was owed to whom years ago, kept her from hating herself and him. She needed to find her strength again, but this place, with its crushing weight of imperial authority, was starting to seem an unlikely place for her to heal.

Briar reached over with his eating sticks and plucked a slice of roast goose from her plate. The maids gasped and giggled behind their hands. Rosethorn frowned at him. "It's bad manners to leave this wonderfully cooked food on the plate, and you're toying with it," Briar retorted, his mouth full. He reached with his sticks again.

This time Rosethorn snatched her plate away and began to eat. "And don't you give yourself airs," she warned when she had finished.

"I wouldn't think of it," Briar assured her. "I want to live to get home."

The waiting-women came forward, bowing and looking anxious. Parahan rose to his feet in a single athletic movement. Rosethorn almost sighed aloud and stopped herself in time. She was no schoolgirl to moon over a handsome man, she told herself. She was just envious because the days when she did not have to first get to her knees, then straighten first one leg, then the other, in order to stand, were long over. Yes, that was it.

"These pretty ladies are telling us that they will get into trouble if they do not have you dressed and to the palanquins soon. As will I," Parahan said. Of course he was totally unaware of Rosethorn's interesting thoughts.

"Then let us get clothed," Rosethorn said, rising to her feet as gracefully as she could. Once she was on them, she could not resist. She stopped, and smiled at Briar and Evvy. "Of course, I *still* only have to wear a shift and a single robe."

Ignoring Evvy's wails, she walked into the airy, luxurious room that was hers for their stay.

Parahan had not been joking. The Hall of Imperial Greetings was a work of art in itself. The chained man led them down a long hallway where the walls and ceiling were lacquered bright yellow. Ornately carved ebony benches were placed along one side of the corridor so nobles could sit, chatter, and be waited on and fanned by serving women and eunuchs. All of them watched their small group go by, their faces emotionless.

They reached the middle third of the hall. On one side large paintings in the Yanjingyi style attracted admirers. They showed lush, beautiful scenes of palace life, gardens, and mountains. These had attracted groups of viewers who discussed them with soft voices. On the other side of the broad corridor, placed under windows cut high in the wall, hung large gold cages. Their purpose was made clear by their size and the ceramic chamber pot on the bottom. There was no screen for privacy, no blanket for warmth. If the absent prisoners were given food and water, the evidence was cleared away. The empty cages swung a little in the thin breezes from the windows and hallway.

"That one is mine," Parahan said, pointing to the last one in the line. "Usually the guides tell guests I am a chieftain from a savage kingdom among the Realms of the Sun. The emperor keeps me here when he has nothing for me to do, or if he wishes to point me out as an example to one of his nobles or generals."

Evvy looked at the cage, then at Parahan, with horror. "That's all the room you have?"

Parahan twined and untwined the chains around his wrists. "It's better than some of the other places he stows his captives. He put me in a couple of those at first."

They had reached a huge round opening framed in teak. Beyond it stood a partial wall that was covered in rough gold silk and embroidered with two-horned, winged lions. A eunuch, his face painted white, his long black hair left to stream down his back, waited there for them. His eyes had been lined all around with black paint. He was gloriously robed in bright turquoise blue, red, and palest yellow.

Parahan bowed to the eunuch. "Master of Presentations, I bring you these most honored guests of the imperial lord of us all." Carefully he introduced each of them in order of their age and expertise in magic, beginning with Rosethorn. He then introduced the eunuch as the Master of Presentations to the emperor, first among the imperial eunuchs. When he was done, Parahan told them, "And that's my part. You'll see me again. Don't worry. The Master of Presentations will look after you well." He grinned cheerfully at all of them, and then walked off, his chains jingling.

Evvy wanted to whimper. Losing Parahan felt like losing a particularly warm and comforting blanket. She didn't whimper, though, not here, not in front of this proud-looking old man who wore more eye makeup than she and Rosethorn put together.

The Master of Presentations looked each of them over as if he expected their clothes to have stains or rips in them. Then he sniffed. "I trust the ladies of your pavilion explained what you are to do when you are presented?" He had a high, fluting voice.

"Of course they did," Rosethorn told him. Her bearing was

suddenly as haughty as that of any noblewoman. "As did the prince. Do you mean to delay us further?"

I will be her when I grow up, Evvy thought joyfully as the eunuch flinched and minced his way past them, through the round opening. I know I will have to work hard at it, but I want to be just like her.

They followed the Master of Presentations around the end of the golden wall. Before them spread a broad, rectangular room, far more splendid than anything they had seen until now. Huge porcelain jars filled with live flowers perfumed the chamber with their scent. The roof was held up by thick pillars in precious woods, all painted with bright red enamel. Their ornate, fish-carved bases and capitals were covered in gold leaf. Overhead, paintings of gods and goddesses at play or doing war-like things among dragons, lions, and other creatures decorated a deep blue ceiling that was otherwise starred in gold leaf. Ornate gold lanterns hung from the tops of the columns to give light. On a dais at one side of the room musicians played the instruments of the empire, including drums, flutes, a lute-like thing called a *pipa*, and the very long-necked lute called the *erhu*. Briar was learning to like Yanjingyi music — the *erhu*'s sweet, mournful sound in particular was growing on him. Evvy loved it, even the singing, as the sound of her childhood, while Rosethorn only sat silent and ground her teeth. Now, seeing the Master of Presentations trot by, the musicians put their instruments aside.

The courtiers who swarmed through the room parted in front of the Master of Presentations, bowing slightly as he went past.

He was bound for a gilded raised platform at the heart of the chamber. Briar fixed his eyes on their host. Like them, he had changed clothes from the yellow robes of the afternoon.

Emperor Weishu Maorin Guangong Zhian of the Long Dynasty was fifty years old. It showed only in the bits of gray at his temples and the startling splash of gray in the beard trimmed close to his chin. His mustache was as black as the rest of his hair. His eyes were the dark brown of Yanjing, his skin the bronze of a Yanjing warrior who spent plenty of time in the sun. He had broad cheekbones and a long nose. Horse nomad blood in the family, thought Briar, but his mother was a concubine and a captive, wasn't she? So maybe she was a horse nomad.

Weishu's robe sported gold embroideries thickly clustered over bright yellow silk. It fastened at the neck and shoulder with more gold silk frogs. He rested his feet, modestly covered with plain black slippers, on a stool. He held a folded blue fan in his lap, though two servants stood on either side of him, wielding much larger, feathered fans to keep him cool. His head was covered with an intricately folded stiffened black silk cap.

"Behold the mighty emperor, sixth of his dynasty, beloved of all the gods," the Master of Presentations began as he came to a halt before the dais. Their small group stopped behind him. This was part of their introduction. The eunuch would list all of the emperor's titles, which would take a little while.

Briar looked briefly to the right of the throne. There Parahan knelt at the foot of the dais. He had been given an addition to his wardrobe, and not one that Briar liked. One more chain was fastened to the big man's gold collar. It led to the throne and looped around the emperor's left wrist. Briar looked down before anyone saw the fury in his eyes. He was surprised to find that he had developed a liking for Parahan. He thought it was cruel to treat him like an untamed beast. In the two years that he, Rosethorn, and Evvy had traveled east, Briar had met a large number of people. He had learned something of warriors. Parahan had not gained his old scars by wrestling with his favorite hound; he'd gotten them by fighting. Perhaps this emperor was too accustomed to his bowing warriors and slaves. Maybe one day he would learn the hard way that putting a man in shackles didn't mean he was tame.

The Master of Presentations reached an end to his gabble at last. Rosethorn bowed only as deeply as she had bowed to the God-King. Dedicates of the Living Circle recognized no masters on the earth. Briar bowed deeper. He liked to let powerful folk think he was a nice, respectful boy. Evvy, who was still a proper daughter of the empire, even if she'd left with her family when she was four, went to her knees and touched her forehead to the ground nine times.

"Dedicate Rosethorn." The emperor's voice was deep and pleasant, the essence of kindness. His *tiyon* was perfect. Briar wondered cynically if he'd had his voice magicked to sound good, then told himself he was being petty.

"We are greatly pleased to welcome you to our court," the emperor continued. "Your reputation came here long ago, borne by Traders who brought us medicines and plant clippings obtained from you at very great cost and trouble."

Rosethorn bowed again. "I trust the medicines and plants gave satisfaction, Your Imperial Majesty," she said.

"They taught us much of your great power," Weishu replied with a smile. "We hope to honor you by introducing you to our gardens, and hearing your opinion. Any advice you might give us will be a gift we could not hope to repay."

"I am greatly moved," Rosethorn said evenly. "I did not believe I would receive such an honor once we had left Gyongxe to come here. The whole world has heard of the imperial gardens."

"We had not realized you intended to visit the lesser gardens of our realms this summer," the emperor said. "Have you family or business here?" He glanced at Evvy.

"Business only as any gardeners would conduct when they venture far from home to new lands," Rosethorn explained. "I had long promised myself a journey east, to see what grows in different climates from my own. I had been forced to put off such travels often. Once *Nanshur* Moss received his certification in magic, it seemed like a good time to journey together."

"Certainly we are glad to take advantage of so great a gardener's visit," the emperor reassured her. "Let us start our tour tomorrow, then. We must warn you, we begin our day with the rising of the sun."

And she stays in bed until noon, Briar thought ironically.

"We are accustomed to early risings, temple dwellers and travelers as we have been," Rosethorn replied as graciously as any courtier.

For someone who hates this stuff, Briar thought with pride, she does it really well.

"We shall send our servants to guide you to us, then," the emperor told her. "We look forward to speaking with you in a less formal setting." The emperor had turned his attention to Briar, who bowed and then gazed at the man with his most innocent expression fixed on his face. From Parahan he heard something very much like a smothered snort. "What did you think of the review of our troops this afternoon? Are you now eager to set aside your trowel and watering can for a sword and shield?"

Briar smiled. "If it pleases Your Imperial Majesty, I already get into plenty of trouble with plants. I shake to think of the kind of mischief I would find with conventional weapons."

"Interesting, to find a youth who does not hanker for battle." The emperor raised a finger. A servant with a tray appeared from the shadows behind the throne. He knelt, offering the tray to Emperor Weishu. Another servant who had been standing just behind the emperor's elbow stepped forward and offered him one of the small porcelain cups on the tray. The emperor drained it. As he returned it to the standing servant, he asked Briar, "Are the stories true? You are a full *nanshur* at such a youthful age?"

Briar swallowed a sigh. He'd been asked this question from Emelan to Yanjing and he was heartily bored with it. Slowly he reached into the front of his robes.

There was movement behind the emperor. Four mages stepped up to stand beside the throne on Weishu's left. Two were men in black scholar's robes and caps, one a woman in scholar's robes, and the fourth a *mimander* of the deserts west of Gyongxe, clad in the head-to-toe gray veil of those mages who worshipped the god Mohun. A knitted screen covered his — or her — eyes. These were all imperial mage guards and warriors, among Weishu's closest advisers. To his right were warrior and slave servants, the former being the only ones allowed to carry weapons in the room, the latter to wait upon their master.

"We must be careful," the emperor explained. "A *nanshur* is the only kind of assassin who could get so close to us."

"Understandable, Your Imperial Majesty, but we have not journeyed so far from home and lived by being stupid," Rosethorn said.

For a moment, Briar knew, their standing hung on the emperor's sense of humor. Then the man laughed, and everyone in the great chamber relaxed. Except Parahan, Briar noticed. He had never tensed up in the first place.

Briar lifted his medallion free of his robes. On the front of the silvery metal, along the rim, his name and Rosethorn's were inscribed. At the middle, his magic was symbolized by the image of a tree. On the back was the spiral that meant he had studied at Winding Circle temple.

It was the Mohunite who came down the steps, walking between the throne and Parahan. The captive man tugged his leash hard enough to make it jingle, hinting that he considered tripping the mage. The Mohunite ignored him and stopped before Briar to extend a gloved hand palm up.

Good of him to ask, under the circumstances, Briar thought. He held the medallion out to the length of the silk cord and placed it in the mage's hold. The Mohunite turned it over in his fingers, saying nothing.

Sometimes Briar wished he'd never gotten the thing. Their teachers had given the medallions to Briar and his three foster-sisters two years ago, before he, Tris, and Daja had set forth on their wanderings. It was rare for mages so young to have them — medallions were the proof that they were accredited mages, able to practice magic without supervision and to teach. The four were forbidden to wear them publicly before they were eighteen, to prevent trouble. At this point, Briar was sure he wasn't going to wear his openly even at eighteen. Older mages were often furious to see it on him, though Dedicate Initiate Dokyi hadn't seemed to care. Most mages didn't receive theirs until they were in their twenties. Briar hated the aggravation.

The Mohunite gently placed the medallion on Briar's chest, gave him a small bow, and then climbed the dais. He raised his robes slightly to climb the steps. When he reached Parahan's leash, he placed one foot on it firmly, looking down at the captive.

The big man replied with a wide grin. He placed his palms together and bowed. The Mohunite shook his head slightly and returned to his place beside the other mages.

"Truly impressive," the emperor said. "I should have expected as much from a student of the great mage Rosethorn."

Briar bowed, wondering if his spine would start to curve after much more of this. "I will never be what she is, Your Imperial Majesty."

There was humor in the emperor's eye as he said, "And modest! Are you certain you are a youth of sixteen years?"

There was a ripple of laughter among the listening courtiers, though no change of expression on the faces of the mages that Briar could see. Briar himself chose to smile — and bow — again. "She has trained me *very* well, Your Imperial Majesty," he explained. "I learned manners under many bloodcurdling threats."

The emperor chuckled. His court responded with more soft laughter. "She does not seem so terrifying to me, *Nanshur* Briar."

Briar smiled cheerfully. "She fools a lot of people that way."

Once more the emperor chuckled and his court followed suit. He did seem truly amused. Briar liked him better for that.

"The messenger who guided you here tells me that one of my former subjects travels with you," Weishu said. "Evumeimei Dingzai, you may rise and come forward."

Evvy did as she was told. Briar could see her hair ornaments trembling. He knew it was probably against protocol, but he stepped closer and put an arm around her anyway for reassurance.

The emperor leaned forward, resting his weight on his elbows. He was the very picture of an indulgent uncle, except for all that gold, Briar thought. Kindly Weishu said, "We are told that you, too, have magic in your veins, unlike these poor servants of mine, who must pull it from spells and potions."

Evvy bowed low and almost lost her balance. Only Briar's arm kept her from collapsing. Gently he drew her upright again. "You're all right," he whispered.

"I get my magic from stones, not my veins, Your Imperial Majesty," Evvy said as she stared at the floor.

The emperor smiled. "And how did you learn to get magic from dull stones?" he asked. "Or do you use those that have been spelled already?"

Evvy glanced up at him, startled, then down again. "All stones have magic in them, Your Imperial Majesty," she said, a little more confidence in her voice. "I can feel it — or I could even before I studied. Now I can see it, too. Just like Briar and Rosethorn see the magic in plants."

"We are taught of *qi*, the power that binds all things." The speaker was the older of the two male mages, a tall, slender old man with silver hair and long silver mustaches. His face was a maze of wrinkles. Like the other two Yanjingyi mages he wore beads of many kinds strung in loops around his neck and worn in multiple bracelets under his full sleeves. Briar closed his eyes briefly, adjusting part of himself. When he opened them again, he saw the light of magic everywhere, enough so that he didn't want to use the spell for long. He did hold it until he saw the blaze of power from each of the beads that were wooden. Even the other mages in the room didn't blaze with power as much as the two men and the woman in black robes. The oldest of the mages who stood with the emperor went on, "It would seem this young student has learned more of *qi* than many of us have forgotten."

Evvy bowed to the old man, to Briar's surprise. "I am certain that cannot be true, Master," she said politely. "I am deeply honored, but I can also recognize the depth of wisdom in a face, a depth I will be lucky to ever attain."

"Such respect, when we are told those of the west are rude barbarians," said the emperor, applauding softly.

The emperor held a hand out to Evvy. It was laden with rings that gleamed with jade, rubies, sapphires, and pearls. "Tell me what my ring stones say," he urged. When his armed guards and mage guards alike stirred, he held up his other hand. "I think I am quite safe. Go on, Evumeimei."

Gently Briar urged Evvy forward. Slowly she climbed the dais and knelt beside the emperor, knowing that her head must never be higher than Weishu's. Then, nervously, she took the emperor's hand in both of hers. Suddenly she smiled at him. "They love you," Evvy explained. "Not the pearls. Well, maybe they do, I don't know. I don't understand pearls because they aren't really stones, just dirt that got in an oyster. Did you know that?" Weishu nodded, his eyes dancing. "I think it's a cheat to call them precious stones when they aren't really," Evvy went on, happy as always to talk about rocks. "But the others, they love you. They just glow from the inside. They've been with you for a long time, and some of them are very old."

The emperor laughed outright. Evvy quickly released his hand. "I'm sorry!" she cried. "I wasn't trying to insult you — I didn't mean —" She looked frantically at Rosethorn, then Briar. "That's not what I meant!"

"Calm down," Briar murmured to his student. "See? He's laughing." He bowed to the emperor. "She's all wound up. She's heard stories of the imperial court most of her life, and she's been scared to death about coming here."

"She has nothing to fear," Weishu assured Evvy, smiling at her. "The stones I believe you meant have come to me from my imperial ancestors. You are right — they are very old. And much may be forgiven so talented a young girl in so overpowering a place. So tell me, *Nanshur* Briar Moss, how can you teach Evumeimei if her power is drawn through stones and yours through plants?"

Briar didn't shrug. That would have been impolite. "I could teach her the basics, Your Imperial Majesty — meditation, reading, writing, mathematics. The names and everyday properties of stones, and what they're traditionally used for. Evvy does the rest herself."

"First Dedicate Dokyi helped me a lot this winter," Evvy said. "He's head of First Circle Temple in Garmashing, and an Earth mage. And so far it isn't too hard once I read the spells and have the sticky parts explained to me. A lot of stone wants to be shaped, even jade, if you know how to explain it right." Her face was brighter and livelier. Briar thought he might swell up completely with pride in her. "Stone gets pretty bored, holding the same form all the time," Evvy explained. "Even mining it doesn't help, because nobody likes being smacked with a hammer. But if you *wheedle* just right, and tell it how it will like being smooth and bouncing light, and feeling its magic ripple along its inner surfaces, it's all you can do to keep it in the shape you want. Sometimes I just let the stone shape itself, for fun."

"And this Dokyi helped you to do this?" The emperor had retreated behind his blank, official mask suddenly. "He showed you how to shatter rocks?"

Evvy screwed up her face and shrugged. Briar nudged her to remind her where she was. "Oh, no, Your Imperial Majesty," she said, bowing swiftly. "No, he said he never tried it my way. He uses spells, and puts the spell on stones. I don't see why. He could probably do it like I do, but he thinks stone is dead."

The emperor laughed, so those who could hear them did so as well. Evvy had that effect on people.

"Did you enjoy your time in Garmashing?" Weishu asked Evvy. "It is a very old and mystical place, I am given to understand, with much that is unusual in the way of temple art."

Evvy bowed. "It's very cold, Your Imperial Majesty," she said as she straightened. "And it's harder to breathe than it is here. The mountains were *splendid*." Her face lit up. "Granite and other stones, scratching at the sky. Have you seen them, Your Imperial Majesty?"

"Sadly I have not," the emperor told her gravely.

"When my family went west, we took the north caravan route, so I didn't see them then," Evvy explained. "We came to Garmashing the same way. It was snowing so bad that nobody would let me get any closer to the mountains than the cliffs along the Tom Sho River, but I caught glimpses on clear days. Now I believe the books that said they're the tallest mountains anywhere." Evvy shook her head. "I wish we'd seen the Drimbakang Sharlog on the way here, but your messenger was in such a hurry, and there were storms that your weather mages were holding off us. I couldn't see *anything* but the storms overhead. I thought I could hear the mountains, though!"

The emperor clapped his hands with delight. "Dedicate Initiate Rosethorn, it is *wonderful* that you have brought Evumeimei and Briar to visit us. I must ensure that Evumeimei has a suitable companion while we absorb ourselves in the wonders of the palace gardens."

The rippling bang of a small gong interrupted every conversation in the room. The emperor looked toward the entry with a frown. Everyone else turned that way with interest except for Rosethorn. Briar saw that she was looking the room over, paying special interest to the plants.

An emerald-robed eunuch, his face painted white like that of the Master of Presentations, stood by the entry with a small gong in his hands. "His Most Glorious Excellency, the War Lion of the Empire, the Sword of the Emperor, Defender of the Long Throne, Terror of the Foreigners, Commander of the Imperial Armies, Great Mage General Fenqi Hengkai!"

A short, stocky man in iron-scale-and-leather armor under a scarlet robe strode across the room without so much as a glance for any of the courtiers. His square, blunt-nosed face was marked with scars and cruelty. He carried a pointed metal helm and wore no weapons. Once he reached the foot of the dais, standing near Evvy, he set his helm aside, went to his hands and knees, and touched his forehead to the floor.

The emperor stood. All of the Yanjingyi courtiers went to their hands and knees, as did Parahan and those who shared the top of the dais with Weishu. Foreigners bowed deep, including Rosethorn, Briar, and Evvy.

"You have met my captive Parahan, have you not, Dedicate Initiate Rosethorn, *Nanshur* Briar, Student Evumeimei? He will entertain you now," the emperor said, motioning to Parahan. The big man sat up on his knees with a jingling of chains. "He might have been the king of Kombanpur, in the Realms of the Sun, one day — if his uncle had not sold him to me." He looked at his mages. "The leash may come off." To Rosethorn, Briar, and Evvy, he said cheerfully, "Once his uncle captures Parahan's twin sister, I will have a matched set. Now, Mage General?"

The emperor snapped his fingers and led his mages down the far side of the dais. His general walked around to meet him there while every courtier nearby backed off in a hurry. That left only Parahan, Rosethorn, Evvy, and Briar near the throne. No one else was within earshot. Briar would have liked to meet some of the other courtiers and listen to the local gossip, but he was not going to get the chance. Everyone had drawn away from Parahan and his foreign companions. If Briar tried to amble away, anyone who looked in their direction would notice, and no doubt report it to the imperial snoops. Briar hated being without information in a strange place, but for now he would simply have to smile and play the part of an overwhelmed imperial guest.

Parahan's leash drew away from him to curl itself at the foot of the throne, snake-like. Evvy glared at it, then asked the man, "Does he keep you chained up all of the time?"

"Evvy!" Rosethorn snapped.

Parahan rested a hand on Evvy's shoulder. "It's all right," he said. "Evumeimei —"

"Evvy," she interrupted.

"Evvy," Parahan corrected himself with a grin, "reminds me *very* much of my sister Soudamini. She is full of questions, too. No, at night I am returned to my cage," he told Evvy.

Evvy's face fell. "It isn't a joke? They really put you in one of those things?"

"I do not joke about the many torments Yanjing has developed over its centuries," Parahan replied, a shadow passing over his face. He smiled abruptly. "My lot has improved since my first days as the imperial captive. Now, if the emperor is receiving guests or out and about, he takes me along. I believe you will see a great deal of me during your visit, particularly if someone grows tired of gardens." He winked at Evvy.

The gong was rattling again. The eunuch who had announced the general came forward to proclaim that an imperial courier had come. This person trotted over to the area on the far side of the dais where the emperor conferred with his general.

Parahan was telling the three of them about the different treasure chambers of the palace when the Master of Presentations found them.

"The Son of the Gods, Light of the Heavens, Glory of His Dynasty, His Imperial Majesty has asked me to say that he must end your audience. The business of the empire calls him away. You should be honored that he deigns to share his reasons with you. He does not explain himself to many. Now come with me." The Master walked away, leaving them no time for polite farewells to Parahan.

Briar knew that Rosethorn would be as aware as he was that they were being steered away from the rest of the imperial court and any other foreigners who were present. Briar had hoped to glean some information on the emperor's plans for Gyongxe, if any, for the God-King, but that would be impossible if the emperor's people kept them buttoned up this way throughout their visit. He also would have liked to examine the many flowering plants set throughout the room. Instead the Master of Presentations shooed them through a side entrance Briar had not noticed before. They were outside; their palanquins waited there on a small side road. No slow walk through a corridor meant to overwhelm visitors! Briar thought cynically. Now they just want to rush us back to our pavilion before we can talk to anyone. But why?

The Master of Presentations didn't even wait to see them off.

CHAPTER
FOUR

THE IMPERIAL GARDENS
THE WINTER PALACE
DOHAN IN YANJING

Slowly Evvy drifted to the end of the procession that followed Emperor Weishu, Rosethorn, and Briar through the series of gardens they had entered shortly after dawn that morning. She was starved. In their rush to watch everything bloom, or whatever reason they had chosen for getting out of bed at this hour, they had not stopped for breakfast. Also, she was bored. The servants wouldn't let her touch the ornamental rocks on the walkway borders and the odd decorations within the gardens. Other than those, Evvy could see no stones anywhere. It was hard to believe that they had all been dug up and carted away, but she felt nothing other than the border stones within a couple of feet of the surface. So where *were* they?

She was so busy pouting that she didn't realize someone was behind her until his hand touched her shoulder. Startled, she jumped with a squeak.

"Easy, easy," Parahan said. "I didn't mean to frighten you!" He was dressed just as he'd been dressed the night before, in the very loose, loincloth-like garment that seemed to be all the emperor would allow him. He still wore chains, too. They hadn't even given him shoes. Drops of water shone in his short hair and on his scarred shoulders.

"Are all those from fighting?" she asked, pointing to his scars.

"No, my mother gave me my shoulders," he said. "Silly, if they look like cuts, of course they're from fighting. I was leading soldiers from the time I was fourteen. I bet you're hungry."

"They didn't give us time to eat this morning," Evvy complained.

"Come on. I'm hungry, too." Parahan put his finger to his lips and steered Evvy down a side path. Two of the guards from the entourage broke off to accompany them.

Evvy spun and glared at them. Parahan turned her back around. "Don't blame them. I have to have guards whenever I'm off my leash," he told her. "Weishu likes me too much to let me escape, though how far I would get in these chains, I can't imagine. I doubt there are many smiths who would take them off or pick the locks. And the palace gardens may be huge, but the wall around them is quite high and well guarded by magic and by soldiers."

Evvy's heart sank. "If he really liked you, he'd give you an army so you could go home and kick your uncle all the way to Namorn," Evvy replied.

"*Now* you sound like my sister. Weishu likes to dangle me over my uncle's head," Parahan explained. "Right now my father lives. One messenger from the emperor, and my uncle dies. So long as my uncle sends gold, opium, and jewels to the emperor, he is safe. When my father dies, if my uncle does not continue his tribute to the emperor, he knows the emperor will send me home, with an army. So I am the emperor's most rewarding toy."

"That would make me angry," Evvy informed Parahan.

"You're free," he replied. "You can afford anger. Besides, I hear many interesting things at the emperor's feet. My father always complained that I spent all my time in school joking around. He would be very pleased if he knew how much I was learning now."

The walkway he'd chosen led through a bamboo grove to the banks of a bubbling creek. They crossed on a high, arched bridge carved and decorated as all Yanjingyi bridges were, following the path to an ancient oak grove. They stopped at the foot of a black-barked ancient tree with branches so heavy some of them bowed to touch the ground before they arched up again.

"Oh, that's better!" Evvy said. Dropping to her knees, she set her palms against two of the lumps of red and yellow sandstone clutched tight by the oak's exposed roots. "What have the gardeners here got against rocks, anyway?"

"Don't blame them." Parahan stretched out on a length of mossy ground that was clear of rocks and roots. The guards sat on their heels a few feet from them. One took out a dice box and they began to play. "It isn't the gardeners, but the imperial will. Unless the garden is supposed to be a little picture of a place, with bridges, a stream, small trees, rocks, and so on, the emperor wants each garden to be absolutely tidy. There can't be anything to distract from the flowers. Not weeds, not insects, not stones. It's a sad gardener who doesn't remove everything but the proper plant."

"I can't like any garden without stones," Evvy murmured, discovering the differences between sandstone here and sandstone in Gyongxe. "It would be like taking someone's ribs out."

"What can *you* do with stones, if I may ask?" Parahan asked. "Can you change the course of a stone hurled by a catapult?"

Evvy made a face. Some of the people who had hosted them on their journey west had asked such questions. Oddly, she didn't mind them coming from Parahan. He was just staring at the sky and making conversation. "No. Catapult stones are too big. I can only help them get to where they're going faster. Look. I can do this." She reached into the sandstone under her hands and sank light into the thousands of grains of quartz, apatite, and garnet that were part of it. When she heard Parahan inhale, she realized that she had closed her eyes. She had not needed them to tell her the sandstones under her fingers were blazing. The guards were babbling in the language of the imperial court to each other. Ignoring them, she opened her eyes and grinned at Parahan. "I can do it with heat, but heat won't stay long in sandstone or limestone. I need pure crystal or gemstone to hold light or heat for very long. I'm really good at lamps. We saved all kinds of money traveling because we didn't have to buy torches or lamp oil."

Parahan got to his knees and, keeping his chains out of the way, crawled over until he could hold a hand over a glowing stone. "Will it burn?"

"Oh, no," Evvy told him. "Rosethorn threatened to send me to bed without supper if I didn't learn to do cold light and hot heat every time."

Parahan grinned as he touched the stones. "No heat at all. She only *threatened* you?"

"I missed too many meals before she and Briar took me on. I don't think she likes taking food from me, even to teach me something."

"Speaking of food . . ." Parahan raised his beak of a nose to sniff the air. "I smell fried cakes and ginger!" He looked at the glowing stones. "We can't take these. The gardeners will get in trouble if anything is missing."

Evvy frowned. "Stones in a wood should be free to go where they want if they let go of their soil. Not that I'd pry these fine fellows loose. They're happy with their tree."

"Stones in a wood that does not belong to the emperor, perhaps," Parahan murmured. He got to his feet and gave Evvy a hand up as the light from the stones faded. "Let's see what we can steal from the cooks."

The guards stood, too. "You can't steal the emperor's breakfast!" said the darker-skinned guard in *tiyon*.

"We won't steal," Evvy told them, all innocence. "We'll borrow . . . from the edges. From the stuff they give people who aren't imperial."

Parahan hooked arms with Evvy and they marched up the path.

Rosethorn had to wonder if she was meant by her gods to spend her entire visit to the Winter Palace in a towering state of vexation. For one thing, when the emperor said they would visit his gardens, he meant that he, Rosethorn, and Briar, as well as a gaggle of mages and courtiers, watched as gardeners dealt with the plants. If she even touched one, the gardeners hovered as if they feared she might break it. For another thing, she and Briar had been forced to wear silk again today, because they were in the imperial presence. She should have known they would not be allowed to get dirty when the maids placed silk clothes before them that morning.

Third, she was deeply unhappy with the mages who dogged their tracks. They drowned the voices of the wind in the leaves and flowers of the garden with the constant click of their strings of beads. She had heard that eastern mages favored beads imprinted with spells and strung together to be worn on neck and wrist. She had seen local mages twirling short strings of spell beads during their journey down from Ice Lion Pass. Court mages wore ropes of them. Apparently Rosethorn and Briar in a garden were considered far more dangerous than Rosethorn and Briar in a throne room.

As if we couldn't have turned those potted plants into weapons, Rosethorn thought as the breeze carried another burst of hollow clicks to her ears. She rounded on the mages. "I can't hear a thing these plants say with that unending *noise,*" she informed them.

All around her the emperor's prized roses, brought at great expense from far Sharen and raised more carefully than most children, trembled and reached for her across the stone borders of the path. The courtiers shrank closer together, terrified of touching those priceless blossoms. Weishu looked on, his face emotionless.

Briar raised his hands to both sides of the path. The roses halted their movement and waited, trembling.

Rosethorn had not taken her eyes off the mages. "What are you doing with those things?" she demanded. "I'm not working magic. If I were, you couldn't distract me with noisemakers."

"They are not noisemakers," said the youngest of them, a woman. "Our magic is inscribed in the marks on each bead. The greater the mage, the more inscriptions — the more spells — on a bead. And the more beads."

Rosethorn squinted at the ropes that ran through the woman's fingers. The small bone-white beads that made up the bulk of her wrist and neck strings, as well as those of her fellow mages, were etched with minuscule ideographs. In between those beads were others, some brown glass inscribed with Yanjingyi characters, some white porcelain with heaven-blue characters and figures, some carnelian with engraving on the surface.

"As I said, I am not using magic. Would you do me a favor and be quiet?" she asked, as patiently as she knew how. "The plants tell me how they are doing — *when I can hear them.*" Even if I did magic, I strongly doubt that you would detect it, you academic prancer, she thought. Like most ambient mages, Rosethorn had little patience for those who drew their power from their own bodies and worked it through spells, though she had studied academic magic in her youth.

"Is *Nanshur* Briar not using magic?" an older mage asked. Not only did this man have two long ropes of beads in his hold, but there were spell figures tattooed onto his hands and wrists. Unlike Briar's, this man's tattoos were motionless.

Briar lowered his hands. "I asked them to stop trying to help Rosethorn."

Rosethorn let her own power flow into the bushes, calming the roses. As she suspected, not one of the Yanjingyi mages so much as twitched. Ambient magic was not only rare here; it was unknown. She called her power back into herself and looked at

Weishu. "If you would like me to tell you if they are well, I must be able to concentrate, Your Imperial Majesty," she explained. "I see you think I am deluded, claiming to hear the voices of plants. Don't your priests hear the voices of ghosts and mountains?"

"Ghosts were once men, and our mountains are ancient," Weishu said. "Blossoms live but a season, and plants a few years at best. Perhaps some of our oldest trees have voices, or the spirits within them do, but it takes ages for living things to gain the wisdom of human beings."

Everyone around them but Briar murmured their agreement. Rosethorn bit her lip rather than call them all fools. Royalty, their pet mages, and their pet nobles seemed to think they knew everything. The mages she was used to dealing with knew instead that they were just beginning to scrape the surface of the world.

And what about you? she asked herself as she followed the emperor along the garden's main path. Weren't you starting to think you had all the answers before Niko brought Briar and the girls to Winding Circle? Before their magics started to combine? We *all* learned there was no predicting how their power would turn out. We couldn't have guessed that four eleven-year-olds could shape the power of an earthquake, or that one girl's metal flower would take root and bloom in a vein of copper ore, or that those children would pull me back from death itself. I could never have dreamed some of the ways Briar has learned to shape his magic, or Evvy hers. I needed shaking up. We all did.

She felt the ailing rosebush before she saw it. Immediately she and Briar stepped off the path. They'd just reached it — only a single branch showed brown and wilted blooms — when they heard Weishu thunder, "What is this?"

They stared at him as courtiers and mages fell to their knees and bowed until their foreheads touched the stone flags of the path. Six gardeners, who had been hanging back among the roses, ran forward to drop to the ground before Weishu and do the same. Briar looked at Rosethorn, waiting for instructions. She clasped her hands and watched the emperor, letting her power trickle gently into the ailing plant all the while. She could feel the touch of the wetlands fungus that had gotten into the roots and was eating it.

"What manner of care do you give our roses?" the emperor demanded. "How is it that we find an imperfect one on the very day we bring important *nanshurs*, great *nanshurs* who know much about plants, to view them? You will be beaten until your backs run red! Head gardener!"

One of them looked up from the ground. He was trembling.

"Remove this wretched bush and burn it. Replace it with another that does not offend our eye," Weishu ordered.

Rosethorn had heard enough. When the poor head gardener touched his forehead to the ground once more, she gave a slight bow. "If I may, Your Imperial Majesty?" she asked. The emperor nodded and she said, "There is no need to uproot this plant. It's been attacked by a mold native to these lands, a fast-growing one. I can tell this damage happened overnight, and we are here quite early. How could your gardeners have known?"

Weishu looked down his nose at her. "It was their duty to know."

Rosethorn tucked her hands inside the sleeves of her robe so he would not see she had clenched them into fists. Of all the silly replies! "Your Imperial Majesty, as a gardener you *know* how delicate roses can be, particularly out of their native climate. This province is lush and green most of the year, I am told, and very damp. The homelands of the rose are in the southern and eastern parts of the Pebbled Sea — dry lands. And like most things that are transplanted here, they grow ferociously fast. In growing fast, this rose helped the fungus grow."

"The bush is fine now, Your Imperial Majesty," Briar said, taking over smoothly. Rosethorn knew he must have seen she was struggling with her temper. She should not have to explain this to someone like the emperor, who claimed to know about gardening.

Briar gestured to the plant like a showman. It was green and glossy everywhere, the blooms a perfect red. "Healthy as ever. Healthier, because Rosethorn made it resistant to your local molds, Your Imperial Majesty," Briar announced. Rosethorn wound threads of her own power throughout the roots of all the plants in the garden to ensure just that as Briar added, "I'll wager your gardeners must run mad, fighting mold."

Without raising their heads, the gardeners nodded rapidly.

"Rosethorn and I can fix that while we're here, Most Charitable and Wise Majesty," Briar said.

Rosethorn refused to give him the fish-eye as she usually did when her boy laid things on too thick. No one else would notice; this was the way they normally addressed the emperor. To her Briar sounded like the flattering, thieving imp who had stolen his way into her garden and workroom five years ago.

Briar told the emperor, "We've got advantages these poor fellows don't. It would be our pleasure to do this for you."

He looks like he swallowed sour milk, Rosethorn thought, watching the emperor. Then he was the smooth, unreadable emperor again.

"You cannot fight these illnesses?" he asked the gardeners.

The head gardener did not look up. "No, Glorious Son of the Gods, Protector of the Empire, Imperial Majesty. It is as they say. The heat and the wet of these southern lands, that make so many things grow so fast, also produce much that preys upon the roots and leaves."

The emperor looked at his mages. "And you? You cannot stop this?"

They looked at one another with alarm. "We do not know, Great Son of the Gods," said one, many of whose thin beads were colored green. "I would have to make a study of such things for the space of months, perhaps years. My field of expertise, as you know, is that of medicines and potions that may benefit Your August Majesty. It is well known that when something causes a plant in the gardens to sicken, that plant is simply destroyed."

"Your Imperial Majesty, I don't understand," Rosethorn said, forcing herself not to sound as impatient as she felt. "There are many Living Circle Earth dedicates here in Yanjing, mages and non-mages, who have studied plant diseases all their lives. You have only to summon them." She had been surprised at first that none of the local dedicates had come to visit her, but the maids in their pavilion had explained it was considered rude to meet guests before the emperor had done so.

Weishu smiled. "We shall have our people make appropriate inquiries," he replied. "The truth of the matter is that the priests of the Living Circle and the priests of the gods of Yanjing, of our state religion, do not fare well together. We fear that, should we invite priests of the Living Circle into our palace, the priests of our state religion would make trouble. It is better for our subjects to be peacefully guided by our priests, keeping harmony in our palace."

Rosethorn gazed up at the emperor's unreadably smooth face. His explanation was believable, but she did not trust it. She suggested politely, "Then, Your Imperial Majesty, for the sake of your gardeners and your plants, I recommend they speak to local farmers. They will know all about this sort of thing. Crossing them with local plants might strengthen the roots of your roses against common molds and funguses. It is something everyone could work on at your pleasure."

"We could make a study of it ourself, given time," Weishu replied with a smile. He looked at the gardeners. "Until Dedicate Initiate Rosethorn and *Nanshur* Briar find the leisure to return and see to the health of my roses, uproot that one and burn it." He pointed to the bush that Rosethorn had saved.

She threw herself in front of it as the gardeners scrambled to their feet. "Imperial Majesty, why?" she demanded, shocked. "It's healthy now — healthier than ever! There's no reason to kill it!"

"There is *every* reason," he told her. "It failed us at the moment of a test, when we came to show the splendor of our works to a foreign guest. Anything that does not present itself in glory and perfection betrays us and must be destroyed."

"But you weren't betrayed!" Rosethorn argued, thinking fast. What would satisfy this absolute ruler? "We have never seen such splendid gardens — have we, Briar?" He shook his head. He'd gone to her side and was keeping an eye on the gardeners. They had yet to notice the tiny green shoots sprouting through the dirt at their feet. She glanced hurriedly at Briar and then at the bits of green.

He closed his eyes briefly. The green sprouts shrank into the earth, seemingly before anyone noticed they were there.

"We'd like your permission to sketch the roses, because we won't be able to describe them," Rosethorn told Weishu quickly. "The king of Bihan will weep with envy when we tell him about your rose gardens and lily ponds. This plant didn't fail you. If you approve, we can create a new color for you from its blooms. One that will breed true, that will be only yours forever."

He hesitated. She had tempted him. "We would take it as a great favor indeed if you were to give us such a gift," Weishu said with a broad smile. Then the smile vanished. Rosethorn hated the way these people had schooled themselves to hide their true feelings behind a blank face. "But the plant dies," Weishu said. "A flaw is not to be tolerated."

A gardener must have laid a gloved hand on the bush when Briar was distracted: Rosethorn heard the plant's cry when the man gripped it hard. She couldn't bear it. She would have felt the rosebush's pain as she walked away. Throwing herself to her hands and knees, she did as the Yanjing people did and touched her forehead to the earth. All around her the ground quivered as roots and sprouts strained to break through.

"A favor, Imperial Majesty!" Rosethorn cried. The bushes trembled as Briar's temper flared. She wrapped her power around him for a moment, squeezing his magic gently in hers as a reminder to Briar to exercise control. Slowly, reluctantly, she felt him relax. As he calmed, so did the roses, sprouts, and roots.

To the emperor Rosethorn said, "It is flawed and an embarrassment to you, with your eagle's eye. But to a humble dedicate from a temple far away it would be an incredible gift. I beg of you, will you let me have it, in memory of my audiences with the great emperor of all Yanjing? It would be an honor beyond all words."

Nothing seemed to move, not even the air. Finally the emperor said, "You truly believe this."

"I truly believe this," Rosethorn said in agreement.

After a long moment's consideration, Weishu told Rosethorn, "This plant will be in your pavilion, with a suitable container, when you return there today. You will carry this thing all those miles home with you?"

Rosethorn straightened to her knees. "It would be my honor," she replied. Her back had gone stiff on the ground; she struggled to get one leg up so she could stand. Briar lunged to help her. To the boy's surprise and Rosethorn's, the emperor himself grasped the arm that Briar did not. Gently they helped her to rise. Once she was on her feet, Briar let her go.

The emperor threaded Rosethorn's arm through his. "Have you a thought as to the color and shape for our rose?" he asked. "Or is it too soon to inquire?"

CHAPTER
FIVE

The Grove of Venerable Oaks
The Winter Palace
Dohan in Yanjing

At the breakfast feast that the emperor had set up in Rosethorn's honor, Briar was finally able to eat his fill. Once that was done he went in search of his vanished student. He found Evvy among the feasting groups of courtiers. She was tucked under an awning, seated on a bench. Parahan sat cross-legged on the ground beside her. Briar had glimpsed him earlier, but hadn't had a chance to do more than nod before the emperor had claimed his attention and Rosethorn's. The young female mage, who had stood with the others next to the throne the night before, was now on the bench with Evvy.

Parahan grinned up at him. Briar took that as an invitation and sat beside him.

"How many cats do you have?" Evvy was asking the young mage. "I have seven —"

"Evvy, I don't think the *nanshur* wants to know about your cats," Briar said. Experience had taught him that not everyone welcomed Evvy's way of chattering on about the subjects she liked.

"But I have cats of my own," the mage explained. "I would have seven if I could, but the servants would frown at me." She smiled prettily at Briar. "I am Jia Jui, one of the imperial mages. It is an honor to meet you, *Nanshur* Briar Moss."

Briar gave her a bow in return. She was very pretty, but he was still jumpy after the goings-on in the rose garden. She was also much too old for him, though she was young for an academic mage — in her mid- to late twenties, perhaps. She wore only a single long string of beads around her neck, and some of them were blank. Could that mean they had no spells? Or were they really nasty, and hidden?

"*Nanshur* Moss, you are staring at my beads," Jia Jui said, her voice teasing. She had produced a fan from her sash and was using it to hide the bare skin above the neckline of her robes.

Briar was rarely caught without something to say. "Actually I was admiring the embroidery on the borders of your outer robe. Please forgive me if I seemed to be rude. Are these bits done with knots? My foster-sister works her magic through thread, and I have to tell her about the beautiful work I see. Are those phoenixes?"

"They are," Jia Jui said with a smile, smoothing the thread-work with pride. "I stitched for years to make this robe. It is such a pleasure to meet a man who takes an interest in these things."

"I'm going to meet his sisters when we go to his home," Evvy said. "One of them braids weather into her hair."

Jia Jui laughed musically. "It is a shame you did not bring your sisters with you," she told Briar. "They would have learned much from my teachers, I know, and we could have learned from you." She looked up at Briar, her eyes twinkling. "I would love a demonstration of your magic. I have never known someone who got his certification from the schools in the west."

She doesn't believe Evvy, Briar realized. She doesn't believe that my medallion could mean I'm as good as a Yanjingyi mage.

Coldly he thought, And maybe that's for the best. Despite the friendly reception, he had that old bad feeling. It was one he got when he was burgling a house, and his instincts told him he had been noticed by guards, or dogs, or magic.

"No demonstrations here, of course," Jia Jui was saying. "It is permitted in the imperial presence only under special circumstances."

"Of course not," Briar replied agreeably. "There's no telling what might go awry, with so many mages present and so many spells for the emperor's protection woven around him."

"Exactly," Jia Jui said. "You grasp what many visitors to court have not, *Nanshur* Briar. Now I will not stop you from din-ing, and Evvy, you may tell me about your cats."

Briar waved off a servant with more food, but he did accept a pitcher of coconut water and a cup to drink it with. Parahan took water and a bowl of steamed dumplings. They listened for a moment as Evvy began to count cats on her fingers. "There's Mystery, Asa, Apricot, Raisin, Ball, Monster, and Ria. They lived with me in Chammur, but they're travelers now. What about your cats?"

"Will you get in trouble for going off with Evvy like that?" Briar asked Parahan.

"Not at all," the big man replied between mouthfuls. "The guards were with us all along. And I was instructed to help keep you three amused. I imagine I will spend a good amount of time with Evvy. There are more flower gardens than the emperor could show you in one morning."

Briar made a face. "Believe me, I'd rather look at plants and trees than armies like we did yesterday."

A eunuch came up to them and bowed to Jia Jui. "Forgive me, great Jia Jui, but His Imperial Majesty, the Glory of the East and the Bane of All Evil, wishes to see the student Evumeimei Dingzai."

Even though Rosethorn was with the emperor, Briar followed Evvy for protection. As she trotted along behind the painted and perfumed eunuch, she grinned up at him. "This is better than all those pavilions and that throne room, isn't it, Briar? You must be happy with these trees."

He smiled. "Yes. And I'm glad you're having fun."

"It's easy to talk to Parahan and Jia Jui. Would you believe Parahan wanted to know what I could do with stone magic?" She chuckled wickedly as Briar groaned. He knew all too well what his inventive student could do with her power.

"Just remember to behave," he cautioned her. "I'll bet there are mages keeping watch all over this place for magic they don't like." But would they recognize our magic? he wondered. Would they even know it was there?

The eunuch led them around other tables placed under the great oaks. Each table was under an awning, and each setting was more ornate than the last, commanding its own group of servants.

At last they stood on an elaborate strip of carpet that led to the longest table. There the eunuch dropped to his knees. Briar bowed to the emperor, who sat with Rosethorn on his right and last night's general, Hengkai, on his left. Like all of the Yanjingyi people, Evvy went to her knees and touched her forehead to the carpet.

"Evumeimei, rise," the emperor ordered. She obeyed, checking to make sure that she hadn't wrinkled her skirt. "How do you find our gardens?" Weishu asked.

"There are no rocks in them, Your Imperial Majesty," she informed him. "Well, there are rocks here, but not in the flower gardens. Rocks don't hurt flowers," she said as the courtiers hid their smiles behind their sleeves.

"Parahan shall escort you to our rock gardens tomorrow. Would you like that?"

"Yes, please, Your Imperial Majesty!" Evvy said respectfully. "We saw a few rock gardens on our way to Gyongxe, but I was told that you have beautiful ones at your palaces. It would be a very great honor to see them."

"Then see them you shall," Weishu replied with a smile. "May I ask a small favor in return?"

Careful, Briar thought at Evvy, wishing she could hear him in her head as his sisters did.

Whether or not she heard him, she said, "If I can, Your Imperial Majesty. I'm only a twelve-year-old student."

"We have seen the power of Dedicate Initiate Rosethorn, and in future I hope to see *Nanshur* Briar display his skill," the emperor explained. "But first I have a little test for you. Mage General Hengkai, will you let Evumeimei hold your neck beads?"

The mage general stared at Weishu, startled. "But — Shining One —" he began to protest.

Weishu raised his brows. "Mage General? Neither your power nor your necklaces helped you to win your last battle in Qayan. Given this is the case, you should have no objection to letting a girl hold your beads. Hand them to her."

Hengkai took in a breath, then slowly let it out. Carefully he unwound three loops of beads from around his bull neck. Clutching them in one knotted hand, he held them out over the table.

Rosethorn leaned forward. Briar, too, was ready in case anything went wrong. The beads had to be protected for people to wear them on a daily basis, or for this general to wear them in battle. Still, Briar felt better when he saw Jia Jui walk into the space behind Weishu and Hengkai. She should prevent anything from going amiss.

Evvy stepped up and took the necklace. "Thank you, Mage General," she said, and gave him a deep bow.

Smart, Briar thought. Just because the emperor can speak to this Hengkai with disrespect doesn't mean that we can.

Evvy backed away until she stood next to Briar, running the long strands of beads through her fingers. They clicked musically, like the conversation beads used by merchants back home on the Pebbled Sea.

"Evumeimei, tell me what they are made of," the emperor said quietly.

The general jumped to his feet. "Imperial Majesty, Crown of Yanjing, only I may use my power on them!" he cried. Instantly two guards who had been standing behind the emperor's table lunged forward. They swung their halberds down, crossing them before Hengkai so they formed a barrier in front of the angry mage general. Then they pulled back on the crossed blades, pressing the man down into his seat. Once he was there, they moved in closer until he was pinned by the weapons. Hengkai could not even raise his arms.

Jia Jui shifted into the space behind Weishu and Rosethorn.

"So long as you remain where you are without moving, Mage General, you will stay unharmed," Weishu said, his voice as smooth as butter. "Evumeimei, proceed."

Evvy gulped. "It's all right," Briar whispered in Chammuri, his lips barely moving. "I don't think this lesson's for you."

She ran the complete string of beads though her fingers twice. The third time, she singled out a section of the most common ones. "These are bone," she told the emperor, forgetting titles in her absorption with her task. "Old bone, *really* old, that's half gone to stone, but it's bone all the same. I know it by the way it feels, but it isn't in my magic." She squinted at the lettering on some of the beads. "This is some kind of scribe work, but I don't recognize it."

"Those are the ideographs our *nanshurs* learn," Weishu replied. "Another bead, if you will."

Evvy chose a cylindrical bead, blue on white. "Porcelain," she said scornfully. Of another, more intricately detailed blue-on-white bead, she also said, "Porcelain." Two more: "Brown glass with white rubbed over the raised marks. General, did you make these?" The general spat on the plate in front of him. "Oh," Evvy said. Briar could tell she was thinking aloud. "You don't make things. You have mages that make your beads for you. But you can use the spells that are put into all this writing?"

"Yes," Jia Jui said. "That is how our magic is taught. Is this not the essence of your magic?"

"Our academic mages write spells on paper, or in books. It's the speaking of them, sometimes with scents, herbs, inks, and other aids, that helps them to complete the working," Rosethorn explained quietly.

Evvy wasn't listening. She was passing the string of beads through her fingers. "Wood. Briar, what wood is this?"

Briar reached over her shoulder and sent out a tendril of his own power. "Willow."

Evvy wrinkled her nose. "Wood's no fun for me, either," she explained to the emperor and the mage general. She seemed to have forgotten that Hengkai was angry. Briar knew that she was sunk into her power, letting her own stone magic spread around her hands. Her fingers sped over more beads. She had missed a big one, but Briar did not call her attention to it. Either it was the detested porcelain, or Evvy would return to it.

"Maybe you asked the wrong student for this test — oh!" Evvy stopped. "Wait a moment. . . ."

She worked her fingers back past flat rectangles of willow etched with circles centered on holes, past bone cylinders dense with ancient Yanjingyi letters, and past three brown glass cylinders. When her hand found a round grayish-white bead studded with small red spots, she stopped.

"Interesting," she said, turning the bead over. "There's spells in each of the red beads stuck in this marble globe. Even though

they're glass I can tell because the magic soaks into the stone."
She looked up at the emperor. "The main bead is marble. It
changes magic. That's how I can tell what's in the glass beads."

"Nonsense." One of the other mages from the previous night
walked up to stand before the table near Hengkai. It was the
older one, the man with silver hair and mustaches. "All know
that marble houses magic and protects it."

Evvy ignored him. "Whatever's in these beads is nasty, and
each one is different. There's illness — smallpox in one and chol-
era in another. Fire in three, one *very* hot, two more normal.
Choking smoke in two, and icy wind in one. The gold rings
around each red bead keep the magic from leaking onto the top
of the marble, so only the general knows he carries these. He's
got . . ." Evvy hauled up the loops of the necklace, her black eyes
scanning it for the pale orbs. She looked at the emperor. "Twenty
of them." She scowled at the general. "And you wear another
necklace and bracelets like this wrapped around your arms, all
loaded with bad magic."

"You dare lecture me on the magic of war, peasant wench!"
shouted the mage general, pushing forward against the halberds.
He glared up at the guards who fenced him in.

"Perhaps Evumeimei only means that the spells in the stone
beads are corrupted," Jia Jui suggested. "As a student she would
understand that far better than war magic or the craft of being a
general." She bowed to the emperor as Weishu turned to look at
her. "In my first years I spent much of my time going over mage
strings to find which beads had gone stale. It is one of the earliest
senses a young mage develops. General Hengkai has fought many

battles recently. Is it not possible that his most personal tools are worn-out?"

Evvy, really interested in her test now, had returned to her scrutiny of the beads. "I never said I was anything but a student stone mage. Oh, more bone, more wood. More glass. Carnelian! Briar, it's carnelian!" She held a large reddish-brown stone up to him.

"I can see it's carnelian," he replied, amused. The emperor, Jia Jui, and Parahan were also smiling at his student's enthusiasm. Briar knew carnelian was one of Evvy's favorite stones because it had been so hard for her to get her hands on any when she lived in Chammur. Even here in the east, where it was more common, she had yet to tire of it. Now she turned the bead around, eyeing it closely. Slowly, so slowly at first that Briar thought he imagined it, her eyebrows drew together. By the time she turned the bead on one end to look at it in a different way, everyone could see that she was frowning.

"Evumeimei, what is wrong?" the emperor asked.

"Who put strength and fear spells in this?" she demanded hotly. "This is *carnelian*. It's for protection and thinking!"

"Perhaps it is so in your benighted teachings, student." The old mage was also frowning as he looked at the emperor. "Your Imperial Majesty, Light of Knowledge, will you humor this peasant infant at the expense of true Yanjingyi mages? She knows nothing of our ancient symbols, of our learning that has been passed down over centuries —"

He fell silent when the emperor raised his hand. "Honored Guanshi Dianliang, I remind you that this western student knew exactly the nature of the spells on the snake-hole bead," Weishu said calmly. "She also recognizes the spells on this carnelian bead, do you not, child?"

"Fear spells, and not just jump-when-a-mouse-squeaks-in-the-dark fear, either," Evvy cried. "This is really bad puke-on-your-robe fear, and the spell's eating away at the stone. If you don't take it off, the stone will go to dust in a year. How many of these do you go through, anyway?"

Silence was her only answer from the general and from the tattooed mage.

"Thought so," she mumbled. She wiped an eye and went threading through the necklace for other stone beads.

It was not long before the older mage the emperor had called Guanshi Dianliang had to speak again. "She could tell us the stone is useful for the growth of fruit trees, Son of the Gods, and we would not know because she studies the learning of the barbaric west. It is true the mage stones last only so long, but it is the strength of the spells. The most ignorant village fortune-teller knows carnelian is a stone of power and strength, lucky for its color, the blood of dragons."

"But —" Evvy began, and stopped. Briar watched as Rosethorn, using her arm on the opposite side of the emperor, leaned her head on the table. Her fist was by her ear, their sign to Evvy to stop. With her little finger she sketched a line from her nose to the edge of her mouth, like a wrinkle. It was their sign for "elder." They'd had to work out a series of signs for Evvy on the road, when her youthful lack of caution started to get her, and them, into hot water.

Evvy saw it. She bowed her head and mumbled, "I'm sorry if I offended anyone, Your Imperial Majesty." From the way she looked only at the emperor, not at his general or at the angry mage, Briar could tell that she had deliberately not included them in her apology. She placed the beads in a heap on the table. "I was only telling what I know from the stone."

"I thank you, Evumeimei," the emperor assured her. "I am delighted and impressed. You have every right — and it is your duty to your teachers and your tradition — to speak what you have been taught. In fact, it would be very wrong of you to speak against your tradition here in Yanjing. We are nothing without respect to our elders and ancestors. You may approach us."

Evvy glanced at Briar, nervous.

"He wants you to walk up closer to the table," Briar whispered.

As she did so, the emperor raised a finger. A eunuch came to kneel beside him. After that, all Briar saw of the man was two hands offering something wrapped in bright yellow silk. The emperor took it, and the eunuch walked away from his master.

"Here is a small token of our friendship," Weishu said, offering the silk-wrapped bundle to Evvy. She took it and dropped to her knees for the usual Yanjingyi bow. Briar glanced at Hengkai and Guanshi, but neither revealed their emotions. Maybe they know they've gotten themselves in enough trouble with the emperor today, Briar decided.

"Rise, Evumeimei," the emperor said. "Open it." He was smiling.

Briar stepped forward. He bowed, then motioned to Hengkai's necklace, which the man had not retrieved. "May I, Your Imperial Majesty?"

The emperor nodded. The general only scowled and looked away. As Evvy carefully unwrapped her gift, Briar scooped the beads from the table. He glanced at Rosethorn, who raised a graceful eyebrow at him. Briar lifted a shoulder to say, "I don't know" to her silent question of "Why?" He ran the necklace through his fingers, watching Evvy.

She draped the silk over her shoulder. Her gift was something carved in bright red stone. "It's a cat!" Evvy cried. "A cat, made of cinnabar!"

"Do not handle cinnabar too much with your bare hands," Jia Jui cautioned.

"I know," Evvy said, using the silk to turn the beautifully carved cat in her hands. "There's quicksilver in it."

"The gift itself is a great honor," Jia Jui went on, smiling. "Cinnabar symbolizes long life in our magical teachings."

Down onto her knees Evvy went again. "Thank you so very much, Your Imperial Majesty," she said. "I'll treasure it always, and I'll remember the lesson that long life and cats are dangerous things."

The emperor chuckled, as did most of those who could hear, but Briar did not. That bow was starting to annoy him. No student of his should have to grovel to anyone.

"How did you know a cat was perfect for me?" Evvy asked when Weishu told her to rise.

"I heard you traveled from distant Chammur with seven," the emperor replied. "Will you tell me about them?"

Evvy hardly needed an invitation to talk about her beloved cats. As she described them and their virtues to her imperial audience, Briar inspected the flat, carved wooden beads with his fingers and his power. He wanted to be sure that, should he ever encounter a warrior who wore such a necklace again, he would know exactly what beads to reach for. He did the same with the oak beads on the string, and the gingko beads, memorizing their feel with the Yanjingyi spells sunk into their grain. Then he looked at Mage General Hengkai. The older man had leaned back, away from the halberds, so he could finger the beads wound around one wrist. What deadly secrets were there? Briar wondered. How many deaths did the general carry in all those strings wrapped around his arms? And for whom were they destined?

Couriers arrived for the emperor just when they reached the lily gardens after breakfast. His guests weren't permitted to know what was in the messages that were so urgent as to take him away from them. He made his excuses and asked Jia Jui to escort them through the beautiful water gardens instead. When they had seen and admired their full share of water lilies, earthbound lilies, trees, flowering vines, beautiful fish, water birds, and carefully landscaped views, the guests returned to their pavilion for a much-needed rest.

Before they retired to their beds, Rosethorn and Briar looked over their new rosebush, which had arrived during the morning. It had been moved into a dark green glazed jar that matched the color of the leaves precisely, a touch even Evvy appreciated. Moreover, the inked Yanjingyi lettering on the inside of the jar's lip appeared to be instructions to the cats. Even Monster, who had learned only with difficulty that he was not to anoint Briar's *shakkans* — miniature trees — sniffed the jar once, sneezed, and stayed away from it. Briar and Rosethorn both sent their power through the bush, finding the traces of Rosethorn's earlier healing of the mold. Neither of them said it aloud, but they both wanted to ensure the gardeners had not been forced to destroy the original plant.

They were joined for supper by Jia Jui, Parahan, and those of the afternoon's party who had actually seemed to enjoy themselves. The group introduced the foreigners to some Yanjingyi games and music, then took them to a terrace that looked out over a long body of water. There they fed the giant carp that swam in its waters until an exquisite display of fireworks — colored flowers and trees made of *zayao* — was set off in their honor. By the time it was over, Rosethorn, Briar, and Evvy were happy to return to their pavilion and their beds.

Rosethorn spent an hour going over the rosebush again. Once she was done she had hoped to write to her beloved Lark, back at Winding Circle, but she could barely keep her eyes open.

A day spent with hidden tensions between Evvy and the general, Evvy and that older mage, and whatever else was going on between the courtiers and Rosethorn's people would do that. The emperor was also the kind of ruler who enjoyed toying with his lords. She would be happy when they left the imperial court and its pitfalls. Rosethorn was asleep as soon as she closed her eyes.

Someone splashed her with heavy, stinking oil. She struggled to shake it off her leaves and blossoms, but the oil clung. Her sisters cried out from its weight on their stems and greenery as the men who cared for them walked between them, throwing this dreadful liquid all over them. The men didn't even care that they broke twigs and knocked petals off their blooms! The men were usually so careful!

Now they came to fling dry reeds down between their plants, reeds that dripped more of the stinking oil. She didn't understand. None of them understood.

The rose plants didn't understand, but the sleeping Rosethorn did. With a cry she thrust her blankets aside and jumped out of bed. She didn't even remember to put on shoes. Still half asleep, not thinking of Briar or Evvy, she raced out of the pavilion through a back door. The first touch of flame to reeds brought her to her knees on a trail that skirted a willow pond. She lurched to her feet again and ran on as light grew slowly in the sky ahead.

When she reached the rose garden, all of it was in flames. The gardeners had been bound and left at its center: They were done screaming. The emperor and his soldiers watched on horseback from the main path.

The emperor saw her as he turned his horse to ride away. "The plants harbored mold and the gardeners allowed them to do so," he said, his face calm. "Surely you understand that no imperfection is permitted at one of my palaces. I did tell you." He looked past Rosethorn. "Slaves will come to escort you back."

Rosethorn felt Briar put his arm around her shoulders. He had felt her magic, wakened, and followed her to discover what Weishu had ordered done. Once the emperor and his soldiers were out of sight, Briar spat on the path.

They waited together on the edge of the burning garden until the slaves came with a palanquin. By then the roses had burned to the gravel and new gardeners had come to dig up the roots.

CHAPTER
SIX

The Winter Palace
Dohan in Yanjing

The next five days were drawn from the pattern of the first. They rose at dawn, for Rosethorn and Briar to pretend friendship as the emperor and his favorites showed them around his prized flower gardens, meditation gardens, and greenhouses. Parahan and sometimes Jia Jui, in addition to Parahan's guards and a few younger courtiers and mages, would join Evvy. First they would play briefly with her cats, then venture out to visit the emperor's wild animal collection, his treasure houses, his artisans' workshops, and his rock gardens. Everyone would gather together for a late breakfast or early midday meal.

After a noon rest, so necessary in a part of the country that was already warming up for summer, Jia Jui would fetch Evvy to show her how the Yanjingyi children studied magic, or Evvy would show Jia Jui what she could do. Briar and Rosethorn retreated to the greenhouse where they and the gardeners would work on the rose they had promised Weishu. There they produced a red-and-yellow-streaked bloom unlike any other in the gardens. The Weishu Rose was resistant to every plant ailment Rosethorn and Briar could think of, including all the molds and funguses known by the local peasant farmers. The blossoms would poison any insects that thought to dine on them, and they would reproduce only from seeds, not cuttings.

They presented the emperor with his rose, and a bush which showed a handful of buds, on their fifth morning, at breakfast. They could tell from his face that he was deeply conflicted.

"Forgive us, that we cannot rejoice more," he said as a eunuch carried the potted plant away and Weishu turned the single cut bloom that Rosethorn had given him around in his fingers. (Briar had been careful to remove the thorns first.) "Even the scent is perfection. Our heart yearns to learn more of our Weishu Rose, but our duty forces us to leave it behind. We depart the Winter Palace in the morning. Our household will continue to look after you as if we were here, but imperial business calls us away. You will find we have left the three of you certain gifts, in thanks for your learning and company, together with the pack animals you will need to continue your journey. We are given to understand you mean to take ship from Hanjian at the end of the month you call Goose Moon?"

Rosethorn bowed. "That is our intention, yes, Your Imperial Majesty."

"You will have plenty of time," Weishu said. "We will ask our priests to pray for your safe journeys by land and sea."

He rose from his table and they bowed to him for the final time. The next morning, the three mages went to the Gate of Blessed Departures to say good-bye, but the emperor had nothing else to say to them. He did wear his Weishu Rose tucked into overlapping pieces of his armor. They watched him ride off with his mages and guards, each feeling a tremendous amount of relief they dared not express.

Parahan joined them as a brigade of imperial troops and another of archers followed their master through the gate. "Things will be more relaxed with the big dogs gone," he remarked. "You can sleep as long as you like."

"What happens to you?" Evvy asked.

Parahan shrugged. "I wait here until he sends for me. If he'd gone to Inxia, like he'd meant to this winter, I'd have traveled with him, but he changed his mind. Where he's going, he won't be settled. He doesn't like taking me places unless he's certain I won't be able to escape."

"Inxia?" Briar asked sharply. "I thought he was fighting with Inxia and its neighbors."

Parahan shook his head. "Inxia and Qayan surrendered over the course of the winter. I suppose they couldn't face another summer's hammering. I can't say that I blame them."

"Their gods have mercy on them," Rosethorn said. "Parahan, will you excuse us? I have some messages to send if we are to leave soon."

"Of course," he said. "Shall I bring supper to you, or shall I take you to supper?"

"Supper someplace we haven't seen," Rosethorn suggested.

Parahan bowed and sauntered off.

"Race you!" Evvy challenged her teachers. She ran down the forested paths that led back to their pavilion.

"If she thinks I am going to run, she may think again," Briar told Rosethorn. "I am going to walk with my most wonderful teacher."

"You won't say that by the time we're done packing," she warned, taking his arm. "I don't want to waste any time, and no lollygagging from you, young man."

"I don't intend to lollygag. If we're on the *far* side of the Realms of the Sun in Snow Moon, we stand a good chance of being home within a year. We can do it if we're in Hanjian by the end of Goose Moon. That gives us plenty of time, if we find a caravan soon." Briar smiled at Rosethorn as they strolled along. "I'll move just as spritely as a rabbit. You'll see."

"Hmm." Rosethorn looked up at a hanging willow branch. The edges of its leaves were brown. She did no more than look, but Briar felt it as her magic washed over the tree and dismissed the illness that was creeping into its limbs. "Boy, you flinched when Parahan talked about Inxia and Qayan. Don't think for a moment that I missed it."

Briar sighed and steered her onto the shady path. The day was getting hot, and Rosethorn wasn't wearing a hat. "The God-King was hoping the emperor would spend the summer throwing his armies at those two countries and Yithung in the northeast, rather than at Gyongxe. He won't like knowing that Weishu now owns Inxia and Qayan."

"Well, with luck the emperor will turn to Yithung, not Gyongxe. There's very little in Gyongxe to tempt him after all. And the God-King should know about Inxia and Qayan by now. Or at least he will know, long before you could get word to him."

Briar knew she was right. There really was nothing more they could do.

For a moment, when they reached their pavilion, Briar thought Evvy was walking away from his bedchamber. Then he decided she'd simply been chasing her lively orange cat Apricot. None of the maids was present to scold if the cats climbed the lacquered cabinets, tables, and chairs. Rosethorn hoisted the cat called Raisin over one shoulder and said, "Start packing," before she sat down at a table to write messages.

Briar rang the bell outside the pavilion to summon a messenger. The girl briefly whined when she learned she would have to ride to the caravansary where the Traders made camp outside Dohan, but was all smiles when Briar held up a silver coin. While they waited for word, they went into their rooms to nap, pack, or both. Before sunset, their messenger returned with word that a caravan would be leaving for the seaport of Hanjian in three days.

"Well, I mean to shift our things to the caravansary as soon as we're packed," Rosethorn said firmly. "That will give us the chance to get to know the people we'll be traveling with."

That night Parahan took them to a small pavilion set on a pond. There they were cool and comfortable listening to night birds and watching floating lamps on the water. By the next night almost all of their belongings had been carried away to be loaded onto horses for their dawn departure. Parahan had the palace staff bring them simple foods, and he rose to leave them as soon as they were finished.

"I know you will want plenty of sleep tonight," he said as the servants withdrew. "And I am not one for long good-byes."

Rosethorn took his hand in both of hers. "Mila and Green Man bless you," she told him. "And may Shurri Flamesword see you home in victory one day."

Parahan kissed her forehead. "You played the part of the agreeable traveler well, but wildflowers don't last very long here. I am glad to see you escape." He clasped Briar's hand, then Evvy's, in a jangling of chains. Crouching in front of Evvy, he tweaked her nose. "I wish you could have met my sister Souda," he said with a smile. "You two are much alike."

Evvy flung her arms around his neck. "I *hate* it that you're his captive!" she whispered in his ear.

"I don't like it, either, but what can we do? We're just little cats in his big house full of lions," he replied.

Evvy let him go and ran into her room, sliding the thin door shut with a bang.

Parahan bowed to them. "May all our gods watch over you on your journey home." He ambled out of the house, fading into the twilight. Briar listened until he could no longer hear the slightest jingle of chain.

Rosethorn went to bed soon afterward. Briar made certain the cats were all tucked into Evvy's room behind her magicked gate stones. Then he went to his own bed.

He was drifting off when he thought of Parahan. Gods curse it, I need to *sleep*! he told himself angrily. We leave at dawn! But there was no denying it; the plight of the man from Kombanpur bothered him. Any other master would have let them buy Parahan from him, but not Weishu. Parahan was some kind of prize. The emperor could give them nine saddlebags full of gold coins for the Weishu Rose alone — and he had — but he wouldn't sell this one captive. Briar would have traded all of that gold for Parahan, and he knew Rosethorn and Evvy would have done the same.

Dawn, he reminded himself. We get up *before* dawn.

Calm thoughts. I'll be able to wear plain old breeches and a tunic again. I look nice in all the silk robes, true, but there's nothing for comfort like the clothes Sandry made for me. Great Mila, I'll be so glad to wear my good old boots instead of slippers, where I feel every rock in my path!

On that agreeable thought he drifted off to sleep.

Something made him pop awake near midnight. He listened, but the pavilion house was quiet. Uneasy, Briar got up and checked Evvy's room.

The cats were draped over her bed. They had moved to take the space she had left empty. They looked up at Briar.

"When I catch her, she's dead!" Briar mouthed to them.

Mystery raised a leg and began to wash.

Swiftly he pulled on breeches and a tunic, then slung his smaller mage kit over his shoulder. Boots in hand, Briar crept to the door of Rosethorn's room and looked in. She was asleep, making the little buzzing snore that he thought was so funny.

Briar sneaked out of the pavilion. There were no servants in the outer rooms or even guards in the street beyond. He put a small bundle of sleep herbs in his tunic pocket in case he met anyone unfriendly on the way, and yanked on his boots. Once set, he began to run, his way lit by a half-moon. He had a very good notion of where she had gone. He should have realized she would not accept leaving Parahan behind, not after she had spent most of five days in the captive's company.

It took him longer than he liked to reach the Pavilion of Glorious Presentations, where Parahan was caged. That was because he kept to the trees and bushes beside the road, making frequent stops to look and listen for guard patrols. He saw and heard none, which only made him more nervous, not less.

He finally reached his destination. Before he approached his runaway student, he scouted the outside of the long hall. Everywhere else around the perimeter of the large building he found no sign of guards. Inside was the row of hanging gold cages, one of which housed Parahan at night. The hall of cages was easy enough to identify on the outside: It squared into the audience chamber, forming an L in the stone work.

When he was certain there were no guards anywhere else around the pavilion, Briar went into the trees along the cage side of the pavilion of Glorious Presentations. There were the small windows high up, higher than a tall man could reach, so the captives had fresh air. There was the corner where the long hall became the emperor's throne room.

Very well, Evvy-knows-everything, he thought grimly as he worked his way through the small wood, how do you mean to get inside?

Then he heard tiny grunts of effort.

She's trying to pull down the wall! he thought in panic. She'll bring any guards within earshot down on us!

He stepped out of the tree cover at Evvy's back. She was kneeling with both hands placed on a marble block two feet above the ground. She wobbled, snorting, but he could see no movement in the stone. For some reason, Evvy — who could guide tons of stones as they fell from cliffs — could not get these blocks to budge.

"Evvy, stop it!" he whispered.

She jumped, but she did not turn around. "No!" she whispered fiercely. "I won't leave him here! What if the emperor turns on him one day and burns him up like he did the roses?"

"How did you find out about that?" Briar grabbed her by the shoulders and tried to yank her to her feet. It was like trying to move a boulder, as he should have remembered from the last time he tried to displace her when she didn't want to obey.

"I heard the servants talking," she told him patiently. "Why don't you stop being silly and help me? I don't know why I can't move these things."

The sight of the gardeners' corpses burning at the heart of the rose garden was still too fresh in his mind. "He can't come with us," he told Evvy. "They'll kill us if they think we helped him to escape."

"I bet he knows a way out of the palace grounds," Evvy said flatly. "The only things that keep him here are the cage and his chains." Then she said the thing that truly horrified Briar. "I brought your lock picks with me. I'm going to pick his locks. But first I have to get in there and these blocks won't budge."

Briar chewed his lip. He knew what Sandry and Tris would say. He even knew what Daja, who was more practical, would say: "What's the matter, thief boy? Lost your nerve?"

"I have plenty of nerve," he muttered to his smith-mage sister. He hesitated for a moment longer, then realized that Evvy was throwing her power into the marble block again. She wasn't waiting for him to decide.

Growling softly, he cast his magic around to see if there were vine seeds in the earth. The gardeners had cut back the local vines, but if he could get their seeds to grow, there was no risk of examiners later finding bits of foreign ones he might have to grow from the seeds in his mage kit. It was in that casting that he felt the ghost of once-living plants at the level of his face. How could that be possible? The only thing in front of him was the marble wall.

He shook his hands as if to clear them of the last magic he had used, a habit Rosethorn teased him for, and let more of his power flow out directly in front of him. Now the entire wall responded with that shadow of life that had once been green.

"Evvy, stop," he whispered. "What's in the mortar?"

"Mostly limestone," she replied, her voice as soft as his. "There are other things in it that I don't feel, though. It clings like the marble is going to run away."

Briar ran his finger over the cracks between blocks. Suddenly he grinned. "And you think plant magic is useless." He crouched on the ground and opened his kit.

"You mean it isn't?" Evvy inquired, being difficult on purpose.

"Apparently the thing you can't feel is rice," Briar informed her. "And that I can manage."

"Rice?" she demanded, outraged.

"I know rice in my bowl and I know it in the mortar. It's the rice in the mortar that makes it cling so, I'll bet. Tell me, were you going to pull the wall down?"

"Nope. I was going to pull out just enough blocks to climb in."

"Then that's what we'll do. But we should make that enough blocks to let Parahan out."

"Three blocks by two blocks?"

"That should do. Let me get rid of your mortar first." Briar ran his hands over the cracks between the blocks, pouring his magic into them and to the openings around their neighbors. He wouldn't have thought the rice would have remained so strong compared to the stone, but it had. When he called it to him it even brought small chunks of the limestone in the mortar with it.

"I should have put down a cloth," he said with dismay, looking at the small heaps of white powder on the ground.

"Should have, would have," Evvy muttered. She reached for a block that sat two feet above the ground. It slid from the wall and dropped.

"Careful!" Briar whispered. He called to vine seeds as Evvy called the next block. This time, as she called it slowly forward, fat, strong vines were there to wrap themselves around the block and steady it as Briar and Evvy put it to one side of the opening. The vines released it and were at the opening, sliding under the next block, before Evvy had so much as a chance to turn around.

As soon as they had finished their opening, Evvy stuck her head inside. Briar heard her whisper something. Then she wriggled into the building. He slung his pack in after her, feeling her — he hoped it was her — take it from him. Then he slid through the opening in the wall. To his surprise, there was a lamp burning inside one cage over. In the cage directly in front of him, Parahan sat cross-legged on its floor.

"Is anyone in this building?" Briar asked softly. Evvy had gone around to the far side of the cage. From the jingle of metal, he guessed that she was using his stolen picks to open the lock.

"No. They usually leave us prisoners alone at night. Who would be boneheaded enough to help us escape? Why are you letting her do this?" Parahan demanded.

"You must think I knew all about it before she did it," Briar whispered. "They let you have a lamp?"

"I'm allowed to read." Parahan lifted a scroll. He glanced at Evvy. "I'd offer to help, but I never learned to pick a lock."

Briar went around the cage. Evvy was scowling at the lock set down beside the bottom of the cage. "I don't understand."

Briar took the picks from her. "Because you've only studied for a year." He reached into his kit and removed a small bottle of specially prepared oil. He let three drops fall into the opening of the lock. While he waited for the cage door's lock to soak, he added oil to those on Parahan's chains: neck, wrists, and feet. Then he turned his attention to the cage lock. It was tricky, but he was far more patient with locks than he was with many human beings. As soon as it popped open Parahan slid out of the cage.

"Close it," he said. "It will lock itself."

Briar handed Evvy the flask of water he always carried with his kit. "Pour some of that into the lock," he told her. "I don't want their mages to get any sniff of my magic from it."

"I doubt they would," Evvy said as she obeyed. "I don't think they even believe in our magic, except for Jia Jui."

Briar had started with Parahan's throat collar. "I try never to count on what strangers do or don't know." The lock was strange — not as simple as the cage lock. He didn't want to spend the rest of the night here. Muttering to himself, he dug through his kit and found another set of picks, one he liked better than the set he used for teaching Evvy. The collar lock popped open after a moment's work.

"You'll be able to escape the palace?" Evvy asked Parahan as she poured water into the collar lock to clean Briar's potion out of it. "I had a feeling . . ."

"You felt rightly," he assured her. "Don't worry about me. You two are taking enough of a risk as it is." He watched Briar open the locks on his wrists. "I don't know if I will ever be able to thank you."

"Just, if you're caught, don't say it was us," Briar advised.

"You understand a man can bear only so much under the questioning of torturers," Parahan said. "I will hold them off as long as I can, of course, but I have already had one experience at the hands of the emperor's interrogators."

"But why?" Evvy whispered, accidentally splashing more water than she needed to. "You weren't an enemy."

"They wanted to see what secrets my uncle and my father had that might be worth stealing, of course. I tried to tell them I was a layabout and my family's fool, but . . ." He shrugged. "Such people only believe your answers once it has cost you some pain to give them."

Briar remembered some of Parahan's scars and shuddered. Within a few more moments he had the ankle shackles unlocked. Parahan was free. He said nothing for a little while, rubbing his wrists as Evvy rinsed the locks. Briar snapped all of the cuffs and the collar back together again and left them on the floor of the cage, then did the cage lock up once more. It would look in the morning as if Parahan had simply turned to mist.

Briar went through the opening in the wall first. He quickly scouted around among the trees, but the area was as quiet as when he had arrived. When he returned to the wall, Parahan seemed to be talking with Evvy. Then he nodded to Briar, turned, and picked up one of the blocks. Carefully he eased it into its place in the wall, his muscles bulging as he worked. One at a time he settled the blocks into the opening. When he finished, only someone who looked very closely would realize there was no mortar between the chunks of stone.

Briar watched Evvy as Parahan worked. The big man had said something to make her think, that was certain. She chewed steadily on her lip until she realized that Briar's eyes were on her. Then she turned her back to him. He would ask her about it later, when they were not so pressed for time.

Briar called on his vines to yank their roots from the ground. He and Evvy then tamped the remains of the rice-and-limestone mortar into the holes the vines had left and filled the rest of the openings with dirt. When they were done, Briar watched as the vines slithered into the trees. They would search through the palace grounds until they found places to grow unhindered. The ability to find homes of their own was part of the bargain that Briar had made with them when he created them.

"Amazing," Parahan said when Briar faced him. Parahan bowed, his hands pressed together before his face. "Thank you both. I am forever in your debt."

"This is all we can do," Briar said. "Don't come anywhere near us while we leave. I won't have this bouncing back on Rosethorn."

"You need not worry," Parahan told them. "By dawn I will be out of the palace grounds. Will you be safe?"

"We will, but you won't," Briar said. "Not if they have dogs that can track your scent. Just wait a moment." He walked out to the main road, where short, broad-leafed palms decorated the way. Silently he called to four of the longest and broadest of the heavy leaves, catching them as they dropped free of their trees. As he returned to his companions, he sent his magic along the stem and heavy veins, strengthening them and drawing them out.

"What are those for?" Evvy whispered when he rejoined them.

"Shoes," Briar said. He explained to Parahan, "You don't want the mages tracking you." He set the leaves down, two pairs by two pairs. "Put your heels an inch away from the stems," he instructed.

"They'll fall apart," Parahan objected softly, though he obeyed. "And they'll give me blisters."

Briar grinned up at the older man. "Trust me," he said, and winked. He folded the long ends of the leaves up over Parahan's feet and held them there as he summoned the woody veins out of the edges. They knitted at his direction, pulling the leafy edges together as tightly as if they had grown that way, binding two tough leaves into one. More veins drew the back and the stems up, closing them up along his heel.

Parahan muttered something in his native language.

"They should last until you're out of the palace walls," Briar said, testing the seams as he made the stems softer. "Then you can switch them for anything else except your own bare feet."

"Won't they be able to trace *your* magic?" Parahan asked.

Briar and Evvy rolled their eyes. Briar replied, "From what we've learned here, they couldn't trace ambient magic if they had torches and hounds. Now, let's be off. May your gods watch over you."

Parahan nodded and vanished into the shadows at the back of the Pavilion of Glorious Presentations.

Briar slung his arm around Evvy's shoulder and steered her down a shortcut through the woods to the rear of their pavilion. "Don't you *ever* try anything like this again without telling me."

"I thought you might say no." She wiped her eyes on her sleeve.

"Maybe I would have." Briar sighed. "You took some really big chances."

"So did you."

"We took them with Rosethorn's *life*," Briar told Evvy sternly. "You know I don't like doing that."

"She's tougher than either of us."

"No, she isn't." This wasn't the first time they'd argued the point. Briar was positive it wouldn't be the last. "She *died*. I was there. I don't want her dying anymore. It's bad for her. It's why she talks slow, sometimes. And why she gets sick so easy."

"You tell me so all the time," Evvy retorted impatiently.

"And I'll *keep* telling you till I'm sure you remember. I'm not going to tell Lark we got careless and that's why we couldn't bring Rosethorn home. And speaking of carelessness, what did he say to you that was so private?"

Evvy flinched. Then she said, "I swear, I'll tell you once we're away from the palace. It's important, but I don't want to talk about it anymore until we're on the road. Please, Briar?"

She hardly ever begged these days except in play. He could tell she meant this. "Don't make me regret waiting."

"I won't. I swear."

In silence they returned to their beds. They saw and heard no one else on the way. No one stirred as they let themselves back into their pavilion. Silent at last, they walked into their rooms and lay down for what remained of the night.

Evvy hadn't even thought she was asleep when she heard Rosethorn say, "Evumeimei Dingzai, we are *leaving*."

She sat bolt upright. A maid knelt beside her with a cup of tea in her hands.

"Thank you," Evvy said. She always thanked the servants. She knew it hurt their pride to wait on someone so much lower in rank than they were. To Rosethorn she said, "It won't take me long to clean up and dress."

The dedicate was dressed in her wool traveling habit and wide-brimmed hat. "See that it doesn't. We still have to load Briar's *shakkans* and your cats." She left the room.

"I *know*," Evvy muttered, and drank her tea. The maid combed out her braid and did it up again while Evvy cleaned her teeth. She left Evvy to dress, having learned the girl didn't like help if she didn't need it. In happy solitude, Evvy pulled on the light cotton tunic and leggings she had laid out the afternoon before. On went her stockings and her comfortable riding boots. Already she felt wide-awake and eager. It had nothing to do with her tea and everything to do with wearing simple clothes again. Once more she was herself, not some street rat pretending to be nobility in the imperial court!

There was a bowl of rice with bits of this and that on a table by the window. Knowing it would be a long time until she got fed again, Evvy made quick work of the whole thing and belched when she was done. She even ran her fingers around the inside of the bowl and licked *them*, just to be sure she had everything. With that seen to, she grabbed her pack and slung it over her shoulders. Others found it heavy, but not her. She had carried it for two years, since Briar had begun her studies when she refused all other teachers. The pack held both her proper mage kit and her stone alphabet, with rocks or gemstones for each letter in its own special pocket. When she traveled, she did not like to be more than an arm's reach away from it. Only knowing that her things were under the strongest protection spells Rosethorn and Briar could weave had made her comfortable enough to leave them while she was on the palace grounds.

As she entered her sitting room, she was greeted with assorted strange cat noises. Briar had freed the cats from her gate spell and lured them once again into their special carry-baskets with his very excellent catnip. Outside she saw Briar carefully stowing the emperor's rosebush and his *shakkans* on the backs of his pack-horses. He had given one of the miniature trees to the emperor when they arrived as a birthday present, letting their messenger present it in case the emperor hated it. Evvy was fairly certain that Briar regretted the gift now, since he loved his *shakkans* like she loved her cats. He had not liked the way that Weishu treated his people and would not like one of his trees in Weishu's hands.

Rosethorn's twin packhorses waited outside patiently, their burdens already tucked away in cushioned leather satchels. Evvy found her riding horse, which whickered on seeing her. She swung up into the saddle and made herself comfortable.

"Anytime, Briar," Rosethorn said, mounting her horse.

"Yes, Mother," he replied. To his obvious surprise, and to Evvy's, the normally straight-faced servants tittered behind their hands at his joke. They sobered immediately and bowed as their guide and escorts set off on the road to the Gate of Imperial Blessing.

Evvy sighed happily. They were on their way out of the palace.

That illusion lasted as long as their ride to the gate. Two groups waited for them there. One was led by the Mistress of Protocol. Behind her stood two hostlers. Each held the reins of a string of three horses, all carrying a full burden of packs sealed with the six-toed dragon of the Long Dynasty. The headstall of each horse bore the same insignia.

A captain led a full company of the palace guard. These soldiers stood across the front of the gate, blocking it, spears planted firmly on the ground. Evvy's skin broke out in goose bumps. They knew! They knew about Parahan!

Rosethorn kneed her horse past their guide. "What is this?" she demanded.

"Evvy, have some tea." Briar nudged his horse closer to hers. He offered her a flask. In a normally loud voice he said, "I bet you didn't even eat breakfast." Softly he added, "Drink some tea and stop looking guilty."

Evvy obeyed. She eased her horse back until she was next to

Monster's carry-basket. She reached her fingers in and stroked the big animal.

The Mistress of Protocol bowed to Rosethorn. "Forgive me, honored Rosethorn, friend of the emperor," she said, not meeting Rosethorn's glare. "This . . . *officer* insists that you will not be allowed to pass until each member of your company is inspected. Please forgive the, the inconvenience. You have my deepest, deepest apologies."

Evvy wouldn't have thought the Mistress of Protocol could ever be so upset. Just after their arrival this intimidating lady had spent several mornings with them, educating them in the ways of the court. At the time Evvy had wondered if she was carved of the same white marble favored for so many of the imperial buildings.

"Inspect, then," Rosethorn said. "Except for the three of us and our guide, everyone is palace staff. The guide was approved by palace officials." She said nothing else as every member of their escort had been inspected top to toe by an armed soldier. Even their baggage was poked, as if the soldiers expected them to be hiding someone in it.

As the guards inspected the pack animals under Briar's eye, Rosethorn nudged her mount over to that of the Mistress. Quietly she asked, "Is it permitted to inquire why one is being subjected to this degrading inspection?"

The Mistress used her fan to hide her face for a moment, then lowered it and leaned very close to Rosethorn to whisper in her ear. Evvy knew that normally torture would be required to get an extra word from the older woman, but she had a bad case of arthritis. A balm from Rosethorn, and its recipe, had made her life much easier. *Very* much easier, Evvy thought, if she was willing to give Rosethorn any information.

The captain was returning; the two women separated.

"Done," the captain said. "They may go."

The men cleared away from the road. The Mistress of Protocol, badly rattled, presented the travelers with the horses and their burdens, gifts personally chosen by the emperor. Rosethorn said a few diplomatic, grateful phrases.

Evvy admired her all over again. Rosethorn said those things, and she acted as any noble lady might, but when she took a drink of tea from her belt flask, Evvy could see that Rosethorn's hand was shaking. Given Rosethorn's nature, Evvy was fairly certain she wasn't scared, but furious.

Were they looking for Parahan? Evvy wondered, nibbling the inside of her cheek. It's early, but maybe they know he's missing. Once they had passed through the last gate out of the palace and were on the long avenue that led into the city, Evvy and Briar rode up to Rosethorn. Their guide had drawn closer as well. "In all my days of service to the imperial palace, I have never seen imperial guests subjected to search upon their departure!" the guide said, indignant. "Did the most honorable Mistress of Protocol hint as to the cause of such extraordinary behavior? The emperor will be furious to learn of this!"

"I don't believe so," Rosethorn said, her voice very dry. "He's missing an even more prized guest." She pursed her mouth, then said, "Apparently his captive Parahan of Kombanpur has escaped. They don't know how. His chains — locked — and his cage — also locked — were discovered this morning when they went to take him to his bath."

"Oh, that's bad," Briar commented, his face and voice suitably grave. "His Imperial Majesty won't like that."

Admiring her teacher more than ever, Evvy decided to add her bit. She sighed, careful not to overdo it. "He won't get very far, not with the whole palace looking for him."

Rosethorn looked at them suspiciously. "Very true. If he's lucky, once he's recaptured, no one will say anything about it," she commented. "No one will want the emperor to know how badly they slipped up."

Their guide shook his head. "That's the kind of secret that always comes out," he said. "But you're right, they'll catch him. They have ways. Now, if you will look ahead, you will see the Gate of Lowly Welcoming. They call it that because anyone who is coming from the palace is assumed to be less happy, even upon entering our glorious city. We will be going around Dohan, though, so we will not pass through."

He trotted on ahead to ride with the leader of their guards. Rosethorn rode for a while in silence, before she said, "We're going to be in Yanjing two more weeks or longer, if the roads aren't good. The imperial spy service will have eyes on us constantly to see if Parahan tries to get in touch. There's no reason why he should. But brace yourselves, all the same."

Good luck, Parahan, Evvy thought. I hope you get out of Yanjing soon.

CHAPTER
SEVEN

The caravansary was the biggest Evvy had ever seen, with beautiful paintings of flowers and fish on the inside plaster walls, and a large square well in the middle. There were two levels of rooms, with the bottom level reserved for the bigger caravans and the upper for smaller traveling parties. This was a Trader place, very clean and in good repair.

The ride leader of their caravan came running as they rode through the gate. As soon as she and her people took charge of their group, the imperial escort bowed to Rosethorn and Briar and left them.

The ride leader, who had introduced herself as Rajoni of Twenty-eighth Caravan Datta, frowned. "That's odd. Usually some of them stay for tea and any news we care to pass on, but this year the imperials have been very . . . distant." She shook her head, as if shaking off bad thoughts. "Dedicate Rosethorn, you and your companions are blessed. I was unable to send a message before your departure from the palace, but as it

happens, we leave in the morning, a day early, for Hanjian."
She looked at their animals. "You have more horses than your
note said."

"The emperor was an overwhelmingly gracious host,"
Rosethorn explained.

"Well, then, we shall make accommodation." Rajoni looked
around. The Trader boys and girls who had taken charge of the
pack animals stood a little straighter, knowing the ride leader's
eye was on them. When Rajoni nodded, the youngsters led the
animals off to the stables. Only those who held the reins to the
cats' horses, the *shakkans'* bearers, and the horses Rosethorn
pointed to, the ones with the mage kits and their next day's clothing, waited and followed as the ride leader showed them to their
rooms in the caravansary. Once they had stowed everything they
wanted to keep with them, Rajoni said, "Midday is being served
now, if you wish to eat. There are tables by the fountain, or you
may carry your food here."

"I can bring the food here," Briar said. "We'll take supper
with the rest of your company tonight."

Evvy sighed. She wanted a nap, but she also wanted time to
herself, to think about what Parahan had told her. She hadn't had
a moment alone with Briar and Rosethorn since they had ridden away from the palace. She had hoped to talk to them here,
but what if there were listening spells on the walls? If they were
Trader listening spells, that wasn't so bad. But what if they
were imperial ones?

Rosethorn said, "Rajoni, I saw a stream outside the walls. Is
it safe for me to meditate there?"

"This area is very safe," the ride leader assured them. "We only ask that you be inside our walls by dark, when we close and lock the gates for the night. We leave at dawn."

Evvy and Rosethorn went inside to inspect their rooms. Using her guard stones, Evvy set the cats up in a corner of the main room by the entry. She filled a shallow basket with dirt in which they could relieve themselves, fed them from the sealed jar of cooked pork scraps the palace servants had left for her, and put down several dishes of water. Constant travel had made Evvy inventive when it came to providing for her companions. When she went to set up her own bedroll next to the cats' place, she discovered that Briar had returned with food.

It had been a long time since the rice she'd had at dawn. Evvy did her best not to slop the bowl of chicken and lemon stew all over her face as she ate, but it was a near thing. She thought she might die happy when she saw the plate of spicy seminola cake that Briar had also brought.

"I *love* Trader food!" she cried.

"Do you know, when I don't particularly want to eat, all I have to do is watch you devour whatever is before you and I feel hungry," Rosethorn remarked.

Evvy and Briar carried the empty dishes back to the Trader washing tubs and did their share of washing up in thanks for the meal. By the time they returned to their chambers, Rosethorn had left in search of her meditation.

"I'll be back," Evvy told Briar and the cats in Chammuri when she saw the woman was gone. "Unless you want to come along. Actually you should."

Briar, who had picked up one of his *shakkans,* looked at her with suspicion. "Go along where? I thought you would want a nap."

At least he's quick enough to speak Chammuri, Evvy thought. "I have to talk to Rosethorn."

Briar's lips went tight and his eyes went hard. "You have to do no such thing. You heard her. She said *meditation.* She needs quiet. She needs to relax. All of that imperial carrying-on was hard on her."

Evvy crossed her arms on her chest. "I know that almost as well as you, Briar Moss. Maybe I'm not a brilliant, dung-nosed *nanshur* like some people, but I'm no paperwit, either. You might think that I have something *important* to say. Something she *ought* to know, even if *I* don't have a cartwheel of metal hanging around my neck." She marched out of the building, bound for the gate.

It wasn't long before the tiny rocks on the path behind her let her know that he was following. She had found the stream and entered the wood before he said, "Evvy, stop. Look at me." She did. "Don't pout," he ordered. "I just don't think she needs to know we helped, you know."

"That isn't what I was going to say," Evvy snapped. "What I *am* going to say? She'll bite my head off if I wait too long to tell her." She set off down the stream bank again. "You don't believe I care about her almost as much as you do."

"I know you care about her," he retorted, trotting until he could walk beside her. "Or I would've just pushed you into the water."

"Do you think you could talk *any* louder?" they heard Rosethorn call. "Because I am reasonably certain my meditations did not include the two of you squabbling like a nestful of birds."

As they rounded a bend in the stream, they saw Rosethorn seated cross-legged on top of a large, flat boulder. "He started it," Evvy replied. "I didn't *ask* him to follow me. He invited himself."

"I was trying to stop her," Briar said.

"What part of *alone* did either of you not hear?" Rosethorn wanted to know.

"I'm sorry," Evvy said, climbing up until she was close enough to Rosethorn to whisper. Briar came to stand beside her. "Bend down, please? Parahan told me something yesterday. This is the first time I think it's safe to tell you."

Rosethorn frowned and leaned toward them. The three were so close that strands of Rosethorn's hair brushed Evvy's head while her sleeve covered Briar's face until he held it back. The woman braced herself gently on Briar's shoulder.

"He said the emperor is going to Inxia to join the rest of the army that's been gathering there since Inxia surrendered," Evvy whispered in soft Chammuri. "As soon as the emperor gets there he's going to invade Gyongxe. They're already near the border. He doesn't trust his generals anymore. He's going to lead the attack himself."

Her legs hurt from standing on tiptoe when she was so tense. She lowered herself until she was flat-footed. Looking up again, she realized Rosethorn had covered her open mouth with her hand. She was stricken, and Evvy had done it.

"I'm sorry," Evvy said, still whispering. "I know it was bad. I told you as soon as I thought it was safe. Briar didn't know. I was scared to say anything in the palace, not when I didn't know what had spells on it!"

Rosethorn stared off into the distance. Evvy wanted very badly to ask what she was thinking, but sometimes it was best to leave Rosethorn to her thoughts. Finally the woman clambered down the boulders.

"So much for quiet meditation," she muttered. "I'll have to consider this for a while. You two will mind your tongues and behave, do you understand me?"

"Yes, Rosethorn," they chorused.

She set off down the path back to the caravansary, her pace brisk. Briar held Evvy back until Rosethorn was out of earshot. He then demanded quietly, "You couldn't have told *me* this before?"

"I didn't dare," Evvy said as they followed Rosethorn, walking more slowly. "It was last night. We were seeing him off. Then we were going back and I was so tired. It's not like there's anything we can do."

Briar rubbed the top of his head, looking tired. "I just hope she feels the same way."

"I'll be glad when we leave Yanjing," Evvy told him. "I'm scared we'll trip over something really bad. It hasn't happened yet, but I keep expecting it."

"There are shrines to the gods in the walls all around the inside of the caravansary," Briar said. "First thing we do when we get back inside the gates, you take an offering to that Heibei luck god of yours. A *nice* offering, mind. And you ask him to get us out of here safely!"

Evvy beamed at her teacher. "That's a splendid idea." She had a piece of white jade that would be perfect, and a piece of lapis lazuli for Kanzan the Merciful. Even gods couldn't be able to resist such fine bits of stone. She would feel better once she had enlisted their help. Heibei had to like her more than he did the emperor, who handed out bad luck to so many, and how could Kanzan like someone who hurt and killed so many people?

At the back of her mind she felt a dark flicker of fear — what about the gods of Gyongxe, and Parahan's gods, who also had something at stake now? She stomped on that flicker until it didn't bother her anymore. Prayers and presents to her two favorite gods would fix all of this, just as giving Parahan's news to Rosethorn had meant passing a hateful burden to someone who could handle it. She could concentrate on the journey, and only the journey.

Later in the afternoon the three of them were cutting vegetables into a soup to share with some fellow travelers when they heard the thunder of horses approaching the gate. They drew together, dropping their knives into the bowls of vegetables.

Caravansary guards ran to the gate, iron-shod staves in their hands. An archer on the wall turned and whistled three sharp notes that sent the men away from the road as a company of imperial troops, accompanied by three mages, rode in. Ten of them galloped through the caravansary in the direction of the rear gate.

Evvy felt her heart begin to hammer in her chest. "Relax," Rosethorn murmured softly.

Rajoni and Changdao, the master of the caravansary, walked up to the haughty man who appeared to be in command. Changdao and Rajoni bowed deeply.

The noble did not speak at all. The younger man who carried his banner did that. The older mage who rode next to him made a series of motions with his hands, forcing Briar to look away. Evvy knew he could see the magic being done. When the bannerman spoke, his voice was loud, much louder than it would have been without magical help. She was certain it was being heard everywhere inside the caravansary walls.

"Travelers and those who keep this place, attend. A valuable slave of southern Realms blood has escaped from the grounds of the Winter Palace!" the bannerman proclaimed. "Remain in your places as the imperial warriors search. No harm will be done unless you are sheltering this runaway. Any who do shelter this Parahan of Kombanpur will receive the utmost of the emperor's displeasure — those persons, their parents, grandparents, families, cousins, to the third degree of relationship both older and younger, no one will be spared."

"Mila, save us," Rosethorn whispered.

"Those who give us useful information will receive great rewards and advancement at the hands of our glorious lord, Wielder of the Dragon Sword, Holder of the Orb of Wisdom, Emperor Weishu of the Long Dynasty," the bannerman continued. "Go about your tasks unless our warriors require your assistance."

The soldiers dismounted, leaving the horses with a few of their number, and dispersed among the stables, supply buildings, and housing. Only the captain, his bannerman, and the mage who had amplified his speech remained where they had halted. Changdao stayed with them, though they did not talk to him at all. Rajoni trotted off in the direction of the brightly painted Trader house carts, presumably to act as middle person between the soldiers and the caravan.

"Back to work," Rosethorn said. "Not you, Evvy, not chopping, anyway." Evvy looked at her hands and had to agree. They were shaking too much for her to risk picking up a knife.

Briar sent her for a bucket of water. She got it, looking at the ground rather than the warriors. She almost dropped it on him when she saw three soldiers enter their set of rooms.

"The cats!" she cried. "They'll knock over the gate stones!" She put the bucket down and ran to their quarters before Briar or Rosethorn could grab her. Two of the soldiers were looking into the bedchambers. One knelt just outside the line of gate stones and was scratching Ball under the chin.

"I'm sorry," Evvy said. It was hard to think badly of anyone who petted her cats, even if it was Ball, who liked everyone. "I just wanted to warn you, the stones are magicked so they stay on that side of them."

"There's a nice trick," the soldier said with admiration. "Useful when you're traveling, I'll wager. But . . . do they run alongside, or how do they keep up?"

Evvy showed him the carry-baskets and the basket the cats used as a privy. He told her about his own cats, to the point where she almost forgot to be terrified. She walked out with the three of them and, once the inspection of the caravansary was done, waved good-bye as they rode away.

Rosethorn and Briar walked up behind her as the other occupants of the caravansary took deep breaths and talked a little too loudly in their relief. "Did they try to get into our mage stuff?" Briar asked.

Evvy shook her head. "Not even enough to get hurt by the protecting spells," she said, "not like those *yujinons* yesterday, looking into our bags like we'd bundled a big man into one."

"Charmed by the cats again?" Rosethorn asked. Evvy nodded. "How many times have we used checking on those creatures to keep an eye on soldiers inspecting our things?"

Briar put an arm around Evvy's shoulders. "They earn their keep, those cats."

Rosethorn gently tweaked Evvy's ear. "They do indeed."

When Evvy turned to protest an unearned ear tweak, Rosethorn tweaked her own ear, then laid her forefinger beside her nose. That was a sign Briar had taught them both, a bit of thief sign from his youth that meant uncanny doings, or mage work. The tweak of her own ear was notice to both of her younger companions that Rosethorn suspected the soldiers had planted spy spells in the caravansary.

Evvy growled.

"You're getting hungry," Briar said wisely. He didn't resent being spied on the way Rosethorn and Evvy did; he expected it. He did sigh when Rosethorn shook her finger, telling him silently he wasn't to try to find and dismantle the spy spells. Evvy giggled despite her resentment. "Let's finish working on that soup."

After the soldiers' departure the Traders retreated to their house carts. Evvy didn't blame them. Too often, when nations were in upheaval and looking for someone to blame, they singled out Traders. In return, the Traders had strict rules in their dealings with outsiders. If Briar's sister Daja, and in fact Briar and all three of his sisters, had not done some notable services for Traders now and then, these eastern Traders would not be so willing to help them now.

The company of travelers was subdued as they gathered for supper. Everyone had something to contribute: bread they had made on flat stones, different kinds of tea, pickled vegetables, cooked eggs, and fried fish. The other diners were loud enough in their complaints about people who broke the peaceful traditions of a caravansary that the silence of Rosethorn and her companions went unnoticed.

"I'll tell you this for nothing," said a merchant from Namorn who was also bound for the Pebbled Sea. Rosethorn had cared for a cut on his arm and he felt kindly toward her. "You won't see anyone from a Living Circle temple between here and Hanjian. The emperor's Magistrates of the Vigilant Eyes announced back in Seed Moon that they had uncovered a fearful plot against the Living Circle faith. For the protection of the temples and those who serve in them, they put them under guard, by soldiers. None of the dedicates or their novices, or even any of those that worship, are being allowed in or out."

Rosethorn stared at him. "But I heard none of this where we were!"

"Yanjingyi people don't talk about the doings of the Vigilant Eyes," the merchant replied. "It's bad luck."

"It isn't only the Living Circle," another diner said. She was one of the drovers who handled the Namornese merchant's mules. "Many of the foreign temples are either closed or under guard.

Only ones for the Yanjingyi gods and goddesses are open to all, and too bad for us that worship other gods. We can only hope they hear us so far from home."

"A pity you couldn't go to Gyongxe," a woman from one of the other groups of travelers said. "They say that even if your god has no temple, you still have a chance of reaching his ear with your prayer."

"Oh?" the Namornese man asked. "How is that?"

"It's Gyongxe," the woman said, as if that made the answer plain. When the people from the Namornese group stared at her, she chuckled and shrugged. "That's why so many build their temples there, even when their faiths have homes elsewhere. That's why the rivers that spring from there are sacred. Gyongxe is the closest you can get to the gods without dying. Everyone knows that. The Drimbakangs, all three ranges of them, they are the pillars that hold the heavens aloft."

"Ha!" Evvy said, poking Briar. "I *told* you the mountains were important! And now I'll *never* get to see them up close!"

"Ow," Briar protested, glaring at her. "Haven't you seen enough mountains?"

The girl who handled mules drew Briar closer to her side. "I'll protect you from the skinny girl who likes mountains," she assured him.

"I think it's time to clean up and go to bed," Rosethorn announced, getting to her feet. "I am sorry to hear your news," she told the Namornese man. "We were in Gyongxe before we came here, and they had no word of this."

"Perhaps he will return the foreign religions to favor as

quickly as he took it from them," the merchant replied. "We can all pray on that."

Yawning, Evvy set about gathering their bowls and utensils, but Briar stopped her. "We'll do it," he said, taking them. "You go to bed." From the look he gave the mule drover, Evvy wasn't sure how much washing up would actually get done, but it was no skin off her neb, to steal one of Briar's sayings. She hurried inside, changed the arrangement of gate stones so the cats could sleep with their favorite people, then prepared for bed. Before she closed her eyes, she sent another prayer to Heibei for Parahan.

She slept, to dreams that Parahan was running ahead of her. She was racing as fast as she could, but she couldn't catch up, no matter how hard she tried.

Long after she could hear Briar and Evvy breathing in sleep, Rosethorn lay wide-awake, absently stroking the lanky Apricot, who lay inside the curve of her arm. She envied the cat. The day's events and discoveries kept her thinking. Duty and wish were tearing at her heart.

Mila of the Grain, what shall I do? she wondered, desperate. I just wanted to go to the places Lark was always telling me about before I was too old to do it. I wanted to see plants and trees and flowers whose names I didn't know in my bones, and I have. I'm bringing home seed and magicked clippings that will keep me busy for years, if I can get them there!

If I can get them there. When Evvy told me about the invasion, I confess to cowardice. I thought that the local temples would have sent word to Gyongxe somehow. Someone among them must be a far-speaker of some kind. But if they've been locked up for months, under guard, I can't be sure if they know the emperor secretly made peace with Inxia, giving him a broad road to Gyongxe. I can't be sure if the temples north of Dohan saw the armies gathering and heard gossip that their new target was Gyongxe. And if I am not sure . . .

Mila, my goddess, I want to go *home*. I want to see my lover again. I want my own food, and air I can breathe without fighting. I want to see Crane, and Niko, and the girls. I want my own garden.

But there is my duty. Somehow I have to leave the caravan and make certain that Gyongxe knows. That our First Circle Temple is prepared. They'll need me when war comes, too. I'll send the children on with the caravan. Briar will go if I tell him he has to look after Evvy. I think.

She lay like that for a long time, staring into the dark.

When the caravan workers came to rouse them in the gray hour before dawn, they found Rosethorn, Briar, and Evvy already awake, dressed, and packed. Most of their things, including Briar's *shakkans* and Evvy's cats, were already on a wagon whose use they had paid for. The rest they loaded swiftly, with the ease of long practice, onto packhorses. Then they saddled their riding horses. Briar elected to drive the wagon for the morning, neither Rosethorn nor Evvy being awake enough to do so. The caravansary workers brought everyone hot tea and steamed buns stuffed with pork or vegetable filling as the travelers finished their preparations.

The sun was just clear of the horizon as Rajoni, the ride leader, raised her staff. Her voice swelled in the trilling cry that was the signal to move out. More and more Trader voices rose from their own wagons and from the guards on horseback, as the caravan passed through the open gates.

CHAPTER
EIGHT

THE ROAD SOUTH, DOHAN TO KUSHI

So relieved was Rosethorn to be out in the countryside, able to leave the caravan now and then to investigate a new plant, that two days of travel and three inspections by imperial soldiers passed before she realized that her two youngsters were behaving oddly. She also had to wait and stay with the caravan to be sure that her instincts were correct. Most of the time Evvy and Briar behaved as they always did when traveling. They rambled up and down the caravan, making friends with Traders and merchants alike. They helped with the horses, the meals, and cleanup. Briar spent idle moments in the back of the wagon putting together seed bombs. These were mixes of lethally long-spined thorny plants that he and Rosethorn had created to grow very fast when the cloth that held them struck the ground. Evvy had her own magical weapons to work on and she did so, knapping sharp edges onto disks of flint. All of that was perfectly normal.

In the second search by imperial soldiers who looked for Parahan, Rosethorn thought both of her youngsters looked uncommonly pale. As the soldiers questioned other travelers,

Briar put his arm around Evvy, when neither she nor he encouraged gestures of affection before strangers. They were cheerful enough when they answered the soldiers' questions, but something was odd. Then Rosethorn spotted a Yanjingyi variant of an herb she used to cleanse wounds and she left the road to get some. By the time she returned, the soldiers were waiting only to question her.

No, she would say, far more politely than she would have done had she been in a friendly country. I have seen no escaped slaves or captives. I have all I can manage keeping up with those two children there. She would point out Evvy and Briar, who watched from their seat on the wagon. Usually the big cat Monster watched, too, blinking sleepily in the sun. No, I have received no messages from anyone who wanted me to hide them on my wagon, Rosethorn would answer. I know better than to break the law in a foreign country. Besides, the Traders discourage it. Are we finished? I need to get these plants in damp wrappings before they wither.

It wasn't true — her magic would preserve the plants as long as she wanted to — but the questions tired her.

The soldiers would let her go.

On the third night, after two more such searches, Rosethorn made arrangements for them to take supper at their own fire in the shelter of their wagon. Briar and Evvy collected their servings of the evening meal while she tied their horses in a picket line near their wagon. If anyone thought they could snoop on the trio's conversation, the horses would give warning.

Once the meal and cleanup were done and they had settled by the fire with a bit of work before bedtime, Rosethorn took a sip of her tea and said in Chammuri, "Do you know what I miss?"

Briar looked up from his night's collection of seed bombs, mildly puzzled. Evvy, who was rubbing Mystery's ears, shook her head.

Rosethorn went on. "The entire time we were in the palace, I don't think I went half a day without 'Parahan said this' or 'Parahan told me that.'" Evvy's head jerked up. Rosethorn said, as if she hadn't noticed, "I heard this mostly from Evvy, but you had some interesting talks with him, too, Briar."

"We miss him, that's all," Briar said, but his eyes were too steady as he looked at her. She was very familiar with that gaze. He was waiting to see how much she knew. It could be a matter of stolen grapes or a missing prince; but her boy was in it up to his elbows.

"When we left Gyongxe, you both talked about Dokyi and the God-King until I thought you wanted me to adopt them. Now we've been away from the palace four days. Your good friend — our good friend — actually managed to escape. It's clear he hasn't been found. Yet you two haven't uttered a word. Aren't you worried? Aren't you wondering how he managed to slip his chains and his cage?" Evvy glanced at Briar, who remained absolutely still. With increasing wrath, because suddenly a few things made very good sense, Rosethorn whispered, "That *is* the wonderful thing, isn't it? You would think that only magic would help him to escape, but if that were the case, the soldiers wouldn't be looking for him still. The mages would have found him. So it wasn't magic that helped him to slip his shackles."

"Please don't be angry," Evvy blurted. "I stole the picks, and

I took them to Parahan, and I moved the blocks so he could get out. And I opened the locks."

Rosethorn looked at Evvy. "You, Evumeimei Dingzai, stole Briar's lock picks and unlocked Parahan's shackles and cage."

"She knows I did it, Evvy," Briar said. "Even if you stole my picks, those were fancy locks. You're not ready for them yet."

"I really did move the stones," Evvy muttered. "We put them back. None of our magic is there anymore, so they won't know we used it."

Rosethorn drew her legs up and rested her face on her knees. Finally she looked at her companions. "Go to bed," she ordered them. "No, wait. Did he tell you his plans?"

They shook their heads.

"Excellent. Go to bed, both of you."

She wished they had gone to their bedrolls under the wagon in utter fear of her wrath. Instead, as she was putting out the fire, she heard Evvy murmur to Briar, "That went better than I thought."

Rosethorn held her hands palm up and looked at the sky. Gracious Mila, help me explain how close they came to the most horrible kind of death, she begged her goddess. Give them knowledge of the world before the world kills them. Give me patience, before I buy two barrels and ship them home that way. I beg you, my goddess, guide me before I do something dreadful and box their ears.

Rosethorn knew very well that these weren't the reasons she hadn't given them a long list of punishments and a royal scold.

She had shown mercy because in two days she would have to tell them that she was sending them on to Hanjian without her.

With dawn came the promise of rain. While Evvy fetched tea and steamed dumplings, Briar and Rosethorn set the ribs on the wagon and rolled the heavy cover over them to protect the most delicate of their belongings. They had scarcely gone two miles down the road when the skies delivered on their promise. The cats, who liked to go for a run first thing after breakfast, returned yowling in complaint and took up positions under the cover. Soon after Evvy had made certain all of them were accounted for, the traffic on the road south came to a halt. There were soldiers ahead, searching and questioning the travelers. Briar tied his riding horse's reins to the wagon and climbed up on the seat with Rosethorn. Gently he took the team's reins from her hands.

Rosethorn decided that now was as good a time as any. She half turned so that both of her companions could see her face under her wide-brimmed straw hat. "Tomorrow we'll be reaching a big market town called Kushi. You might remember it from the map I showed you. We're going to have a small change in our plans after that. The caravan turns southeast from there, going on to Hanjian. You two will take our things and stay with the caravan, understand me? Briar, you're to get Evvy, the cats, your *shakkans* —"

"No." Briar held the reins tightly, so much so that his knuckles had gone white, but he wasn't pulling too hard on the horses' mouths. She made sure of that.

"Don't argue with me, boy," she warned.

"No," Evvy said. She knuckled an eye before a tear could escape. "I'm sorry, I'm sorry, but I couldn't leave him in the cage. Please don't send me away." She crawled to the back with the cats. "I won't leave, you can't make me."

Rosethorn turned to Briar. "You have to take her back to Emelan," she said, trying to hold his eyes with her own. He would not look at her, keeping his gaze on the team that pulled the wagon. "Briar, you heard what they said, Weishu has kept the religious people in the local temples prisoner. Unless there was a miracle of some kind, no one has been able to smuggle word to Gyongxe. I don't know if I'll beat the imperial army there, but I have to try."

"It's a horrible long way," Evvy argued. "It'll be dangerous, with bandits and rock slides and border guards. You'll *need* us."

"Be sensible," Briar said. "Even with people being locked up and all, you're going the long way around. They probably will know by then. What will you do, turn and walk back out?"

Rosethorn stared at the horse's ears. "I have to help. You won't understand. If the First Circle Temple falls . . . It's sacred to everyone of the Living Circle. This is my faith, and my devotion. My vows."

"Now we come to it," Briar said bleakly.

Rosethorn glared at him. "*My* vows. But I won't risk your lives because I swore to defend my faith and those who take shelter in it. Neither of you is a believer. I am not dragging either of you into a war, and that is my last word on the subject!"

Rosethorn looked around the inside of the *gilav*'s wagon with admiration. The home of the head of the caravan and his family was ornate and as organized as the caravan itself. Each inch of space was put to use, with no clutter allowed on any surface. Rosethorn always took away ideas for her small workshop at home.

She exchanged her greetings with Rajoni and her mother, Nisha — the *gilav* himself took over as ride leader while Nisha and his daughter had their midday with Rosethorn and talked business. The women invited Rosethorn to take a seat on a fold-out bench as she surveyed the food set on the table between the three of them.

Since this clan of Traders had its roots in the Realms of the Sun, Rosethorn was braced for the spicy vegetable stew with fish and green chilies and the pickles flavored with mustard seeds. Silently she thanked Mila of the Grain for the rice that took some of the bite off the chilies and mustard. She even managed believable thanks to her hosts for the excellence of the meal.

She always thought of Lark when she ate food like this. Lark could eat spicy food by the bucket, the hotter the better. She'd acquired a taste for it as a traveling player on the roads between the Pebbled Sea and the Storm Dragons Ocean. It was thanks to Lark that Rosethorn had at least a little preparation for some of the deadlier dishes of the southern and eastern countries.

Once they had cleaned their hands, Rajoni was pouring a final cup of tea when Nisha asked, "You said you have business with us?"

Rosethorn picked up the small cloth bundle she had put beside her when she took her seat. Carefully she set it before them, centering it with her hands. She knew that she had the two Traders' absolute attention. Negotiating business with Traders was a ceremony, one that Rosethorn, Briar, and Evvy appreciated. It involved gifts, which showed respect, and money, which showed thanks for the extra time and trouble those who conducted the caravan would be put to.

"To our sorrow, we have realized we must change our plans," Rosethorn told the other women. "For reasons we may not discuss, we must leave the caravan at Kushi, but our goods, including Briar's miniature trees, must be conveyed to Hanjian, and placed aboard the next Trader ship for Summersea in Emelan, on the Pebbled Sea. We will need to purchase our pack animals and riding horses from you as well." She didn't mention that she would be selling or trading their horses for others in Kushi. The less that was known of their plans, even by tight-mouthed Traders, the better.

"What of the cats?" Nisha asked with a frown. "It seems to me that your Evvy exercises a control over the cats that will not be possible for strangers. It would be difficult to convey them. Not impossible, given proper consideration, of course."

"Of course," Rosethorn said. She sighed. "No, the cats will be coming with us." In fact, the battle over the cats had been almost as bad as the battle for Briar and Evvy to stay with Rosethorn. It was Evvy's threat not to travel with them, but to follow them, *with* the cats, that had forced Rosethorn to agree.

"These are all very difficult and unusual requirements to fulfill," Nisha said. She folded her hands on the table. It was time for the real bargaining to start.

Rosethorn opened the topmost folds of cloth on her bundle to reveal two rubies the size of pigeon's eggs. Evvy could call forth the magic that was part of any stone, which meant that others would pay highly for what she had handled. She accepted precious stones in trade, which had come in handy on their way east. Hidden deep among the girl's things was a store of gems that the three of them had accumulated against emergencies during their travels in exchange for magical work.

Rajoni and Nisha were interested in the rubies. Their faces were expressionless, but Rosethorn could read the signs in the twitch of Rajoni's shoulder and the hitch in Nisha's breath. Now Rosethorn opened another fold in her package to reveal a vial and a small cloth bundle.

"A drop of this" — Rosethorn touched a finger to the vial — "on the lips of one you believe to be lying to you will result in truthful speech. A pinch of this" — she touched the bundle of herbs — "in a cup of tea for a laboring mother will ease her birth completely. They are our gifts, a thank-you in advance for the trouble we will cause."

"We will need a list of your requirements," Nisha said. "Written instructions for the transport of your goods to Hanjian, and another for the ship that will take them to your home."

Rosethorn reached into a pocket in her habit and brought out folded papers. There had been plenty of time that morning, while waiting for the imperials to search for Parahan, to write everything out. "I will have the instructions for the ship's captain later this afternoon," she said, handing the papers over.

Rajoni looked her over. "*You* will need magic on your face," she said frankly. "Briar and Evvy are fine for this country, but you stand out."

"I could go veiled," Rosethorn suggested.

"Our *mimander* can place a spell that is hard for other mages to detect," Nisha replied. "We've had to use it before. It will last a week, and those who look on you will believe you come from their country."

Rosethorn frowned. "I thought *mimanders* could only deal in one kind of magic."

Rajoni shrugged. "You are able to work a spell from another mage if it is complete and needs but a word from you, yes? It is the same here."

Rosethorn grimaced. "I understand. There is another thing."

The women raised their brows in the same expression. Up until that moment Rosethorn would have said Rajoni resembled her father, the *gilav*. She did her best not to smile, because now it was clear the daughter was her mother's child as well. Rosethorn took a sip of tea and opened another fold of her bundle. There lay some of the emperor's farewell gift, ten pieces of gold, each the length and width of Rosethorn's hand and twice the thickness of her cup.

"I need a map of the country between Kushi and the end of the Snow Serpent Pass in Gyongxe," she said quietly. "And I need a map of Gyongxe. I will copy yours or Briar will, but we need them."

Nisha looked at Rosethorn, then at Rajoni. Trader maps were sacred documents, kept secret among Traders. Rosethorn saw refusal in the women's eyes.

She opened the last fold. The mage back in Laenpa had traded Evvy three Kombanpur diamonds for a handful of stones that Evvy had prepared for magical use. In turn, Evvy had spent one month of her spare time that winter doing nothing else but thinking about those stones when she was not carrying them in her pockets, bathing with them, and even sleeping with them. The next month she had turned one of the diamonds into ten shards, which one of the local stone merchants happily traded for two small diamonds. The month after that, with further thought, she had tried to shape a large diamond again, carefully running her power down chosen fissures in the gem. The result lay on the cloth before them: a clean, many-surfaced stone like a jewel-cut ruby, sapphire, or emerald, with a brilliant white fire. The cuts and stone were uneven, but Rosethorn could tell that made no difference whatever to the other women. She reached for it, saying, "I do understand the maps are —"

Nisha beat her to the diamond. "We will copy the maps. You will have them by the time we stop for the night. Be assured, they will be correct in all the ways you will require."

Rajoni reached for a small basket nearby and placed the gifts in that. "It is true, then? The emperor means to wage war on Gyongxe?"

Rosethorn said nothing.

Nisha was turning the diamond over in her palm. She looked up when Rosethorn did not reply. Seeing that Rosethorn hesitated, she pointed to the unlit lamp that hung over the table. "What is said under the lamp is repeated only to those who are trusted," she assured Rosethorn.

Rosethorn nodded. "He is going to invade through Inxia."

The Traders exchanged looks. "We were supposed to cross roads with Third Caravan Gerzi fifty miles north of Dohan," Rajoni said, her voice just above a whisper. "But only two of their people came by stealth to warn us. Imperial troops took the caravan. They now hold everyone but the two who escaped. Very slowly our people are leaving Yanjing. Our imperial treaty states clearly that we are permitted to trade without harm. Either this emperor thinks we do not know our own treaties, or he believes we fear him too much to punish him by refusing to trade."

Rosethorn felt a chill run down her spine. "I pray you will escape Yanjing before he sees that is what you are doing," she replied. "It will go badly with your people if he realizes you are fleeing altogether."

Rajoni made a V of two fingers and stabbed them at the floor. That was the way Traders signaled spitting when they were unwilling to soil their carpets.

"Even though you are not one of ours, your prayers are welcome," Nisha said. "Now, let us begin to make your arrangements. And do not worry that the other travelers will tell any imperial soldiers about those who left us unexpectedly in Kushi. We will make sure that they understand it is against their best interest to speak of it."

Rosethorn thanked them for the meal, and for the excellent bout of trading. Tying her wide straw hat to her head, she walked back to her wagon and her two unruly students. There was much to be done yet, even if the Traders had taken on the burden of copying the maps. Briar and Evvy had better have gotten their packing under way while she was gone, Rosethorn thought. She was still unhappy that they had been so impossible about continuing on to Emelan. She knew what Moonstream and her fellow dedicates back home would say when they learned she had dragged a child Evvy's age into a war.

Those two impossible young people would never hear that she was secretly glad they were coming with her. The only thing that had frightened her more than taking them into a land soon to be invaded was the thought of letting them travel back to Emelan without her. She trusted the Traders: The ties that bound Briar, his foster-sisters, their teachers, and the Traders were many and strong, too many and too strong to be erased by outsiders' money and magic. But they were not Rosethorn, and they were not aware of the special kinds of peril that followed those who wielded ambient magic.

It was almost dawn when the three of them finally gave up on sleeping and finished their last preparations. Briar and Rosethorn had spent time before bed working with their traveling clothes. Sandry had made them from an unusual cloth, both the wool that most people wore and linen spun together with the wool. It was the linen that had mattered on delicate occasions, when Rosethorn or Briar could call on it to look more elderly, worn, and hard-used than it was. Their neat, clean traveling tunics and breeches turned into the weary clothes that poor farmers wore for days on end as they went about long hours of work. The braided trim came off, to be packed away. The wooden buttons lost their polish and developed cracks and splinters. Briar planned to send Evvy to buy straw sandals for them while he and Rosethorn swapped their horses for others more suited to poor farmers.

Using Evvy's light stones they dressed, then quickly readied the horses and the cats. Two years' of experience at having to leave some places quickly had made them good at being quiet.

They were drinking tea made over some of Evvy's hot stones when Rosethorn raised the cat issue again. "Evvy, they'll know to look for the cats. Can't you —"

Evvy stared at her. "Then I'll follow on my own. You don't know. All those years in Prince's Heights in Chammur — my cats were all I had. You never spent all your days with strangers looking to wallop you just for living. They were my blanket when I didn't have anything else. When I had to eat rat, they shared with me. I am not dumping them with strangers in a foreign place."

Two of the hot stones cracked and went to pieces.

"Sorry." Evvy walked away from them, over to the wagon.

"We'll grow plants from the carry-baskets," Briar told Rosethorn soothingly. "If anyone asks, we'll say we bought the plants at the market and we're going to try them in the garden. No one will notice there's cats inside."

Steps — quiet ones — made them turn. Rajoni approached, carrying the smallest of lamps. She also had an old Trader woman with her. When they reached Briar and Rosethorn, Rajoni said, "When Grandmother learned what was going on — she had to log in your payment, understand — she told us we were fools."

"My children sell a charm to disguise the woman and never think of seven cats," the old woman remarked, and shook her head. "The soldiers capture you because of cats, then see charm to disguise woman and punish Traders. No."

"She came to offer her help," Rajoni explained when she realized Rosethorn thought the old woman was going to create problems.

"For a price," Briar said quietly.

Both women raised their eyebrows as if to say, What else? Money was the main thing that kept Traders free and alive in the hostile lands where they made their living.

"Isn't it the *mimander* who handles all spells, even purchased ones?" Rosethorn asked. He had come the night before and set the disguise spell before she went to bed. It had changed the look and feel of her from top to toe, everything about her but the way she spoke.

"The *mimander* still snores in his bed," the grandmother replied crisply. "And we have no charms to sell that will disguise baskets of cats as crates of gabbling chickens. This is work that must be done over the baskets and over the cats."

"But you can do it," Evvy said. Her hands were bunched into fists. "Even their sounds?"

The old woman looked at her. "What do you offer, girl who changed the nature of diamonds?"

"But I didn't," Evvy said. "I just broke them in the way they want to be broken. What people call flaws in stones, those are really just opportunities, you know."

"Diamond opportunities are beyond other *lugshai*," the old woman said, using the word for non-Trader craftsmen.

Evvy grinned. "I have a few opportunities, then." She went to the pack with her mage kit and dug in it. She soon returned with a piece of cloth. When she opened it, she revealed four long pieces of diamond that sparked in the light from Rajoni's lamp. "These are diamond splinters. Your *lugshai*, or whoever you get, must fix these really well to a metal grip, then use them as a chisel on one of the flaws in a diamond. Diamond will cut diamond. It will cut the surface, too, so they have to grip the stone tight in some kind of vise, and it will break diamond, so they can't hit too hard, understand? Have we a bargain?"

"Show me the cats. Then you can tell me if we have a bargain," the woman told her.

Briar and Rosethorn stayed with Rajoni. "I still don't understand," Rosethorn murmured to the other woman. "We were always told about *mimanders* and their one specialty."

"But they do not hold all the magic for the clan, any more than one mage holds all the magic for the village," the ride leader replied. "Some of us have more or fewer talents for different kinds of magic, and some don't want to limit themselves to one thing all their days. Grandmother discovered she could hide things when there was a killing riot against Traders and she hid her whole family. She was only five. She can un-sour and sour milk, tell if a well has gone bad, cleanse a water source if it is bad. And she can make my mother back down as fast as a monsoon rain, which looks like magic to *me*. Are your horses ready?"

By the time the cats had come to look and sound like chickens — and their baskets had come to resemble crates — Evvy and Rajoni's grandmother were on good terms. Evvy was even allowed to kiss the old woman on the cheek before Rajoni took her back to the Trader carts. Then it was time for the three travelers to mount their riding horses, the weariest, scruffiest animals the Traders would allow them to keep, and lead their four packhorses to the market gate.

It was a matter of a bit here and a bit there. When they emerged from the city some time after noon, they had sold the horses they had taken from the caravan at one horse trader, then bought shaggy, sturdy ponies to ride and four bright-eyed, wary mules for pack animals from another. These were farm mules, used to humans and animals alike, which barely blinked at the false chickens they were forced to carry. The ponies, the trader had assured Rosethorn, were bred in the mountains and used to breathing there.

After a trip to the sellers of used clothes, Evvy once again had the bright head cloths she loved. Rosethorn chose the more sober colors of a married woman. Both had put on long skirts made of odds and ends, but their breeches were underneath them, just in case.

Their packs could have been supplies for a farm or the things they needed for a long visit to relatives. As they left the town they presented the picture of a family that knew how to travel. Each carried a cloth sling across the front of their chests. Other travelers used their slings for food, water bottles, cloths for wiping away sweat, or coin purses. Rosethorn and Briar carried round balls of seed made to explode into thorny, strangling vines when they hit a target. Evvy carried her stone alphabet, razor-edged throwing disks, and honey candies. She was always afraid of being hungry.

Once they had passed the guards at the south gate on their way out of Kushi, Briar let Rosethorn and Evvy ride ahead. He purchased steamed plum buns, pressed-rice cakes, and ham at the vendors who kept shop beside the road. It was there that he saw an old beggar or madman hobble through the gate, propped by a long staff. His sack bent him half over. He was utterly filthy, barefooted and bareheaded, missing teeth and blind in one eye. His mingled gray and black locks were lank with greasy dirt. He offered a begging bowl to one of the soldiers on the gate, but the man just pushed it away and ordered the poor creature to move along. The beggar stumbled on and offered his bowl to travelers who were passing him by. Several wrinkled their noses and pretended he wasn't there. Others walked far around him.

Briar shook his head. People assumed they would always be well fed and well clothed. The beggar lurched toward him, bringing a wave of piss-stink and other smells with him. Briar breathed through his mouth and beckoned so the man could see him with his good eye. The beggar approached on stumbling feet, his staff clicking on the stones of the road. His feet, like his hands, were wrapped in stained and dirty rags.

"Good afternoon to you," Briar said. "Here you go." He put a handful of coins in the man's bowl first, then covered them with one of his many clean handkerchiefs. On top of that he put two of the plum buns and three pressed-rice cakes. The man could chew those even with some of his front teeth missing.

"Thank you, young master," the beggar said, lisping through the gaps in his teeth. "May Kanzan the Merciful smile on you all your days."

Briar put his palms together and bowed. "May she smile on us all, friend," he said politely.

The beggar stopped to tuck his food into various places in his upper garments. The coins vanished into a breeches pocket. Then he limped on, chewing a rice cake.

Briar turned to collect the rest of the food he'd bought for his girls.

"You waste your money on the likes of that," the cook said. "He'll just spend those coins on wine."

Briar shrugged. "If it makes him warm and happy for an hour or two, I'm not the one to judge." He bowed to the cook and tucked the bundle into the sling over his chest. Excusing himself to those he bumped, he wove through the walkers, wagons, and riders as he searched for Rosethorn and Evvy. He thought he would overtake the beggar in only a few yards, but he was well along before he passed the man. The beggar had managed to hitch a ride on the tail of a farmer's cart, and was dozing in spite of the faint drizzle.

Briar grinned and passed the cart. Every step he took away from Kushi and their last ties to the caravan and the palace made his heart lighter. The Traders had been decent — they always were — and the people traveling with the caravan were pleasant enough to talk to, but it was hard to keep an eye on Rosethorn and Evvy among so many people. Here, too, it would be difficult, but soldiers would not be palace troops, fearing for their lives when the emperor learned that Parahan had escaped. Soldiers here would be bored and uninterested.

He soon caught up to Rosethorn and Evvy. They ate in the saddle while keeping a sharp eye on the pack animals. None of them had much to say. The cart with the sleeping beggar passed them by, but they passed him before too long. He was afoot again. The cart had turned down a smaller road away from the main one. The beggar, it seemed, wanted to go south, but not the farmer who had given him a ride.

More and more of those on the main road turned off it as the day drew to its close. Still, there were plenty of travelers remaining to enter the caravansary near sunset. Here, Rosethorn's group was not far from the banks of the Grinding Fist River and the high bridge they would be crossing in the morning. The sound of the river's thunder as it descended from the Drimbakang Sharlog was intimidating, though Briar would have bitten his own tongue rather than admit it.

Briar and Rosethorn told those few fellow travelers who had taken an interest that they could not afford the prices of a caravansary, and they set their small camp up not far from the gates. Briar wasn't worried about bandits or wild animals here. Other travelers couldn't afford the caravansary or chose to save money, so the camp outside the walls was a good-sized one. The guards atop the caravansary walls could see them and come to their rescue if there was trouble.

Rosethorn sent Evvy to a nearby stream to fill their teapot and soup pot. The girl returned to tell Briar, "You know that beggar fellow? He's soaking his feet in the stream. He stinks. I got the water upstream from him."

Briar and Rosethorn looked at each other. "You could put him downwind," Briar suggested.

"Go get him," she growled. "And keep him away from our chickens."

"Oh, no, no, young fellow, thank you, no," the beggar said when Briar made his offer. "I won't bother anyone here."

"You won't bother us. It won't be easy to see in the dark, and you're off on your own. We're making soup." Briar used the voice he called his "best wheedle." He could get things out of Rosethorn with that voice. "My mother can do very good things with soup. There will be ham in it."

The beggar, it seemed, was made of sterner stuff. "I know what I smell like." His lisping, slightly husky voice was gentle in the growing shadows. "I will be fine. Kanzan shower blessings on you and those kind women you travel with."

Briar returned to Rosethorn, shaking his head.

The night passed quietly. When they woke, Briar returned to the stream for the morning's tea water. The beggar was gone. A bowl that looked just like one of their own sat under his tree, freshly cleaned. Briar carried it back with the pot full of water.

"I took him a little soup after you went to bed," Rosethorn said. "That's all."

Guards in imperial colors left the caravansary with the rest of the travelers that morning. Those who had camped outside were already lined up at the bridge, waiting for them to unlock the tall gates. Briar, Rosethorn, and Evvy were near the end of that line with a pushy merchant behind them. They waited as the guards looked through many wagons before they finally unlocked the gates and people began to stream through.

"What were you looking for?" Briar asked one guard as he was about to ride onto the bridge.

"Escaped prisoner," the man said, and yawned. "As if he'd come this way."

"Gods pity him when the imperial torturers get him," the merchant in front of Rosethorn said bitterly.

Everyone murmured agreement. Then they rode onto the bridge, where the thunder of the river below drowned out the sound of their crossing.

CHAPTER
NINE

The gorge of the Snow Serpent River

Company continued to thin as people scattered to other roads. The land now was steep and hilly, with terrace farms on the slopes. Beyond them were mountains. By the map, Briar saw they were in a kind of funnel that would take them into the Snow Serpent Pass. Evvy would have no cause to complain after that. They would be traveling down a gorge through the Drimbakang Lho, the highest mountains in the world.

Briar kept a keen eye on the people around them, knowing that Evvy was too busy looking at the stones beside the road. The others were commoners by and large: an occasional priest on donkeyback, merchants on mules or horses followed by servants, peddlers, farmers, and the occasional beggar. Two days after they had crossed the bridge, Briar saw the man he had come to think of as *their* beggar again. They overtook him around mid-morning, when a large wedding party left the road to cross the river. The beggar was seated by the road, digging a stone out of the wrappings on his feet. Successful, he rose and hobbled off, leaning on his tall staff.

"He moves fast for someone with a bad back," Rosethorn murmured.

"Maybe he's used to it," Briar suggested.

Suddenly she stiffened. "Look at his neck."

The rags the beggar wore for scarves had come undone. The morning's stiff breeze blew them onto the hillside. He was struggling to climb after them when Evvy galloped uphill to grab the flyaway rags. She had learned some riding tricks in their two years of travel, and she loved to show off.

Like Rosethorn, Briar was staring. The beggar's neck was as dirty as the rest of him. What his dirt could not cover was the shackle gall around his throat, the kind of scar that would come from years of wearing a metal collar.

As Evvy rode over to the beggar with his neck scarves, Rosethorn murmured, "Without the pack he carries . . ."

Briar replied, "Could the long hair be a wig? It's a good one."

"The rags on his feet and hands could be as much to cover scars from his chains as to keep him warm," Rosethorn added. "But the blind eye?"

"Oh, that's easy," Briar told her. "This beggar we knew, back when I was with the Thief Lord, he would take the white lining of eggshells. He'd cut pieces of it to the right size, then punch a hole in them with a pin to see out of. It made me go all over goose bumps to watch him put them in his eyes, but he made money. It's the beggars that have something wrong with them that get the coin."

"Let's invite this one to supper," Rosethorn suggested.

"Let's. I'd like to know what he's doing out here."

Briar kept an eye on the beggar all that day as they progressed along the road. There were no inspections. It seemed that those who were hunting for the emperor's missing captive did not think he would be heading west.

Yet again they camped outside a caravansary. The beggar was the only other person there to use the well and fire pits set up in the shelter of the wall. Briar started supper and Evvy saw to the animals while Rosethorn went in search of him. By the time Briar had a thick, hearty soup bubbling over the fire, Rosethorn returned triumphant, the beggar in her wake.

Briar looked at them. "What, you aren't towing him by the ear?"

Evvy frowned. "Howcome you always do that to us and not to him?"

Parahan gave Briar and Evvy a sheepish look and a wave. His big satchel had lost its cover of rags and revealed itself as a couple of packs. These he put by the fire, as well as his staff, before he went to the well with an empty bucket. Once he filled it, he began to wash. The wig came off; the eye coverings came out. Rosethorn sent Evvy over with a cloth and a jar of soap. By the time Parahan joined them, all that remained of the beggar was his robes. He sat downwind of them to correct for the scent of his clothing.

"I don't understand," Evvy complained, once they had eaten enough hot food to be pleasant to one another. "Why are you going the same way we are?"

"It's simple enough," Parahan told them. "A man has to eat. I haven't a copper to my name, and if I try to go home, I doubt that I'll get there. I imagine my uncle has his spies out looking for me by now, or he will soon. Weishu will pay him to get me back this time, to show the Yanjingyi nobles that no one can thwart the emperor and get away with it."

Evvy shuddered. "If it looks like the emperor will get you, kill yourself first."

Parahan nodded. "I have seen what he's done to others. Trust me, if I know I cannot escape, I will not let myself fall into Weishu's hands a second time."

"And the eating part?" Briar prodded.

Parahan shrugged. "Gyongxe will be hiring fighters soon. The temples have plenty of money and treasure from pilgrims. I've seen the list of the jewelry my family has sent to the temples so the priests in Gyongxe will pray for my ancestors. They can afford me. I may be rusty, but I used to be considered a good warrior. It would have been even nicer if I could lead troops, but I'll take what I can get. They won't know I used to be a general." He grinned at Rosethorn. "Maybe you'll put in a good word for me if I don't make it to the temples dedicated to my own gods?" Less cheerfully he added, "I imagine I'll be able to give you a demonstration of my skills at the border."

"What do you mean?" Evvy had been about to serve herself another bowl of soup. She sat back down instead. "What about the border?"

"He's planning a war with Gyongxe," Parahan replied. "You don't think he's left the border with the remaining eastern pass wide open, do you?" He looked at Rosethorn. "What I don't understand is why you people are here. Why didn't you just send some magical message to Gyongxe and go home as you planned?"

"Just because we have magic doesn't mean we can fly," Evvy told him scornfully. "And even if we could talk through plants or stones, there's no one in Gyongxe who could hear us!"

Rosethorn raised a finger in admonishment. "That we know of."

Evvy rolled her eyes. "Yes, teacher. I have to be precise, teacher. That we *know* of. And even if we could, Rosethorn swore vows, so she has to go to help, and we'll be *yujinon* dung if we'll let her go without us."

"Do I want to know what *yujinons* are?" Parahan asked, chuckling.

"No," Briar assured him. "Not with it being night and all."

The big man looked at Rosethorn. "You shouldn't have brought them."

She rubbed her temple with her fingers. "You have my permission to send them back."

Parahan looked at Briar and Evvy, taking a breath to speak. He hesitated when he saw the blazing light in their eyes and the hard set of their mouths. "You saw only one of Weishu's armies."

"The God-King is our friend," Evvy said. "Dokyi is our friend. Rosethorn is going, which means we are going."

Parahan sighed. "Then we should sleep. It's always better to go to war if you've had proper sleep."

They offered to rearrange things in the morning so that Parahan could ride, but he was far too tall for the ponies, and he protested that his dignity forbade his entering Gyongxe on mule-back. With his packs redistributed to the mules, his stride was long enough that they were able to keep pace with one another without losing too much time. They left before dawn so none of those who had seen any of them the day before would suspect that the tall man walking alongside Rosethorn was the same bent beggar they had passed during their own journeys.

The four also improved their pace simply because there were ever fewer travelers. By the time the sun dropped behind the looming mountains and the evening cold set in, they were alone.

There was no caravansary when they decided to make camp, only swaths of ground left bare by those who had stopped in the same places before them. Considerate travelers had left piled wood and stacks of dried dung for campfires. Rosethorn chose a spot with its own stream, well situated against a stony cliff that protected them from the wind. Even with summer on the way, the Drimbakang Lho got cold at night.

Parahan disposed of his stinking rags. From one of his packs he produced the same general sort of tunic and breeches they wore. He hadn't been able to get boots that would fit him, he said, so he donned long socks and sturdy leather shoes from the same pack. Evvy set the gate stones and released the "chickens." Once they were out of their "crates," the cats took on their normal appearances. Parahan, caring for the ponies and mules after his change of clothes and a cold wash, shook his head in amazement. "And these are *Trader* spells?" he asked.

Evvy scowled at him. "They'll cook you and eat you if you tell," she said, repeating an old lie about Trader habits.

"I'm old and stringy," the man replied. "Don't be cranky, Evvy. I thought you liked me."

"That was before you got us into this mess," she grumbled.

"The gods would have found another path for us to enter this mess," Rosethorn said as she stirred the pot. "Can't you tell fate when it bites you?"

"No," Evvy and Parahan said at the same time.

"She has to talk like that," Briar said. He was mixing and baking flatbread on a heated rock. "She took religious vows and everything."

Once they were seated with their meal, Parahan sighed. "Warm feet. I had forgotten what warm feet were like. Now, I need to ask, how are you three fixed if it comes to a fight?" The three looked at him. "Evvy, stay back with the animals. Rosethorn —"

"What part of 'mage' did you not understand?" Briar reached into the sling on the ground next to him. Taking out a seed ball, he flipped it to the edge of the firelight closest to the road. It burst, immediately sinking roots into the ground. The vines shot up and out, sprouting their long thorns as they grew, spreading around the ground where they struck. By the time they stopped they were three feet in height and covered a circle of three feet in rough diameter. With no target, the thick stems had formed large curls around one another. Even in the flickering firelight the thorns could be seen. Some were four inches long. Others were two inches long and two inches thick at the base, curled rather than straight like the longer ones.

Parahan, fascinated, got up and started to walk toward the plant.

"Don't do that," Rosethorn said as the vines rustled. "They're still awake."

Parahan stopped. The vines settled. "You could kill a man with that," he said, his voice cracking.

"We don't carry them for toys," Briar replied. "Don't be so upset. I only let a couple of the seeds grow."

"Want to see what I have?" Evvy asked eagerly.

"No," Parahan said suddenly. "No, I don't think I do."

"But you think I'm a kid!" Evvy protested, using Briar's slang for child. "You don't think I can help protect us!" Rocks rose from the ground and began to whirl around Parahan's head.

"Evumeimei," Rosethorn said dangerously.

"Sorry, Parahan," Evvy apologized. The stones fell to the ground. "But — you *did* know we're mages."

"I'm not sure I thought about what you three do in terms of war," he admitted. Sitting on his heels by the fire, he grinned. "We may have an easier time getting past the border than I thought."

Rosethorn served out the tea. "What do you expect once we're there?" she asked as she warmed her hands on her cup.

"It's a small post, from what I learned," Parahan explained. "If things were normal, we might expect caravans coming through southern Gyongxe in another month, but not this early. Figure no traffic coming from the Gyongxe side. There's a village that supports the border post on the Yanjing side. They keep perhaps five guards on duty at a time. We're going to have to fight if they've received word to stop anyone from crossing. If they've gotten word about you leaving the caravan, or about me, we'll *really* have to fight."

"We might scare them into running," Evvy said cheerfully, giving Ria a scratch.

Parahan grunted. "We might, though if they're imperial regulars, not locals recruited to stand still and look tough, they won't scare." He looked at the staff on the ground beside him. "I wish I had a sword to go with this thing."

Rosethorn looked at him in horror. "You mean to take on armed guards with a *staff*?"

He wiped his bowl with the bread that Briar had made. "But I have three mages at my back." He stood and stretched as they stared up at him. Then he bent double at the waist and grabbed his ankles, bouncing a little without bending at the knees. Turning halfway, he put his right leg out in front of him as if he were lunging, and did so until his right leg was at a right angle and his left was stretched all the way out. After he had done that a number of times, he switched his front leg to the left. Rosethorn and Evvy began to clean up, while Briar tried to do similar stretches.

Finally Parahan picked up his staff and pulled one end of it off to reveal a long, slender, double-edged blade. "Not much as a throwing weapon," he told Briar as he began to spin it in both hands, "but I could jab fish if I was in the woods with no supper on my way south. I tried to stay off the roads, at least till I got to Kushi. When I finally got tired of fish, I tried the beggar disguise. That hurt as much as it helped."

"I wondered how you did that," Evvy said, on her way to fetch dung for the fire. "Once I had to go through this tunnel that wasn't quite high enough for me in Prince's Heights, where I used to live. It was really long. When I came out I had a terrible ache in my back and my neck."

"I still do," Parahan admitted. He got the spear twirling over his head. Stepping well away from Briar, he spun it rapidly down along one side of his body, then up, over, and along the other. As the firelight sparked off the blade, it gave him the appearance of wings.

He did other exercises while Rosethorn and Briar prepared more thorn balls and Evvy more disks of flint and quartz. Off and on they would look up to see him kicking and punching into the air, spinning to kick at the side, or to lash out with a fist so fast it was a blur. Finally he came over to the fire with one of his packs and settled in to sharpen his belt knife.

Rosethorn gave him the cup of tea that was steeping beside her. "This should help those aching muscles," she explained.

As night fell, Briar drew the line of ponies and mules closer to their camp. Evvy gathered her pack with her extra gate stones and created the enclosure where all of them would sleep. At first, Parahan balked at the thought of sleeping as part of a pile with the others.

Briar waited until Rosethorn went off into the dark to explain about her lungs, and how she needed all the warmth they could give now that they were in colder lands. "We did it sometimes on our way to Gyongxe, when sleeping alone didn't keep us warm enough. She'd start coughing otherwise," he explained.

When she returned, and Parahan and Evvy had gone in separate directions for the last errands of the night, Briar had to cajole Rosethorn into sleeping at the center of the huddle that would include Evvy, the cats, Parahan, and himself. At first Rosethorn insisted on taking an outside position with Parahan.

The big man, overhearing as he returned, said flatly, "We need every one of us at their best in the morning, woman. You may sleep on the outside and freeze tomorrow night, if we're alive and free."

Rosethorn stared at Parahan for a long, worrisome moment, and then placed her bedroll on the ground. Parahan proceeded to bank the fire. Briar wondered if he ought to say he would pray for the man in the fight to come, or something of the sort. In the end, he simply put his own bedroll next to Rosethorn's and crawled into it. Evvy chose Rosethorn's free side and Parahan Briar's. Rosethorn went to sprinkle her herb circle around the camp, including the ponies and mules. It was something she'd done several times on their way east: create a kind of magical curtain that hid them from any predator, human or animal, that might come by. Once the circle was finished, she murmured her spell over it, and returned to wriggle into her bedroll. Only then did the cats fit themselves into every comfortable spot that they could find.

Briar was drifting off when Parahan said, "Why don't we take the border at night? If we muffle all our clanking things, we might just sneak past. They'll expect us during the day. We could avoid a fight completely."

Briar yawned. "We can't do it."

When Parahan spoke, he sounded peeved. "I may only be a simple soldier, not an educated *nanshur*, but I'm sure if you do it in small words, you can explain it to me in a way I can understand. Why should we not try the strategically far more sensible move of attempting the border crossing by night?"

Briar growled. He was tired and he was worried about the border just like everyone else. "We're *plant mages*, oh strategist."

"Stop it, you two," Evvy complained.

"Plants require sunlight. Surely even simple soldiers know that," Briar went on, ignoring Evvy. Parahan might be a prince, and a warrior, but he wasn't going to bully them into trying something when Rosethorn was not at her best. He also didn't need to know Rosethorn's secrets.

It was Rosethorn, of course, who ruined it by telling the truth. "He's only half lying, Parahan," she said. "I don't see as well in the dark as I used to. I was . . . ill, six years ago. It's why I speak as I do, and why I have trouble catching my breath the higher we go, and why my night vision is limited."

"She *died*," Evvy said with relish. "Briar and his sisters went to the Deadlands and brought her back, only she left part of her speech and her breath and her sight there as a promise to the White Jade God that she would return."

Parahan's voice was shaky when he spoke again. "That's a story, isn't it?"

"It is not," Rosethorn said. "I nearly died of the Blue Pox. We leave in the morning. Now go to sleep."

That was the end of the night's conversation. They settled between the banked fire and the picketed mules and ponies, warm with their blankets, cats, and one another. Their night was so undisturbed that Parahan's only complaint in the morning was that Monster snored.

The road was empty. None of them was happy with that, though they found no other signs of trouble. Eagles and buzzards soared overhead searching for a meal. In the distance they saw a herd of goats moving on a looming hillside.

As the hours passed, the lands ahead on their side of the river began to flatten. By mid-morning they noticed distant fields off to their right and the kind of isolated barns used for sheltering herds and storing hay.

It was almost noon when they crested a rise in the road.

Before them a small river had cut a little flat-bottomed valley to the north as it hurried to join the Snow Serpent on their left. A quarter of a mile away and to the north, a walled town stood on the sloping hills that shaped the western side of the valley. Near it were grain fields and herds of the large, shaggy cattle known as yaks.

Where the road and the smaller river met, there stood a guard- and tollhouse. It was built like the local dwellings, two stories tall and curving inward from ground to flat roof. The shutters were open on the narrow windows since it was a sunny day. Ivory plaster covered every chink in the walls. It was bigger than most of the houses and there was a watchtower on the roof. A couple of horses grazed in a fenced-in field at the side of the building. If this place was like others in this area, Briar figured, the stables would be on the ground floor.

One soldier in imperial livery stood by the barrier on the road. Four more lounged on benches on the side of the guardhouse. Briar squinted against the sunlight that shone into his eyes. A flag on the tower snapped in the wind. All he could tell was the color, a bright, imperial yellow. "Border crossing?" he guessed.

Two of the seated warriors rose and took up halberds that leaned against the guardhouse. The other two gathered quivers and crossbows that had been on the ground next to their feet, slinging the quivers onto their backs before they stood to set a quarrel in their crossbows.

"I think so," Parahan replied.

Rosethorn and Briar double-checked the slings on their chests. Their seed bombs lay ready. Their mage kits were open and strapped tight on the saddles in front of them, in case they were needed. Evvy was leading the pack mules. She had her own cloth sling ready, with disks of quartz and flint ready for use.

"This may be nothing," Rosethorn cautioned.

They said no more until they were within shouting distance of the guard on the barrier. He was a strongly built older man who kept all of his attention on their small party.

"Hello!" Parahan cried cheerfully. "It must be a dull day for you fellows with no one else on the road!"

"Halt for inspection!" the oldest man shouted back. "In the name of our glorious emperor!"

"Gladly," Parahan called, not slowing his pace forward. "Only, would you ask your fellows there to lower their crossbows? My wife is in the family way, and they're making her nervous."

"Rogue," muttered Rosethorn.

"Your endearments make me yearn for our nights together, my sweetest," Parahan whispered.

Briar choked, trying not to laugh aloud, as Rosethorn turned crimson. "How can you joke at a time like this?" she demanded.

"If not at a time like this, when?" Parahan asked.

Briar fingered the cloth balls in his sling, skipping from the killer thorns to the ropey ones. He supposed Rosethorn would want him to use the ropes, though the thorns would ensure that none of these people followed them into Gyongxe. If the emperor was declaring war after all, why should they care if they broke the laws of the border?

But Rosethorn would care if Briar killed anyone he didn't absolutely have to. He wondered if she'd discussed that issue with Parahan.

"Halt!" shouted the leader again. "Dismount and raise your hands."

"Is there a problem, sirs? As I have said, my wife is in a delicate condition," Parahan called. They were crossing the bridge over the lesser river. "Get ready," he told his companions once they reached the other side. "Stop right here. If we get any closer they'll win the fight." He swiftly brought down the top of his staff and removed the cap, sliding the wooden tube into the front of his tunic.

"You answer to the descriptions of criminals wanted by the emperor!" cried the leader. "Put down your weapons, dismount, and kneel!"

The crossbow archers leveled their weapons at their group. Evvy snapped two pieces of quartz into the air. They flew straight at the archers, who threw up their hands to protect their eyes. Their weapons clattered to the ground. Their bolts began to sprout leaves.

The commander shouted an order. The archers grabbed their bows and put fresh bolts from their quivers to the string. The men with halberds ran toward Rosethorn and Evvy, who had moved to the right to deal with anyone who came from the house. Rosethorn whispered something to the cloth ball in her hand and threw it at the spearmen. It burst as it struck the ground, throwing its burden of seeds into the air. Vines that went thread-like to thick shot from the ground at their feet. They wrapped around the spearmen's feet and crawled up around their legs.

Briar trotted his pony forward. The crossbow bolt that came for him dropped to the ground and sprouted roots. The second bolt struck a disk of quartz in midair and fell to the ground. The disk returned to Evvy. Briar didn't thank her. He had gotten close enough to throw his own ball of seed where he wanted it to go. It landed between the two archers and exploded into thorny growth.

The older soldier, the one in command, had unsheathed his sword and run forward the moment the archers released their second round of bolts. He met Parahan's spear with his sword, baring his teeth in a growl.

For a moment Briar stared as Parahan blazed into action. The big man reversed his spear. He slammed the butt end up under the commander's jaw hard enough to break it, then swept it down, jamming it into the side of the soldier's right knee. The Yanjingyi man's leg buckled. He slashed sidelong at Parahan, but the bigger man had continued his motion, smacking the staff of his spear hard into the back of the soldier's head. The Yanjingyi man hit the ground and rolled away from Parahan.

Briar could look no longer. More yells were coming from the direction of the guardhouse. Four soldiers spilled out of it, wiping their mouths on their sleeves or fumbling with weapons. Evvy pitched a ball at the fresh arrivals as if she played at ninepins. It was quartz, the size of both of her fists, and it rolled swiftly across the flat ground toward the new soldiers. They didn't see it until it reached them and exploded into a number of sharp stone needles.

The four men split apart. Two fell screaming to the ground. They tried blindly to pull the sharp stone slivers from their faces. The third ran toward Parahan and one toward Rosethorn, both drawing their swords. Rosethorn pointed to some of the vines that had completely covered the two spearmen near their bench.

The green ropes reached for the swordsman who came at her and grabbed him by the throat.

Briar looked for the mules. Evvy had them on a long rein with one end tied to her waist. Doesn't she know they could pull her out of the saddle? he thought, panicked. He dismounted and ran back to the animals, who were on the verge of panic. Digging in a pocket, he found the handful of calming herbs he'd put there. Carefully he blew some over each animal's nose until they had lost that white ring around their eyes. He checked on Evvy again. She was steadfast next to Rosethorn. They waited for the enemy's next attack, Evvy with a second stone ball in her hand, Rosethorn with another thorny vine ball in hers.

Parahan seized the commander's sword and dagger and turned to greet a soldier who rushed him, a sword in his fist. The big man was grinning, his teeth bright against his brown skin. The soldier who had come to attack him halted just out of reach, his sword at the ready. Parahan feinted to the side. The soldier was stupid enough to swing that way, bringing his weapon up to guard. He never saw Parahan cut his head off.

Evvy glanced at movement in the windows on the second floor of the guardhouse. Archers hung out of two of them. She reached into her sling and brought out two flint circles, handling them carefully. Briar only had a moment to register their color before she sent first one, then the next, flying through the air just as she had the rounds of quartz. They flew straight at the archers. One circle embedded itself in the archer's chest. He vanished from view. The other circle struck the second archer as he lowered his crossbow after shooting. His bolt went over Rosethorn's head and narrowly missed a peacefully grazing mule. The dark circle the girl had thrown hit the archer's throat. He pitched forward, out of the window, and lay still on the ground.

At last everything was quiet except for the soft roar of the river and a hawk's distant shriek.

Parahan wiped his mouth on his wrist and groped at his waist for his water flask. It startled him and his companions to see that his belt had fallen off, cut in two by the commander. His flask had gotten trampled at some point. He looked at the women and Briar, confused.

"Wait," Briar called. He took his own flask over to the big man.

"Thanks," Parahan said. He set the sword he had taken on the ground, gulped half of the water, and then poured the rest over his head.

"Were they waiting for us?" Rosethorn asked.

Parahan shrugged.

Briar saw sheets of paper flutter under a stone near where the commander of the soldiers had first been standing. He wandered over and pulled them out from under the stone. He couldn't read the Yanjingyi writing under the drawings on each paper, but the pictures were perfectly clear: Parahan on one; Evvy, Rosethorn, and Briar on the other. He gave them to Rosethorn, then went to make certain that the mules were unharmed.

Rosethorn remained in the saddle, watching the guardhouse. Once she had looked at the papers, she stuffed them in the sling on her chest and took out more thorn balls, just in case.

Evvy dismounted from her pony. She let the reins trail so the animal wouldn't wander, then trudged toward the guardhouse.

"I don't think that's a good idea," Rosethorn called.

Evvy looked back at her. "Are you joking? Do you know how long it takes me to knap an edge on those flint pieces so I can throw them just right? I don't think I'm going to find more flint here, either." She looked at the fallen archer, gulped, and bent down to pry the dark stone circle from his throat.

Parahan followed and took it from her fingers to wipe it clean on the dead man's clothing. "Beetle dung. It *is* flint," he said. "I'll get the other one, Evumeimei. You wait here."

"I'll go with him," Briar told Rosethorn. "Evvy, come watch the mules." He waited until Evvy took the reins before he ran into the guardhouse after Parahan.

The downstairs was empty of animals except for chickens on their nests. Upstairs was the main living room. Midday for the guards sat half eaten on a long table. Pallets were rolled up and stacked in a corner. The archer who had fallen inside lay in a heap on the floor, plucking at the flint circle stuck in his chest.

Parahan killed him with a sword thrust. "We can't have them reporting who did this," he told Briar. He retrieved Evvy's second flint circle and wiped it off. "Perhaps you shouldn't tell Rosethorn, though."

Briar grimaced. Rosethorn would not like to hear of the killing of a wounded man, but Parahan was right. "We'd best get out of here, then, before the townsfolk come."

"Yes, you're right. Ouch!"

Briar saw that the big man was sucking blood off a fingertip. "Oh, sorry. Those things are nasty sharp." He took a handkerchief from his pocket and slid the circle from Parahan's hold. Carefully he wrapped the flint and put it in his sling, but even so, he could see it was cutting through the linen of the handkerchief. Evvy owed him a fresh one.

As they went down the ladder, Parahan said, "I confess, even with their magic, I am . . . impressed with how strong-hearted our ladies are in battle. Will they need time to calm themselves? We can't linger — the herd boys will report trouble here to the town."

When they went outside, they found that Rosethorn had tethered her pony. She had managed to catch one of the horses and saddled and bridled it. From the length of the stirrups, she meant the brown gelding for Parahan. "Are you finished?" she asked them. "Because I would like to put some distance between us and this, now."

"Yes, Mother," Briar said. To Parahan he said, "See? She's calm." He skittered out of the way when Rosethorn mimed a swat at him. Smiling, Briar took Evvy the flint disk Parahan had recovered. She tucked it into the pocket with the other flint after wiping off the last traces of blood. Briar said nothing to her about the vomit he could see a few yards away. Evvy never faltered in battle, but blood still set her back on occasion.

Moving quickly but without fuss, Parahan resupplied himself from the dead soldiers until he had two swords, a belt, an iron-covered leather jerkin, and leather boots that fit. After testing a couple of the spears used by the Yanjingyi guards, he fashioned a quiver for them and his spear, and slung it across his back. Evvy found a spare water bottle for him. She and Briar swiftly searched the food packs for some kind of midday meal before they swung into their own saddles.

The four of them shared out cold rice balls wrapped in leaves and cold red-bean buns. As they were about to leave, Rosethorn trotted her pony by the open windows and tossed two of her thorn balls inside. Vines began to sprout through the doors and windows as she joined the other three on the road. Chickens erupted from their side of the house, squawking in alarm.

As they moved on, Briar tossed a thorn ball of his own onto the road behind them. In the house, spiked vines were shooting out of the upper windows. Those vines that grew from where dead men lay now crawled over the ground, snake-like, bound to meet their friends in the guardhouse. There was no sign of bodies anywhere. The vines had spread to cover them all.

"They'll know we were here," Parahan said.

"Too bad," Briar and Rosethorn said at the same time.

"I was tired of sneaking around anyway," Briar added. "Let's teach Weishu to keep his greedy hands to himself."

Snow Serpent Pass

They trotted forward as the mules complained. "I don't see what you're whining about," Evvy told them. "You just stood around while we did all the work." She had put her rice ball half eaten and her bun untouched back into the cloth sling over her chest. Though she had done her part without flinching earlier, the memory of the man whose throat she'd cut kept rising past any other thoughts or pictures in her head. He joined her vivid memories of a handful of people she had killed, trying to survive before she had met Briar and Rosethorn and in bandit attacks on the road to Gyongxe. It never got easier.

When the road curved around the edge of a hill, she looked back. Thick green thorn vines covered everything between the tumbling river and the fence behind the guardhouse. The chickens and the horses that had grazed inside the fence had gotten away, the chickens to huddle on the bridge, the horses to gallop through the fields.

Someone would notice the problem sooner or later, but by the time anyone came to look, the thorns would have reached the water's edge, blocking the road completely. They could try to go behind the guardhouse to get at the road, Evvy supposed. She wasn't really sure when the thorns would stop growing. Rosethorn and Briar created very determined magic.

She looked ahead once more. At least the dead men were covered. That was something, since they hadn't had time to give them a burial or prayers.

They trotted a mile before the jolting and the image got to Evvy. She cried for a halt. She dashed behind a boulder on the hillside and lost what food she'd eaten. Once she'd covered that mess, she heard Rosethorn call, "I'm coming up. Nobody watch."

Since that meant Rosethorn needed to take care of business, Evvy thought she might as well do the same. She had her complaints about dried grass, but it was what was available. She was tugging at the ties on her breeches when Rosethorn asked quietly, "Are you all right?"

"It's just . . . I don't like killing people," Evvy whispered, ashamed of her weakness.

"None of us *likes* it. There would be something wrong with you — with us — if you did. You know Briar jokes to cover it up sometimes. You know he also has nightmares."

"Oh," Evvy breathed. She had been so caught up in the picture of the dead man that she had forgotten all the times she had been roused in the night by Briar — and Rosethorn — crying out in their dreams.

"Parahan will be different. He's a soldier. We saw that today. It wasn't just bragging from him. It may not bother him as it does us. But you aren't weak because you threw up, girl. You're human."

"Thank you," Evvy whispered. Feeling less like slime, she scrambled down the hillside to wash her hands. They went numb as soon as she dipped them in the icy brown torrent. She got to her feet and tucked her fingers into her armpits to warm them, glaring at Briar and Parahan as she walked over to the mules. It wasn't fair that men didn't have to twist themselves into knots to pee!

Rosethorn looked up the gorge, her eyes narrow. "My boy's restless. Not you, Briar, my mount. I don't think he likes what he smells on the wind."

Evvy gulped. Their long travels from Chammur had taught them respect for the animals that worked the trade roads. She went to her pack and searched for the bag that held her exploding quartz balls.

"We have no choice but to ride on," Parahan replied. "Wait here." Without stopping for anyone's reply, he hung his sling of spears from his saddle horn, taking only one as he climbed the dip between two hills to their right. Evvy could see him long after she stopped hearing him. Her respect for the big man went up several more notches. It took plenty of skill to move so silently over loose gravel and long grass.

She, Briar, and Rosethorn continued to load their ponies with the magical weapons they might need for another, perhaps bigger, battle. She and Briar had their daggers as well. Evvy wore two blades inside and two outside her belt in addition to one at the back of her neck inside her jacket. She didn't know where all of Briar's were except for the obvious ones.

As far as Evvy knew, Rosethorn didn't carry extra weapons. A kit with blades in it hung at her waist, but they were supposed to be used with plants. The only non-plant use Rosethorn had for her belt knife was to cut her meat. Of course, Rosethorn could turn most plants into something nasty. Evvy hoped that would be enough.

She feared that it would not be. Here in this steep gorge with its single road, she could not forget that for her entire life the one fixed idea in her world was that the emperor of Yanjing was as powerful as any god and more powerful than some of them. She had seen nothing at the Winter Palace to teach her any different. When they had destroyed the guard station, they had declared their own war against the Yanjing empire. All she could do was pray that Gyongxe could somehow do what no other country had managed to do when the imperial armies marched: defeat them.

A few stones rattled down the hillside, distracting her from her dark thoughts. Parahan was coming back.

"I don't know what's on the road ahead," he told them when he reached their group. "I only saw about a mile's length of it. But there's a game trail that way" — he pointed uphill — "that takes us out of view while still allowing us to travel along the line of the river. We might be able to skirt anyone on the road itself."

"Tie everything down that might make a noise," Rosethorn ordered. "Muffle the harnesses, whatever jingles. Evvy, your chickens must take a nap, I'm afraid."

Evvy grimaced, but she took out the packet of cat-sleep herbs and sprinkled some over the crates. She used only a pinch for each: The spell was powerful. Normally the Trader spell that disguised the cats was enough to make people think they heard hens, but Rosethorn didn't want to risk any noise as they moved to higher ground.

Rosethorn continued to say, "We'll walk. Check your own gear. Nothing that clanks. Parahan, muffle those spears."

When they were ready, Rosethorn told Parahan, "Evvy leads."

His eyes went wide with surprise. "Evvy! But —"

"You'll see," Rosethorn told him. "Go on, girl."

Evvy said nothing. She was already summoning her magic. With her in the front and Rosethorn in the rear they set off, each of them leading a pair of animals. Evvy slid the reins up over her elbows so she could stretch out her hands. Gently she flicked and twitched her fingers, shaking them to and fro lightly at the same time as she sent her power out to the many bits of stone uphill of her. Inside her head she could feel the stones in the cut between the two hills giggle as they shifted and slid, all sizes easing around one another. They had never had this kind of energy before, but it was more interesting than just tumbling down, pushed by streams of snowmelt or rain or the feet of animals. They liked it. The only sounds the rocks made were faint clicks as they edged into position, each one sliding into the right spot next to another. Behind her Evvy left a smooth stone path under the horses' and the mules' feet. Better yet, the new footing gave way just enough to cut the sound their hooves made.

Up and up they climbed. At last she heard a soft bird whistle. She glanced back to see Parahan point off to her left. There, in a dip on the far side of the western hill, was the game trail.

She turned onto it, hands still moving. The trail itself was beaten earth. This time she urged the stones to either side, letting them roll into deeper grass.

The ground began to rise again. To their right, to the northeast, hill after craggy green hill rose, stabbing into the sky. Behind them were the mountains of the Drimbakang Sharlog. Evvy could hear Rosethorn was struggling to breathe. She needed her special tea for managing in the heights. Evvy or Briar would make it when they stopped for lunch.

They must be higher than Evvy realized if Rosethorn was having trouble. These were mountains, for all they looked like hills close up. They hummed in Evvy's bones. What would she do when she came to the big ones, those with rocky sides that had been swept of almost anything but stone and snow? Those mountains would sing in a voice that would surely rattle her poor head clean off her neck.

Short of the top of the fourth hill, another soft whistle from Parahan brought her to a stop. This time he left his horse and mule and crept ahead of the others. Evvy sat in the grass and even ate a bit after she thumped the muscle cramps from her thighs. Working her magic and teasing those stones had thrust the horrors down where she didn't have to think about them. Briar had made a cold mix of Rosethorn's breathing tea and was pouring it for her. It was just as well they had gotten a chance to rest.

Parahan returned and beckoned them close. "There is half a company in the road," he said, his voice barely a whisper. "Fifty soldiers. Yanjingyi regulars, curse it! Not locals."

"If we're quiet they'll never know we were here," Briar replied, his voice just as soft. "The game trail will put that next ridge between us and them. Even if they look up they won't see us. We've *got* to take word to the God-King about Weishu's plans. Guaranteed he doesn't know these *kaqs* are here, either."

Parahan grinned at Briar's use of the Trader slang; Rosethorn nodded at his thinking. Once more they went forward with

Parahan in the lead. Evvy reached farther ahead with her power, shooing the rocks away. Even the animals seemed to understand that the alternative to silence was death if the enemy caught them.

Between more hills they went, the green shoulders rising sharply on both sides of their group. The biggest worry came when they reached a stream. It ran along the foot of a tall ridge on their right. They couldn't avoid a little splashing as the animals crossed. When they halted on the far side, there were no sounds of movement anywhere. Parahan crawled to the shoulder of the hill on their left, to see if he could glimpse the road and the enemy. When he came back, he said they were now beyond the soldiers below. If their present trail kept on parallel to the road heading west, they might evade the Yanjingyi soldiers completely.

Rosethorn and Briar weren't listening. Like the ponies and the mules and even Parahan's horse they had pointed their noses into the wind that came down from the north and over the stream. "Bamboo," Rosethorn whispered. "Seaweed. Vinegar."

Briar frowned. "Peony? Pomegranate for certain."

They turned their heads to stare uphill at the ridge.

Parahan said a few things in his own language and drew his swords.

"Wait," Evvy told him. She threw her magic up the slope and let it spread. When it spilled over the top of the ridge, Evvy felt weight on the stones there, the kind of moving weight that said people to her. She shifted the rocks, straining to pull the bigger ones toward the edge. Someone above shouted.

Briar knocked Evvy down. Still wiggling her hands, her power, and the rocks, she looked around. Arrowheads lay on the dirt as long wooden splinters, the remains of their bolts, sprouted tendrils and leaves. Rosethorn smiled grimly and muttered, "Try to catch *me* unawares, will you?"

Getting to his knees beside Evvy, Briar glared at the ridge. As weeds and grass sprouted madly along the sloping ground, five people looked over the edge. Two wore black scholar's robes with the gold sashes of mages. Ropes of beads hung around their necks and in their hands. Two more were archers; the fifth was armed with a halberd. All five were struggling to keep their feet. The archers also did their best to fit fresh arrows to their crossbows.

Evvy yanked her hands up. Rocks flew into the air above the ridge. The archers dropped their bows as they covered their eyes with their hands. She tugged her hands forward. The mages had protected themselves from the airborne stones, but it was another matter to have the ground pull away from their feet. They stumbled, trying to stay upright. Something was going wrong with the long strings of beads in their hands. They twisted together around the mages' wrists, binding them like rope. The loops of beads around each mage's neck spun swiftly, winding tighter and tighter, strangling the wearer. The mages struggled to pull their traitor necklaces away from their necks, without success. Their faces got redder and redder as they fought to breathe.

Evvy gave all of the stones on the ridge one last, savage pull. This time it was the ponies and mules that saved her and her companions, hauling them away from the landslide by the reins looped around their arms as the entire ridge came down. They scrambled with the animals to retreat from the tumbling earth and rock. The stone of the ridge roared past them through a dip between hills, dragging the Yanjingyi mages with it. When everything settled but for a haze of dust, there was no sign of the warriors who had stood with them. The two mages lay on the heap of fallen rock where it had come to a halt. They were clearly dead.

Evvy crept to the southern hilltop to see the road. There was no sign of the enemy. She was starting to grin in relief when she saw movement at the crown of the western hill. She scrambled back to Parahan and pointed west.

Yanjingyi warriors in domed helmets and armor galloped over the hill's crest. Evvy guessed they'd heard the rock slide. Now she strained to give them a rock slide of their own, struggling to find and move the medium and big stones in front of them. She was too tired for small ones at that distance. She flinched when the archers among them raised their crossbows, as if the bolts had struck her already.

Parahan scooped up a couple of round, hard stones and threw first one, then the other, with vicious accuracy. Each hit an archer in the face, knocking him out of the saddle and under the other horses' hooves. Parahan grabbed two more stones.

Suddenly Evvy saw the bows leap from the remaining archers' hands. The crossbows broke apart in midair, raining stocks, lathes, arrowheads, and splintered shafts down on the other riders. She laughed in spite of herself as lathes and shafts grew and sprouted leaves, then wound around the arms and necks of the soldiers. Stocks planted themselves in the ground and grew as trees. Horses reared and slipped, trying not to run headfirst into trees that had not been there a moment before. Briar and Rosethorn were hard at work. Parahan grinned at Evvy, then snapped his rocks at one soldier each, striking their heads with deadly accuracy. Down they went.

The horses that missed the growing trees slipped, losing their balance on moving stones and pebbles. They went down; those behind them piled on top. Evvy ground her teeth and kept the stones on the slope under the riders moving.

Men were screaming. She opened her eyes. Briar had run forward to pitch seed balls as far and high as they would go into the air over the charging soldiers. The cloth balls burst at his command, sprouting deadly vines with sword-sharp thorns in midair. The falling, deadly net trapped the remaining soldiers and their mounts together with the ropes grown from pieces of crossbow and the fast-growing trees.

Evvy shrieked as more arrows arched into the air from the far side of the hilltop.

Parahan, at her side, laid a hand on her arm. "Evvy, look. What are you screaming for?"

She had *thought* they were fire arrows. In truth they were crossbow bolts dyed bright orange. These struck short of her and her companions, into the ranks of Yanjingyi soldiers. More followed, again dropping into the net and the enemy beneath.

New soldier-archers, these in pointed helmets, charged over the hill in the wake of the arrows. Deftly they split apart to avoid the fallen enemy and the trap of thorny vines. The newcomers' leather armor was worn over flame-colored silk. The metal pieces fixed to the leather in tidy rows were bronze, not iron, and they were rounded, not flat, as the Yanjingyi soldiers wore their metal. Their horses were smaller, nimble, and less dismayed by sliding rock. Where had she seen them before? Garmashing! These were Gyongxin soldiers!

Half of their allies split off and galloped downhill, toward the road. Parahan swung into his own horse's saddle and followed.

Evvy released her stones and collapsed on the ground. She watched blankly as the Gyongxin soldiers who stayed behind killed any living Yanjingyi soldiers. Two Gyongxin warriors rode over to Rosethorn and Briar.

Now that she had a chance to catch her breath, Evvy looked at the trickles of blood that emerged from beneath the heap of thorns and felt unclean. She scrubbed her hands on her breeches. We *had* to kill them, she told herself. The emperor's soldiers were going to kill *us*, them and their mages. To stop us from getting word to Gyongxe that the emperor is coming. So the emperor can torture Parahan to death.

Why did we bother? she wondered, swimming in self-hate. She trembled from top to toe. All of this means nothing. These dead horses and dead men, it's all camel spit in a high wind, because the *emperor* is coming. Gyongxe is so small. Gyongxe doesn't have a chance against Yanjing.

The two warriors dismounted before Rosethorn and Briar. They put their palms together before their faces and bowed low to Rosethorn. "Dedicate," the taller of them said, "I had the honor of seeing you in Gyongxe over the winter. I am Captain Rana, sent by the God-King and First Dedicate of the Living Circle Jangbu Dokyi to ensure your safe arrival in Gyongxe. This is my sergeant, Kanbab. I beg your pardon for our lateness. We did not know the beast Yanjingyi had crept up the gorge to lay in wait. Excuse me." He turned and held up a hand. A warrior trotted forward. "Get to General Sayrugo. Tell her the enemy is here.

We surprised a company and are dealing with them. There may be more moving northwest above the road. As fast as you can ride, and I know that's fast."

The soldier bowed and ran to collect his horse. To Sergeant Kanbab the captain said, "Take half of our people. Help Sergeant Yonten mop up on the road. We must take the dedicate and her companions to the general as soon as possible."

Rosethorn took a drink from the flask at her belt. "Forgive me, Captain Rana, but we are on our way to Garmashing. We have important news for the God-King and First Dedicate Dokyi."

The captain smiled. "The First Dedicate has anticipated you," he replied. "He waits at Fort Sambachu, at the end of this gorge — our home base."

"A fort? Not the temple in Garmashing?" Rosethorn said.

"I am certain the First Dedicate will explain when you see him," Rana said. "If you will excuse me, I must see to my wounded."

Rosethorn and Briar walked slowly over to Evvy, towing the mules and their ponies. Once the animals were tethered, both of them sat beside her in silence. After a moment, Evvy leaned against Briar's shoulder. A glance told her Rosethorn had stretched out on the grass and cradled her head on Briar's knee.

"Do you want to lie down?" Evvy asked Briar. "I don't mind."

"I'll just lean against you," he said. "We can prop each other up."

"Good," Evvy whispered. She let her eyes close. If she had her way, she would never fight again.

Evvy slid off his shoulder at some point. Briar woke in time to catch her and lowered her to the grass. Rosethorn had rolled away from him and curled up in a knot. Once awake, he felt too itchy to rest. One of the Gyongxin soldiers offered him a flask of tea. Briar had a drink and looked around at the mess they had made — they and the emperor's soldiers — of a beautiful mountain cove.

Now that he had time to think and remember, something puzzled him. He went back to the rock slide Evvy had made of the ridge. At first his feet simply went out from under him as he tried to reach the two dead Yanjingyi mages. Suddenly the sliding rocks held still. He turned to see Evvy's eyes on him. He smiled at her and pursued the short climb to the corpses.

He hadn't been mistaken. Their bead necklaces had strangled them while he had bound their hands using the wooden beads in their bracelets. Briar knelt and touched a bare spot where the cord lay exposed against a dead mage's throat. Cotton. The necklace had been threaded on cotton. Not only that, but the cord tingled with the remnants of a magic he knew very well.

He scrambled down to solid earth and walked over to his teacher. She was sitting up and talking with Captain Rana. When they stopped and looked at him, Briar said, "Cotton."

Rosethorn raised an eyebrow at him.

"You strangled them with the cotton thread on their own mage necklaces. They didn't even try to stop you?"

"They couldn't even tell I was there," Rosethorn replied calmly. "Briar, they truly don't understand ambient magic. We will be very useful here." Her voice was perfectly reasonable. "You could have done it just as easily." She looked at Captain

Rana. "Would someone build us a small fire? We need to collect these beads and burn them, before they fall into someone else's hands." She and Briar went to collect the beads as the captain gave orders.

It took some of their supplies of herbs that kept magic from spreading, but they saw all of the Yanjingyi mages' beads destroyed in a nice, hot fire. They were even able to destroy the enemy's mage kits. A part of Briar wanted to go through them, for curiosity's sake. Rosethorn pointed out that just as they left special surprises in their own mage kits for snoops, the Yanjingyi mages could be expected to have something similar. Briar and Evvy both sighed at the missed opportunity and let the kits burn.

By the time they were finished, Parahan and the other Gyongxin warriors returned to report success at the road. There were no Yanjingyi soldiers left to carry word of Gyongxin soldiers in the pass. Just as good, from Briar's point of view, those Gyongxin who took wounds were not badly hurt. Rosethorn, Briar, and Captain Rana's healers were able to patch them up quickly before they all rode out.

They had not gone far before Briar noticed that Evvy was swaying in the saddle. Rana allowed him to switch to one of the surviving horses so he could take Evvy up in the saddle in front of him: Briar's pony would not have appreciated the extra weight. Evvy was exhausted. Lately the work didn't wring her out as it had today, but she had not shaped the paths of so many rocks in such different ways before this.

Briar asked Rana if they could stop long enough to make hot tea or soup, but the man refused. Briar understood — if there was one company of the enemy in these hills there might be more — but he was desperately worried for his two companions. Parahan finally caught Rosethorn when she began to slide from her mule and pulled her up to ride with him as well. At least the captain sent riders ahead to his camp to prepare hot liquids and food in advance of their arrival.

In camp Parahan and Briar wrapped Rosethorn and Evvy in blankets and propped them in front of the captain's fire, where Captain Rana and Sergeant Kanbab joined them. Briar was startled when Kanbab removed his helmet to free a tumbling waist-length braid of black hair. She grinned at his obvious surprise.

"Sergeant Kanbab is my right hand," the captain said. "I would be in bad shape without her. A good number of Gyongxin women serve in the army before they marry. Some of them stay even afterward, like the sergeant and General Sayrugo."

Kanbab bowed to Rosethorn. "The men wish to know if they may eat the honored dedicate's chickens."

"My cats!" Evvy cried wearily, trying to struggle out of the blankets. "They're really cats. You can't eat them!"

"I'll take the spell off," Briar told her. "Finish that tea and have another cup." He rose, trying not to groan. He had put out a lot of magic, too, without being able to draw more from his best *shakkan,* which was now on its way to Hanjian. Every muscle in his body ached.

The crates had been placed beside the small round tents that were to serve Rosethorn, Evvy, Briar, and Parahan. Approaching them, Briar shook his head at the soldiers who stood nearby. "Sorry, lads," he said in *tiyon,* hoping they understood. "They aren't as tasty as you'd think." Kneeling among the cackling crates, he murmured the words he'd been taught by the *mimander*.

Suddenly crates, chickens, and chicken noises were gone. From the look on Asa's and Ball's faces, Briar knew they were going to make their humans pay for the extra-long nap they'd had from the dose of sleeping herbs.

Monster stuck his head through an opening in the side of his carrier and squeaked. For a large cat, he had a very tiny voice. Briar grinned. "You don't hold a grudge, do you, old man?"

Evvy staggered over, her eyes swollen with exhaustion. "I can't do gate stones to keep them from straying," she whined. "I'm too tired!"

"I'll do herbs," Briar said. "Don't worry. That tent's for you and Rosethorn. Go to bed."

Evvy managed to crawl into the small tent. When he looked in shortly afterward, Briar discovered she had collapsed onto her open bedroll without crawling into it. He tugged her blanket off and covered her, silently thanking whoever had set up the tents.

Once he'd made the herb circle around the women's tent so the cats could roam inside it, he released them from their baskets and fed them dried meat soaked in water. Then he went in search of a meal for himself.

The soldiers invited him to share theirs: a cup of butter tea and a bowl of dough mixed with cheese and tea, apparently the normal ration meal. Briar had eaten worse, and more unusual, dishes. He devoured his and thanked his hosts.

They chuckled. "Usually foreigners just spit it out," the cook explained in *tiyon*. Briar wasn't about to tell them he hadn't spat out far weirder things served by the emperor. They had agreed to keep silent about their time in Dohan, for one. For another, he didn't want these people thinking he was a snob.

"You won't catch me wasting decent food," he said truthfully. He bowed and returned to the captain's fire.

Rosethorn was gone. "She went to bed," Parahan told him. He was sharpening his swords. "Captain Rana here says the emperor's troops attacked in strength up the Ice Lion Pass, the Green Pass, and out along the northern plain a week ago. General Sayrugo only had word of it two days ago. She wasn't convinced until today that Yanjing might have sent forces up the Snow Serpent Pass. Most people have left it alone for attacks in the past. It's too narrow for getting real numbers of troops into Gyongxe."

"We didn't see any soldiers before today, so they were ahead of us for certain. If they try to send more soldiers, they'll have a fun time," Briar said. "We choked the border crossing with thorns. They won't get through those without a really good mage. We made the plants to resist axes, fire, and a lot of magic, Rosethorn and me."

"The emperor hasn't sent an army this way," the captain replied. "Still, he can bleed us a bit, and tie up our troops here in the south with only the smallest portion of one of his armies if he chooses. He can afford to waste soldiers here; we can't." He got to his feet. "We ride before dawn and we'll be riding hard all day. Get some sleep."

By the time their journey into Gyongxe was done, Briar never wanted to hear the words "ride hard" again. His bum and thighs, used to the slow pace of caravan riding, were as blistered and chafed as if he had just sat on a horse for the first time. Rosethorn and Evvy were no better off, and Parahan, after years afoot in Weishu's palaces, was even worse. Night after night the four applied salves to their sores and did their best not to complain. It was too important to reach the people who had been their friends for those long winter months.

Rosethorn and Briar also patched wounds on their companions. Twice during their ride up the pass they were cut off by Yanjingyi soldiers and had to fight their way out. Rana said with grudging respect that these Yanjingyi warriors were enemies to be respected. They had seen Rana and his company ride east and done nothing. It was Rosethorn and her companions who brought them out of hiding to attack.

Every day the hills around them rose ever higher. Trees grew straight up, clamoring for each bit of sun. There were fewer broadleafs and more pines. Scrub and grass clung to the lower slopes where wild goats and yaks grazed in between ribs of naked limestone, shale, and granite.

It did not help Briar's peace of mind in this land of stone that Evvy twice dropped loads of rock onto Yanjingyi attackers. In his head Briar knew that even if the cliffs and ridges that soared above the road were unstable, Evvy would redirect loose stone if it fell. In his heart he waited for a ton of boulders to drop on him. If he could do it without Evvy noticing, he sent a screen of tough ivy crawling over any area that looked like it might be inclined to fall, just in case.

After supper the night before they were due to reach Rana's base, Fort Sambachu, Evvy walked out beyond the picket line of sentries. Sergeant Kanbab came running for Briar.

"The men chased her, trying to get her to come back. They didn't dare call to her, and they kept tripping in the dark," she explained as she led Briar to the place where his student had last been seen.

"On rocks," he said. He didn't need to ask.

"On rocks," Sergeant Kanbab agreed. She left him when he could see the pale gleam of Evvy's yak-skin coat. Briar followed Evvy until she halted on the edge of the riverbank. He called for some of the grasses there to sprout up in case Evvy slipped and tumbled into the icy water. She could control rocks, but not dirt.

When he reached her, he had to shout in her ear. She had chosen a spot right over a series of rapids. They boomed in the night.

"What are you *doing*?" he cried. "The enemy could be nearby! And you scared the sentries!"

"The mountains sing." Strangely enough, her voice was perfectly clear. "Not like the Yanjingyi singers do, or the Gyongxin warriors. It's in my bones. They sing of caves and snow and vultures."

"No, thank you!" Briar shouted. "I'm sure it's lovely, you bleat-brained stone mage, but we're going back to camp now! I bet your pocket stones will sing to you if you ask them nicely!"

"All right," she said, as if he'd asked her to feed the cats. She linked her arm in his and walked peaceably back to the cook fires with him. She even apologized to Kanbab and the sentries. Briar was shivering by the time they sat down to get warm. These mountains weren't like any others they had seen. She had liked the heights and the occasional glacier, but she hadn't been strange about the mountains themselves. He remembered the skeletons stepping out of the cliff face not so long ago, and the knowledge that, in Gyongxe, this kind of thing happened over and over. Evvy had been friendly with Gyongxe's rocks all winter. What if they survived this war, and Evvy was too entangled with the stone and mountains of Gyongxe to leave? What could he say to her that would compete with the highest mountains in the world?

CHAPTER
ELEVEN

The sunrise was just touching the river the next day when the hills in the east ended in towering cliffs. They were free of the gorge. Half a mile on they found a wide bridge that crossed the Snow Serpent River. They turned south and rode across it, off the main road. A lesser road following a deep stream took them to a short and jagged hill where Fort Sambachu was built at the feet of the Drimbakang Lho mountains. By then Briar was leading Evvy's pony. Her eyes were fixed on the soaring peaks ahead. In the gorge the hills had obscured the mountains beyond. Here Evvy saw the immense, snowy heights that stood between Gyongxe and the Realms of the Sun.

"See those three?" Kanbab asked Evvy, pointing to the nearest mountains. "According to the worshippers of La Ni Ma, our sun goddess, those mountains are her husbands. The east one is Ganas Rigyal Po, the Snow King. The west one is Ganas Gazig

Rigyal Po, the Snow Leopard King. And the one in the middle is Kangri Skad Po, the Talking Snow Mountain King."

"What does that mean, the 'Talking Snow Mountain King'?" Briar asked. He wasn't sure if Evvy even heard.

Kanbab looked at Briar. "I think the worshippers feel he is the most conversational of the Sun Queen's husbands."

"The sun isn't a queen in the Living Circle," Evvy murmured.

Kanbab smiled at her. "But this is Gyongxe, the home of many faiths. Surely they told you that when you were here for the winter. Garmashing itself has more temples than even the God-King can count, it is said. People come here to build at least one temple for their faith because our realm is closest of all to the heavens, and our mountains hold them up."

"And why do people want to be close to the gods?" Evvy wanted to know. "Back home, Shaihun does *horrible* things to people."

Kanbab gave Briar a strange look.

"Shaihun is a god of the deep desert," Briar explained. "Is that Fort Sambachu or a temple?"

"It's the fort," Kanbab said in confirmation. "Let those lowland creepers come against us there and see what they get!"

Briar had to admit, the fort looked promising. Its hill and its towers commanded a view of the pass, the road, and the grassy plain for a good distance. The curtain walls sloped inward and climbed the hill in steps, which would allow the archers on the highest level to shoot above the heads of those lower down. Around the outer walls an army of five hundred or more tents was camped, flying banners of crimson, turquoise, and emerald silks.

Evvy yelped and reined up, almost forcing her mount to rear. Briar instantly reached for her horse's bridle, though he was trying to keep from pulling too hard on his own animal's reins.

"Wait! Wait!" Captain Rana called, raising a hand. "It's all right! They are allies, and welcome ones at that!"

Kanbab rested a hand on Evvy's elbow. "If you're this jumpy now, what will you do when you get to the war?" she asked. "We're just getting ready for it. Garmashing is where you'll find the real danger!"

Parahan rode up beside Evvy. "These — these are Kombanpur flags, but not my uncle's or my father's. What is going on here?" He dismounted and walked into the tent village.

"He'll catch up with us," Rana said. "Come on. The general's waiting for you."

Once inside the fort, they barely got a chance to wash up and release the cats in the rooms to be shared by Rosethorn and Evvy. Rana shooed the three travelers along the halls of the fortress to General Sayrugo's audience chamber. There the notables were seated on one side of a long, worn table behind pots of the ever-present tea and teacups. Rosethorn, Briar, and Evvy watched as Rana marched up to an imposing bronze-skinned woman in a fire-orange tunic jacket. He presented her with the reports he had written each night on the road.

Then they saw the older man on the general's right and forgot all about her and Rana. Evvy squeaked and threw herself around the corner of the table to hug First Dedicate Dokyi. Rosethorn and Briar were more restrained, but every bit as glad to see the older mage.

"Evumeimei, where is your dignity?" her most recent teacher asked as he patted her on the back.

"I don't have any," Evvy said, her voice muffled by the cloth of his habit.

Dokyi looked up at Rosethorn and Briar. "General Sayrugo has been good enough to allow me to read the reports she received from Captain Rana," he said. "I understand you had a difficult time. Evumeimei, did you bring your cats?"

She straightened up, indignant. "Of course I did!" Then she saw his smile and realized that he was teasing. "Sorry, Honored Dedicate. You can visit them whenever you like."

"Perhaps a little later. I should very much like to hear Monster purr again. Now." Dokyi looked up at Rosethorn. "Captain Rana wrote that you came to warn us, but as he has told you, your warning was not needed. Weishu made secret treaties with both Inxia and Qayan, which freed his armies so he could launch an invasion here. He is a greedy fellow, is he not?"

Rosethorn smiled wryly and told Dokyi, "That is one way of looking at it, Honored Dedicate."

"Is it true, then, that you are also determined to fight here?" the older man wanted to know.

Rosethorn nodded. "More than ever after our time at the Winter Palace," she said. Her belly griped. Her heart cried out for Lark, but her answer had to be the one she had given Dokyi and the reason she had taken her two children and brought them back to Gyongxe. After what they had seen of Weishu and his court, she had to do all she could to stop him. The emperor of Yanjing was a monster in human skin.

"Good," Dokyi said. "I have an errand of utmost importance. You are the best person I know of our faith who can carry it out." He came out from behind the table and gripped Rosethorn gently by the shoulder. "Forgive me. I did not let you walk into peril on purpose. I did not know that war was inside our borders until the God-King did, and I did not let this errand wait until you were the only one who could do it for me. At first I undertook it. A week ago I set out from Garmashing. For each step I tried to take due south on this errand, there were Yanjingyi troops to drive me south and east. To here, in fact, where I would find you." He turned to Briar. "They are bringing food for you and Evvy, if you will sit over there." He nodded to a bench against the wall. "I must speak with Rosethorn privately. And then all of us can have a proper midday."

"She's tired," Briar said flatly. "Her breathing —"

"I understand," Dokyi replied. "She will sit, and I will have tea brought."

Rosethorn caught Briar's gaze with hers. When she was certain that she had it, she raised an eyebrow. It was a warning, and her boy knew it. He was not to push any further. He stared back at her, hard, and then guided Evvy to the bench Dokyi had indicated.

"He is a faithful son," the First Dedicate said as he led the way to a side door out of the general's meeting room. "You have been unstinting with your own love, that he is so unstinting with his love for you."

She ducked her head and hoped he didn't notice she was blushing. She and Briar only rarely talked about affection. Both of them had learned the hard way when they were children that many people would take any affection they offered and use it to get everything they had.

The older man brought her into a room next door that also seemed to be laid out for meetings. He sat on a bench on the nearest side of the long table and indicated that she should sit beside him. There were no windows here and only two doors. The only thing on the table was a leather pack.

Dokyi gestured, deep black fire trailing from his fingers. He and Rosethorn were instantly enclosed in a shadowy globe that almost touched the room's ceiling. Suddenly Rosethorn, who had been cold since they left Kushi, felt warm. She drew her own power within her skin, not wanting her plant sensitivity to be entangled with the great man's stone magic.

"Your children are not as carefree as they were when you left for Yanjing," Dokyi said.

Rosethorn sighed. "No, Honored Dedicate. The emperor was more overwhelming than we liked. You warned us it would be so."

"But I am sorry to have been proved right, all the same." He hesitated, then asked, "Rosethorn, are you still heart-whole in your vows?"

"Of course, Honored Dedicate!"

"As I said, I tried to take care of this matter myself, but no matter how I tried, I could not place my feet on the road to my destination. I have not been so thwarted in my designs since I was a dedicate of only ten years." Using great care, he opened the pack on the table and slid the leather down over the sides of the contents. He revealed a large peachwood box that contained four drawers. Letters were carved in the sides as well as the top.

Rosethorn shrank back from the waves of power that seemed to flow away from the box. "What is this?" she asked.

"This box holds the greatest treasures of our religion," he said quietly. "Without them, the Living Circle falls apart."

Goose bumps raced over Rosethorn's skin.

Dokyi touched the small gold knob on the bottom-most drawer. Carefully he pulled, and the top three drawers separated from it. The drawers were not set into a single frame, but were interlocking pieces.

"Look at it," he told Rosethorn quietly.

The contents of the bottom drawer, or open-topped box, were wrapped in silk that had not been dyed. Gingerly, using the tips of her fingers, Rosethorn separated the leaves of cloth that lay on top. Underneath them lay a cup. At Dokyi's silent urging she picked it up, gasping as magic flowed up her arms and through her veins.

The cup was the size of her palm and made of baked reddish clay with no glaze on it. Four twisting branches of carved white aspen seemed to grow around the cup from a round, flat base. The base itself was secured to a thin granite circle. More signs she did not recognize were cut into the outside of the clay, but not the inside. It was the simplest of objects, but the power within it made her bones shiver. Somehow she managed to gently place the cup in its box and cover it again.

"Honored Dedicate?" she whispered.

"The Cup of Water," he told her. He slid the three drawers into place on top of the cup until Rosethorn heard a faint click. Now the man touched the gold knob on the third drawer and pulled the top two off it. He motioned for Rosethorn to remove the silk cover from the drawer's contents.

"No," she said. She still shook from her contact with the cup. Frowning, Dokyi motioned again.

Rosethorn reached out a trembling hand and uncovered the drawer's contents. There lay a clear stone or crystal ball in which a flame burned, seemingly without air or fuel.

"Pick it up," Dokyi ordered. Sensing that she was about to refuse, he ordered, "Each guardian must handle them. Pick it up!"

Rosethorn closed her eyes and wrapped her fingers around the ball. It was warm.

And then she was furiously hot, burning inside her own skin. Swiftly she put the globe back and gulped the remains of her tea. It did not put out the heat inside her. She was afraid to speak, expecting flames to come out of her mouth.

"The Blaze of Fire." Dokyi covered the ball with silk and slid the two remaining drawers over it. He pointed to the knob on the third drawer.

Rosethorn looked at him and gasped, covering her mouth with her hands. She saw Dokyi as she had known him that winter. She also saw a towering tree, a soaring fire, a jet of water, all whipped by a gust of air. She didn't dare argue. It occurred to her that he had been these things all along and she, a dedicate initiate of Winding Circle, had never suspected it. Embarrassed for her ignorance, she stabbed the gold knob with a finger and let Dokyi lay the third drawer bare.

It held a green jade bowl. Inside it was a motley collection of seeds, large and small, many belonging to plants that Rosethorn had never seen before. She felt the magic in each as she ran her fingers through them, but no pain. Either she was worn down, or this Earth power was friendlier to her. She raised the bowl and carefully inhaled the dry scent of the seeds, wondering how old they were. What she wouldn't give to plant some of these!

Gently she set the bowl in its drawer and covered it with silk.

"The Seeds of the Earth." The man covered the bowl with the last drawer and nodded to Rosethorn. She took a deep breath and touched the gold knob for the Air treasure. The wooden top of the drawer flipped up.

Under its silk covering lay a feather that was many colors and none. Every time Rosethorn's eyes moved she saw different shades ripple across its surface. Even the feather's shape changed as she held it in her fingers. A great wind assaulted her. Thunder rolled in the distance; lightning struck nearby. The skin all over her body rippled.

"The Feather of Air." Dokyi's voice was a comforting growl as Rosethorn covered the feather and replaced the lid. "Now these boxes will open only for you. These are the four sacred Treasures of the Living Circle. There are no other beauties like them. These are the embodiment of all we hold sacred. Each temple we build is touched by them, and they are in every temple. As long as we have these, our faith will not fall. As long as we labor in our charge to preserve the beauties of the world, to worship all of it in life and death, these Treasures and their blessings will be ours. Should they fall into the hands of a destroyer, however — into the hands of one such as Weishu — our temples will lose their strength. Our works and our people will become corrupt. The Treasures must be hidden outside a temple of the Living Circle."

Rosethorn blinked wearily at him. "Why not?" she whispered. Tides dragged at the blood in her veins and in her womb.

Another kind of tide, hot and molten, surged in the marrow of her bones and within her eyes. She felt its long, slow roll countless miles below her feet, under the pathetically thin skin that covered the earth's surface. "Why not . . . to another Living Circle temple?"

"First Circle Temple in Garmashing is the only one of our houses built to keep the Treasures without revealing their presence," Dokyi told her. "If I had been here, or in your Winding Circle, with these boxes for a week or more, everyone would feel their nearness in the air they breathed, the fire they warmed themselves with, the water they drank, and the earth under their feet. Every bit of magic within them would strain to find the Treasures and touch them. They would appear in dreams, water puddles, in the surfaces of metal. A week more and others would come. No, there is only one other safe place for them here in Gyongxe."

Rosethorn covered her face with her hands. Water laden with ice coursed through her veins. Flocks of birds flew south below her as she slid from wind to wind.

She didn't notice when Dokyi left the room and returned with a tray of tea and buns. She came a little to herself when he wrapped her hands around a warm cup. "Drink. Do you understand, girl? You will take them to the Temple of the Sealed Eye in the Drimbakang Lho, west of here. Their priests are the only ones who can hide such things so no others can sense them. They are immune to the power that great magics possess over others. Only a dedicate of exceptional will and power can carry such a burden. Only a dedicate with strong reasons to return can take the Treasures there and come back."

Slowly Rosethorn looked at him. She could have sworn she heard Lark ask someone to fetch Comas home from the looms. "What if I didn't have such reasons?"

"Drink." Dokyi helped her to lift the cup to her lips. A few sips and she began to feel as if she was more herself. "You would become a priest of the Sealed Eye. As I told you, I did try to take the burden myself. Thanks to the gods, I have to suppose, I failed. You must not."

Rosethorn emptied the cup and set it down. "What if something happens to me?" she whispered. "The emperor's soldiers . . ." She turned her head. There — that was Niko's voice. He was talking about Tris, and Lightsbridge University.

Dokyi gripped her chin and made her look him in the eyes. "You will stop hearing the sounds shortly. It is the winds that carry them to you. Or perhaps it is the life's blood of all the plants that link roots beneath the surface of this world. The sounds will fade. Listen." His voice made her blink. "I was right about you," he said with great satisfaction. "They can be distracting at first. But I knew the acceptance of the Treasures would not drive you mad."

"Surely someone from Garmashing could have . . ." Rosethorn began to say. Then she saw the complexity of the table's wood grain. She sensed a grain within the grain, and patterns inside that. Gently she followed the whorls with her fingertips. She might follow them to the tree that had supplied the wood for the table, if she concentrated hard enough.

"You are not listening. One of my dedicates perished in the attempt to hold the box, and another lost his mind. No other dedicate had both the strength to go and the need to return,

Rosethorn." Dokyi spoke into her ear so that she could hear nothing else. "Only a very strong mage can survive the Treasures *and* the Sealed Eye temple. But *you* — half of you walks in the sun, and half of you walks in shadow. You will need the shadow in the Temple of the Sealed Eye."

"What!" Rosethorn yelped. "That's not true! I'm a plant mage! I *need* sunshine, I *thrive* on it —"

"Then *how did you die and return*?"

She opened her mouth, inhaled, and thought the better of whatever she had meant to say. Instead she exhaled and rubbed her temples. "It's a long and difficult story."

"Then I will live through the fighting, because I want to hear it. In the meantime, I am First Dedicate of the Living Circle faith, First Dedicate of *all* of the Living Circle temples, and your vows of obedience are vows to *me*. I need you to do this because if the emperor, if any evil person, seizes these Treasures, they will poison our temples first, and then the world. No more arguing!"

She bowed her head. "No, Honored Dedicate."

"Eat something."

"Yes, Honored Dedicate." She picked up a bun and bit it. Red bean. She hated red bean. She ate it anyway.

As she chewed, Dokyi explained, "In a day or two General Sayrugo will send troops on a sweep of the villages between this fort and the Drimbakang Zugu. The people here in the south must be moved to safety, should imperial armies come this far. You will ride with the soldiers as far as the turnoff for the road to Sealed Eye. They will guard you."

"Will the children and I have a guide?" Rosethorn asked. She bit another bun. This was very spicy meat. She ate it dully.

Dokyi shook his head. "No. The fewer people who know of this, the better. Briar and Evumeimei must remain behind."

That pierced the fog in her brain. She sat straight. "Dokyi, no. They're my charges."

"Briar is a man as such things are judged here. Others will look after him and Evumeimei. You cannot take them with you."

She remembered their restless nights on the way through the pass, when she had roused them both from ugly dreams. Did Dokyi even understand the weird effect the mountains were having on Evvy? Briar was watchful, but he hadn't spent years of his life raising young mages. "You've forgotten what they're like. Briar seems tough, but he worries himself sick over me. Evvy's still a child. And the mountains are pulling at her. She should be watched carefully."

"They will not be able to accompany you. I swear it. No, I will not prevent them," Dokyi said in response to her glare. "The magic of the Sealed Eye itself will do so. Once you set foot on the path to their temple, your young people will lose you in plain sight. This friend of theirs, this Parahan, will keep them safe. Or they may remain here, but you must take these Treasures into hiding!"

Rosethorn bowed her head, feeling very weary. "I am really the only person who could have done this?"

"I am one of Garmashing's defending mages," the man replied. "I took precious time to try to do it myself and failed. I am needed in the capital now."

"Oh. Forgive me, Honored Dedicate," Rosethorn whispered. Her heart twisted. Briar would *not* understand. Sadly, Evvy would understand all too well. Evvy expected everyone to leave her sooner or later.

All you can do is deliver this thing and hurry back to her, Rosethorn told herself. Get a grip on yourself, Niva!

She looked at Dokyi.

"Look," he said, understanding that she was ready to listen. "This pack will keep the Treasures concealed for ten days or so. Anyone who snoops will think it holds clothing. Place the Treasures inside it." He held the leather pack open for Rosethorn. At first she hesitated to touch them, afraid of what the combined Treasures, even in their silk wraps and boxes, might do to her. When she saw Dokyi's glare, Rosethorn glared back, wiped her fingers on a handkerchief she kept in her sleeve, and gripped the box by the sides. It felt like any other wooden container, cool and smooth. Rosethorn set the box inside the pack.

Briskly Dokyi did up the ties and buckles that secured it. Once he was finished, he placed it on the table. "Now you must take the map to the temple from my mind. This is why you require no guide. If the map is behind your eyes, no one can steal it from you."

Rosethorn nodded. She had done spells like this twice, though she did not care for them. She closed her eyes and found the core of her power, the part that was pure magic. It surged up through her arms and into her hands more fiercely than ever before. Carefully she pressed her fingers against Dokyi's temples.

His Earth magic answered hers. Once again she saw a landscape. She knew it for southern Gyongxe in vivid detail. The Snow Serpent River flowed over its rocks and hollows, plunging into the gorge. The fort lay just below her, with the army camped around it. Now she turned west, following the Snow Serpent River deeper into the country. There were villages on both sides and temples dedicated to gods she did not recognize. Only once did she spot a Circle temple to the north on the plain. She recognized it by the four-colored banner that flew from the bell tower.

When the Snow Serpent met the Tom Sho River, the map spell drew her south, into hills that were just lower rises of the massive Drimbakang Lho mountains. Inside the first line of peaks the magic pulled her along first one gorge, then another. At last she found the shadowed spot that was her destination, the Temple of the Sealed Eye.

She took her hands from Dokyi's head. "I should tell Briar and Evvy something," Rosethorn murmured. She felt dizzy and strange. "Where's the pack?"

Dokyi gave it to her. "You must rest and have a proper meal. Soudamini wishes to meet you and thank you for saving her brother."

Rosethorn blinked at him. "Souda-who?"

"Parahan's twin sister is camped before our walls with troops she has brought to join us. Her name is Soudamini."

"Oh." There were mountains in Rosethorn's head. She rose and swayed.

Dokyi stood and supported her by one arm. "Forgive me. The map is complex. Together with the Treasures, you have borne too much all at once." He snapped his fingers. The dark bubble around them vanished. "I can only say in my own defense that we are all desperate. The emperor took the God-King by surprise."

"How bad does it look?" Rosethorn asked, leaning on Dokyi as they walked out into a hallway.

"Soudamini's warriors have shown they are worth more than their numbers. The eastern and western tribesmen and their shamans have been coming in to join our armies. I don't think the emperor has planned for them," Dokyi explained. "And we still await the armies of the northwest." He led her somewhere in the fort; Rosethorn wasn't certain where. If she closed her eyes, she saw the Endless Ocean and the unexplored lands far to the west of Emelan. She tried to keep her eyes open.

Dokyi handed her over to two female dedicates, who gently took her arms. "Let her sleep and eat. Give her a hot bath. Treat her with all honor," the man instructed them. "And put this among her things."

To Rosethorn's drowsy surprise, he casually handed the pack with the Treasures to the younger of the two. "Rest," he said, and kissed Rosethorn on the forehead. "I will see you later."

The older dedicate led Rosethorn into a large room. All Rosethorn noticed was the bed, strewn with Evvy's cats. Promising herself that she would never let Dokyi talk her into anything more than a fishing trip again, she tumbled onto it.

Briar and Evvy had finished their snack and were wondering what would happen next when the main door opened. Parahan came in, his arm around a much shorter person in a yak-skin coat and boots. They were chattering in the language Parahan often used for swearing. While his companion waited to see the general, Parahan came to see Briar and Evvy and filch a couple of their leftover dumplings.

"Who's that?" Evvy demanded, feeling a little jealous. She could see that Parahan's friend was female. She wore a long braid of black hair pinned at the back of her head, and a tiny row of rubies that followed the line of her brows somehow. She also had large golden-brown eyes, a perfect nose, and full lips. She made Evvy feel even more like a grub than she did already. "That's my sister," Parahan said gleefully. "That's Souda — Soudamini! She's the fierce one and I'm the layabout. There was gossip that the emperor might invade Gyongxe this year or next, so she came from Kombanpur to offer her services and two hundred warriors to the God-King. She heard what happened to me. So now I have my own clothes and weapons, because she prepares for everything, and we are going to fight Weishu, if the God-King will have me." Parahan indeed had his own clothes: a red silk tunic embroidered with a multitude of birds, blue silk breeches, and proper riding boots. He asked, "Where is Rosethorn?"

"First Dedicate Dokyi took her away for a talk," Briar said, leaning against the wall. "In that room." He pointed to the door.

"There's some kind of magic going on in there, but it's behind a wall," Evvy offered. "We can't even get a peek."

"Far be it from me to try to peek at mages," Parahan said. Then he frowned. "Is she all right?"

"Dokyi's our friend," Evvy told him. "He wouldn't hurt her."

"He's her, I don't know, he's the First Dedicate of First Circle Temple," Briar explained. "That means he's sort of the head of all the Living Circle temples in the world. And Rosethorn is a Living Circle dedicate."

Parahan nodded. "I understand."

"Maybe he's telling her that she doesn't really have to fight the emperor," Evvy suggested. She sighed. "I would like that."

"Prince Parahan," General Sayrugo called.

"Excuse me," Parahan told them. He went to the table and bowed. "Please, General, here I am only Parahan, a soldier."

Sayrugo looked him over. "Well, only Parahan with one hundred of Soudamini's troops to his name, the God-King sent me a message about you."

"But the God-King doesn't know me," Parahan said, unnerved.

"In all my years of service to Gyongxe, I have learned never to try to guess what the God-King does and does not know," the general replied. "The answer to your question, he says, is yes, you have a job. You may begin here in the south. Soudamini and you are to go west with two of my captains. Move as many villagers as possible into the fortresses between here and the Temple of the Serpents on the Tom Sho River." Evvy saw that General Sayrugo was showing the road to Parahan on a map on the table. "With those same troops you may then proceed north. You have my permission to cut down every unsanctified piece of Yanjingyi worm bait that gets between you and the capital."

"Where does that leave us?" Evvy asked Briar in a whisper.

"Wherever Rosethorn says we go," he replied comfortably.

Evvy wasn't comfortable. Dokyi had plans for Rosethorn. What if they didn't include her or Briar? And now that they were indoors, with thick walls between her and danger, she was suddenly too tired to get up. She felt as if she had been pulling rocks out from under the feet of killers for months. She had been sleeping cold at night for years. She'd been hungry again, and terrified. This was a comfortable place. The mountains sang even through the walls. Why did they have to leave? Let soldiers deal with the emperor.

They slept most of that day, and bathed, and put on clean clothes. Evvy introduced the cats to Soudamini. Parahan introduced his rough-voiced twin to the people who had been his companions on the road to Gyongxe. When Souda learned that Evvy and Briar had freed him from his shackles, she insisted on pressing her forehead to their hands, which flustered both Evvy and Briar, though for different reasons. She was fascinated by the tale of their journey and their battles along the Snow Serpent River.

Serious conversation came over that night's supper with Dokyi, the twins, and General Sayrugo. The discussion about the imperial soldiers in the Snow Serpent Pass, and plans to get villagers to safety along the Snow Serpent River, went smoothly. Then Rosethorn began to explain her plans.

"No!" Briar cried. "This is the most bleat-brained idea you've *ever* come up with! You can't!" He glared at Dokyi. "Find someone else. Look at her! She's worn-out! I won't let you do it!"

"Such an ill-behaved child," Sayrugo commented, looking at her pakoras — ball-shaped dumplings — with a suspicious eye. The Kombanpur cooks who had come with Souda and her troops had provided the meal to welcome Parahan.

"I am not a child!" Briar snapped.

Dokyi tried, unsuccessfully, to hide a smile behind his finger. "Such a bad student, then."

"I'm not a student, either! Exactly! I'm certified in my own right, and she can't tell me to go or stay anymore. She has trouble *breathing* up here!"

"Actually, I feel better," Rosethorn said. She took a deep breath and raised her eyebrows. "*Much* better." She had eaten all that was put before her and was taking seconds.

"There are benefits to the burden I passed to you," Dokyi said, though his eyes were on Briar. "I will not tell you my age, because I am vain. I am older than I seem, however, and stronger, due to its influence. She is healthy enough for whatever trials the land may put before her, young man. And it is not your place to question a duty for which her vows have fitted her."

"Enough," Rosethorn said when Briar opened his mouth again. "Not *one more word*, understand me?"

For a long moment there was silence and tea drinking. Then Evvy said, "My cats can't take any more travel. Between sleeping herbs and galloping along they're not looking so good. I am a bit tired myself." She rubbed her thumb along the table's edge. "Might we stay here? I could help defend this fort and the cats would be all right. It's a mountain fort. There are rocks I can use here, big ones. Maybe Rosethorn and Briar could do more thorns and bar the road to the pass."

"That is a *splendid* idea," the general said unexpectedly.

Everyone looked at her in shock. "It is?" Rosethorn asked.

Sayrugo smiled. "I am taking troops northeast along the Drimbakang Sharlog," she explained. "Parahan and Souda will have two companies of my people as well as their own two hundred to ride along the Snow Serpent Road going west. We all have to move villagers to safety and fight any imperials that have come so far south. But Captain Rana's company will remain in charge here to defend the pass and the local villagers. A barrier of thorns on the pass will make Rana's work easier. There will be no more Yanjingyi soldiers to come through that way."

Rosethorn frowned.

Briar smiled wryly. "I don't think any trade will be going down the Snow Serpent for a while, Rosethorn, if that's what's wrinkling your face. It won't matter if the pass is blocked."

She nodded slowly. "We could do thorns, then. I'll go with Parahan and Soudamini as far as the Tom Sho River, provided they don't slow down too much alerting the villages and temples."

"And I'll go with you, since Evvy will be snug as a flea in an armpit here," Briar said cheerfully. Soudamini choked on her curried rice.

"Briar!" Rosethorn cried. "Where are your *manners*?"

"In the same dung hole you left your bleating brains when you said you were going off without me!" Briar shouted back, jumping to his feet.

"Boy, you cannot go to the Temple of the Sealed Eye with her," Dokyi said. "It will not be permitted."

Briar stared at Dokyi in white-hot rage, wondering if he should tell the old hand waver what he could do with his permission.

Dokyi stood and put an arm like stone around Briar's shoulders. "Let us confer outside," he said agreeably.

I'm not even one of his precious dedicates! Briar thought, indignant. He did not argue. At the moment standing this close to the old man was like being close to Rosethorn when she was in the depths of her magic, only stronger, like stone.

Outside the room with the door closed, the First Dedicate released him. Softly he said, "I know that you have lived under terrible strain since you reached Yanjing."

"So?" Briar demanded. He kept his own voice quiet. He didn't want Rosethorn to hear, either.

Dokyi folded his hands in front of him. "I honor your care for her, Briar, but this is now something only she can do, and it concerns survival for many. She wanted you to come with her, but it is quite truly not possible. If you love her, you will help her, not hinder her."

"Is there no one else?" Briar whispered.

Dokyi shook his head. "The task requires someone extraordinary. She is that person. Do not make her duty more painful."

He walked back into the supper room, leaving Briar to think and kick the wall. When he returned to his seat, Evvy was saying, "The emperor has plenty of riches. He doesn't need Gyongxe. The farming here isn't very good. What can he want here?"

Dokyi shook his head, smiling. "But he *isn't* the heart of the world. He hears Gyongxe is the spindle on which the world turns, but he does not understand it. He thinks if he takes Gyongxe, people will say that he is the spindle."

"He thinks Gyongxe means wealth, and magic," General Sayrugo explained. "He thinks that people build temples here to be close to magic. In truth they come to be closest to the sky, where the gods dwell. When our ambassador reminded him that five holy rivers, that feed hundreds of thousands, rise here, he only said that was interesting."

"He must not be allowed to control our temples or to handle the gifts of our gods," Dokyi said. "He will do what he has done to every other realm he has conquered. He will loot its treasures and destroy all the signs of its history. That is what the emperor does to his conquered nations."

Evvy stared at the man, her eyes wide. Briar glared at him for frightening her and put his arm around Evvy.

They picked at their food in silence for a time before Parahan said, "Do you know, I would like Briar with us." To Soudamini he said, "You must see what my friend here can do with a handful of seeds, Souda."

"Truly?" she asked.

Evvy nodded. "There's plenty of the emperor's soldiers that won't be buried with their ancestors because of what Briar can do."

Souda smiled wickedly at Briar. "Impressive."

Briar looked at her. Parahan's twin was a couple of inches shorter than Briar and well curved. Tonight she wore her blue-black hair in complexly twined braids secured with gold pins. A wicked dimple accented her mouth. Briar was the first to admit he was a fool for a dimple.

"Ride with us and find some Yanjingyi dogs to fight," Souda proposed. "Show me these skills of yours. A *prebu* is always welcome."

Briar looked at Parahan, confused by the strange word. "A *nanshur*," Parahan explained in *tiyon*.

"We're going to have a splendid time deciding which language to speak," Souda murmured.

Briar shoved his hands into his pockets to give himself a second to think. If he went with the twins, at least he could watch Rosethorn for part of her journey. He could see Evvy was worn-out. There was also her un-Evvy-ish drifting off as she stared at the vast mountains. Perhaps if she stayed here for a time, to feed her cats and rest, she would get used to the tall peaks and come back to herself again. With the pass closed off, and Gyongxe armies roaming in two directions, the fort ought to be safe for her.

He hated to think it, but maybe Dokyi had a point as well. Watching Rosethorn until she left the twins for this strange temple was probably all of the orange he was going to get. Half of the fruit was better than none. With luck, he would find her when she returned from her strange errand. He would be able to sense her as she came down from the mountains: The very grasses would tell him.

He glanced at her. She had actually cleaned her plate. Her color was better than it had been since they left the Traders.

"You need to go to bed if we're taking the road again soon," he said gruffly. He looked at Dokyi, Parahan, and Soudamini. "We can't wait another day?"

"You may wait," Dokyi said. "I leave at midnight."

"Alone?" Souda asked, alarmed.

"Alone is best," Dokyi said. "Souda, I *am* the First Dedicate of the Earth temple of First Circle Temple. Midnight and the dark are my elements. I will be fine." He stood and went to Rosethorn. "Do not wait for more than a day. The new magic will strengthen you as you travel, and the emperor is on the move. Good fortune and the gods' blessings to you, my daughter." He kissed Rosethorn on the forehead and looked at Briar. "If all things go well, soon we will meet again."

As he walked from the room, Parahan, Soudamini, and the general followed to ask their own questions. The moment the door closed behind them, Rosethorn began a scold that blistered Briar's ears.

CHAPTER
TWELVE

Briar rose at dawn the next day after a night filled with foul dreams of Rosethorn and Evvy in the hands of imperial torturers. Rather than go back to sleep and risk more dreams, he borrowed a mare with a stable girl's permission and rode out of the fort.

He had thought to go uphill, but the sight of the Sun Queen's three mountain husbands towering over him made him feel uncomfortably fenced in. Instead he rode down, past the tent village where most of the army was camped, over the Snow Serpent River crossing, and out onto the grasses and brush of the Gnam Runga. The light in the sky was pearly and seemed to come from everywhere in the east. It would be a while before the sun crested the topmost heights of the hills and mountains there.

His horse startled a pair of pheasants, who drove horse and rider away from what turned out to be a parade of peeping youngsters. Snow finches, wagtails, and larks also gave their opinions of the rider and his horse as their day was interrupted. Briar wasn't sure, but those opinions sounded like bird insults. He scanned the sky for the famed Gyongxe buzzards and steppe eagles, but there were none in sight.

"Too cold," he told the mare. Gloomily he added, "Or they're out where the fighting's going on. They'll get plenty of food at those places, enough for every carrion bird in Gyongxe." Normally he grudged no one a meal, having often gone without for the first eleven years of his life, but it was hard to wish a buzzard well at a battlefield.

Once he could no longer see the village on the eastern hills or the fort on the southern ones, Briar dismounted, letting the mare's reins trail. The horse, a sturdy animal bred for the thin air of the mountains, began to graze. Briar walked on until he heard only the wind in the grass and the insults of the smaller birds.

Someone had told him that Gnam Runga meant "Sky Drum." It was a vast plain between the Drimbakang Lho and the Drimbakang Zugu, the long finger of mountains that curved out of the southern heights and around the capital, Garmashing. The enemy was aiming for that wide plain, where his generals could put their catapults to good use. First they would have to fight the emperor's army in the north and the tribes of the Drimbakang Sharlog around the eastern passes. No one wanted the imperial armies to mass on the Gnam Runga.

Briar would have preferred to fight in the canyons, where he could have put trees to work, but the plain was what he would have, first when he rode west with Parahan and Souda and later when they rode to Garmashing. Now he crouched and tried to dig his fingers into the dirt of the Gnam Runga. The grass was interwoven and tough. It fought his intrusion, just as it fought the death of the winter freeze.

"I'm a friend," he told it. "I just want to meet the dirt. Let me in a little." He spread his magic over the bed of plants. There were patches of bare earth here and there, but he could feel the plant roots running under them, nourished by the trickle of moisture from the distant river.

The grasses trembled and then gave way.

"Thank you," Briar told them gravely. "You're very strong. Those lowland grasses would never stand a chance against you."

The grasses were scornful of fat, water-soaked plants beyond the mountains. Only here, next to the sky, could they reach for the infinite.

Briar shook his head and looked around. A line of boulders stood close by. There were images painted on them in bright colors and outlined in white: a many-headed god, a snake twined about itself to make an intricate circle, a goddess riding a beast whose antlers were tipped with stars, a spider that wore a crown. It wasn't the first time he had seen such paintings on rocks. Then, as now, he wondered who went to such trouble, and why. The Snow Serpent Pass was bare of them. Now that he thought of it, the Ice Lion Pass, which they had taken on the way to Dohan, had also been bare of the paintings. It was as if the artists had not wanted to share them with foreigners.

Shaking his head at the idea, possibly a leftover of his nightmares, he scooped up a little dirt. The grass closed over the space it had made for him. Briar said his thanks, rubbing the dirt in his palms to get a feel for it. If he was going to be fighting on these plains, he needed to understand his battlefield. He spent his ride back to Fort Sambachu smelling that earth, rolling it between his fingers, and dusting it onto his cheeks. Finally he rinsed it off in the little river that ran past the camp. By then he understood the earth of the Gnam Runga and what grew there, if not the stones and their paintings.

This dirt was very young and energetic, thrust up by the same force that made the Drimbakangs themselves. That same youth filled the roots and stems of everything that grew in it, making it more inclined to do whatever he — or Rosethorn — might ask of it.

He was considering the possibilities on his return to the fort when a soldier in the armor of the Realms of the Sun hailed him and informed him that Their Highnesses Parahan and Soudamini desired his company at breakfast. By the time Briar left Parahan and Souda, they had equipped him for any fighting they might encounter as they got the villagers to the safety of the temple fortresses. He now had three horses assigned for his use, extra packs, a tent, an armored vest, riding gauntlets, leather riding breeches, and an armored cap with a tassel of bronze eagle feathers. He also had a short, potbellied rider named Jimut, who had been assigned to care for Briar's horses, tent, and even Briar himself.

He and Jimut had just dumped everything in Briar's room when Rosethorn banged on the door. Briar could hardly believe what he saw when he opened up. Rosethorn looked fresher and brighter than she had in a couple of years. There was an extra gloss to her short-cropped hair. Even the natural red of her lips was more vivid than it had been in a long time.

"What are you gawping at, boy?" Her voice was louder and crisper, as if she had more wind in her lungs. Briar forgot himself and hugged her. She pushed him away. "What has gotten into you? Don't think I've forgiven you for your rudeness to First Dedicate Dokyi last night!"

He grinned at her. "Never crossed my mind," he reassured her.

Rosethorn looked at Jimut. "And who's this?"

"Jimut, this is my teacher, the *nanshur* Rosethorn," Briar said. He'd been lucky that Souda had found a man who spoke *tiyon*, since Briar had only a scattering of words in Banpuri. "She'll be riding with us."

Jimut pressed his palms together before his face and bowed deeply to Rosethorn. On their walk to the fort Briar had tried to explain that it was important to be polite to her.

"Whatever he told you, I'm much worse," Rosethorn said.

Jimut kept his palms together and bowed again.

Rosethorn made a harrumphing noise and looked at Briar. "Bring a seed ball and some strong-grow potion," she ordered. "Captain Rana has horses and guards waiting. We're going to block the pass."

"May I come?" Jimut asked. "If I am to attend *Nanshur* Briar —"

Briar sighed. "It's just Briar." He'd already said it to Jimut twice.

"I should take every chance to become used to his sort of magic," Jimut continued politely.

"I have no problems with that," Rosethorn said. "Only Briar, if we can move this along? We need to root them more deeply than usual, and I want to get it over with."

"Evvy?" Briar asked.

"She would rather take a bath, she says. She *has* seen us do this before."

They were out the door with Rosethorn before she had time to get testy. She said nothing, sinking into a distant, thoughtful mood as they joined Sergeant Kanbab and a squad of ten soldiers at the stables.

As they rode past the camp, they saw that everyone was now up and busy shining armor, sharpening weapons, bundling crossbow bolts, and doing up packs. In the open ground between the tents and the river, archers practiced their shooting while spearmen and swordsmen dueled under the eyes of their commanders. The cavalry jumped their horses over obstacles in unison on the plain. Refugees were arriving: They carried children and belongings, or fetched them in carts and on the backs of mules and yaks as they climbed to the fort.

Once they reached the narrow place in the pass where the road first entered the river gorge, Rosethorn emerged from her deep silence. "Sergeant, take your people over to that rock," she yelled over the roar of the fast-moving water. "If you'd hold our horses until we're done?"

Kanbab nodded and motioned for her people to take the animals as Briar, Jimut, and Rosethorn dismounted. Jimut stayed back as the mages went into the bottleneck where the hills were closest to the road.

The task was easily done. Briar sprinkled strong-grow potion on the seed balls held by each of them, but the seeds were already quivering before the liquid touched them. The balls had soaked in the wakefulness and swift growth of the others used in the fighting on their way to the fort. Now it took just a whisper from Rosethorn for them to leap to the ground. The cloth burst, showering seeds everywhere. Plants slammed roots into the earth and sprouted even as Rosethorn and Briar walked forward with their water flasks. By the time they had emptied the water over the scattered seed, the growing vines were up to their shins. The green whips did not try to snag the two mages, but those would be the only people the vines left alone. Thorns an inch long showed on the lowest parts of the stems as the vines rose and sprouted more branches. Their various flowers budded and bloomed, then scattered still more seed in a burst of air.

Rosethorn and Briar had withdrawn to the clear ground near Jimut by the time the first blossoms showed. Everyone could see that green stems had crawled across all of the open ground between the rise of stone to the hills and to the river. They could hear the rustle as petals and leaves unfurled and heavy stems wove together with their neighbors.

Kanbab, who had at least seen something like this before, offered Rosethorn her flask. Rosethorn took a gulp of butter tea, grimaced, and passed the flask to Briar. He took two good drinks, having acquired a taste for the local beverage, and returned the flask to Kanbab with a quiet thank-you. He never took his eyes from the barrier, feeling with his power for any weaknesses. Rosethorn left that to him as the kind of basic work a junior mage ought to attend to.

"Will the enemy be able to cut through the vines?" Kanbab wanted to know.

"With a sharp enough sword or halberd," Rosethorn said absently.

Briar grinned. "And then the stems will grow back three times as fast. And they will look for the one that chopped them, and grow straight through him."

"Or around," Rosethorn murmured.

"Or around," Briar agreed. "And around, and around."

"And the emperor will know you did this," Kanbab said.

Rosethorn and Briar looked at each other. "Let him," Rosethorn said.

The barrier was now two feet thick and three feet high. Thorns pulled themselves up the hillside, drawing stems with them. Roots shot down from the stems, lancing deep into the stony earth. More blossoms gave up seed that filtered to the ground among the thickly woven stems.

Briar waited for word from Rosethorn. She watched until the barrier was four feet tall and five feet wide on the road, and had climbed ten feet up along the hillside. No horse, mule, camel, yak, or human would be able to pass between the barrier and the river without losing skin, or between the river and the cliffs that edged it on the far side. They both knew the thorns would continue to grow for days, leaving the flanks of the hills on the north side of the road impassable by mount or by foot. No one would be crossing into or out of Gyongxe until Dokyi, Sayrugo, or those with whom they had trusted the opening spell came to clear the pass again.

Briar glanced at Jimut, who had turned gray under his dark brown skin.

"Jimut, mount up," he told the rider. "And have a swallow of something, before you faint."

"I never faint," Jimut said, but he wobbled as he walked to his horse.

One of the other soldiers held the mount's reins. It took Jimut two tries to get into the saddle.

"This will do, I think," Rosethorn said, turning away from what they had set in motion.

"Good," Briar said. "I want my breakfast."

By midday, General Sayrugo and two hundred of her troops were gone, on their way northeast to warn the villages and get the people to safety in the temple fortresses. Briar, Rosethorn, and Evvy spent the afternoon with Parahan and Soudamini, playing with the cats, watching their troops exercise, reading maps of the Gyongxe basin, and refusing to speak of anything gloomy. Supper was a grand feast in the style of the Realms of the Sun. Captain Rana and his squad were invited as thanks for bringing Parahan to Gyongxe and his sister. There was juggling, sword and fire dancing, and music from the Realms and Gyongxe. In the end, Parahan carried Evvy back to her room in the fort. She had fallen asleep by the fire. The cats, used to these things, followed them.

Evvy woke as Parahan set her down to open her door. Since she was leaving at dawn, Rosethorn had moved her things down to the camp. Evvy now had the room to herself. Parahan held her up with one hand as he walked her inside.

"Are you coming to say good-bye to us in the morning?" he asked as she fumbled to feed the meowing cats.

Evvy shook her head. "I don't like good-byes. They're bad luck. I feel small enough about not going to fight." She sat cross-legged on her bed.

"You helped fight all the way here," Parahan told her. "And Rana may need you to help defend this place. Just take care of yourself and the cats, so I have my friends to come back to. Will you promise me?"

"All right. I promise." Evvy grabbed Parahan's sleeve. "And you look after Briar and Rosethorn? As much as they'll let you." She felt a bad quivering in her lip and in her eyelids.

Evvy turned over and buried her face in the pillows. She only looked up, and wiped her wet eyes on her sleeve, when she heard the door close.

That afternoon she had placed her small statue of Yanjing's god of luck, Heibei, on the room's shrine. Now she used one of the coals in the hearth to light a stick of incense. Applying that, she lit two more sticks in the jar that already stood on the shrine, then left hers with them. Putting her palms together, she bowed and prayed silently to the plump, grinning god. She knew that Parahan, Souda, Dokyi, and Rosethorn didn't pray to Heibei, but she didn't think the god would mind, and Briar always said he would take help from wherever he would get it. She wasn't sure about General Sayrugo's gods, but she included her as well. She'd heard Captain Rana's warriors say that soldiers could always use a friendly god's attention.

Once she had finished praying to Heibei, Evvy turned in the direction of the Sun Queen's husbands. She knew exactly where each mountain's peak rose behind the fort. Now, in the quiet of the room, with the cats settled on the bed without fuss, she even thought she could hear their voices. One of them especially had a kind and musical voice, a low, burring hum. She tried to copy it low in her chest, reaching for that magical sound. On and on she hummed, making a kind of prayer of it, a prayer to the Sun Queen's husbands to look after her friends.

CHAPTER
THIRTEEN

THE PLAIN OF GNAM RUNGA
SOUTH AND WEST, ALONG THE FOOT OF
THE DRIMBAKANG LHO

Jimut roused Briar at a painfully early hour to help him put on his new half armor. Briar donned the sling with his seed balls and other odds and ends himself, not wanting his helper to get in the habit of handling his mage's gear. Breakfast was hot bread stuffed with spiced meat and rice, something he could eat as the soldiers dismantled and packed up his tent. He drank hot tea with Rosethorn, Parahan, and Soudamini, none of whom seemed to believe in chatter before sunrise. He was drinking a second cup of tea when Rosethorn bent down and lifted the strange pack she had gotten from Dokyi two days before: the thing she had to take someplace that Briar was not allowed to go. She slung it on her chest in place of her own bundle of deadly plant magics and ran her fingers over it, her face thoughtful.

Briar scowled.

"Don't start fussing again." She met his eyes. "I took care of myself long before you met me."

"Carrying something like that?" He tapped the pack with his finger.

The next thing he knew he was flat on the ground. His ears and head rang. Something cold and wet lay on his forehead. Above him the sky was the color of gray silk.

Rosethorn bent over him, her brown eyes rueful. "I had no idea it would knock you down," she said. "I would have warned you, honestly."

Parahan knelt beside him. "Are you all right?" he asked. "There was a flash of light and you flew through the air." He looked at Rosethorn. "We'll warn the troops to keep away from you and your burden."

She nodded.

Briar took a breath and coughed. Rosethorn helped him to sit up. Jimut knelt beside him with a flask. Briar hesitated, then drank. It was cold water. "Thank you, Jimut. I believe you would have told me," he said to Rosethorn. "And you think *you* are safe with that thing?"

"Safer than you," she said. Parahan and Jimut hoisted him to his feet.

Souda waited nearby with men who held their saddled horses. Their small army was ready to march.

Briar felt better in the saddle. He didn't complain when Jimut rode close to him and collected the reins so he could lead Briar's mount. That seemed like a good idea, too.

It was hard to concentrate on what anyone said, or on anything but the strange pictures that rippled through his brain: lions that seemed to be carved of ice and snow, tiny metal serpents with skulls for heads, and orange fanged gods with flames for hair. Blue goddesses danced on the mountaintops with a different weapon in each of their six arms. A yak whose head was as big as he was tall snuffled in his ear. He had wanted to know what Dokyi had foisted on Rosethorn — what all the secrecy and risk was about. Now it seemed like ignorance might not be such a bad thing. At least, not when it came to that pack. Clearly Rosethorn could carry it without problems, but he thought he would leave it alone.

Briar opened his eyes to full daylight. He found himself at the back of their group with the pack animals and their crossbow-wielding guards. The rest of their numbers trotted ahead. Briar twisted frantically, looking for Rosethorn. That was when he discovered someone had tied him to the saddle.

"You're back with us," Jimut said cheerfully. He rode between Briar and an attendant who led a train of supply mules. The reins to Briar's horse were in his hand. "You *are* back?" His furry eyebrows inched up toward his hairline.

"I never left!" Briar retorted, annoyed by the question. Then he looked at the sun. It was almost noon. "Did I?"

"Your eyes were closed. You didn't move. Forgive me," Jimut said, bowing as Briar yanked at the long scarf that secured him in the saddle. "I didn't want *Nanshur* Rosethorn angry if you fell off." He edged his own mount over to Briar and traded Briar's reins for the scarf once Briar untied the knot.

"I . . . was in a mage trance," Briar announced, trying to recover his dignity. "Don't your *nanshurs* have trances?"

"Weeelll, yes," the older man drawled. "But usually they shake rattles and hum and chant for a long time first to give us warning."

"Mine caught up with me fast," Briar replied, thinking quickly. "I had no time to warn anyone." He looked ahead. "Shouldn't we be riding up there if I'm to help guard the warriors?"

Jimut looked at his friend, shrugged, and led the way as Briar nudged his own horse into a trot. They picked up the pace to a gallop. A few of the warriors they passed called out jokes to Jimut, suggesting that it was nice of him to join them. Jimut only turned his beaky nose up haughtily.

"I'm sorry," Briar called. "You should have roused me."

"I tried!" Jimut replied. "It didn't work!"

"I don't normally sleep like that," Briar said as they slowed. "I really don't."

"Whatever *Nanshur* Rosethorn carries, it must be as strong as the great river Kanpoja — the Thundering Water," Jimut explained. "You can hear her in Kombanpur from miles away. She comes to us from here in Gyongxe. The hero Ajit Robi fought the Drimbakang demons to set Kanpoja free. He cut a path for the goddess through the mountains, and she leaped from Gyongxe into Kombanpur. All of our great rivers are born from her."

Briar looked at the tumbling band of the Snow Serpent. "*This* river is the Kanpoja?"

Jimut shook his head. "Farther west. Along the Drimbakang Zugu and through the Drimbakang Lho. Maybe we will see it, where the goddess's temple stands." He sighed. "I have always wanted to see it."

He and Jimut had just caught up with Rosethorn, Parahan, and the others when they reached a bridge across the Snow Serpent. Here Rosethorn, Briar, Jimut, Souda, the Gyongxin Captain Lango, and two companies of warriors turned off the road and crossed the bridge. A large village several miles up this road had to be evacuated. Parahan rode on to collect people on the south side of the road and ensure they reached safety, while the other Gyongxin captain, Jha, left them to do the same errand on the north side of the road.

At the village, the officials were not impressed with the warning carried by Souda and Captain Lango. They did not like the arrival of two hundred-odd soldiers at their gates, half of them southern foreigners. They did not believe that the Yanjingyi emperor had declared war on Gyongxe. Yes, the headman said, messengers had come from that fortress to the east, but messengers were excitable. They would claim a caravan was an enemy army. The headman said his village wall would hold off any invisible army.

Finally Rosethorn had heard enough. She rode forward to Souda's side. "Excuse me, Your Highness," she told Souda, her voice carrying to the villagers, "but if they don't want to leave this place, they don't have to. If they want to trust their safety to logs that have been eaten hollow by insects, let them. Surely there are other people around these parts who will be grateful for the warning."

Briar hadn't thought the bug munching was that bad, but it was his and Rosethorn's pattern to reinforce what the other said. He dismounted and walked to the wall beside the gate. With one hand he reached out to a log he guessed wouldn't bring the gate down and pushed. No one had to know that he asked the weak wood at the base of the log to give way for him. The log groaned, and then toppled onto the ground outside. He shook his head, *tsk*ing to himself.

"When did you last replace these logs?" Rosethorn wanted to know.

"Magic!" the headman shouted, his face red-bronze with fury. "You used magic!"

Briar turned and looked at the man. "I can't magic the kind of bug damage that got done to this log," he said. "Rosethorn can't, either. We're plant mages, not bug mages. Look at this wood yourself."

"We just came up the Snow Serpent Pass with the emperor's warriors chasing us," Rosethorn snapped. "We didn't have time to spell your logs. Believe us or not, but ask your wives and children if they mean to wait here with you behind your rotten walls."

"We come at the bidding of the God-King," Captain Lango said last. "Why would we be foolish enough to use his name for a lie?"

The village leaders were finally convinced, and the soldiers set up camp outside the wall. Rosethorn vanished. Briar could tell she had walked outside the wall, probably to listen to whatever songs her burden was singing.

He found work helping a woman and her children pack. Jimut, seeing what he was up to, obtained a mule the fatherless family could use for their burdens. While Jimut helped to load the mule, Briar gathered piles of sticks and what twine was available and made carry-crates for the villagers' birds and pets. If he didn't have enough twine, he simply persuaded the sticks to grow through one another to make the joins he needed.

The afternoon was half over when he heard a crash from a hut and a child's screams. He ran to see what was wrong.

Inside the hut, two women were bent over a wailing child who lay between several wooden boxes. The little boy clutched his left shin with both hands, shrieking. Blood leaked between his twined fingers.

Briar pulled off the sling he wore on his back. "Excuse me," he called loudly to the women. "Please, I can help. I'm a *nanshur*. I use medicine."

The women moved aside. Briar felt inside the sling for a roll of linen bandage and a potion he kept for bleeding wounds. He leaned close to the child's face and yelled, *"Hah!"*

The boy threw up his hands to protect his face. Instantly Briar gripped his leg. He felt it gently to see if it was broken — it did not seem to be. He used a touch of his power to tug a square of linen off the bandage roll. Carefully he pressed the cloth against the wound. After a short wait he took the cloth away for a quick look. The boy had cut himself from his knee halfway to his ankle, but the wound was a shallow one. Quickly Briar pressed the cloth to it again.

The older of the two women, assured that he knew what he was doing, got a wet cloth and set about cleaning the child's bloody hands. The younger woman began to carry the fallen boxes outside.

When he heard steps approach, Briar looked up from his patient. A much older woman came over with a small kettle of steaming water and a bowl. "I think you will need this for your work?" she asked. "You are very good to come to the help of strangers."

"I used to scream like that, too," Briar said, grinning

at the child. "When it looks so bad you think the healer will cut your leg off, you get scared. It is just a very ugly scratch."

"We should have watched him better," said the woman who had cleaned the child's hands. Now she had given him some kind of sweet. He was sucking on it and watching Briar's every move. "There is so much to put in the wagon that we forgot."

With the two women to help, Briar cleaned the wound, covered it with his medicine, and bandaged it. The only thanks he accepted was a couple of very good dumplings that he shared with Jimut. After that he settled by the well and continued to make carry-crates.

The soldiers and the villagers combined resources for a large meal after dark. Though everyone was friendly enough as they came together to eat, the villagers' faces showed their worries. The scramble to pick what to take and what to leave continued long into the night. Briar was dozing over a half-finished crate when someone nudged him awake with a booted foot. He looked up at Souda.

"Bed," she ordered with a friendly smile. "In the camp. Come on. I'm turning in, too."

Saddest of all, he was so worn-out he could not think of anything witty to say to impress her as they walked out of the village and into camp. Jimut was waiting. He bowed to Souda and took Briar to his bedroll.

They left in the early morning. Captain Lango detailed two squads of warriors to keep the villagers moving. The rest of his company and all of Souda's, together with Rosethorn and Briar, returned to the main road. They halted that day only to rest the horses.

It was twilight when they reached the Temple of the Sun Queen's Husbands. As a fortress, it made Fort Sambachu look like a collection of crates. Its walls, painted with blue and green many-armed men, were thick and lined with men and women armed with longbows. The walls were built in step fashion like those at Sambachu; so, too, was the temple itself, building up to a tower that gave a view of the road and plain. The heavy gates, each one painted with what Briar assumed was a husband who held weapons in every one of his eight hands, stood wide open to admit the villagers.

When Rosethorn approached the gates, her burden set up such a high, tooth-hurting screech that Briar covered his ears, almost falling off his horse. The ever-alert Jimut caught his reins just in time. The noise only stopped when Rosethorn turned her horse away from the gate.

She conferred with Souda and Captain Lango briefly, explaining that the magic in the temple's walls and gates was uncomfortable with the magic she bore. In the end, only Captain Lango and his warriors accompanied the refugees inside for the night.

"Uncomfortable," Briar muttered to Jimut, rubbing his aching jaws. "Uncomfortable, she says. I've heard two ships scraping against each other that didn't make such a noise."

"It's not that the magics are fighting, or the temple is evil," Rosethorn explained to Briar and their friends over roast goat, flatbread, and cheese. "Magic isn't evil of itself, only the ends to which it's put, like a dagger. But the shape their magic holds doesn't match mine." She didn't really mean her own green magic. Briar knew he could have walked through that gate if he had wanted to. It was Rosethorn's burden that had put up the fuss.

"No," said a voice just outside the light of their fire. A man of Rosethorn's age in the long scarlet tunic worn by this temple's priests walked closer to their group. "Our magics enclose us to protect us, with only the opening at the gate to allow other magics to enter, if they are small ones." He looked at Rosethorn, then around the circle until he found Briar. "We would have been forced to ask both of you to remain outside. I have brought our chief priest's apologies to you. Normally this is not such a problem, though your burden" — he nodded to Rosethorn — "is more than our spell walls can handle at any time. But there are so many small magics now. We already have two villages and their shamans, and there are always the midwives and healers."

Rosethorn got to her feet and bowed. Briar did the same, though his sore body complained.

"We understand," Rosethorn told the priest. "These are things that happen in times of upheaval."

He bowed; she bowed, which meant Briar had to bow. Then she wandered off with the priest to talk magic. The others began to talk about fighting they had done before. Briar listened until he got so bored that he decided to go for a walk. It would stretch his legs and give his ears some blessed quiet.

He ambled down toward the river, waving to the sentries as he passed them. Once he reached it, he found the bank was lined with large boulders. He didn't remember them from the ride in, but that was no surprise, as tired as he'd been. He slipped between the boulders and sat on the rocky verge, listening to the fast-moving water and thinking of nothing else for a while. It was a relief to have some time to himself.

When he turned to climb uphill to camp, he saw images in softly glowing paint on the sides of the boulders that faced the water and the plain. Each stone showed a different figure: dragon, yak, many-armed god or goddess, snow cat.

Then he saw motion. First the painted eyes followed him, and then the painted faces.

He stopped in front of the largest stone. The picture on it was a nine-headed cobra. It was a very big nine-headed cobra, taller than Briar by twelve inches at least. The paint glowed a moon-pale white. Briar wouldn't have liked the thing even if it had held still. Then the middle head of the nine, the one that bore an ornate crown, left the safe grounding of the rock and stretched forward until her flickering serpent tongue touched Briar's nose. He thought he might howl like a herd dog. He was far too scared to move.

"Please go away," he said. His voice cracked.

"Briar?" That was Jimut. "Who are you talking to?"

"Are there any nine-headed snakes that crawl around after dark here?" Briar called. "One head is a woman's?"

"Naga," Jimut whispered. He had to be close for Briar to hear him. In fact, Briar was certain Jimut stood on the other, unpainted, side of the boulders. "But they're stories. And the ones up here are different from the ones at home."

Briar winced as all nine faces grinned down at him. "What do you mean?"

"In the Realms of the Sun they're evil." To Briar's horror Jimut climbed on top of the boulder beside the naga. The three-headed goddess that was painted on Jimut's rock stared upward as if she could see him. She slid a hand up along the curve of the stone, reaching for Jimut's foot. "Here a naga can be a human head surrounded by snake heads, or crowned by snakes. They're the gods of whole mountain ranges," Jimut explained, "or several rivers that flow into one, or —"

Briar's knees gave way and he knelt, unable to stay up anymore. The naga sank back into its boulder and went flat again. The three-headed goddess held her arms out to either side, as she had posed originally, and stared into the distance.

"You're tired," Jimut said, jumping off his stone. "You must go to bed."

Briar did go to bed. His dreams of imperial armies that marched on Winding Circle were mixed with dreams of naga women dancing among fields of dead soldiers. He woke when dawn was just a pink gleam in the sky and walked back down to the stones by the river.

In the pearl-like early light, the naga queen was blue with partly scaled skin and very red lips. Her companion heads were yellow snakes, their tongues the same red as her mouth. Her crown was orange flames.

"Excuse me, please," Briar said politely, "but I have to ask, were you joking around with me last night? It's addled my head a bit. Well, more than a bit, since here I am when I could be sleeping, talking to a painting of a snake lady. A very *beautiful* snake lady," he added hurriedly. "The most beautiful I've ever seen." He waited, but there was no response from the painting.

"Addled," he said at last, turning to look at the river. "That's all it was. That thing of Rosethorn's plain scrambled my poor —"

Something tapped his shoulder. He looked. It was one of the snakes. Slowly he turned. The naga queen leaned forward from her boulder and kissed his forehead.

"Real," Briar whispered.

The queen and all of her snakes nodded.

"Have a good day," he said, entirely unsure of what else to tell her.

She smiled as they all retreated back to their flat, painted selves. As flummoxed as he had ever been, Briar trudged uphill to the camp. He couldn't even tell Rosethorn. She had too much on her mind for him to worry her more.

When they took the road, Briar carefully did not look at the stones until they had safely crossed the river. Only then did he turn to gaze at them. A number of gaudy, painted figures in shades of orange-red, bright green, and deep blue sat on top of the stones, waving at him. Atop the biggest stone, the naga swayed as she stood on her muscular tail, eight of her heads looking at their neighbors or the air. The crowned head blew a kiss at Briar. Gingerly, trying to do it so no one else would see, he waved at her.

A hard hand smacked him in the ribs. "What is the matter with your hearing today?" Rosethorn demanded. "I said your name three times! Captain Lango says we should reach the junction of the Tom Sho and the Snow Serpent sometime tomorrow. I'm leaving you there."

Briar frowned. "You didn't see —"

"I've had visions till my eyes want to pop. So what?"

He looked at the toe of his boot. A handful of sparkling snake scales lay on the leather. He would let them serve as a reminder that what he'd seen weren't visions in the least.

"I should go with you," he said, once he collected his thoughts. "There are strange creatures up here, Rosethorn —"

"No," she interrupted. "I won't argue the point anymore." She turned her mount away from his and rode up to the head of the column.

Souda moved into the spot at his side. "I'm sure she'll feel better once this errand of hers is done," she told Briar softly.

Will she? he wondered. Will any of us?

They had ridden three miles when they saw buzzards circling near the road. In a shallow gully where a creek ran into the Snow Serpent, they found the remains of a group of villagers, one of Captain Lango's squads, and some Yanjingyi warriors. Lango dismounted and walked down among the dead along with a few of his people. Briefly the Gyongxin soldiers stood there or along the edge of the road, their palms pressed together in prayer. Then the captain and those who had gone down to look climbed out of the gully.

Rosethorn and Briar approached him. "We know you haven't time to bury them," Rosethorn said, "but we can grow plants over them, all of them, until they become part of the earth."

Lango shook his head. "We have sky burial. The buzzards will have them, and the other creatures. In that manner they will become part of our holiest of lands and remain close to all the gods."

"This sky burial is your tradition?"

Briar envied the polite curiosity in Rosethorn's voice. He was clenching his fists to keep from yelping his disgust. He had seen the buzzards haunting the gorge as they had fled into Gyongxe, but he hadn't thought they were following meals left by Captain

Rana. Or by him and his companions. He knew the Yanjingyi soldiers had their own elaborate funeral rituals that did not include being left to rot in the open. At home, the dead were buried to return to the earth.

"Sky burial is a practice of thousands of years," Lango replied. "Commonly we have more ceremony for our dead, but war leaves us little time for the celebrations of peace. The ending is the same. The creatures feed and return us to Gyongxe." He nodded to Souda and her captain. They came closer to hear what he had to say. "You see the danger. Here we have Yanjingyi soldiers who have come this far into the plain. We must press on."

That night they were forced to camp in the open, together with two small villages' worth of refugees. Briar saw Soudamini the commander for the first time as she chose the camping ground and selected sentries, both ordinary and mage. The mages among the soldiers and the villagers placed their protection spells, while Rosethorn and Briar sprinkled lines of thorn seed all around the outside of the camp, to be woken if things came to a fight. They took guard shifts with the other mages, watching and listening in the dark for the enemy.

No one came.

By noon they had caught up with Parahan's company. They were escorting a long train of refugees to the Temple of the Tigers, a massive fortress that guarded the meeting of the Tom Sho and Snow Serpent Rivers.

"We've seen scouts in the distance," Parahan told them when they had a chance to talk. "They ran from us. Captain Jha sent scouts to me last night. He has found two villages burned in the northeast and planted with the emperor's flags."

"When does Jha mean to return to us?" Lango asked, worried. "If the enemy is in this area, I don't like him being out there alone."

"His message said he'd meet us at the Temple of the Tigers," Parahan assured him.

Briar drifted back until he could ride without having to talk to anyone. His gut was tight; his hands trembled. During the night he had dreamed of the imperial birthday celebration, and the field of Weishu's soldiers that had seemed to go on forever. It wasn't the first time since they had left the palace that he'd dreamed of them. Today, though, the dream had a more ominous meaning.

Captain Jha was out there with one hundred warriors. They had looked like a lot before, when they were all crowded together on the road west. Now, imagining them against the emperor's thousands, he realized the number was pathetic.

Stop panicking, he ordered himself, when it seemed he might vomit. The emperor has his thousands at the capital, not all the way down here. He's got his main force guarding his own silky self, not burning a clump of wood-walled villages!

And what happens if Weishu catches *you*? a nasty little voice inside his head inquired. You were his guest, and you helped his pet captive escape. Then you carried word of the attack to Gyongxe, and now you're fighting against him. You didn't just take a vase from the guest pavilion. Weishu is going to want to do very bad things to you. And Rosethorn. And Evvy.

What he wouldn't give for a few of those nagas and many-armed gods to send Weishu back to Yanjing!

The sky was turning gray and they had ridden another three miles or so when Briar saw something bobbing in the river. At first he thought it was a boat. He rode down to the water's edge for a closer look. The thing that had gotten his attention was brown and muddy. A log or a branch? Several like it followed, rolling as they came over the rapids. One floated close to the edge and turned, showing him a swollen, eyeless face. Two of the corpses were missing heads. All had either ugly blade wounds or carried the crossbow bolts that had killed them. Behind them came the carcass of a yak, its hooves sticking in the air.

"Say nothing," Rosethorn murmured. Briar flinched. "Our soldiers have orders to keep the villagers away from the river or they'll panic. We're only a mile from the temple."

"What if the temple's under attack?" Briar asked. "What if imperial soldiers are there already?"

Rosethorn shook her head. "Scouts came to tell us all's safe. The dead are coming from west of there. No one's been reported on the south side of the river."

"You aren't still going on alone!"

"I'll be fine," Rosethorn said. "You stay with Parahan and Souda and do as you're told, understand? They know more of war than you do."

Briar glared at her.

"When we go home, I am giving Vedris a big hug and kiss," Rosethorn remarked. "I never appreciated what a fine ruler he is before we made this journey."

"Me neither," Briar agreed. "There's a lot to be said for a king who isn't greedy."

They rode together in silence, trying not to look at the other bodies that came down the river. At last they reached the two bridges at the meeting of the Tom Sho and the Snow Serpent Rivers. The temple rose on a rocky hill high above both of them. Their people didn't wait. Soldiers and villagers streamed across the Tom Sho Bridge on their way up the hill.

Rosethorn leaned across the space between her mount and Briar's to kiss him on the cheek. "Travel safe, travel well," she told him. "We'll see each other soon enough. It takes more than the likes of Weishu to come between my boy and me."

Parahan rode over to wait with Briar as Rosethorn crossed the Snow Serpent Bridge alone. She looked small and lonely as she followed the lesser road away from them.

"I should go with her," Briar said, gathering up his reins. "Someone will see her by herself like that —"

Parahan grabbed his arm. Slowly, from the edges in, Rosethorn and her horse disappeared from sight. All that remained was an empty road.

CHAPTER
FOURTEEN

Evvy soon learned that it was one thing to be the companion of Rosethorn and Briar, the *nanshurs* from the west, and quite another entirely to be a student *nanshur* of eastern blood who had been left behind without them. For her first day after her friends' departure, she had slept, eaten, explored, slept, and eaten some more. Even the cats were happy to laze and stuff themselves. On the second day she wandered among the refugees who were coming in from the villages on the eastern hills and plain. Unlike Briar or Rosethorn, she could do that without inspiring awe or fear. Here near the border, her Yanjingyi face was common enough to cause no extra interest. She admired babies, helped the families to settle in the fort's empty rooms and sheds, and — when no one was looking — shored up crumbling walls in the rooms by packing the pieces they had lost back into the crevices. On the third day she wandered idly between the buildings, sending gravel and larger stones to fill in cracks.

It was when she looked at the fortress walls that she began to worry. They were not as solid as they ought to be. She started at the gate. There were gaps between the wooden frame and the wall that surrounded it. This close to the mountains, the builders had used stone in the walls instead of the brick preferred by house builders, to Evvy's great approval. If she was to make repairs, she could do more with stone. She would need to do a great deal to make up for all this neglect and age.

Shaking her head, she climbed up to the battlements for a look around. Things were no better here. There were holes in the plaster on the walkway where running men could easily trip. Brick edging in the crenels had fallen away: Soldiers leaning out for a look below could slip on gravel or crumbling plaster and fall to their deaths. Anxious, she began to usher loose stones into the gaps on the walkway until one of Captain Rana's mages caught her.

"You are a student!" he shouted. "Students do not practice magic without their teachers!"

"My teachers let me do the magic I'm best at!" Evvy shouted in return. "I don't need a teacher for filling in gaps!"

The mage marched her straight down to Captain Rana's office. They had to wait as the captain listened to complaints from refugees ahead of them in line. Finally he gave them his full attention.

The mage stood haughtily straight. "I caught this *student* practicing magic, unsupervised, without permission, on the wall. She was meddling with the walkway. She could have destroyed everything!"

"I am certain that she did not. I am familiar with her skills. You may go," the captain said.

"But, sir —"

"Dismissed," the captain said firmly. The mage stalked off, and the captain sighed. "Evvy, you can't carry on here as you did with Briar and Rosethorn to back you up."

"But you knew I didn't do any harm! And the walls here *need* shoring up!" cried Evvy. "I can pack stone into the holes so tight it'll be as if there's new rock in place!"

"A few holes in plaster do not mean the fort will collapse," the captain said patiently. "I have seen your work. I was impressed, but I am not prepared to do battle with my mages every time you want to fuss with things. This fort has stood for centuries."

"It *shows*."

Rana held up a hand. "We can use some more of those glowing stones you made on our journey," he said kindly. "Why don't you do that? It will help us save torches, and you'll be useful." Firmly he added, "That will be all, Evvy. Try to stay out from underfoot."

Like the mage, she knew she had been dismissed. She stomped back to her room to sulk for the rest of the day. She made several handfuls of her spare pieces of quartz glow, then go dark again, just to be spiteful. Finally, knowing Briar and Rosethorn would both raise their eyebrows at her if they knew she was carrying on, she made them glow again. She put them in a basket and carried them out to the gate, where the sergeant in charge of the watch could be found.

"Captain Rana wants these," she announced, and left the basket at the astonished man's feet. Without another word she climbed up to the southern wall. Several of the guards saw her, but they were from Rana's company and knew her. They nodded and left her alone. For the rest of the night she listened to the mountains sing.

A few of the tones almost made sense, she thought as she listened. One was water trickling over rock. Another was water streaming over it, and another was water roaring over it. That tone was rain falling on stone. She thought one might be snow falling on granite, but she would have to be closer to granite during a snowfall to be sure. There was a click that had to be a mountain goat setting a hoof on limestone, and a long, soft brush that she would bet was a snow leopard's tail passing over gravel. But what was that metal scrape on granite, the tone that wavered? And the ringing clop like horseshoes in a cave, but not exactly?

A guard sent her to her room finally. Her cats curled around and on her. Monster's cheeping mew of worry intruded on her thoughts and she petted him to comfort him. Ball settled between her shoulder and ear and purred loudly as if to drown out the mountains' singing. She couldn't do it; Evvy could hear them even in her room now. Apricot and Raisin covered her feet, Mystery her belly, and Ria curled inside the curve of her free arm. Asa settled on top of her head. Their combined purrs led her into sleep. She dreamed of the Sun Queen's husbands. The cats climbed the mountains and laughed at her for not going with them.

Perhaps that was why, after feeding them and letting them out in the fort's grounds to do their business in the morning, she took a small pack, filled it with dumplings and a water bottle from the fort's mess kitchen, and strolled out of the rear gate.

"Don't go too far," the guard cautioned her. "And if you hear a trumpet, come running."

She nodded and ambled on. The herd boys had already gone out with the villagers' goats, sheep, and yaks. Everyone felt safe with the southern mountains at their backs and the massive wall of thorny vines blocking Snow Serpent Pass in the east. She'd heard the soldiers say that by the time any Yanjingyi warriors came over the plain, everyone would be inside the fort with the gates closed and barred.

Evvy meant to go only as far as a ridge she could see from the southern walkway. It was home to a waterfall that fed the little river by the fort. She would take her lunch there, listen to the mountains a while, and return.

It was a glorious day. The sun warmed all the stone surfaces around her as she walked. She inhaled the air, scented with granite, limestone, and quartzite. The mountains' chorus rang out in her ears, louder than the cries of the eagles and the singing of the smaller birds, louder even than the waterfall as she approached it.

The trees at the foot of the waterfall hid a canyon on the other side of the small river. Exploration would have been out of the question had a large pine not lain across the water, forming a perfect bridge. Evvy looked up at the ridge, where she had planned to have lunch, then down at the fort and the plain. There was no sign of any horsemen or trouble. She climbed onto the pine and across the river.

The canyon led her deeper into the stone reaches at the mountain's foot. It made an echo chamber for the birds and the singing. Evvy felt like she was inside magic. She finally stopped for lunch by the creek that ran along the canyon floor, ravenous after her morning's explorations. She was ready to swear that the mountain husbands and the Sun Queen herself sang to her as she took a nap.

Then she was yanked out of pleasant dreams. Soldiers in Yanjingyi uniforms grabbed her and bound her hands tightly behind her back. When she screamed, she was slapped. "Are there any more of you out here?" one of them demanded. "Speak up! Are any more of you out here?"

Evvy kicked and caught him on the thigh. She twisted her head and savagely bit one of the soldiers who held her. He cuffed her so hard she saw light flashes inside her head. The man she'd kicked grabbed her legs and tied them.

"Who else is with you?" he demanded.

She fell back on Chammuri to tell him what his mother ate for breakfast. He lifted her and dumped her over his armored shoulder. When she screamed, he pinched her leg hard and said in *tiyon*, "Silence, or you'll wish you were as dead as my mother."

Evvy called to the canyon rocks. They began to fall. Men shrieked as they were battered by the stony rain.

"Well," someone out of her view said, "this is where she got to. You will talk eventually, Evumeimei Dingzai, but in a more comfortable setting." A hand thrust a bottle of something smelly under her nose. Evvy tried to turn her face away, but the bottle was too close. Fog traveled up her nose and into her brain.

When she awoke, a man was bending over her. She yanked away only to discover she could not move from the neck down. They had taken her clothes and tied her to a table. Her legs were raised on a board above her hips and tied at the ankles so her bare toes pointed back toward her head. She couldn't move her feet.

Her mouth was dry. She wanted to scream; she wanted to weep, but she would give these snot-suckers neither of those things.

The soldier who leaned over her wore the tan tunic and breeches of a regular foot soldier in the Yanjingyi army. "Here's water." He supported her head as he put a cup to her lips. Evvy drank the liquid greedily. "If you want my advice, girl, you'll answer any questions you're asked. Otherwise they'll torture you. Nobody is hard enough to take that."

"Why do you baby her?" Another soldier sat on a chair by Evvy's feet. He stood. Like the other man, he wore the tan uniform. This one had an untidy mustache and carried a leather strap in one hand. "She's going to get the full treatment sooner or later." He drew back his arm and slapped the soles of Evvy's feet with the strap, hard.

The pain shot through her like fire. She gasped, then bit her lip.

"Please, take my advice," the soldier next to her head whispered. "Tell him what he wants to know." He looked at the other man. "She's just a girl! Ask your questions — you don't have to hit her!"

"You're an idiot, Musheng. Why are we here if we don't teach them respect for the emperor? She came to this country to carry information against him and fight for his enemies, didn't you, Evumeimei Dingzai?" He struck Evvy's feet with his strap again. She screamed and tried to imagine a stone where she could keep her secrets. She had done so before. Another blow, or two, might make her blurt out something important, like where the others had gone, or the thing that Rosethorn carried. That was the problem with being quick with her tongue. Sometimes she spoke before she thought. She couldn't do that now.

The soldier Musheng took Evvy's hand and clasped it tightly. "Dawei, she could be your daughter!" He looked at Evvy. "Please, child. You came here with three companions, Briar, Rosethorn, and a dangerous slave, Parahan. Tell us where they are. We'll have a mage see to your feet —"

"Let them heal like my arm had to heal when the northerners poured boiling oil on it!" snapped Dawei. He drew the strap lightly across Evvy's burning, bleeding feet, making her flinch.

"A mage will tend your wounds," Musheng said with a glare at Dawei. "But my captain won't allow it unless you tell us what we need to know. These people abandoned you here when they knew trouble was coming, didn't they? You don't owe them anything."

Evvy didn't listen. She had the stone in her mind. Inside it she hid her cats, and her friends and where they went: Rosethorn and the thing she carried, Briar and the soldiers moving the villagers to safety, Dokyi and his lonely journey to Garmashing. Souda vanished inside the stone as well. Maybe these *zernamuses* didn't already know she had come to Gyongxe with two hundred soldiers. Finally she blinked at Musheng. "What people?"

Dawei snorted. "That's what you get for your kindness! Insolence! A Zhanzhi gutter rat lies to you about information she knows perfectly well you already have!" He slapped the strap harder over the soles of Evvy's feet twice, grinning at her screams. "Tell him the names of your companions, and apologize!"

"I don't know their names anymore," she said.

Musheng sighed. "Why don't you know their names, Evumeimei?"

"They told us she was a mage student," Dawei said. "She did some magic."

"Forgetting things is a high degree of magic for a student," Musheng said. "I think you're lying to us. Girl, you don't help yourself this way."

Evvy didn't answer. Now she was trying to think her feet to stone. She had done it before. Someone — she couldn't remember who — had told her to imagine herself as stone, though he'd woken her just as she had it worked out. That part she remembered.

Dawei lashed her again. She lost the feeling of stone. Pain washed up her legs in bloodred waves.

"Tell the emperor you have me," she whispered. She remembered the emperor. "He likes me. He gave me a cinnabar cat."

"Who do you think sent us in search of you and your friends?" Musheng wiped her face with a cold cloth. "Where are they, Evumeimei?"

"I want my clothes," Evvy said. Her feet throbbed. In spite of herself tears trickled from the corners of her eyes. They ran into her ears. How could feet hurt so much? "I feel bad without any clothes."

"You don't need clothes," Dawei told her. "Talk, and you'll get them back." He looked at Musheng. "She ought to have said something useful by now."

Musheng nodded. "Let's see what the mage thinks."

Dawei scowled. "It's past midnight. She hates to be woken up."

"She'll want to know the girl hasn't talked, late hour or no. Wake her."

Dawei left the room. Musheng leaned against the wall. "If I were you, I'd tell *Nanshur* Jia Jui what she wants to know, right away. She isn't patient like Dawei."

Jia Jui — she knew that name, but she wasn't sure where she knew it from. She thought Jia Jui was another friend of hers who had cats. It was hard to think when she hurt so badly. "I don't know what you want," Evvy said. "I wouldn't tell you if I did, but I don't."

"They were at this fort with you," Musheng said. "The other prisoners told us that much. They said the First Dedicate of the Living Circle temple was here, too. Dokyi left before they did. What did he want?"

When he said "Dokyi," Evvy saw a stone in her mind. "I don't know," she said, trying not to whine. "Would you put water on my feet?" It was hard to concentrate on making them feel like stone when they burned so badly. "Really, I'm just a kid. Why would these people you're talking about tell me anything?"

"You're a baby goat?"

That confused her. "I — I heard it somewhere. It's street talk for somebody young."

"Kid or no, you're a prisoner now," Musheng said. "Tell me something that *Nanshur* Jia Jui will think is useful and I'll pour water on your feet. I had mine lashed once. I know how much it hurts." He sighed and drank some water. "None of the villagers or soldiers we questioned knew why First Dedicate Dokyi was here, but you were with Rosethorn. He talked to her for a long time. Tell me what he wanted, and I'll help you."

"Anything to report?" A beautiful young woman entered the room with Dawei just behind him. She wore a bed robe of soft peach silk rather than a mage's usual black robes and hat. There were no mage beads on her neck or wrists.

"She is very stubborn, *Nanshur* Jia Jui," Musheng replied, bowing deeply. "She did not respond to the strap or to kindness."

Evvy's thinking, sluggish with pain and the effort she needed to maintain the stone around some of her memories, finally placed the young woman. "Jia Jui," she mumbled. "Where are your cats?"

Jia Jui smiled as she bent over Evvy. "You remember me. That is good. Sadly, my cats are at home. They are too unhappy when I travel. But I understand you dragged your poor cats all the way here."

Evvy frowned. "They're used to traveling. Why are you in Gyongxe?"

Jia Jui shrugged. "The emperor my master has begun the conquest of this country. I must say, Evvy, I am sad to find *you* here. You do not show your appreciation for the Son of the Gods and the favor he showed you very well, do you?"

"I don't know what you mean," Evvy replied crossly. What Jia Jui said and what Evvy remembered were not the same. "Where's Captain Rana?" she demanded.

Jia Jui sighed. "He threw himself off the wall of this fortress rather than let us question him. I hope we may do better, Evvy, but you must not force me to be cruel. Answer our questions, please, and spare yourself further pain. Tell me where Rosethorn and Dokyi have gone."

Evvy remained silent and tried to make her poor feet feel like stone.

Jia Jui ran a finger along Evvy's cheek. It broke the girl's concentration. "Jia Jui, I don't know who you're talking about!" she protested.

The young woman frowned. "Evvy, have you worked a spell while my foolish friends stood by?"

The two men protested frantically, telling the mage that Evvy's hands were bound so she couldn't move them, and that the only words she said were normal talk. Jia Jui held up her hand and they shut up. Evvy shivered at how instantly the two men went silent.

Then Jia Jui held her hand out. Dawei put something into it — not a strap, but a rod. Her face calm and thoughtful, the woman struck the soles of Evvy's feet with it.

It made the strap seem gentle. Evvy's stone spell vanished. She cursed Jia Jui with every bad word she knew in several languages until the mage struck her again. Evvy howled in pain.

"Please, lady mage, stop!" Musheng cried. "Give the child a chance!"

Jia Jui lowered the rod.

Musheng leaned close to Evvy and whispered, "You see? I tried to warn you. She is pitiless. Answer like a good girl — you don't want this, do you?"

"Where *are* they?" Jia Jui demanded. Musheng sprang away from Evvy. "Dokyi, Rosethorn, Parahan, Briar, Soudamini. Yes, we know the princess joined her brother here. Why do you think we bothered to take *this* honorless dump? We can't even use it to get more troops and supplies here until we clear your *chetu* thorn spell from the pass. Where are your friends?"

Evvy licked blood away from her lip. She must have bitten it. She didn't know who those people were; she didn't care. She told Jia Jui to do something very bad with a yak.

The mage struck her feet three more times with the rod. In the gaps Evvy fumbled until she had her stone spell again and hung on to it, keeping it not in her mind but in the ceiling above where she could see it. The pain was white-hot in her feet and head. Her throat burned from screaming. Where was the song of the mountains? "Take over, Musheng," she heard Jia Jui say. "I don't care to weary my arm."

That was when she learned that Musheng was not truly her friend.

He struck her for some time. He would stop. Jia Jui would ask questions, and Evvy would insult her. After three stops when Evvy said nothing, not even curses or insults, Jia Jui sighed. "Let her think while I fetch my mage beads. And you two, have someone take you to her room and fetch two of her cats. Preferably the biggest one, that she calls Monster, and the smallest one."

The two guards followed her out of the room.

Evvy tried to breathe. It was hard. Her nose was filled with snot and the air hurt her throat. The cats. They would hurt the cats in front of her. She remembered the beads she had handled, General Hengkai's beads, the ones for killing and destruction. Jia Jui had a necklace and bracelets of beads like that. She would use them on Monster and any of the others, maybe all of them.

She thought about pulling down *these* walls with her power, but she could not do it. Her legs throbbed and burned. Would she ever walk again? She couldn't stop crying, though she bit her already sore lip to keep any noise from coming out.

Think! she ordered herself. What can you do if you can't wreck this room and you can't stop the pain in your feet? How can you escape? How can you stop her from hurting your cats?

She was Evumeimei Dingzai, a stone mage. If she couldn't turn herself into stone, what if she took herself, her spirit, and put that *into* one? There would be no one in her body to hurt or to answer questions.

If I was cold and stiff, they would think I was dead, she thought. Not cold like stone. They'd know that was magic and Jia Jui would break my spell. But if they thought I *died*... There wouldn't be any reason to hurt my cats if they thought I was dead.

Small pebbles lay in the corners of the room. Evvy found one to her liking. She began to concentrate. Her leg twitched; the wave of pain that resulted made her gasp. She tried again. Against her will she swallowed, making her throat burn even worse. Once more she tried. A noise outside made her jerk in fear: Was Jia Jui coming back? Were the men coming? The noise faded.

Now, she told herself fiercely, *now,* or you'll fail and the cats will die!

Her power was a needle, darting across the room and into her particular stone. Her magic followed. With it went her thinking, most of her breathing, most of her heartbeat. Her body stilled and cooled as she found room for herself around each and every grain of rock in her particular sanctuary. She settled into it and rested.

Something sang to her. It was deep and comforting, but it boomed, too, shaking her loose from her hiding place. Her spirit and power flowed toward the singing, shivering to the deep hum beneath the song and dancing to it, too. Following the song, she entered a space that was hers.

Slowly she began to fill it, though it hurt. She knew, and the song knew, that her last hiding place was only temporary. This was her proper shape, pain and all.

Briefly it warmed. The warmth entered some of the places that hurt, making them loosen. Something inside made her wait. She must not rush, though she had no idea why she shouldn't. The warmth faded. Perhaps she had imagined it, because once more she was *cold*.

She lay facedown on a lumpy hill. For a while she did nothing else, though the songs called to her. It took time for her body to remember the uses for fingers, arms, and legs. Any attempt to move hurt beyond words to describe it, but she knew that now she *had* to move.

She groped around her. She felt cloth, icy in spots. There were other, painless feet, stiff feet, stiff arms, stiff heads, all of them as cold as stone. She lay on a heap of corpses.

That was when she cried.

The mountain songs made her stop crying. They had changed. The deepest song spoke of safe caverns no bad soldiers could reach, where no killers went, where no pain could be found. It sang of safety and stones that healed, of water that was so cold it numbed pain.

She had to go to that song. It steeled her to do what was needed, and soon, before the sun rose. Using the sliver of the moon for light she began to tug clothes off the dead bodies around her. There were scarves for her to bind in layers around her poor feet. She found jackets and breeches and more scarves for her head, until she began to warm up at last. Among the bodies of so many adults — she couldn't count how many — she also found the bodies of children, infants, and animals, including cats.

There was enough light that she recognized all seven of her cats among them. She nearly gave up then and there, weeping into Monster's fur. She was at Fort Sambachu, and the Yanjingyi beasts had killed everyone. They were going to kill her if they saw her again. Maybe she ought to let them, or maybe she ought to go permanently to stone.

As if the singers knew what she was thinking, the mountain songs grew louder. The deepest song was loudest of all. It demanded that she hurry away from all the death. She must bring her song to the stone heights, to the dwellers inside. They would take her in, their sister of the mountains. They would bring her home.

She rolled down the rest of the cold heap rather than look at any more of it. The soldiers had dumped the dead outside the fortress, behind the rear gate. Evvy reached the little river, where she found a long stick under the trees. It became her staff. After a drink of water, she was able to turn her soles to stone. It was all that she could do for them. The rest of her feet throbbed. Even the scarves she had wrapped around them did not keep them from hurting with every step.

She fixed her mind on stone in the soles of her feet and on the song of the mountains, and kept going.

By sunrise she reached the canyon where the Yanjingyi war party had captured her. The deep song had called to her from there. She stopped to drink again from the stream. She wanted to sleep, but the mountain song was too loud now. There was no sleeping with that racket going on in her brain. She staggered upright by the water and looked back the way she had come. With horror she saw bloody footprints marked her trail. Panicked, she stumbled forward, wanting to run and unable to. The song was so loud that she did not hear the clatter of hoofbeats in the canyon.

Turning a bend in the stone, she saw an opening in the side of the canyon: a cave. Could she go there? There was plenty of loose rock above it and to the sides. Did she have the strength to close the opening once she was inside, hiding where she had gone?

She halted. The deep song had stopped. In front of the cave she saw the strangest thing. On the dirt was a polished lump of fluorite: deep green, deep purple, and clear crystal. It looked like an eighteen-inch bear sitting on its haunches, one that had been smoothed by years of running water until all of him was rounded. His muzzle was only a gentle point, not a sharp nose. It was the friendliest-looking piece of stone she had ever seen.

It cocked its head knob at her. "Evumeimei Dingzai, welcome to my home," the living stone said. It spoke with the voice of the deep song, making every bone in Evvy's body shiver. "Will you enter?"

Evvy stumbled toward it. "Who are you?"

"My name is very long, and I will say it for you at some time, but not now. I am the heart of the mountain that the meat creatures here call Kangri Skad Po." The stone creature turned and trundled deeper into the cave on very short legs.

Evvy followed, leaning on her stick. Glowing moss on the walls of the cave lit their way. As they walked the tunnel opened up. Normally she would have gasped as it grew larger, but not today. Today she desperately held to the feeling of stone at the bottoms of her bleeding feet as they descended into the earth. So intent was she that she didn't notice when the cave's entrance closed behind them.

She did notice a mild grumbling overhead. A few rocks fell and the floor shook slightly, making her stumble.

"What was that?" she cried, steadying herself with her make-shift staff.

"It is nothing," the crystal bear assured her, his amazingly deep voice making her think of icy underground rivers and hidden hot springs. "Soon you will rest and heal. Then you will tell me what you are. I have never felt anyone like you in all my millennia."

Normally Evvy would have demanded to know how many millennia the living stone had, and what millennia were. Now she clung to her staff and limped onward, biting her lip until it started to bleed again.

In the world above the mountain roots, Jia Jui led the search party into the long canyon. On the walls of Fort Sambachu, the bodies of Dawei and Musheng hung as a warning to every idiot in the army who did not know the difference between a dead girl and a mage in a deep trance. She had already left sizable offerings to several gods that the emperor would never learn that she, too, had examined Evumeimei's body and pronounced her to be dead. She would have *sworn* the girl was dead, and if the emperor's spies ever learned differently, she would pay very painfully.

She could still save herself. The bloody footprints showed that Evvy could not go much farther. With the girl back in her hands, Jia Jui meant to shackle her to her own wrist and take her to Emperor Weishu herself.

So deep in her plans was Jia Jui that she didn't notice the quiver in the ground until it was much too late. Driven by the living heart of Kangri Skad Po, the canyon collapsed on soldiers and mage. None of them would be seen again.

CHAPTER
FIFTEEN

THE TEMPLE OF THE TIGERS,
THE DRIMBAKANG LHO, AND
THE TEMPLE OF THE SEALED EYE

Once he had gotten used to the fact that Rosethorn and her horse had simply disappeared, Briar listened to Jimut's pleadings and turned to help move the refugees into the Temple of the Tigers. He busily sent runaway toddlers, goats, and the odd group of boys across the Tom Sho Bridge and up the rugged hill. It was when he reached the temple fortress at the top of the hill that he saw why the place had the name that it did.

Two giant tiger figures stood on either side of the front gate. One, painted orange with black stripes, snarled realistically at anyone who rode toward it. The other, carved of pure white stone with black stripes, looked as if the sculptor had caught it in midleap, forelegs and claws extended. Briar could even see every hair in the animals' carved fur. Captain Lango's Gyongxin people did not care for them. Parahan and Souda's people only bowed as they passed: Jimut explained that tigers were common, respected animals in the Realms of the Sun. The local villagers, unlike Lango's fighters, were clearly used to these tigers and even rubbed them on the side or paw. Briar only relaxed once he was well inside the curtain wall. He had half expected the tigers, like the naga queen of the Temple of the Sun Queen's Husbands, to act unpleasantly alive.

He went with Parahan for a look around when they were settled: The plan seemed to be for the soldiers to patrol a circle around the place while they waited for Rosethorn's return. They also expected the arrival of more warriors from the west, the southern part of the Drimbakang Zugu mountains and beyond. Knowing that, Briar agreed they ought to familiarize themselves with their newest temporary home.

The place was big, with the stepped outer wall that was common to Gyongxin fortresses. A small village already fit in the lower courtyard as part of the temple, together with barns, stables, mews, chicken coops, fenced gardens, and roaming herds of goats and fowl. In the upper courtyard loomed the main house of worship with its dormitories, side temples, and kitchens.

Briar wandered into the temple. It was lit with hundreds of small lamps. Parahan explained this was the sole Temple of the Tigers in Gyongxe: All of the others were in the Realms of the Sun, where tigers made their home. It was hard to keep tigers here, a priest told them. They missed the warmth and the ability to roam that was theirs elsewhere. Also, the snow leopards resented interlopers.

Briar was fascinated by the artwork that covered the temple's interior walls. The borders set around each large painting were made of dozens of smaller ones: pictures of prophets, gods, demons, teachers, and tigers shown in every aspect, from infancy to godhood. Like the main scenes, the border images were done in vivid colors, showing their subjects in various poses. What bothered Briar was that the small figures seemed to move in the corner of his eye. They turned to chat with their neighbors. Worse, some leaned forward to get a better look at him, Parahan, or Souda. When he whipped around to stare at the paintings dead-on, they were still — except that the little border folk had changed position. Some of them were rude enough to cover giggles with one or several hands. One tiger had rolled onto his back. Another urinated in Briar's direction.

He just had to ask. Fortunately a priest-artist was nearby, touching up the colors on a large painting. "Excuse me," Briar murmured when the man set his brush down, "but weren't the figures in the border over there placed differently before?"

The priest smiled tolerantly and came to look. "Sir, it is dark here. With the torchlight and the many shadows our paintings *appear* to change. . . ." He stared at the section of paintings that had moved for Briar. One crimson-fanged warrior-demon now showed his bare behind to anyone who cared to see it.

Briar looked at the priest. The man blinked, then backed up a step. He leaned in closer and inspected a broad section of the paintings with borders that had moved. Finally he scowled at Briar and hurried off, telling his novice to put his paints away.

Briar turned his back on the paintings and tried not to look at any more of them. He said nothing to his companions, just as he had not mentioned the boulder paintings and the naga queen before. If they thought his twitches and flinches were strange, they were too polite to comment. Mages were expected to be odd. He would ask Rosethorn what was going on when she came back.

He had an idea that it had something to do with his touching her cursed burden.

Briar also refused to sleep inside, despite the arguments of Parahan, Souda, and Jimut. There were just too many paintings to avoid. In the end, his friends gave him an assortment of furs to use as well as his bedroll, to keep off the early summer cold. Briar didn't care. There were no paintings inside the curtain walls, and the stars above moved only as they were supposed to move. He fell asleep looking at them and asking Rosethorn's gods to watch over her.

When the morning sun touched his eyes, Briar opened them to find a shaven-headed priestess in heavy robes squatting beside him. She grinned, showing off a scant mouthful of teeth. "Don't worry, *emchi* youth," she said, and offered him a bowl of butter tea. "Once you return to the thicker air down below, you will no longer see things. Whatever touched you was powerful. I can see its blaze all around you. Its power calls to the little gods whose doors are on our walls."

Briar sat up and accepted the bowl. "Thank you. You're very kind. I would prefer not to have been touched at all."

She cackled. "But then they would not have their fun with you, the little gods, and it is so rare that they may play! The power in you makes it possible for them to enter our world for a time. They have been stirring for years, knowing that the evil was coming. At least now the waiting is over, and we will all see."

Briar sipped the tea for a moment, thinking. She was a nice old woman. Perhaps she wouldn't mind a question or two from a silly foreigner. "May I ask — why do even the temples here in

Gyongxe have walls, like castles and big cities do? From what I've heard, you aren't attacked very often."

The priestess chuckled. "We aren't worried about enemies outside our borders — it's our neighbors who are trouble too much of the time," she explained. "Our walls and fighters are to keep the tribes and warriors from the other temples out. If god-warriors take your temple, your priests must become priests of their god, and your temple becomes the temple of the enemy's god. And the tribes are always fighting."

"But you weren't fighting when I was in Garmashing before, and no one's fighting each other now. We've got at least five different tribes and warriors from four different temples riding with us. I heard Parahan say so."

The priestess straightened. "When were you here before?"

"This winter."

She snorted. "Nobody fights in winter. Everyone would die. And no one fights now because we all have the same enemy. Gyongxe belongs to us, not to that lowland emperor." She nodded and said, "I would rather fight Weishu."

Briar had finished the bowl of tea. "Thank you for telling me about all of that," he said, returning the bowl to her with a bow.

"Don't let the little gods worry you," the priestess told him. "They are on our side. Mostly."

She left Briar. He dressed under the covers in the chilly air. It unnerved him that she spoke so blithely of the things that moved on her walls. The priest-artist hadn't seemed used to them. What else was she accustomed to seeing?

And what of these little gods? he asked himself as he struggled into his boots. If they could leave their walls and boulders, might they be convinced to fight Weishu? Could they even damage him and his armies? Might as well ask Lakik or Mila of the Grain to pick up weapons and fight!

He did up his furs and bedroll, and went to breakfast with Jimut. They were about to see if Parahan or Souda had orders for them when a horn sounded a long, low call throughout the temple compound. Everyone stopped what they were doing and waited, their eyes on the central temple. The highest tower there was capped by priests wielding horns so large and long that the curved ends rested on the ground.

The biggest of the horns sounded again, a long call, then three short calls. A long call, and three short calls. This second repetition was picked up by every temple horn. Briar didn't have to ask what the calls meant. Every temple warrior was scrambling for the walls, crossbows in their hands. Briar's warrior companions did the same.

Priests ran to bar the gates. Others backed wagons full of stones up against the gates once they were closed. Priestesses covered the large courtyard wells to keep arrows or stones from landing in the precious water. Novices guided the herds back into the barns just as they had begun to lead them out for the day. More temple workers gently urged the refugees that had come outside back into the buildings, where they might be safer.

Briar and Jimut gathered up their own weapons. Then they, too, ran up to the walls. They found their commanders on the southern wall, just over the main gates. There, together with the warrior-priest in command of the temple troops, they watched as three hundred Yanjingyi soldiers galloped up the road and fanned out before them, just out of shooting distance. A novice ran along the walkways to speak quickly in the warrior-priest's ear.

"Two hundred more at the north gate," the commander said to Souda, Lango, and Parahan. "We are nearly evenly matched unless they have others hidden on the far side of the ridge. I doubt this. None of our watchers has reported movement, and our guard changes have occurred without incident. The last change came just with the morning bell."

"They could have used magic to get closer," Parahan said uneasily.

The commander had a rich, deep chuckle. "It would have to be very unusual magic to get past our watchers, their dogs, and the guarding spells in the tunnels the watchers use to return here," he assured Parahan. "A spy did get into the tunnels last year. He did not get out. They never learned where he vanished to. Captain Lango, will you reinforce my people on the eastern wall?" The Gyongxin captain nodded and ran down the walkway, beckoning for his soldiers on the ground to follow him.

A Yanjingyi soldier was riding up to the gate. He bore a white flag.

"They're coming to talk," Souda remarked. She slung an arm around Briar's shoulders. "But he doesn't need five companies just to talk. Maybe we'll see action against these curs, eh, Briar?"

What a bloodthirsty girl! he thought in admiration.

The Yanjingyi messenger halted his mount and waved his white peace flag on its long pole. "Honored priests of the great Temple of the Tigers, I bring you salutations from General Jin Quan of the Imperial Army of South Gyongxe!"

"The blessings of our tigers be upon his head," the commanding priest replied.

"I wonder if that's a good thing," Souda whispered to Briar.

"Our glorious general is merciful, and our mighty emperor, sixth of his dynasty, beloved of all the gods, Weishu Maorin Guangong Zhian of the Long Dynasty, holds this realm of Gyongxe close to his august bosom," the messenger went on.

"So it was strangers that killed all those people in the river and the gorge?" Briar murmured to Souda.

"The blessings of our tiger gods be also upon the head of your emperor," the commander replied. "In the Heavenly Time to Come, they will surely reward him in the most fitting manner."

If the messenger thought this, or any of the commander's replies, to be strange or double-edged, he did not show it. "My master the general bids me to say, we hope to make our visit to your glorious temple a brief, peaceful affair. Give to us the smallest of tokens of your esteem for our lordly and puissant emperor. If you do so, we shall proclaim our desire for peace between our great empire and your gods, and leave here."

"Interesting," murmured the commander. "What exactly are these small tokens?" he called.

"Four people," the messenger replied. "The runaway slave Parahan. His sister Soudamini. The woman Rosethorn. The boy Briar Moss. Your peace, and the peace of all those within your walls and on your vast lands, in exchange for these four, who have offended against the imperial majesty."

"I may not answer this," the commander said. "Only the head of our temple may do so. You will have to wait." He went to the steps. Instead of taking them to the ground or sending a messenger for the head of the temple, he sat there. A novice who waited with a large pot of tea and a basket full of cups poured one for him and handed it over. The commander seemed in no hurry to pass the message to anyone.

The rest of their group on the wall turned away from the messenger and sat on the walkway, where they could not be seen.

"Just like a Yanjingyi." To Briar's surprise, the old priestess who had roused him had somehow made the climb up to them. Now she sat cross-legged in front of him, Souda, and Parahan and let Jimut pass a cup of tea to her. At her side was a tall, gangly young tiger cub on a leash. "Because they trade people to and fro like trinkets, they believe others will do so." She patted Briar on the knee. "What did you do, boy? Twist the imperial nose?"

"I did no such thing!" he protested. "I was perfectly nice! Rosethorn and me even made him his very own rose, unique just for him!"

The old priestess chuckled. "Doubtless he wants you back to make another. This Rosethorn is separated from you?"

"Just for now," Briar replied. "She had an errand."

The woman looked at him as if she knew Rosethorn's errand was a secret, very magical one. Then she said to Parahan and Soudamini, "And you two troublemakers?"

"We are not slaves," Parahan said quietly, his hands whiteknuckled in his lap. "My uncle sold me to the emperor, but I escaped."

"It does not matter," the old priestess said. "Emperor Weishu believes threats will make us crumble like dried mud. Last year, he sent me a beautiful box, carved all over with snakes. It was a very splendid gift." She shook her head. "It is thanks to my friend that I lived after I opened it." The old woman stroked the cub's back. He butted her shoulder with his big head. She balanced with the ease of long practice. "He ate the small viper the emperor had tucked into my lovely box. We were up all night with his belly ache, but now he knows not to eat vipers."

"But why?" Souda asked. She looked at the cub with longing. "Why did the emperor send you a viper?"

"I believe he thought that my successor would be likely to forget the debt of gratitude we owe to the God-Kings for allowing our temple to be here. He thought that if he killed the cranky old woman, he would have a friend in Gyongxe. Instead he still has a cranky old woman who now holds a grudge against him. We sent my would-be successor to him in a box of our own." She stood and went to the wall. The cub stood beside her, his forepaws planted on the ledge. "Messenger! Your imperial master knows who I am — he tried to kill me last year. He failed." Though she spoke in normal tones, her voice rang in the air. It startled not just the messenger's horse but those of the mounted soldiers behind him. "Tell him this for me: His palace will crawl with angry cats before I surrender anyone. Gyongxe has many surprises for you people. Get out while you can!" She stepped back from the wall and beckoned to the commander. "Are you ready?" she asked quietly. Her voice only reached those near them. Briar got to his feet. Souda and Parahan were already up.

"If you are," the Gyongxin soldier replied.

Briar looked out. The messenger was galloping back to his own people. The archers must have set their bolts and drawn their crossbow strings earlier, because their weapons were raised and ready to shoot.

One Yanjingyi soldier, a burly fellow in gold-painted armor, raised a crimson banner. Several men shouted orders as the archers aimed over the temple wall. The soldiers trotted their horses forward.

Then the priestess — the head of the temple, Briar knew now — and the commander began to chant.

The immense orange tiger statue that sat by the gate shook itself and roared at the charging horsemen. The white tiger that was already leaping into the air finished its jump, landing in the middle of the attackers.

The horses went mad with terror. They reared and plunged, screaming as they threw their masters to the ground. The tigers whirled and swung their huge paws, sending horses and men alike flying through the air.

Parahan's and Souda's warriors froze at the sight before them, but not the temple archers. They aimed and shot. As their bolts flew, Briar looked at Jimut. He was already aiming his crossbow. Briar turned back to the tigers and saw their weakness. They were anchored near the gate somehow. Once at their limit, which seemed to be about three hundred yards, they could keep the enemy at bay, but they could not pursue them. The Yanjingyi soldiers also figured it out. They formed up out of the tigers' range and waited for their own mages to have a turn. These worthies had kept far back all along. Though Briar couldn't see them closely or hear them, he guessed they had taken their beads in hand and were chanting the words that would wake the spells in them.

The Gyongxin and Kombanpur archers launched their arrows high in the air. For some reason they fell short of the mages and even the soldiers. The archers on the wall tried a second time.

The bolts still fell short. The temple's priest-mages came forward with small pots and boxes. Novices followed with mortars, pestles, cloth bags, and fists full of incense. They set their belongings on the wall and began to mix substances for the priests to burn and chant over. Briar felt their power press against his skin. The next time the archers on the wall shot, their arrows hit the enemy.

Briar ignored what his allies were doing and sat cross-legged on the wall.

"Don't let anyone trip over me, Jimut," he said. He sank into his magic, flowing through the roots under the temple and out below the battlefield. Here was a weight of rock that had to be one of the stone tigers. On he went until he sensed the small magics that went into the good-luck charms carried by soldiers.

Overhead now he felt bead-shaped willow with magic dug into its grain: exactly what he wanted to find. Weishu had not warned his mages to remove their wooden beads. There were other wooden beads, but for now the willow ones would serve his purpose.

Briar surrounded those beads with his own magic. They welcomed him. He brought them the memory of their life as trees, before someone had cut them into pieces and forced strange magic onto them. Willow magic healed and united. It was power that bent before it broke. Instead of flowing streams and falling rain someone had jammed killing and destruction into the wood, the kind of spells that burned and thrust.

Willows didn't understand that magic. They wore it uneasily. Feeling themselves in Briar, remembering what they were, the bits of willow shook off the foreign power. They took up the green magic that had been theirs when they were trees. They grew. Briar guided their power to veins of water underground. Here they found the fierce strength of the Snow Serpent and Tom Sho Rivers. Briar bound their magic to his, sank both deep into the water, and let go.

Saplings shot from the willow beads worn by the Yanjingyi mages. Rapidly the new trees grew. The mages tore off their strings of beads, but not fast enough to keep from being enveloped by fast-growing willows. The new trees followed their power to heal by uniting the mages' arms with their bodies and forcing the humans' two legs to become one. They wrapped the humans in their trunks.

Feeling that he had exacted a little vengeance for the dead who had lain in the gorge and the river, Briar ran down the steps down into the courtyard. He wanted to see what he could do if there were mages at the north gate.

By the time the stone tigers had returned to their poses as statues, Briar had calmed the new willow groves he'd made north and south of the temple. He had lost his chance to ride with the warriors to capture what remained of the enemy after the last soldiers had fled. No one wanted the escapees to reach General Jin Quan.

Since he couldn't chase soldiers, Briar searched the grass around his new willows and collected the rest of the mages' beads. The thought of someone with a little power stumbling across them gave him the chills. He also preferred the voices of the new willows to the noise of the villagers after the battle. They were boasting about the valor of Gyongxin warriors and their allies from the south. Briar didn't want to listen. This war party had been tiny compared to what the emperor had to send, and it was magic that had won the day. Next time there might not be enough magic to turn the tide. The image of the imperial soldiers in their thousands was never far from his mind. Next time they might not have such an easy victory. Or any victory at all.

Rosethorn rode quickly as she left Briar. The sooner I go, she told herself, the sooner I return to them. Who knows what mischief they'll get into without me to keep an eye on things?

She looked back after ten yards for a last glimpse of her boy, but a heavy fog had come from nowhere to hide the north bank of the Snow Serpent River. She faced south again and let her patient horse follow the trail. As they moved into the canyons of the Drimbakang Lho, she prayed to Mila of the Fields and Grain, the Green Man, god of growth that was orderly and chaotic, and even Briar's own Lakik the Trickster to look after him and Evvy.

One thing she had found while carrying the Four Treasures was that her path was always clear. Since leaving the fort she had seen it as a shining pale ribbon along the main road, across the bridge, and now on the simple one-mule track. She only had to stay on it.

Her burden was company of a sort. It carried myriad voices to her. Most of them spoke languages she had never heard, even after all her years of life on the Pebbled Sea. Some bits of conversation came in tongues she knew quite well, speaking of trade, the governing of nations, the weather, the condition of crops, or the behavior of children. The voices held her attention so well that the horse would nudge her when he required rest, water, or the chance to crop grass.

She brought out one of Evvy's glow stones for light once the sun had set, not for herself, but for her mount. Finally he dug in his hooves to let her know he had walked enough for the day. She made their camp in a stand of trees and rubbed the easygoing animal down, then covered him with a blanket against the mountain cold. She ate yak jerky and cheese for supper, though she wasn't particularly hungry. Her own common sense, at least, was still working.

Best of all, she breathed easily. She might resent the detour to Gyongxe and the separation from both of her young people, but it was good to fill her lungs again.

The package wasn't even that much of a burden in a physical sense. She felt its light pressure on her chest, but it wasn't heavy. She slept on her side with the box still around her neck, one arm draped lightly over the Four Treasures.

She woke at dawn, fed her horse and herself, and continued her upward trek. The gleaming path turned away from the one-mule road onto a game trail some time after noon. Wild mountain goats and yaks politely moved aside to let them pass.

The trail led to a slender ledge over a deep gorge. On her side the cliff rose over a hundred feet into the air above her. "I hope you're nimble," Rosethorn told the horse. She gulped when she looked down. The gorge plunged far deeper than she had expected. A ribbon of blue-and-white water tumbled over rocks.

The horse calmly followed the trail around the curve on the ledge and onto wider ground again, deep into shadowed lands. The mountains rose higher, and the path rose with them. Rosethorn relaxed and returned to her dreaming state. That night it was cold enough that she built a fire.

The next day the trail took them down a thin canyon. It was so narrow that Rosethorn could touch both walls when she stretched out her arms. She could tell her mount did not like the close quarters.

"What can we do?" she asked him softly. Even so her voice echoed. "See the path? This is the way we have to go."

"Few have the gods' blessings to come here." The deep male voice boomed between the stone walls. Rosethorn reined in, unsure of what was going on. "You are expected, bearer of the Living Circle's Treasures. You have come to the Temple of the Sealed Eye. Ride on."

After she caught her breath, she decided there was nothing else to do. She nudged her mount, clicking her tongue between her teeth. He snorted and tossed his head, but he did advance. The path descended as the canyon widened. Rosethorn could hear a waterfall.

A clearing opened before them. Soft grass grew around a wide pool. It was supplied from a waterfall that dropped thirty feet from a cliff. Three caves opened into the cliff face beside the waterfall.

"Leave your horse," the voice ordered. "He will be cared for. Enter the temple — if you choose the correct entry."

"And if I do not?" Rosethorn asked. Really, this is absurd, she thought impatiently. I have the Treasures; I found this hole in the wall — these *holes* in the wall. What more do they want of me?

"The temple protects itself," the voice replied.

"Did you hear that?" Rosethorn muttered to the horse as she dismounted. "The temple protects itself. The rest of us can enjoy our nice little mountain vacation that we took when others need us." She went about removing the horse's saddle.

"Grumbling will not assist you," the voice told her. "The animal will be looked after."

"Grumbling makes me feel better," she retorted. "If you don't like it, you should have given the First Dedicate instructions, or made it possible for *him* to bring this burden to you. And I was taught that it's proper to look after your own mount." She did so, rubbing him down, feeding him grain, and settling him on the grass. Once that was done, she moved her pack to her chest, having placed it on her back to care for the horse, and looked at the three openings. The glowing path went straight through the smallest opening, the one that was covered with cobwebs.

Lark, Rosethorn thought, bringing her lover's face before her mind's eye in case this did not go well. She took a deep breath, picked up a stick that lay on the ground, and advanced on the cave. Using the stick, she cleared away most of the cobwebs before she walked inside. The glowing path led her down a narrow tunnel, so narrow that in some places the stone brushed her shoulders. Rosethorn bit her lip and went on.

As the daylight faded behind her, she saw light from another source. A fungus she did not know grew high on the walls and the roof of the tunnel. The farther she came from natural light, the brighter glowed the fungus. It gave off a whitish-green illumination, one that was not favorable to her skin. She grimaced at the sight of her corpse-green hands, but consoled herself with the thought that no one would possibly care about her looks down here. As a religious dedicate she knew it was a weakness to be vain of her creamy skin. It was doubly so because she spent nearly all of her time in the sun.

"Concern for appearance is a folly of the world," the voice said, as if he'd read her mind.

Rosethorn spun. Behind her stood a black-skinned man so large he had to bend to keep from bumping his head on the roof. He wore a plain Gyongxin jacket, breeches, and boots. A white mark in the shape of an eye was painted on the middle of his forehead.

Rosethorn clutched the Treasures tightly. She didn't want him to see that she was shaking. No man had seen her frightened since she had run away from the chains in her father's farmhouse. "I don't know how you read my mind, but it's rude," she snapped. "And my weaknesses as a dedicate are between me and my own First Dedicates."

"In the Temple of the Sealed Eye all is known," the man said. "Continue to go forward. Keep to the left of the tunnel."

She didn't like to turn her back to him, but it was a question either of staying here or going ahead. She certainly couldn't go back, through him. As she moved on, the Treasures gripped her mind. They showed her strange images: a great city under attack; a young black man trying to get two girls who resembled him out of a beautiful house; soldiers in Yanjingyi armor surrounding them. They were separated and sold, the girls and the young man, in a Yanjingyi city. The young man was made to work on a rice farm. Then he found his way through forests and up into mountain passes, starved and half naked, until he collapsed. The last thing Rosethorn saw was a Gyongxin woman with the white eye painted on her forehead: She was bending over the fallen young man.

The vision faded.

"Is that you?" she asked, forgetting the big man most likely couldn't see what she did. "You were an escaped slave?" She looked back at him.

He sighed. "Your Treasures could leave me my secrets." He reached out. "Careful!"

She bumped a tall rock on her right. Something there hissed and scraped, darting at her. She stumbled back. The thing retreated, hissing still. Rosethorn turned to face it and carefully backed up until she struck the opposite wall. On the flat top of the rock was a serpent-like thing with a human skull. Its body seemed to be all vertebrae. It had no skin, no flesh, no muscle; its material was shaped like bone, but it looked to be a combination of metals.

"The cave snakes are the substance of the Drimbakangs," the man told her. "In the beginning they made themselves of tin, copper, and gold."

"They *made themselves*?" Rosethorn asked.

"At first," the man replied.

She didn't know if she was unsure or astonished. The cave snake rose up on its coils and hissed again, leaning out until its face was immediately in front of Rosethorn's. The thing's breath was cold, wet, and scented like the depths far underground. To her horror, Rosethorn saw movement beyond the beast's small skull as several more of the snakeish things rose up inside her coils, hissing softly.

"They are very irritable when brooding a nest," Rosethorn's companion said belatedly.

Rosethorn took a deep breath. "I am sorry that I disturbed you and your nest," she told the cave snake mother, fixing her eyes on the eye hollows in her skull. The thing must not know she was frightened. "It was not my intention. I would not like to see this become an argument between us."

"It would be a shame on both sides," a newcomer said as the cave snake drew in tight around her nest.

Rosethorn silently cursed the cave that gave her no warning of someone's approach and looked to her left. Here the tunnel opened up into a good-sized chamber. A Gyongxin man an inch or so shorter than Rosethorn stood there, dressed like her companion in tunic and breeches. Also like the black man, he wore the white eye on his forehead, though it did not look like it had been painted on. As Rosethorn watched, the white eye blinked at her.

I want to go home, she thought dizzily.

The small priest said, "Welcome to the Temple of the Sealed Eye, Nivalin Greenhow, whose name in religion is Rosethorn of Winding Circle temple. I see why Jangbu Dokyi trusted you with your faith's Four Treasures. In the wrong hands they would be powerful forces for ill, but you would never allow them to pass into those hands, would you?"

Rosethorn frowned at the man before returning her gaze to the cave snakes. She didn't trust them. "I'm not sure how I could stop the wrong hands, past a certain point, though I would give it my best."

"Your best is most formidable, my dear. Come. I am Yesh Namka, High Priest of the Temple of the Sealed Eye. Our warden of the gate behind you is Tegene Kess." Rosethorn looked at the big man, who nodded to her. "We must go deeper into the mountains' heart together before you can put down your burden," Namka said. "What you see and hear beyond this point you may tell no one, not the children of your heart, not your lover, not Jangbu Dokyi."

She heard ringing sounds in the dark behind the high priest. Out of the shadows walked three more creatures, eagle-headed, cat-bodied, spindle-legged, horse-hooved. Dark in color, they were speckled with spots that shone with a pale gold light, as did their wicked, hooked beaks. They halted beside Namka and cocked their heads to eye Rosethorn. The cave snakes chattered at them.

"Where did they come from?" Rosethorn asked Namka when she felt she could speak without her own teeth chattering.

"The mountains grow bored, sometimes," Tegene Kess explained. "They have eons of time to build themselves and their children. At first they follow the nature of the world, but there are times when they wish to try something different. Or the lesser gods who enter this realm feel it needs something unusual, and they make it. Do you understand?"

"Not at all," Rosethorn said.

"You will," Namka said, beckoning to her. "Come." He turned and shooed the strange hooved creatures out of the way.

There was nothing for Briar to do. Those few warriors who had been wounded on the wall by enemy archers were being well cared for by the temple healers. He had collected all of the fallen mage beads he could find. He scrounged a midday meal and hunkered down near the north gate with his finds. Once he had eaten, he worked on spells that would turn the oak and gingko beads against their holders. One such spell depended on the sex of the gingko tree that made up the bead. To test the spell Briar threw two beads several yards downhill and worked the magic he had placed on them. Within seconds they popped, turning into rapidly growing female seeds that reached the size of a small goat, ripened, and burst. Briar cackled wickedly even as he covered his nose with one elbow and backed away from the vomit-like smell.

He bumped into something behind him. Turning to apologize, he choked. He hadn't really expected the sitting orange stone tiger to be awake, but it had walked up for a closer look at what he was doing.

"I take it you can't smell," he said.

The tiger shook its head.

"Lucky you," Briar said weakly. Of course they know what I say, he thought. Since he could do nothing about it, he resumed his seat to consider what to do with the male gingko wood beads.

While the great creature was there, he thought to ask it a question that had hovered in his mind all morning. "Did you two come from the canyon behind Garmashing? In the Drimbakang Zugu?" In case the tiger did not recognize the names, he brought his memory of the morning when shamans had danced a pair of giant skeletons to life to the front of his mind, in case the tiger could see it in him, somehow. He concentrated, trying to capture the sounds and scents of that chilly moment in time when stone shaped itself and walked out of the cliff.

A scraping noise made him open his eyes. With a single large claw the tiger had drawn two smooth lines with a waving line between them. It was a map of the canyon behind Garmashing.

"When did they dance you out of the cliffs?"

The tiger shrugged, making its well-marked fur ripple.

"But it was a long time ago."

The tiger nodded and lay down beside Briar.

"Thank you," Briar said politely, awed. "That's what I thought." He returned to his experiments with the male gingko beads, though his heart wasn't really in his work. If he didn't watch it, he thought, he would start to think the gods really were closer to Gyongxe than they were to any other part of the world, if they could gift native stone so that it defended the temples of lands far away.

He may have been deep in thought, but he still noticed the orange-and-black tiger as it got to its feet again and walked by him. Several moments passed before his curiosity overcame him and he looked up. Both tiger statues had gone downhill to eat the remains of the oversized, vile-smelling gingko berries.

"Well," Briar said. "I suppose they don't care if it's meat or not. I wonder if they just like the magic?" He continued to work with the other wooden beads.

The tigers had eaten all of the berries and returned to their guardian positions to wash themselves when the grasses told Briar that horses were coming. A glance at the sky showed him that the day was drawing to a close. He gathered his beads and the remnants of his midday and walked to the gate. The tigers had taken still positions, but not the ones they had held before.

The white tiger sat on its hindquarters, washing a forepaw. The orange tiger stretched out on one side.

Briar waited until the soldiers who had ridden after the enemy passed through the gate, then followed them inside. He stopped briefly to give each stone tiger a pat. Evvy would expect it of him, he knew. They had gone solid.

The twins and Captain Lango greeted him as they dismounted from their horses, but they seemed preoccupied. They withdrew to Souda's tent and sent for a handful of their own people while the temple captain trotted up to the temple. Not long afterward he returned with the temple's warrior-commander, the chief priestess, and her young tiger. They all entered Souda's tent; guards were placed to keep anyone from coming close enough to eavesdrop.

The returning hunting parties had brought wounded. Briar swapped his mage kit for his healer's kit and offered his assistance to the temple workers. With the addition of those who had been hurt on the patrol, the temple healers were glad to have Briar's assistance as well as his medicines.

"We got all but two of the ones we were chasing," Atori, one of Souda's archers, told Briar as he cleaned her arrow wound. "Those Yanjingyi *seps* can ride!"

Briar grinned at her use of a Banpuri curse word he'd heard Parahan use many times. She ground her teeth as the cleansing potion he had applied bubbled deep into the wound. He murmured, "Not long, now. I've yet to lose someone to infection with this."

"Well, there's the goddess's blessing," she gasped. "Aiiiii!"

"Done," Briar said, and began to bandage the wound. "When you take this off tomorrow, around noon, say, your arm will look like you never got shot. Give it a week, and it won't even be sore."

"I'll be able to shoot with it?" Atori wanted to know. Her face was anxious. "That was a big camp we found. Bigger than ours. Signs of an army in the area."

"You'll be able to shoot," Briar assured her. "Get some of the healing tea, and keep drinking that."

She had been sitting on a stool so he could work on her arm. Abruptly she stood, grabbed him by the ears, and kissed him well. "Oh, if only I weren't betrothed," she said mournfully. "Thank you, Briar!"

He stood there, grinning for a moment. She was twenty or so, definitely too old for him, but it was nice to have a pretty girl kiss him among so much insanity. Better than nice!

"Say, *emchi*," growled the next patient in line, an older Gyongxin warrior, "if you don't want me kissing you, would you have a look at this?"

Startled out of his happy state, Briar apologized and beckoned the soldier forward.

It was almost midnight when he emerged from the barn that had been made over into an infirmary. He'd given his slumbering patients a last check, and then cared for those who were awake and asking for help of some kind. He had just seen his bedroll and furs, set up beside a shed where they wouldn't be in anyone's way — thank you, Jimut! he thought gratefully — when he heard noise outside the gate. It was a horn: not the great horns on the temple's walls and roof, but a normal-sized one, blowing several notes. It halted, then sounded the same notes again.

Briar watched as guards hurried to open one half of the gates, which had been cleared after the battle. A rider in Gyongxin armor stumbled through, leading a weary horse. Attached to his saddle was a long bamboo wand with a blue silk banner attached. He was a messenger from one of Gyongxe's generals.

A temple novice ran forward to take the messenger's horse. Another came to lead him to those he needed to see. For a moment Briar wished the man brought word of Rosethorn or Evvy, but he knew better. He would not hear from Rosethorn until he saw her again, so secret was her task, and no one would send a wartime messenger for a student mage and her cats. For anything else, Briar was exhausted more than he was curious. He washed his face and hands at the courtyard well, then stripped off his boots and crawled into his bedroll.

As so often happened, he found himself too tired to sleep. After staring at the stars for a time, he sat up and pulled his boots back on. Perhaps the healers could spare some ordinary tea and maybe some food. He had not eaten supper. No doubt the temple kitchens were closed. He went back to the well for a drink of water and to clean his teeth.

It was there that Parahan and Soudamini found him. The twins looked as weary as he felt. He noticed they had taken time to comb the dust from their glossy black hair and change into comfortable Realms-style tunics and baggy breeches. Parahan carried something bulky in his hands.

"Why aren't you abed?" Briar asked, his voice froggy from weariness.

"We could ask you the same," Souda replied. She sat beside him on the edge of the well.

"Oh, no," Briar said, giddy from a lack of sleep and food. "I've been kissed by one pretty girl today. I couldn't take it if I got kissed by another."

Souda laughed quietly and put her arm around him. "It would be like kissing my brother," she said. "Briar, listen. We have news."

He looked at her, then up at Parahan.

"We chased some of the soldiers to a camp. They got the warning in time and ran, but their general left some letters and other things." With shock, Briar realized that Parahan was weeping. "Briar, Fort Sambachu was attacked two days after we left. The Yanjingyi enemy had enough mages to blow down their gates. They wrote to their general that they killed the refugees and the animals."

Briar clenched his fists. "Evvy?"

Souda took up the story. Parahan was wiping his eyes on his sleeve. "They had orders to send Evvy to the emperor's camp once she told them where we were, and where you and Rosethorn were. But — she died, as they questioned her. They had one of the emperor's best mages with them, just for that."

Briar heard a voice. It turned out to be his own. "You mean tortured."

Souda bowed her head. "Tortured."

Parahan held the bundle in his hand out to Briar. "She showed me this, one of the days when you and Rosethorn were making the flower. It was in the general's tent with his letter. He was going to send it to Weishu."

Numbly Briar took it and undid the ties. It was Evvy's stone alphabet. Not the one she had begun recently, made of stones that she had found herself. It was the one he had made for her, back when he realized he would have to teach a stone mage somehow. The stones lay still and dead in the dim torch- and starlight.

"A for amethyst," he whispered, running his fingers over the stone. It wasn't high in quality; it wouldn't have fetched much in the market, but Evvy had loved it. It was her first step into her new life as a mage. She had kept the alphabet where the cats couldn't play with it. . . .

"The cats?"

"The letter said they killed the animals. We can hope they escaped," Parahan said, his voice cracking.

He had spent time with Evvy and her cats, Briar remembered. "Might I be alone now?" he asked politely. "I'll be all right."

"Are you certain?" Souda wanted to know. "We can only imagine how bad this is for you."

"Really, I'll be fine," Briar said. "I do this best alone." Or with Rosethorn, and Lark, and my sisters, he thought, and *none* of them are here! None of them are with me! They've all gone off to do their whatevers and left me to face this!

It wasn't fair. He knew it wasn't fair. He didn't feel like *being* fair just then. He climbed up the wall and walked along until he could look north. Right now he hated everyone, the First Dedicate and the God-King, Lark for not making Rosethorn stay home, Rosethorn for not refusing the emperor and the First Dedicate, Evvy for being unwilling to come along with him. Himself for not insisting that she come, or for not staying with her.

Especially himself. He hated himself. He was her first teacher, and he had dragged her into the path of the huge imperial armies and the legions of imperial mages. He stood by and watched as Weishu smiled and played games with their lives. Briar had left his Evvy to be tortured and to die alone. She was good with her power, but these people were masters of theirs. She was only twelve.

He clutched the stone alphabet and stared at the grasslands beyond the north gate. They were gray in the starlight. Somewhere across those were the imperial armies. That way lay the torturers, the murderers, and those who would steal other people's countries. They would pay. He would make sure of that.

In the dark the grasses strained upward, their blades trembling with the power that filled them. Their roots swelled and stretched. For a long moment the land shook, then sank back.

CHAPTER
SIXTEEN

The Temple of the Tigers, and

Kangri Skad Po Mountain in the Drimbakang Lho

Dawn found Briar with the orange-and-black stone tiger at the southern temple gate. He had managed to talk the guards into letting him out at some point; he didn't remember when. The tiger was good company in his present bleak mood. Wrapped in a fur from his bedroll, he had told it about Evvy, how aggravating she could be, how protective she was of her cats, how much she loved new clothes. The tiger had curled around him, forming a bowl to hold Briar. At last he had slept.

It was the chief priestess who found him. She spoke with the stone tiger gently, thanking it for its care of Briar, until it slowly uncurled and took its normal place by the gate.

As Briar looked at the old woman sleepily, she told him, "I think we must treat the gate tigers differently after this. It is written in our books that they are mindless slaves of our magic, but apparently they are otherwise. We have you to thank — perhaps." She touched one of his swollen eyes. "You have been weeping."

For a precious moment he had forgotten. Tears spilled down as he told her, "They killed Evvy. My student."

"You shall have revenge," the old woman said. "Last night a messenger came from the west. Your people will wait here another day for the wounded to heal. By this afternoon warriors from the western temples and tribes will join you. Parahan and Souda want to go east, to trap the enemy in Fort Sambachu. We shall see. General Sayrugo is closer."

"I want to go there," Briar said, struggling to his feet. "I want to serve them at the fort like they served Evvy!"

The old woman helped him up. "When you agreed to help Parahan and the others, you put yourself at the orders of the God-King. You may not have a choice."

Briar glared at her, but he was too weak with grief to argue. Instead he thought of something else. "Wait — I can't go. I have to wait here for Rosethorn. She'll be returning from the mountains soon, I hope. I said I would meet her."

"And you will," the priestess said patiently. "When was the last time you had any food?"

He shook his head, not because he didn't want to eat, but because he couldn't remember his most recent meal.

"As I thought," she said. She towed him into the temple complex.

They fed him egg soup and *momos*, scolding him when he picked at his food. When he'd eaten enough that the cooks let him be, he went to the healers' tent and helped there. Midday was curry. Jimut sat on one side of him, Souda on the other. Between them he ate all that was set before him, just to stop them from nagging him to death.

He was about to leave the temple to say prayers for Evvy in one of his new willow groves when a squad of Gyongxin warriors carrying the yellow banner of messengers galloped up the road. He knew a couple of them from Fort Sambachu.

"We almost did not come up here," the woman who carried the banner told the gate guards. "Those trees weren't on your road when I was here last! How —" Looking past the guard's shoulder, she saw Briar. "Oh. I thought Rana made that up about you growing trees from nothing. Never mind. I bring messages for Prince Parahan and Princess Soudamini, and Captains Lango and Jha!"

Only when Lango identified the newcomers as General Sayrugo's warriors did the guards open the gate. The messenger and her guards led their horses inside. Briar felt distantly sorry for them. They would soon learn of their own losses: the slaughter of Captain Jha and his company. At least they had been soldiers. They had known they were expected to die in war. Evvy had not. She had been dragged here by Briar and Rosethorn. She had not wanted anything to do with the emperor. All she had wanted to do was see the mountains.

Evvy slept a lot. She dreamed, too, and they were the strangest dreams of her life. The fluorite bear was in most of them, trundling beside her from her head to her feet, watching as snakes made of backbones and skulls unwound her bandages. Lions made of ice and packed snow licked her feet. A spider at least twice her size leaped down from a roof she couldn't see and bandaged her feet in its webs.

In some dreams, when the bear wasn't present, a woman with a white eye painted on her forehead came and argued with her about food. Usually Evvy would drink the soup brought by the woman just so she would go away. Evvy knew that dreams didn't work like that. People didn't go away because you did the things they wanted you to do in dreams, but these dreams were as odd as the strange things that she saw in them.

In one, she asked the fluorite bear, "Which is weirder, the nine-headed snake, or —" Suddenly she was wide-awake and saying, "— the giant spiders that come from above?" She sat up and looked around. She was *definitely* awake. She could feel her ragged clothes against her skin. She could smell herself. When had she last bathed? "Can you smell me?" she asked the bear.

"No," it said gravely.

"Oh, good." Swallowing, terrified of what she might see, she made herself look at her feet. They were there, looking like her ordinary, everyday feet. She wriggled her toes. They were stiff, but not painful. "I dreamed the Yanjingyi *yujinon* flayed my feet and killed everyone in the fort, but that part was so real," she murmured. "I dreamed they killed my cats. And then I came here and a big spider wrapped my feet in its webs. I *know* that part was a dream."

"It was all real, Evumeimei Dingzai," the bear told her. "I called to you so you might find safety here in the mountains. The webs dropped from your feet a sunrise ago, when your feet were healed."

Tears trickled down her cheeks. "My cats really are dead?"

"Once I understood why you called for them in your dreams, I showed their images to one of my snow leopards," the bear said. "She went to the dead pile behind the stone cave. She found the seven little cats that matched your dreams in the pile."

Evvy turned over on the soft pile of rags where she had been sleeping and wept harder.

When she finally dried her eyes and sat up again, she found the bear had not moved. "I don't usually cry like this," she told him belligerently. "Just so you don't go thinking I'm some kind of watering pot."

"What is a watering pot?" he asked.

"It's a jar. You put water in it and pour it on plants so they grow."

"Is not the rain enough?"

Evvy rubbed the dried blood on the back of one foot. It flaked off. "People have plants in their houses. They use watering pots for indoor rain." Slowly, grimacing because she was so stiff, she drew one foot up onto the opposite knee so she could look at the sole. It was puffy with scars that crisscrossed the flesh, but when she poked them, they were merely sore, not as painful as they had been when she had fled the fort. "You cured them."

"The webs of the peak spider cured them," the bear explained. "Forgive us for keeping you in slumber. We felt that it would be less unnerving for you if you did not see how you were healed."

"I don't care about how I was healed," Evvy said bitterly. "I care that I was hurt in the first place. I care that they killed all those people in the fort. I *care* that they killed my cats." She opened and closed her hands, remembering the feel of the stone-cold dead cats under them as she crawled over bodies, looking for clothes. "What did the villagers ever do to deserve dying like that, tell me! They had little ones with them, babies, and those imperial *qus* killed them and dumped them in a pile to rot!" She glared at the fluorite bear, who had cocked his head knob once more. "What! You think I'm crazy, don't you?"

"I do not know what crazy means," the creature said in his slow, thoughtful way. "What I think is that we healed the hurt in your feet and the hurt in your body, but now your spirit is sick. I want to heal that pain for you, but I do not know how. I can heal the meat creatures of my mountain, but I leave two-legged meat creatures to their own kind."

"Do you always talk this way?" Evvy demanded. She wasn't being polite, or grateful, but if her cats were dead, why couldn't this thing just have left her to die? *Briar and Rosethorn have each other,* she thought. The memory went through her like lightning. Briar and Rosethorn! If the enemy got around General Sayrugo and her troops, or killed them all, to reach Fort Sambachu, maybe they caught up to Briar and Rosethorn, too! *How will I ever know?*

The stone thing said, "My difficulty is that you are not entirely of the meat creature kind."

"Of course I am!" Evvy retorted.

"No. If you were, I would not have heard your approach when you were still in the lowlands of the Ice Naga River."

"The what?"

"The river that flows below my mountain, before the stone place where they tried to kill you, Evumeimei Dingzai."

"We call it the Snow Serpent River," Evvy told him. "And you can call me Evvy."

"I could not begin to say such a name before I would have finished it. Will you accept Evumeimei?"

She sighed. "I suppose I have to. What do you call yourself?"

He tipped back his head knob and gave voice to a series of sounds she could not even begin to remember. Her mind caught on to two syllables she knew she could say.

"I'm going to call you Luvo. I'm sorry, I know that's not your whole name, but I can't say it all, or even remember it." She hung her head. "I'm not trying to be rude or disrespectful. I suppose being a mountain is a big thing, like being a god. I can't do big things."

"I am only the heart of this mountain," Luvo said kindly. "And part of you is of my kind, the mountain kind. Though it saddens me to say that you are impaired. Too much of you is a meat creature. I cannot understand how you came to be."

Evvy wiped her nose on her arm. "Rosethorn and Briar say I'm an ambient mage. We draw our power from different parts of the world. They get their magic from plants and growing things. Briar has one foster-sister who gets hers from the weather, and another one who takes it from metal and fire, and one who draws it from making and working with cloth. I get mine from stones."

"I did not know that this could ever be true," Luvo said, fascinated. "This magic is of a different kind from that used by the chanting people, or the people of the white eye."

"I think those are academic mages and shamans," Evvy said. "I know Briar's somewhere west of the fort with Parahan and Soudamini. They have mages with them, but I think Briar's the only ambient one. If *he* isn't dead." She twisted her hands in her ragged shirt. "What am I going to do? How will I find him or Rosethorn? They don't know where I am. I can't go back to the fort — they'll torture me again!"

"You could not return to the fort," Luvo told her. "It no longer stands."

Evvy blinked at him. "Did General Sayrugo come? Or the God-King's army? What happened?"

"The hill that it was built on shook," Luvo said. "The fort fell down."

Evvy looked at the stone creature for a long moment, not exactly sure what he meant. Then she asked, "How did that happen?"

"Our mountains are young and still growing." Luvo's deep voice was bland. "Growing mountains may shake the land around them."

"Why?" Evvy demanded. She had a feeling this was not an accident.

"The land and its guardians do not care for intruders who damage and kill those who belong here, or those who would bring good things here." Evvy could have sworn she felt the ground quiver beneath her. In fact, she was sure of it. Nervously she eyed the stalactites that hung from the cave's ceiling.

Then she screamed. A giant spider was leaping from one stalactite to the next, coming lower and closer, until it dropped to the ground only a few yards away from her. Evvy looked at its hairy body and its large black eyes and screamed again. It held one great foreleg in the air as if it were hurt. Evvy realized it held a bag even as she scrabbled backward off her bed of moss and scraps.

"Evumeimei, stop it!" boomed Luvo. "You frighten Diban Kangmo!"

"*I* frighten — whatever that is?" Evvy shrieked.

"Her name is Diban Kangmo. She is bringing food for you," Luvo said firmly. "Stop that dreadful noise. You must thank her. She did not want to feed you. She did not like the idea of bringing a meat creature so far into our mountain."

Evvy clapped her hands over her mouth and stared at the spider. She was six feet tall if she was an inch. Her mouthparts would easily crush Evvy's arm. Once the girl caught her breath and was certain of what she would say, she moved her hands to ask, "Dee-what?"

"Dee-bahn kang-moh," Luvo said even more slowly than he normally spoke. "One of her daughters healed your feet."

Evvy gulped at the thought of something so huge working on her body. She was so very grateful she had not woken up then. "What is she? What are they?"

"Peak spiders," Luvo replied. "The gods and goddesses of the utmost heights of the Drimbakangs."

Evvy shuddered. She did not want to think about gods shaped like spiders. Slowly she knelt and touched her forehead to the cave floor. "I am very, very sorry, Diban Kangmo," she told the giant spider. "I guess I am still upset by what has happened to me. Please thank your daughter for healing my feet." This she meant with all of her heart. "I would have died, probably. And thank you for feeding me. I swear you won't regret it."

She peeked at the spider. Diban Kangmo took two steps forward — her feet made clicking sounds on the stone. Slowly she uncurled the leg with which she held what Evvy saw were several cooking pots. She carefully set them on the ground. Then she stepped back a couple of yards.

Evvy looked at the pots. She wasn't quite sure what to say, or do. "Where did she find them?" she whispered to Luvo.

For a moment Luvo said nothing. Then he told Evvy, "There is a place on the Ice Naga — what you call the Snow Serpent River — to the west, like the . . . fort . . . that fell down, only with more — You do not like it when I call your people meat creatures. What do you call them?"

"Humans," Evvy said. "Or people."

"People can be anyone," Luvo argued. "Diban Kangmo and her kin are people, as are the ice lions, the cave snakes, the nagas, the deep runners, we mountains. Humans are those meat creatures on two legs?"

Evvy nodded.

"The place like a fort where many humans are gathered just now. It is a place that reaches for the sky in spirit, and the humans who live there all of the time make pretty noises with long tubes and metal plates."

"It's a temple, maybe," Evvy said. "I heard Parahan say that the first stop on the Snow Serpent Road was the Temple of the Thunder Horses."

"That is where she found your food."

"Did the humans there see her?" Evvy asked, wondering if she was the only one to scream at the sight of the giant peak spider.

Luvo sounded amused. "No one sees the spirit people of this realm if those people do not desire it. They prefer quiet lives. Stop asking questions, Evumeimei!"

Gingerly, keeping an eye on Diban Kangmo, Evvy crawled over to the pots. All of them were cold. She did not care. She started with tea, gulping it down. It soothed her dry and raw throat. She then turned her attention to the food, scooping up the barley-flour balls called *tsampa* and stuffing them into her mouth. These had butter and milk curds. Normally she would have spat such things out. Today they tasted better than anything she had eaten in her life, even her beloved fried eggplant. Another pot contained spicy rice curry with lamb. She alternated handfuls of that with the *tsampa* until she could eat no more. Only when she couldn't even look in the other pots to see what was there because she was so full did she lurch to her feet and go to the great stretch of water near her resting place.

"I'm dirty," she told Luvo. "I'm going to wash." Since she was fairly sure he wouldn't know what dirty was, she explained, "I'm all over blood and piss and dung and sweat. I don't normally smell like this." She fumbled with her clothes, peeling them off layer by layer. It didn't occur to her to be shy. A talking rock and a giant spider were hardly the sorts to make her nervous about baring her skin. "I wish I had clean things." It was hard to tell in the green light from the glowing spots everywhere, but she was nearly certain there was blood on some of her clothes. That made sense, given that she had taken the garments from the dead.

The water was *very* cold. After all of the cold-water baths we took as we traveled, I should be used to this, she thought gloomily, but I'm not.

The memory of her cats, seated to watch on countless stream banks as she and Rosethorn yelped in cold waters, struck her like a knife stab. She sat on the bottom of the cave lake and silently let her tears flow.

At last she began to drag her fingers through her knotted hair. Once it was straight again and fairly clean, she lurched up onto dry land.

Her dirty clothes were gone. Beside her mossy bed lay a pile of fabric in various green-tinted colors.

"There is an enclosed place," Luvo said as she approached. "It is like the 'temple' place for the Thunder Horses, but it is for my mountain and those of my brother and sister. Your humans come to it and leave things for the humans that sing there and light lamps and bow up and down as you do, only more. They use fire to make smoke that smells interesting, too."

Evvy gave him a tight smile. "The humans here worship your mountain and the other two as gods. They think you three are the husbands of the Sun Queen."

"Ridiculous!" Luvo said. "The sun is not even part of this world!"

Evvy knelt clumsily and sorted through the pile. Soon she wore multiple layers of gaudy silk robes lined with fur. Somehow Luvo had also brought away several pairs of breeches that fit once she had rolled them up, and two pairs of fur-lined boots. She could wear one pair. Once she was clothed, she drank some more tea and fell asleep again.

The western army, made up of over five hundred tribesmen, priests and priestesses, and shamans, mounted on small, tough horses or driving carts, arrived around noon as Briar was brewing medicines in a temple workshop. One of the children brought word of the new arrivals, but Briar was busy keeping the greatest strength of his potions from cooking off. Once, when he took a

rest, he walked up onto the wall to a view of many tents and soldiers inside and outside the temple. The sight alone made him
cross. He wondered if he could ask his new friend the orange
stone tiger if it would let him sleep there again that night.

The village child returned later to let Briar and the other healers know that a messenger had arrived from the east. Briar was
not interested. He could not feel Rosethorn's approach. With
Evvy's death, he doubted the east held any good news for him.

Jimut brought Souda's dinner invitation to him. Though he
was done for the day, Briar refused it. He meant to beg food
from a cook and go somewhere private to eat. But Souda marched
into the workshop as he finished his cleanup and seized him by
the arm.

"No more hiding," she said firmly. "You will eat with us,
without arguments." She did not release him until they were
inside the tent that she and Parahan seemed to use as an audience
chamber. Guards had set dishes on the carpet. Cushions were
strewn all around them. Parahan was there already, scooping
something into his mouth with a piece of flatbread.

"You couldn't wait?" Souda demanded.

He swallowed and said, "Briar, sit. Don't hide, will you? I'm
missing her, too. I know you knew her longer, but you know I
wouldn't be here without her." His smile trembled. "She was
too young to consider all the consequences, as you and I would
have done."

Briar nodded. He took a cushion next to the big man and
picked up a plate. He spooned curry onto it, then looked at it
blankly, having lost track of what he'd meant to do with it.

Souda took the plate and loaded meat, flatbread, and dumplings onto it beside the curry. "Eat!" she ordered. "We have work to do!" She sat cross-legged on a cushion of her own and served herself. "While the westerners were getting settled, another messenger from Sayrugo arrived," she told Briar. "She wants us to meet her at Melonam. It's northeast of here, on the road to Garmashing. Her soldiers moved as many people to the eastern temple fortresses as they could before they ran into more imperial troops than they could handle."

"They tried to fall back to Fort Sambachu," Parahan said abruptly. "Well, they *did* fall back. Except the fort isn't there."

Briar stared at him. "What do you mean, the fort isn't there? It didn't just get up and walk away."

"The general's letter says that maybe there was an earthquake," Souda explained. "Only she doesn't know how they didn't feel a quake that was strong enough to make the entire fort collapse in on itself."

"Could Evvy have done that? If she was dying?" Parahan whispered.

Briar shook his head. "That place was big! We pulled down parts of a house, her and me, but nothing that size."

"I wish she *had* done it!" Parahan shouted. Two soldiers stuck their heads inside the tent flap. Souda waved them out again. "I wish she'd pulled it down on those murderers!" her twin snapped, his voice softer this time.

Briar hooked a hand around one of Parahan's shoulders for comfort. "We'll come up with some surprises for their friends, you'll see," he promised. When Parahan looked at him, Briar gave his friend a small, nasty smile. "We'll make Weishu regret he ever heard of any of us."

Parahan wrapped his hand around Briar's. "Yes. Yes, I think that sounds like a most magnificent idea."

"Briar, can you sense Rosethorn yet?" Souda asked.

He shook his head. "But if we take the road north from here, it'll be easy enough to feel for her. I'll let the plants know where I'm going. She can follow our trail."

Evvy woke to find Luvo in the same place he had been when she had gone to sleep. The giant spider was gone. She was relieved, though Diban Kangmo had been nothing but kind to her. Still, being watched by all those eyes was nothing short of unnerving.

There was food remaining in the pots that Diban Kangmo had brought. Evvy ate a good amount of what was left. Would the spider steal more? Surely the temple inhabitants would start to wonder where their food was going. Also, the temples were supposed to be housing refugees. Was Diban Kangmo stealing food that should go to them?

She emptied the teapot and realized she had another issue that had to be addressed.

"I, um, need a privy," she told Luvo. Then she had to explain what privies were for, and why she couldn't just go where she stood, like the animals of his mountain. Once all of that was said, he showed her a cranny in the wall of the cave where the flooring was more sand than rock. Afterward she bathed again. Binding her hair in a scarf from his pile of offerings, she steeled herself and said, "Luvo, I can't stay here. I have to find my friends. Sooner or later they'll learn the enemy took the fort. They'll think I'm dead, or that I got tortured and told where everyone is. I have to find them."

Luvo rocked back and forth on the rounded pegs that served as feet when he wanted them. "Do you know where they are?"

"I know which way they went," she said honestly. "The places they were going to stop at, the people there should be able to tell me where my friends went afterward."

"How will you go?"

"I'll walk, I suppose." She tested the sole of one foot on the stone. They were still tender, but she had the boots, and the longer she waited, the farther away her friends would be. "I'll steal a horse or mule if I get the chance." It would have to be in an open field around the temples where they were grazing, and she would have to pray that the herders didn't have any dogs.

Luvo hummed to himself. "I could find your friends."

"How? They don't have stone magic like me."

"You said that the fire around your stone self is magic that lets you draw on it. I did not know of this reason for the fire in some meat creatures — humans — before. Now that I know it, I can tell which fires I see on the plain are simply magic and which are wrapped around part of the world. I can see the magic around your plant people if we are close to them. I think it is best that I go with you. Are you able to carry me?"

Evvy walked over to him. Excusing herself, she bent, wrapped her hands around him, and lifted. She heard her spine crackle, but Luvo did not move. "You're so heavy!"

"Forgive me. I am a mountain outside this heart aspect." He grew warm under her palms, though not hot. "Try again."

Evvy tugged. She lifted him an inch, no more.

301

He warmed a second time. "Try."

She was able to hoist him into her arms that time, but she staggered when she tried to move a few steps. "I'm sorry!" she said, placing him on her bed. "I'm more worn-out than I realized. All of my packs weigh as much as you, but . . ." She turned away so he wouldn't see her mouth quiver.

"That is the lightest I can make myself. I shall think of something." He climbed off her bed. "Rest. I will reflect on this and resolve it." He watched as Evvy curled up on the rags. "You cannot understand what a joy my moments of speech with you are. Each one presents me with a new idea or a new problem, when I have seen nothing new in ages. I have not felt so alive in millennia, Evumeimei."

"Huh!" she said, disbelieving. "I'm not the interesting one. That's Briar, and Rosethorn, and Parahan. They've done all these things, and they know languages, and books, and different people. I just know stones. Not even all of those." She yawned.

"Then I look forward to our meeting with your friends. Truly, Evumeimei, do not value yourself so little. You are a bright light in my underground home."

"Thanks, Luvo. That's a really nice thing to say." She pulled some rags over herself and slept before her new friend even walked away.

She dreamed she could hear Diban Kangmo talk with him.

She will be dead before you know it, the peak spider advised from a position high on one of the cave's stalactites. *It is folly to become attached to her.*

I think it has been folly for me to keep myself separate from them, if they can produce young like this one, Luvo replied.

Will you guard her for me until I return? I worry about the cave snakes.

She needs more food, the spider said as Luvo waddled into the dark. *Get some for her. Make one of my children carry it.*

When Evvy woke, she smelled cooking. She also smelled musk and dung, and heard the restless shift of hooves on stone. She opened her eyes and saw a large yak drinking from the lake. Luvo sat near her bed, next to a smaller peak spider — only three feet tall — and two covered pots.

"This is Diban Kangmo's daughter," Luvo explained as the smaller spider scurried off into the far end of the cave. "She is very shy of humans. She is the one who bandaged your feet."

"Thank you so much!" Evvy called after her.

"She also brought food for you and a bag for me to ride in."

"Ride? Ride what?"

"Big Milk," Luvo said. "She is the queen yak. It is a great honor to you that she chose to do this for us, and our luck that she has no young to prevent her from helping. We cannot ask a male. They are too restless."

Evvy thought she was going to cry. Big Milk had turned her head to stare at them with one eye. Or rather, she stared at Evvy.

Finally the girl thought of something safe to say, other than that the rock had lost his mind. "Luvo, she doesn't have a saddle or bridle."

She had to explain what those things were between bites of onion-and-mushroom dumpling. When she finished her description, Luvo said, "I could not ask one of my friends to take metal in her mouth and bind her head in leather. She might become ill.

Poor thanks that would be! Besides, I have never seen anyone ride a yak in such a way. You will tie the bag around your waist and shoulders, and hold on to Big Milk's fur. She has plenty of that. She will not even feel it if you pull. Her undercoat is quite thick and packed firmly beneath the outer fur."

"But how will she know which way we're going?" Evvy asked. "The reins are so you can pull right, and the horse goes right, and so forth."

"I will tell her which way to go," Luvo said confidently.

"Where will I sit?" Evvy didn't say that the animal's back looked as broad as if she could lay down on it and sleep without rolling off.

"The herd boys ride on the necks of the tame yaks. You have trusted me so far, Evumeimei."

"I didn't have a choice."

"Do you have one now?"

Evvy looked at Big Milk, who swiped a thick tongue around furry jaws. The girl sighed. "Not really."

Evvy hated to do it, but she used one of Luvo's silk offering scarves to wrap up the leftover dumplings. The cloth was made of brightly dyed patches, and now it would have grease stains. No doubt it would also stain the crimson shirt she wore, since she was hanging that small bundle on her chest. Once she was ready, she lowered Luvo into the bag he had brought. It was a picking bag, big enough that she could slide one strap over her shoulders and under her arms. She wrapped the coarse upper strap in a scarf so it would not chafe her neck, and wore the upper strap there.

Luvo must have said something to the yak. She ambled over and knelt on her forelegs. Impulsively Evvy scratched Big Milk between her curved horns as she would a cow. She felt a bit better when the yak turned her head and rubbed it against Evvy's belly.

"I think we're going to get along," the girl said. "Now, be patient with me, all right? I've never ridden anybody as wonderful as you before."

"She likes the compliment," Luvo told Evvy. "Swing your leg over, carefully!"

With a bit of experimenting and a little struggle, Evvy managed to get herself and Luvo onto Big Milk's back. Then she gave the great yak another forehead scratch and settled her grip into the fur on the animal's neck. "Now what?" she asked.

Slowly Big Milk straightened one foreleg, then the other. Evvy squeaked, then bit her lower lip to keep from doing so again. She yelped. Her lip was one of the injuries from the fort that was not completely healed.

Big Milk ignored both noises. She set off briskly along the shore of the lake, headed deeper into the cave.

SEVENTEEN

The Temple of the Tigers

The confluence of the Tom Sho and Snow Serpent Rivers

It was clear that Soudamini would go half mad before all of the western troops had packed up and ridden north.

"We've been through this before," Parahan told her, an arm around her shoulders. He and Briar had taken her up onto the roof before the westerners could hear her mutterings. "These people don't fight for a living. Well, perhaps the temple folk do. As the war goes on, they'll understand the importance of starting the march at dawn, not starting to pack at dawn."

Souda gnawed a thumbnail and swore to herself in Banpuri.

"Our people are all ready to ride," Briar said in consolation. He stared toward the distant river, hoping for the slightest hint that Rosethorn was coming. He wasn't unhappy that the westerners were holding them up.

"They may as well have slept late for all the good it will do us!" Souda replied, her husky voice a soft growl. "Who drew the short straw so we left last, anyway?"

"You," Parahan said.

"You may as well tell our people to unsaddle their mounts and run some weapons practice," Souda told her twin.

"Already did," he replied.

Then Briar felt it, the lightest touch of green. He inhaled and forgot to breathe out, waiting. There it was again. Suddenly his chest hitched and he began to hack, unable to catch his breath. Parahan shoved a flask of tea into his hands. Briar gulped half of it down. When he could breathe properly again, he stretched his power as far as it would go. That touch was a little stronger. It connected to his magic; he knew it like his own.

"I think you'll be happy we're last," he said casually.

Parahan's face lit. "Rosethorn?"

Briar nodded.

It was almost noon when Captain Lango's people rode through the gate on their way north. Briar went to the twins, whose companies were next. "I'll meet her and catch up with you," he said. "I think she'll reach the river crossing by midafternoon."

Parahan beckoned to Jimut, who came forward with saddled horses. "I have a fresh mount for her," Jimut said. "And you do not go without a guard."

Briar was too nervously eager to even consider an argument. After everyone said their farewells to the chief priestess and the temple commander, Parahan's and Souda's companies rode out the north gate. Briar and Jimut went south together with the squad of ten warriors that Parahan had insisted upon. Before they left the temple behind, Briar stopped and said good-bye to the orange stone tiger, ignoring the odd looks of the soldiers.

They walked their horses down to the river to wait and ate the meal they had cajoled out of the temple cooks. Two of the soldiers stood guard, watching north and east, while the others rested and talked. Briar paced the riverbank. He had no idea of how he was going to tell Rosethorn about Evvy. The idea of doing it made his stomach twist.

Clouds were spreading across the sky when Briar saw a flash of green — real green — atop the road that led into the Drimbakang Lho. He yipped, then clenched his hands so tightly his nails bit into the tattoos on his palms. The blooms and stems of his tattoos, swiftly turning into roses of every color, protested his grip. He apologized, silently. The enemy was supposedly gone from the area, but he and his companions had agreed to be cautious. Making noise at the sight of Rosethorn was not anyone's idea of cautious behavior. Instead he leaped up and down, waving frantically. He stopped only when she raised an arm to indicate she had seen him, and urged her mount to a trot.

They met on his side of the bridge, where she swung off her horse and hugged him very hard. She smelled to him of pine, wood smoke, and the chamomile she used for headache tea. He saw no sign of that nasty leather pack she had carried away with her. She looked like his good old Rosethorn, fixed on the here and now. Her brown eyes were sharp as she looked him over.

"What is it?" she asked. "Your eyes are puffy. You look like you've been dragged backward through a bush. Tell me."

"Evvy," he said, and his throat closed up.

Jimut took charge of her horse. Rosethorn guided him to the riverbank, where they sat. Once he could speak again, Briar told her about the letter and Evvy's stone alphabet. Then he held her. For too short a time they mourned.

"We should go," Briar said hoarsely at last. "We have to catch up with the supply train by dark, just to be safe."

Rosethorn went to the river and soaked two handkerchiefs in the cold water. She wiped her face with one and gave the other to Briar. A light rain had begun to fall. "At times like this it's hard to be a good dedicate and to trust in the gods that all things happen for a reason," she said, her voice hoarse. "She had such a hard life. I feel that the gods owed her something better for longer than she had it." She looked at her handkerchief and twisted it dry. "Since I never get an answer from the gods, I shall have to work my frustration out on Weishu and his armies."

Briar nodded. She had put his rage into words. They would make Weishu pay.

Rosethorn put her arm around him as they walked over to the others. They were already mounted up. Jimut passed her the reins of the fresh mount they had brought for her. The one she had ridden this far was with their spare horses. Rosethorn stopped briefly to give him a handful of oats, then swung into the saddle on the fresh horse.

Briar looked at the drizzling clouds, wishing he and Rosethorn had the wide straw hats they usually wore in the rain. Where had the hats gone? East, probably, with the Traders. He hauled himself into the saddle of his own mount.

"Are you up to a trot?" the sergeant in charge of the squad asked Rosethorn. "So we can cover some ground?"

"I'll keep up," Rosethorn said. "Don't worry about me."

Briar rode beside her, one careful eye on his teacher. He could tell she was upset, but he knew her. To the others she must look as if she were deep in thought. That's good, he told himself. She hates people feeling bad for her.

For his own part, he had Evvy's stone alphabet in the sling on his chest, tucked among the seed balls he used for weapons. Now and then he would slip a rock or crystal from its pocket and hold it, reminding himself of what he owed the emperor and his soldiers.

They set a rhythm of trot, walk, trot, rest. They would water the horses, drink tea, check to make sure their weapons were ready for use, and then mount up again. That steady pace brought them to the supply wagons by late afternoon. At day's end they found Parahan, Soudamini, Captain Lango, and their soldiers. They were raising their tents at the far end of the ground where the western tribes and temple warriors had set up camp. Their friends greeted Rosethorn, expressed their sympathy for her loss, and invited her and Briar to join them for supper.

Free of her temple's burden, Rosethorn was happy to share a tent with Briar. Jimut saw to the arrangements, placing it to one side of Souda's far larger tent. While they waited for the call to eat, Jimut also brought out Rosethorn's packs, which had traveled with their supplies. She and Briar sat quietly, going over what they had.

Finally Briar had to ask. "What was it like?"

Rosethorn sighed. "I can't say."

"Wasn't it just a temple?"

"It was and it wasn't. I can't put it any better than that."

"You could try."

"Briar, it's not permitted. I had to swear an oath."

He knew she meant it. "I *hate* that, you know. Just once you could break an oath."

"Then how would you ever trust me, boy, or I you?"

"I'm not your *boy*."

In a shocking burst of affection, she leaned over the seed balls between them and hugged him. "You will always be my boy. And you would never listen to me again if I broke an oath."

"You know Parahan and them will ask." He hugged her back, and let go at the same time that she did.

"They will have something like the same answer." Rosethorn sighed. For a moment they were quiet together before she said, "I will be so glad to go home."

"I know what you mean," he said fervently. "This country is just too odd, Rosethorn. The paintings come to life and make fun of you —"

"There are mysteries I was never taught in my temple," she added.

"Statues move around."

"I hear voices that shouldn't be there. Emelan is wonderfully ordinary," Rosethorn said. "We'll go home, and this place will seem like a distant dream. It has to."

In the morning word spread through the army like wildfire: The scouts had found plenty of hoof prints on the road ahead and on the ground to the east. The enemy had been here before them. With the news that the enemy had come so close, the westerners were eager to be up and moving at dawn. Their fires were out and their tents packed at the same time as Souda's and Parahan's troops.

That day saw the Realms troops and Lango's company in the middle of the line of march, since they'd had the rear the day before. Briar yawned without letup. He had joined Rosethorn for her midnight worship, knowing she would conduct prayers for Evvy in the darkness. He did not begrudge Evvy's spirit some of his sleep, not when he and Rosethorn could now burn the proper incense and say the prayers that felt like balm to his heart.

The day was uneventful but tense. They rode by a walled village: Its gates were closed and its people positioned on the wall, armed with crossbows. A small party of villagers rode out to confer with Captain Lango. The commanders of the various portions of their group stopped beside the road to talk while the rest of them rode on. Then they rejoined their people. Immediately scouting patrols were increased, riding in all directions around their small army.

Briar eased up through the soldiers until he rode next to Souda when she returned. "How close to them are we?" he asked.

She frowned at him. "Perhaps you are new to armies. Perhaps you don't know that it's not common for commanders to share information with soldiers unless it's absolutely necessary."

"But you have to share information with your mages, don't you?" he asked, giving Souda his most innocent look. "It might be something we can work with."

"You're *plant mages*," Souda replied. "What can — oh, Raiya, give me patience. The riders who came too close this morning are a rear guard. There's a small army two days ahead of us and moving a hawk's anus faster than we are, because they don't have a monkey-spit supply train to worry about! It's those swine who attacked the Temple of the Tigers, from what the people in the town told Lango. You'd think they'd turn around and give us a nice straight-up fight!" She glared at the open lands on her right, then frowned. "Now who do you suppose that is? Don't tell me I'm going to get my wish!"

Briar squinted. A new rider watched them from a distance, far enough that Briar couldn't see what the observer wore or if he carried weapons. He sent his power into the grass roots, reaching for the watcher, but the man wheeled and rode away before Briar's magic got to him. He glanced at Rosethorn, who shook her head. She hadn't touched the watcher, either.

Souda whistled sharply. This time she sent two of her soldiers after the stranger. They soon returned. They had lost him.

One of the tribesmen spotted the next watcher; Parahan's scouts reported a third. By nightfall a total of six watchers had been seen. None had been caught.

"Theirs or ours, do you think?" Briar heard Parahan ask Captain Lango.

The Gyongxin man was grim. "Yanjingyi armor, Yanjingyi spies."

All the commanders put the soldiers to digging a broad ditch around their camp that night. Rosethorn sprinkled a few seeds at the bottom of the ditch, just in case. They would take the place of abatises if the enemy attacked. A word from Rosethorn or Briar and the seeds would send thorny branches shooting up to surprise anyone who tried to cross the ditch. The only side of their camp not so defended was on a wide pond.

The creation of a tighter camp seemed to make the soldiers feel more like one army. When Briar volunteered for guard duty, he found himself trading nods of greeting with tribesmen, temple warriors, and Realms soldiers who had the same duty. One tribesman even offered Briar a chew of betel nut, though Briar politely turned him down. He thought orange teeth might ruin his appeal for girls at home in Emelan.

Staring at the stars, he realized that the constellation called the Herdsman was starting to rise over the horizon. He picked out the ancient hero's head and earring, his shoulders, his belt, and the one visible arm with its sling, ready to drive a rock straight between the eyes of the Lion of Shaihun. It was one of Evvy's favorite stories. On their road east, she had insisted on pointing out the Herdsman every night she could see it.

Briar's eyes filled as he looked at it. He wiped them on his sleeve.

I'm not going to get all weepy every time I see a shepherd with a sling, he told himself. That's not fair to Evvy. And this country has herders with slings everywhere I look.

Then he frowned. It was hard to shoot a seed ball from a crossbow. The archer drew the string until the head of the bolt almost touched the stock, leaving scant room to tie the ball. A seed ball was too light to go far on its own, but a sling could throw a seed ball if the ball were weighted somehow.

Briar looked at the earth under his feet. There were stones in it. He picked one up and tossed it in his hand.

Rosethorn took his place when the guard changed, sending him off to bed. Once he pulled his blankets up around him, Briar slept without dreams.

He woke in the morning to a normal camp. No one had tested the sentries. While Jimut grumbled about it as he brought tea for Briar and Rosethorn, Briar was just as happy. He prized his sleep.

He helped Rosethorn to do up the laces on her cuirass and greaves; she returned the favor. Both of them settled their carry-bags full of seed balls over their chests.

Briar nearly collided with Jimut when he walked out of the tent. His aide was bringing the dumplings called *momos* for their breakfast. "Do you know anyone who is good with a sling?" Briar asked him. "Someone who can put a rock close to a reasonable target."

Jimut shrugged. "I can," he replied, offering *momos* to Rosethorn as he emerged from the tent. "I helped my father and uncles with the herds before I decided to be a soldier. When I hunt for the company I save arrows with my sling."

"Would you start carrying one with you?" Briar asked. "I'd like to be able to work at more of a distance."

Jimut frowned, and then bowed. "Of course."

"I think I would like a slinger, too," Rosethorn said. She ruffled Briar's short hair, which was starting to grow out. "Clever Briar."

Briar pulled a tuft of hair out to see how long it was. "I need this cut." He was strict about keeping it an inch long. That way it never curled and it dried fast.

"Just don't let the emperor's barbers do it," Parahan said cheerfully. "They could make a mistake and take your whole head." He turned his beak of a nose into the wind from the east. "I smell battle coming. It's about time."

"Savage," Rosethorn told him.

"We are civilized about wars in Kombanpur," Parahan replied. "We study long and hard for them so we do not dishonor our enemies by giving them a bad fight." His dark face went a shade darker. "And we do not kill their little girls."

"I wish every warrior was as tidy about it as you," Rosethorn said.

"I wish some little girls I know were here to help fight," Briar said. "They'd give these muck-snufflers a lesson they'd never forget." He saw some likely looking stones and bent stiffly to pick them up. It was hard to do in armor.

"We use what we have," Rosethorn told him. "It will be enough."

After breakfast the small army set forth once again. Souda had placed their three companies in the middle of the march. "If we're attacked, I want regular soldiers in the middle," she explained to Rosethorn and Briar as they rode along. "We worked out that the temple soldiers will bring the supply animals up with us and guard them in the event of a fight. The tribes will ride into the enemy flanks. If we hold here at the middle, we might just make a battle plan of it."

Rosethorn nodded. "If we have to fight, it's a good plan," she replied.

"But I have seen you fight," Parahan commented with surprise. "You did not hang back."

"I am like most who take up a religious life in our wicked world," Rosethorn said. As she and Briar rode, they used their magic to open the seed balls and drop thumb-sized stones into them. Another touch of magic wove the cotton together once more. "I will not surrender to evil, or allow anyone in my charge to be harmed by evil, and violence that kills the helpless and destroys the beauties of the world is evil. But I am also a healer. It can be depressing to have to repair what you took apart that morning."

"There are religious orders that live in isolation and refuse to commit any violence," Souda remarked.

"I hope they are mages who can defend or hide themselves, then," Rosethorn replied. "I and mine, we live in the real world."

Everyone ate midday in the saddle. Not long after that a cloud of dust rolled toward them across the flatlands from the east. The tribal shamans began a heavy, droning chant like that Briar had heard in the temples and in the canyon behind Garmashing. It was a song with a buzz under it, much like the sound of the great horns. As the shamans chanted they pounded small drums or banged little gongs. Goose bumps prickled all over Briar: They were raising Gyongxin magic.

He passed a cloth seed ball to Jimut, who already had his sling in hand. Rosethorn's slinger balanced his cloth ball in his hand, noticing the weight. He raised his brows, then settled it into his sling.

Whatever the other mages had put in motion, it seemed to be working. The dust cloud was breaking up and drifting skyward. As it thinned, it revealed several companies of imperial horsemen.

"Archers!" cried Parahan, Souda, and Lango at the same time.

"Wait," Briar murmured to Jimut. He heard a change in the chanting of the shamans. Lango's mage had also begun something of his own.

Briar shifted his attention to the grasses that grew ahead of the enemy horses' hooves. Under the earth's surface, he followed his power into their roots.

He didn't hear the commanders giving the archers the order to shoot. In the part of him that stayed with his body he noticed that Jimut and Rosethorn's slinger released their balls of weighted seed at the same time. Seed and arrows soared high, then fell among the enemy soldiers even as the Yanjingyi archers shot. The Gyongxin tribes and temple warriors on the right and left attacked, charging under most of the Yanjingyi volley of arrows. Those were aimed for the commanders and mages on the road.

Parahan, Souda, and Lango barked the order for the archers to prepare to shoot again. Briar urged his body to hand a second thorn ball to his slinger, as Rosethorn was doing, and returned to his work on the grasses ahead.

He heard shrieking war cries: The tribal and temple warriors were colliding with Yanjingyi horsemen on the right and the left. The center of the Yanjingyi line began to charge, bellowing in return.

Lango and the twins yelled the order to shoot; the archers obeyed, aiming at the heart of the charging line. Riders and horses went down. Jimut and Rosethorn's slinger released their seed balls to strike the enemy soldiers who still galloped on.

They were falling even before the balls hit the ground and exploded. Growing ferociously, the grasses enveloped the horses' hooves. The animals went down, throwing their riders. In the heart of the army, warriors screamed as thorny vines shot through and around them. Horses reared, trying to shake the grip of the tough grasses. They dropped under the hooves of those horses galloping up behind them.

Some of the thorns and grass went gray. Some burst into flame, burning the soldiers in their grasp. Briar fumbled as he passed another ball to Jimut, his fingers going numb. A strange green veil was falling over his eyes; his throat had gone too tight to breathe. He clawed at it, gasping.

Suddenly air rushed into his throat. He inhaled several times, filling his poor lungs, then looked for the cause of his sudden cure. Jimut was holding an oblong disk in front of his face. "Are you all right?" the man asked.

"Better, thanks. What *is* that?" Briar wanted to know.

Jimut turned the disk around for a moment, then turned it back so the polished side faced the enemy. It was a metal mirror. It had reflected the enemy's spell back to them.

Briar checked Rosethorn. A temple mage with her face tattooed all over with interesting patterns had ridden her horse next to Rosethorn. She wrote signs on the air between her and Briar's teacher. As she worked, Rosethorn sat with her hands palm up in her lap, peacefully gazing at the battle before them. Vines were growing rapidly, twining around enemy warriors and yanking them from the saddle to be trampled in the fighting. Whatever the temple mage was doing, she held the Yanjingyi mages off Rosethorn, it was plain.

Briar let Rosethorn work with the vines. There was a cluster of stillness in the spot where the Yanjingyi soldiers had waited before their charge. He would wager that was where the mages and perhaps the commanders watched the fighting. He closed his eyes and poured his magical self through the grass roots between him and that stillness. The grasses lent him their strength as he ran from root to root.

The Yanjingyi mages' power shone like a beacon even underground, guiding him to them. Below them in the earth, Briar drew on the vast network of plants that stretched out around him and carefully reached up with his power. There were the above-ground grasses that grew around the horses' hooves. Out of habit they tried to eat a mouthful or two, but these were the finest products of the army's stables. The plants of the Gyongxin plain were a little too tough for their liking. Sensing Briar's presence in the grass, they huffed and stamped, only to be slapped by the soldiers who held their reins. Neither the generals nor the mages wanted to be disturbed by restless animals.

Briar stretched himself above the grasses, searching for the beads wrapped around the mages' throats and wrists. He could not tell if the general was also a mage, as General Hengkai had been. He could only sense the wooden beads. In his magical vision they hung in midair, shaping three necks and three pairs of arms. He gripped his power for just a moment, then flooded the beads with it.

The willow beads shattered, breaking the strands around the mages' necks and arms. The oak beads sent roots shooting into the ground. The grasses told him that the horses had gone frantic at the sudden appearance of fast-growing trees. They reared and flailed at everything around them. The mages were thrown to the ground. At Briar's command the grasses seized the mages, weaving around their throats. Strangling would teach them to kill little girls!

His rage fed strength to the grasses. They grew and tightened like rope.

That's it! Briar told the grasses. Don't give way for an instant!

Rosethorn was calling him. He refused to go. He wasn't going to leave just when he was paying the Yanjingyi beasts back.

Then he got that bad feeling, the sense of fingers wrapped around his body's real ear. The fingers twisted. Only one thing would make that pain stop. Slowly, so he wouldn't frighten his grasses and oak trees, he retreated across the field and back into the body that hurt with Evvy's loss.

He opened his eyes. Rosethorn released his ear after an extra hard flick with finger and thumb. "What if we'd had to escape?" Rosethorn demanded. "Do you know how many mages get trapped away from themselves?"

"You never said anything before," he muttered, rubbing the sore ear. He wondered if the grasses had succeeded in killing those mages.

"It wasn't a danger with you before." Rosethorn sighed. "Revenge is as bad for the one practicing it as it is for those it's practiced upon, Briar."

He didn't agree. She probably has to say such things because she's a dedicate, he thought, gulping tea from the flask at his belt. But I ain't no dedicate, and I'm going to get me a piece of the empire.

He looked to see what other damage he could do.

The enemy was fleeing, or rather, those who were in good condition had fled already. Those who remained swayed in the saddle or sported arrows in their own bodies or those of their mounts. Some were on foot, fighting back to back as they tried to hold off the Gyongxin warriors.

All across the ground between the road and the remainder of the Yanjingyi troops lay the fallen of both sides: horses, the wounded, and the dead. The Gyongxin healers were driving their wagons around the troops in the road and out onto the field.

Briar shook his head. "I won't do it. They killed Evvy."

"All of them?" Rosethorn asked.

"They killed other people here, too."

"How many of them were given a choice about it?" she asked him. "You know the emperor. How many of them have families in Yanjing who would be punished if they refused to serve in the army? Besides —"

"I don't want to hear besides." He sounded like a kid even to himself.

"The more of them that have decent treatment here, the more of them will know that Weishu's is not the only way. The more of them will realize that these people are not monsters." Rosethorn dismounted and unbuckled her saddlebags. "You don't have to come," she said. "I'll understand." To the woman who had guarded her from the Yanjingyi mages' spells she said, "Mila and the Green Man bless you, Servant Riverdancer." The shaman pressed her hands palm to palm in front of her face and bowed. Rosethorn turned to her slinger and thanked him as well. He offered to take care of the horse. Rosethorn nodded, then proceeded out onto the battlefield.

Briar sighed. He could look after the Gyongxin wounded. That wouldn't make him feel as if he betrayed Evvy's ghost.

"Do you know what wagon has my mage kit?" Briar asked Jimut.

"The part with your medicines?" the older man inquired. He patted the bags behind the saddle of his own horse. "Right here." He handed them down to Briar, who took them and went in search of the small army's healers.

The soldiers raised big infirmary tents where the healers could work, then fetched empty barrels and filled them with water. Those who did not bring the wounded into the tents gave the injured horses a merciful death. They then dragged the animals' bodies to the side of the battlefield opposite that where they laid out the human dead. Cooks set up outdoor kitchens for soup and tea for everyone as the rest of the camp was built around the healers' tents.

Briar, Rosethorn, Riverdancer, and the rest of the healers labored well past midnight in the chaos that filled the tents. The screams of the wounded were enough to make Briar want to scream himself. To make sure that he didn't, he bit the inside of his cheek until it bled, then found a piece of rolled bandage to chew on. There weren't enough medicines to ensure that everyone could have their pain eased. The healers were forced to keep such potions for the unfortunates who had to have a leg or an arm cut off, or a weapon pulled from their bodies. Mage after mage was sent from the tents, worn to exhaustion, while more wounded were brought in or came to consciousness.

Jimut and a number of other people Briar recognized from the road worked in the tents together with the mages and healers, helping to hold patients for stitching or surgery, wrapping bandages, carrying water, and sitting with the dying. Briar even saw their commanders throughout the night. They came to talk to their people and even to fetch water or soup when everyone else was busy.

At last Riverdancer ordered both him and Rosethorn to bed, reminding them through a translator that they had used their power in combat as well as in healing. They needed rest. Their medicines could continue to work without their presence, she informed them tartly, and there was less risk of a medicine collapsing onto a patient.

In his bedroll, Briar was staring at the roof of the tent, listening to Rosethorn's sleep-breath, when he realized that he hadn't seen any wounded Yanjingyi soldiers. The other healers must have steered him away from them.

Just as well, he thought. That way I don't have to make any hard choices.

He felt around until he found Evvy's stone alphabet by his packs. With his hand resting on it, he slept.

CHAPTER
EIGHTEEN

Under and on the Gnam Runga Plain
Between the Temple of the Tigers and
the town of Melonam

Under Gnam Runga, Evvy lost track of time. It was hard to remember days without sunlight. Her companions did not help: One counted time in thousand-year chunks and the other didn't talk. Except for brief stints running and necessity halts, Evvy stayed on Big Milk, even to sleep.

Luvo told her about the coming of the Realms of the Sun and how that slab of land had shoved the edge of what would be Gyongxe higher and higher to form the Drimbakangs, youngest of all the world's mountains. She told him about Briar, Rosethorn, and the things they had seen as they had traveled east. That seemed to require many more explanations than Luvo's stories. He found humans mystifying, particularly the human need to take things from other humans, and to put an end to other humans' lives without the need to eat them. He was also curious about what Evvy had learned to do with stones. She managed to collect a few new stones from the walls and floor of the tunnel, teaching some to produce light or warmth if they had the capability for either.

The tunnel had plenty of strange pictures on the earthen walls, pictures given odd movement by the green fungus that was the sole source of light. Evvy examined the pictures every chance she got at first. She was eyeing one that seemed to be a spindle-legged horse with a bird's head when she turned to find a creature just like it staring at her.

She screamed. So did the creature. It clattered into the dark on impossibly thin legs, followed by three others that would have been colts if it had been a horse. Big Milk, who was eating one of the heaps of grass that someone had left at intervals, looked at Evvy with a reproachful eye.

"Evumeimei, you must not scream at the deep runners because they are not what you are used to," Luvo told her mildly. "This is their country after all."

"Their country?" cried Evvy, clambering onto Big Milk's back, where Luvo already waited. "It's a tunnel underground!"

"Underground is where they and their kindred live, unless danger brings them to the surface."

"The God-King and Dokyi never said anything about horse-birds!"

"Forgive me, Evumeimei, but from what you have told me about your friends, it seems to me they did not tell you the greatest part of the secrets of Gyongxe."

Evvy sat cross-legged on Big Milk's broad, solid back and propped her chin on her hands. "No, I suppose not. Please don't feel insulted, Luvo, but even though you have the most splendid mountains I have ever seen, I will be glad when I leave here. Gyongxe is too strange for me."

"Would you not become accustomed to things?"

Evvy started on a little braid in Big Milk's fur. She had made quite a few of them so far out of the yak's hair and brightly colored threads from her clothes. Luvo had said the giant yak did not mind. Evvy found it was good to focus on braiding in the green-lit gloom of the vast tunnel during those bad times when she might otherwise dwell on the smiling Jia Jui as she raised the rod over Evvy's feet.

"No, Luvo," Evvy said. She couldn't tell him the cold winds would always remind her of the piled dead, or that the jeweled night sky would show her the picture of her cats' limp bodies. "I'm sorry." Something scampered by overhead. She bent close to Big Milk's fur so she wouldn't see what it was.

The army remained in camp for a day, to give the wounded a chance to rest. After a heated conference and some back-and-forthing of messengers, two companies of warriors took the Yanjingyi prisoners and wounded back to the village they had passed the day before. They could not spare soldiers to guard captives as well as their own wounded on the road. The companies returned well before sunset.

Briar heard all of this from his friends among the twins' and Lango's companies. He did not wake until twilight. When he joined them at their cook fire, they hooted at him.

"I overreached, that's all," he growled. "I got a little tired."

"You had best make a decision," Parahan said, handing him a full bowl.

Briar accepted the bowl and blinked at the big man. "Decision?"

"Fight or heal once the serious battles start. You can't do both without half killing yourself. Most mages don't even try," Parahan said.

Briar frowned. He had always thought mages chose to be healers or war mages because they hadn't the talent to do both. It hadn't occurred to him that they might simply be conserving their strength. "But me and Rosethorn fought and then did healing on our way east, when bandits attacked our caravans," he said. "And Rosethorn fought the pirates back home and then did healing after."

"I used my medicines when we fought pirates," Rosethorn corrected him. "I cleaned wounds and bandaged them. I didn't put added strength into my medicines, not when I might need it for the thorns on the beach. Parahan's right. We won't be able to do much healing and fighting at the same time, not once we face real armies. We didn't do anything like that on the way here."

"Do you have to choose?" Briar asked.

"Of course," she replied. "Moreover, I'm sure General Sayrugo will prefer we use our abilities as battle mages. This army is short of them."

"Not that you're exactly battle mages," Souda remarked.

Rosethorn chuckled. "We aren't what the generals order when they call for battle mages at all. We can't throw fire, we can't make things explode, and we can't send a hundred catapult stones flying through the air at once."

"Hey!" Briar said, offended. "We can do better things than that!"

"Oh, he's a man, all right," Souda said, rolling her eyes. Riverdancer laughed once her translator relayed what the princess had said.

"We can," Briar argued, grinning. "We can put acres of thorn vines down among the enemy in a flash. We can ask the grasses to tangle the soldiers' feet and the feet of the horses. We can make their wood useless to them. You'll see!"

"They *will* see," Rosethorn agreed. "And I have a few other ideas. Most of the temple mages and shamans are healers, and they can use our medicines. We'll help in the tents when we can, but when it comes time for armies, we are battle mages." She got to her feet and wandered off into the darkness.

Briar returned to their tent to make sure his armor was in order and he had plenty of seed balls ready for the next day, then went over Rosethorn's things as well. When he began to yawn, he went to use the privy for the last time.

On his way back to bed, Briar saw Rosethorn and Parahan talking in the shadows near one of the supply tents. They stood close together — very close. He squinted, trying to get a better look without going over to them. Something in their postures said they would not welcome an interruption. Then Parahan rested a hand on Rosethorn's hip.

Briar turned away and briskly walked to his tent. He knew that Rosethorn sometimes slept with people other than Lark. He knew that *Lark* knew that Rosethorn sometimes slept with other people than her. Rosethorn had done so twice since they had left Winding Circle. Briar simply was never certain how he felt about it. This was the first time he actually knew one of those someones before anything happened.

Why am I surprised? he wondered as he pulled off his boots. They've been circling around each other since we met up near the border. And it's Parahan. If I was *damohi*, I'd give Parahan the eye myself.

Am I worried she'll decide to stay here? Because she won't. She doesn't love the plants here like the ones back home; she hates the emperor; Gyongxe doesn't have near enough trees, and I don't think she'd ever let go of Lark.

He was still trying to decide what his feelings were when he fell asleep.

By the time she left Parahan's tent at dawn, Rosethorn felt more normal than she had in some time. Evvy's loss remained an ache deep in her heart, but overall Rosethorn felt as if her body was her own once more, not a puppet that moved at the directions of the Treasures and the priests of the Sealed Eye. For the first time, with Parahan, she had not heard the faint whispers that had been in her mind since she took charge of the Treasures.

He'd been every bit the lover she had hoped, too, humorous and caring, attentive without smothering her. His queen, whoever he chose one day, would be a lucky woman. She sent a prayer up to Mila of the Fields and Grain that he would find someone who could appreciate him.

They had deliberately not spoken of the war all night. Now Rosethorn's awareness of it returned as she greeted her friends in the camp. Everyone was up and preparing to move, packing the tents and loading supply animals and wagons. Briar must have gone to breakfast, she decided when she walked into their tent. His gear was ready. Only his armor and her own lay out. Her things, of course, had not been touched since she had put them in the tent last night.

She could hear the creaks and groans of thawing ice and snow in the mountains as the thin sunlight warmed everything. Somewhere closer a horse grumbled deep in his chest. She frowned. It seemed too far away to be one of their own horses. Had they sent out scouts, or were these enemy spies? She cursed the day she'd touched the Treasures. The lingering effects made her life so confusing. Namka of the Sealed Eye said they would wear off in time. The problem was that his idea of time seemed to be very relaxed by her standards.

She was struggling with her armor when Briar returned from breakfast. Seeing his knowing smirk and realizing he knew where she'd spent her night, she cocked an eyebrow, daring him to give her sauce about it. Only once had he questioned her right to choose sleeping partners as she wished. They'd had a nice talk about choices being between someone and that someone's lover, and there had been no more discussion. She had only had to lightly slap the back of his head for foolishness once.

Apparently Briar remembered their talk, because all he said was, "Did you have breakfast?"

"Spicy eggs and rice with that puffy white flatbread," she said. "I think my eyes are still watering from the chilies." She shook her head. Her mouth was still burning a little. "It wakes me up better than tea, though. You could have joined us. Parahan and Souda asked where you were."

Briar shrugged. "We had mushroom pancakes over at Riverdancer's fire — very nice." He saw her struggle with the side lacings of her cuirass. "Here, I'll manage that, and you tie mine." She lifted her arms so he could see better. As he tightened the woven silk cords he inhaled and murmured, "I smell sandalwood."

She slapped his head lightly. "I smell impudence."

Once she had tied Briar's armor for him, she gave him one of the cloth bags she had prepared while he slept like a statue the day before. "I was able to bring some of our thorn plants to full seeding growth to stock us up again. I wasn't exhausted as you were. Of course, I didn't send my magical self halfway to Yanjing and try to fight a battle that way."

"Complain, complain, complain," Briar muttered as he tucked the bag into the sling he hung over his chest. She knew he had spare rocks and squares of cloth in it, as she did in hers. They could create more thorn balls in the saddle if all remained quiet this morning.

"No, caution, caution, caution," she retorted. It was an old argument between them. "We aren't invulnerable, and you won't avenge Evvy if you're dead as well." She turned away. "I don't want to tell Lark I lost you." The absence of Evvy throbbed like the loss of a tooth. The loss of Briar would be so much worse. If anything happened to him that she could have prevented, she didn't know how she would live with it. Jimut poked his head into the tent. "If the honored *prebus* will come out, I will pack you up," he said cheerfully. "Their Highnesses want to ride soon, and we're at the front today."

Once they were packed up and riding, Rosethorn found herself near the very head of their group where Parahan and his guards rode. She had Riverdancer, her translator, Briar, and Jimut for company. Souda and the western chief called Glacier Cracks each took fifty volunteers and split off, Souda going east, Glacier Cracks riding west. They were scouting to see if they could find any stray Yanjingyi raiders. They had promised to catch up with their northbound comrades sometime during the afternoon.

Rosethorn heard Briar and Jimut sigh enviously as they watched Souda go. "Don't be so eager to find battles," she warned them, not wanting to mention the soft grumble she heard from very far in the north, near the ceaseless temple horns and gongs of Garmashing. "There will be enough for everyone eventually."

"This is just march, march, maybe a squabble, healing, and then more marching," Briar explained. "Why don't they just settle down and *fight*?"

Parahan overheard. "Why should they, if they can tire us out first?"

Rosethorn, who had been through a few large battles, didn't tell Briar she was just as happy to put off the next one. She knew he would think her spiritless. He was young.

They halted to water the animals and to eat a midday meal, albeit a cold one. Glacier Cracks and his people returned halfway through the afternoon. They had found an empty village and a fortified temple with its gates locked and armed warriors on its wall. They had not seen any sign of the enemy between the road and the Tom Sho River.

Rosethorn and Riverdancer, through her translator, struck up a conversation about healers' spells. Rosethorn was getting some interesting ideas from the shaman. The conversation also distracted her from the nagging question: Where were Souda and her fifty riders? Had they found trouble east of the main road?

Troops on their way to join whatever was making that noise so far ahead?

The afternoon dragged. The sun inched down with no sign of the eastern group. With the wind blowing from the north, the pesky leftover effects of the Treasures gave Rosethorn no sign of whether there was an army in the east or not.

She was better able to hide her fidgets than were Briar and Parahan. The men of Souda's company who had not gone with her grew even testier with the passage of time. Leaving the column to ride back to the water barrels, Rosethorn saw that the healers were preparing for wounded, piling their supplies on the sides of their wagons so they could lay a few of the injured flat. Refilling her water flask, she noticed how very quiet everyone was, even the tribal warriors. The temple soldiers had prayer beads out and were softly chanting as they marched.

When she rejoined Riverdancer and her translator, she saw that several Kombanpur warriors were talking with Parahan. One of them waved his arms and shouted.

"They want to go search for the missing. Lord Parahan says they're fools to ask." Jimut translated the Banpuri for them. "He says if the lady and her people are taken, any searchers will be captured, too."

The sun's edge had touched the distant peaks when Rosethorn saw Riverdancer look to the east. A hill stood between them and anything that might be going on, but when the shaman reined up, Rosethorn did as well. Within a moment everyone heard the drawn-out blast of a battle horn, not one of the Gyongxin horns.

"Jimut?" Briar asked.

"Enemies!" Jimut said, reaching for his crossbow. "Er — do you want me to use a sling?"

Rosethorn shook her head. If the enemy came over the hill, or even around it, their chances were too good that the balls would roll back to the Gyongxin troops. "Not this time, I think," she said. "Too risky."

Briar could see what she saw. "What, then?"

"Off the road on the left," she told him. "We're healers today." She turned and waved her arm over her head to let the columns of Banpuri warriors know she wanted an opening in the road, a split in their numbers. Slowly, with perfect discipline, they opened a corridor for her.

To the east, soldiers galloped into sight along the shoulder of the hill. These were their people, clad in the earth-colored tunics of the western tribes or the armor of the Realms of the Sun and Gyongxe. Some of them barely clung to their saddles. Others were riding double.

"This way!" she cried, backing her horse down the opening between the soldiers at her back. The healers would come to her, as they had discussed in planning as they rode.

"This way!" yelled Briar. Riverdancer, her translator, and Jimut were shouting the same thing in their own languages. There was a ripple among the eastern edge of the column of soldiers: They beckoned the galloping soldiers to them. Behind their racing allies came the enemy, several hundred Yanjingyi swordsmen and archers.

Rosethorn grabbed one of their wounded as he came through the opening in their front ranks, dragging him across her saddle with a care for the arrow that jutted from his back. A soldier ran forward to seize the reins to the wounded man's frantic horse. Briar grabbed the bridle of the next mount. The rider was able to stay upright; she had a sword cut that bled into her eye.

Healers ran forward to take Rosethorn's wounded soldier from her saddle. "Carefully," she cautioned them. "He's got an arrow in his back." They nodded and carried the soldier facedown to a wagon.

Rosethorn looked for Briar. He had turned his mount over to a soldier and kept his medicine packs. He began to examine those with lighter injuries as they came in, mostly cleaning sword cuts. Riverdancer's translator stood beside him, a roll of bandages in her hand.

One by one everyone on the opening in their lines caught one of the wounded and guided them to the healers. Once they were relieved of their charges, they returned for more wounded, if any came, and to fight. The Yanjingyi archers were raining crossbow bolts into their ranks.

Rosethorn glanced at the returning warriors who rode to Parahan. One was a dusty Soudamini. She held a bloody sword, but showed no injuries herself. She spoke rapidly to her twin as the small army's archers shot into the oncoming enemy troops.

Rosethorn turned at the sound of a cry and ran to help two wounded on one horse as they came through the opening in the lines. The air around her filled with the sergeants' yells for archers to take aim, then shoot. After that she was too busy to keep track of what took place along the battle lines.

As a plant mage who had also studied healing, she had learned her fair share of basic surgery. Riverdancer came to help as she began to remove arrows from the flesh of the wounded. It was nervous work. To stay calm, Rosethorn focused only on her assistants. She had been known to cut while a temple was falling down around her. It was a useful skill to have that day. They had no sooner cared for Souda's wounded when those hurt in the more recent fight with the Yanjingyi soldiers began to come in.

Finally Rosethorn stopped to catch her breath. She hadn't realized that it was already dark. Someone shoved a large pottery mug of tea, heavily buttered and sweetened, into her hand. She gulped it thirstily.

"How are you managing?"

She looked up and blinked at Souda. "Well enough." Her voice came out a croak. "How goes the fighting?"

Souda shrugged. "The enemy has retreated to the other side of this ridge. Parahan split his warriors. Half of the archers are up there." She pointed to the top of the hill. "They have them pinned down, I think, but it's too dark to tell. . . . What's that?"

Over the hill a greenish light bloomed brightly enough to show the archers Souda had mentioned. Rosethorn finished the mug of tea, forcing herself to stay calm. That green light was mage work. None of the mages in their small army was capable of that kind of spell and neither she nor Briar did magic that cast a light.

"I'll go look," she heard Briar say. "If they have willow or oak or gingko on them, I'll put a stop to that."

"Briar!" she cried, but he'd taken a saddleless horse and ridden off around the side of the hill. The hill itself was too steep for a rider.

They were bringing another wounded victim from the

battlefield. This one had a gash down his chest. If she didn't clean it and get it sewn, he would die of infection. She could treat these people, or she could go after her boy.

An open sword cut that bared ribs had to come first. Briar was sixteen and a man in the view of the world. She raised a prayer to Yanna Healtouch for the warrior before her and to the Green Man for Briar's safety. Then she got to work.

Riverdancer sent her off much later; she didn't know what time. No one had seen Briar. They promised to look for him if she would only rest. Rosethorn hesitated, but her hands were shaking; she needed food and a break. The tents were up, including one for the healers. She lay on a mattress there and told herself to wake in two hours, no matter how tired she might be.

Someone was shaking her awake. It was Jimut. Seeing the look on his face, she struggled to her feet. Then she followed him at a run. He took her straight to the healers' tent.

Two assistants were caring for a warrior by lamplight. One of them cleaned his bruised face. The other was carefully trying to cut his leather breeches away from the gash in his thigh.

The warrior was Briar.

Jimut was talking to her, but his words could have been thunder for all she understood him. For a moment she thought she would go to pieces. Her bones felt loose and watery. Her father's ghost shouted in her ear, "Don't you come the pretty princess, Niva! Get your arm in there and ease that calf out or I'll give you so many stripes you'll sleep on your belly for a month! There's a chamber pot because I won't let you so much as go to the privy, so do as I bid!"

Thanks, Da, she thought as she stepped over to the cot. She felt for Briar's pulse — strong — and his warmth — colder than she liked, but he was wounded. She glanced at his thigh. The healer cutting the leather breeches off was carefully pulling them away from the wound. It was deep and dirty.

Rosethorn peeled back one of Briar's eyelids. They had given him something for pain already. His pupil was wide enough that she could barely see his gray-green iris. That was good. She would have to hurt him to clean the slash, and she preferred that he was not awake for that.

Hot water. She would need —

One of the assistants stood on the far side of the cot, a pot of hot water cushioned by wrappings in her hands and clean cloths over one arm. Briar's clothes were cut away and dumped elsewhere. For a moment Rosethorn turned her back to the cot, closed her eyes, and prayed to Yanna Healtouch of the Water temple for healing, the Green Man to ward off the racing growth of infection, and Shurri Flamesword of the Fire temple for a steady hand. Then she turned back to the cot and began to clean the gaping slash. Blood followed. As soon as Rosethorn was done, Riverdancer swiftly placed a padded bandage on Briar's thigh and pressed to control the bleeding. They waited for a few moments. The woman lifted the pad and they replaced it with a clean one. Rosethorn pressed this one, counting to herself for what seemed like forever. When she lifted it, there was blood, but less of it.

"Praise Yanna," she whispered. In *tiyon* she added, "It appears no big veins were cut." She switched for a clean pad and let someone else press. She went through her medicines for one to cleanse and one to hold the inside of the wound together.

This time, when they removed the pad, Rosethorn warned the others. "Hold him, please," she said. "He's going to jump." When they had him by the hands, shoulders, and legs, Rosethorn said, not caring if Briar was awake or not, "This will hurt, my lad, but not as much as you will hurt when I talk with you in the morning." She swiftly dribbled the cleansing potion in the open wound.

Briar arched against the cot and the hands that kept him on it, his eyelids flying open. He let out a screech. Riverdancer leaned over his head, a vial in her hand. She showed it to Rosethorn, who sniffed and recognized it as a potent sleep and pain medication favored by Gyongxin healers. She nodded.

Riverdancer let three drops fall into Briar's open mouth. He swallowed, coughed, and relaxed back onto the cot. As his eyelids fluttered down, Rosethorn added a thin line of the medicine that would hold the inner muscle of his thigh together like a line of stitches. By the time she was done, Briar was snoring.

Rosethorn smiled grimly and turned back to her medicines. She would need a needle and gut to sew up Briar's skin, and then a healing potion for that.

By the time she had finished, she felt dizzy. "Would someone bandage him?" she asked in *tiyon*.

Kind hands steered her away from the cot as Riverdancer took over. Someone pressed a cup not of tea but of broth into her hands. She sipped from it carefully. From time to time she wiped away tears that ran down her face on her sleeve.

When Briar awoke, he felt as if someone had used his head for a drum. Worse, Daja had taken one of her white-hot irons from the forge fire and shoved it into his thigh. He demanded that she remove it or suffer the consequences, or rather, he tried to demand it. The words left his mouth as mush. He went back to sleep.

Evvy turned over, screaming as Musheng held up Asa and brandished a knife. She opened her eyes, stared at the low earth ceiling above her, and screamed again.

Five little silver snakes with skulls for heads vanished into the ceiling of the tunnel.

"Evumeimei," Luvo said calmly in her ear, "they are only baby cave snakes."

"They're dead!" Evvy cried, sitting up on Big Milk's back. "They're all bones!"

"Nonsense. They are made of metal and earth. They cannot be dead. Big Milk says you bawl more than her young ones."

Evvy glared at her small traveling companion. "I'm sorry, Luvo," she told him. "I'm sorry, Big Milk," she added, stretching out so she could scratch the giant yak on the poll. "I was dreaming again. Are we going *up*?" She squinted at the tunnel ahead of them. Even in the scant light of the glowing mold, she was certain. The tunnel was sloping upward for the first time in their journey.

"It is my hope that you will do better under an open sky," Luvo said. All around them the earth began to groan. "I believe you will dream less."

General Sayrugo's camp was on alert. The enemy's scouts had been seen to the north and to the west. She ordered triple sentries and prayed she would unite with Captain Lango and the twins from the Realms of the Sun the next day. All the signs pointed to a big fight before she even reached Garmashing.

Suddenly she heard an uproar. Cursing, she grabbed her sword and raced to the source of the noise. On the southern line of defense, her guards stood and pointed at something. With a roar of command she sent the onlookers back to their posts and squinted into the growing twilight. At least the other sentries had kept their positions, she told herself.

Then she blinked, and blinked again. The plain was tearing itself in two a hundred yards away from their picket line. The ground was trembling under her feet. She turned to yell for her shamans, only to feel the quivering stop. She stared at the hole that had opened in the — up until now — solid, reliable earth.

The biggest yak she had ever seen in her life plodded out of the hole and began to graze on the grass near it.

Then, as Sayrugo and her sentries gawped like farmers in Garmashing for the first time, someone slid off the yak. The someone removed some bags, or packs, slinging one off his or her shoulders. Then the someone scratched the yak on the forehead. Sayrugo knew there was another word for a yak's forehead, but she was a city woman; she didn't know these things. She did, however, know all the words for the pieces of a crossbow. She held out her hand, groping for one in the empty air.

A huge voice boomed in the air. "Do not attack us, defenders of Gyongxe." It was deep and musical. It could not belong to the person who walked toward them, hands — holding bags — in the air. "We are allies to you and foes to the invader from Yanjing!"

The huge yak turned and ambled south on the plain. Sayrugo wished she could do the same.

The second time Briar woke, someone was ordering him to drink. He obeyed, then tried to spit the nasty sweetness of spirits laced with opium from his mouth.

"Drink it, or *I'll* use you for sword practice next time," Parahan told him. The big man sat on a camp stool beside his cot, bracing Briar with one arm as he held the cup in his free hand. "You were supposed to be healing people — what were you doing on the battlefield?"

Briar drank the rest of the cup's contents. "I went to see . . . what the green light was," he mumbled. "It was our people. Gyongxe. 'N then I stayed to work on the wounded. 'N someone whacked me with a sword."

His brain wasn't so muzzy that he couldn't remember *that*. He had been checking a fallen temple warrior by the light of one of Evvy's glow stones. Suddenly, nearby, a Yanjingyi warrior had lurched to his feet.

"You!" he'd cried in *tiyon*. He was hardly more than Briar's own age. "You're one of their demon mages!" He had stumbled forward, raising his sword as he fell. Briar had felt something hot in his leg. He'd looked at the Yanjingyi boy to find that he had fallen because he was dead. He had been dying of a big wound in his chest when he attacked Briar. Only crazy luck, Lakik's luck, had made him chop Briar's leg instead of something more important.

For a wound that wasn't vital, it had made Briar scream

anyway. People from his own side had found him. When they lifted him to bring him back to camp, the pain had been so bad that he had fainted like some temple archive lily.

He was trying to tell Parahan all this when the potion hit and he slept.

THE GNAM RUNGA PLAIN
THE ROAD NORTH TO GARMASHING

The next time Briar came around, Rosethorn sat by his cot. She said cheerfully, "I'd box your ears, but apparently you're being punished enough."

He glared at her. "You aren't usually so happy when I foul up this bad."

"I'm not happy because you got hurt," she replied tartly. "I realize your motives were good, but you shouldn't have been out there."

Briar covered his eyes with his arm. "I figured that out," he admitted. "I just didn't want anybody to die who didn't have to. Well, our people."

"General Sayrugo found us," he heard her say. "Her scouts spotted the Yanjingyi warriors and she cut them off. None of them survived."

"That's good," he said dully. People were moving around the tent. He didn't want to see them talking about what a bleat-brain he'd been.

"Briar, look at me," Rosethorn told him. "Sayrugo brought us company."

He heard a scraping noise. A very deep voice said, "This is Briar? From your conversation, I had thought he would be as large as Diban Kangmo."

"Go away, company," Briar said. "I don't want to be gawped at like some daftie in a show."

"I thought I had come to understand the odd words that you use, but he is incomprehensible," the deep voice complained.

Someone tugged on his sleeve. A voice he thought he would never hear again said, "Please look at me, Briar. I traveled such a long way to see you, and on a yak named Big Milk, too."

It couldn't be Evvy. Evvy was dead. He had her stone alphabet, taken from her by her murderers. She never would have let them have it unless she was dead.

Briar lowered his arm. Evvy stood at the opposite side of his cot from Rosethorn, wearing a tunic that was big enough to be a dress. A gaudy, multicolored silk scarf served her as a head cloth, but under it was Evvy's same pair of bright eyes and her same flat-tipped nose. A smile quivered on her mouth.

"You're alive?" he asked her.

She nodded. Tears filled her eyes. "But they killed my cats, Briar." She knelt beside the cot and put her head on his chest.

Despite the pain he turned and hugged as much of her as he could reach. He murmured silly things, about how they'd pay them back, and she told him about what they'd done to her. It set a dull heat of fury burning in his chest.

"But you can walk?" he whispered.

She nodded and drew back, wiping her eyes on her sleeve. She was about to wipe her nose, too, when Rosethorn reached across Briar to thrust a handkerchief into her hand.

"Luvo fixed me. Well, Diban Kangmo's daughter fixed me. I hardly limp at all," Evvy explained. "Luvo's a mountain. The mountain's heart."

"Who's Luvo?" Briar demanded. "Who's Diban Kangmo?"

"Diban Kangmo is the goddess of the peak spiders," the deep, calm voice said. Evvy moved aside a little. Next to her, on a stool that brought it up to the level of the cot, was a rock of clear, purple, and pine-green crystal. It was roughly the height of Briar's forearm and hand together, and it had the shape of an animal, though it was that shape after the rock had sat in running water for years.

A bear, maybe, Briar thought. A bear worn down by water.

"Briar, this is Luvo," Evvy told him. "Well, Luvo isn't his actual name. His real name is a lot longer, and I couldn't remember it, so I call him Luvo. He's one of the Sun Queen's husbands — the one called Kangri Skad Po, the talking mountain."

The rock nodded to Briar. "I did think you would be larger, from Evumeimei's descriptions," it said. Briar did not see a mouth move, but the voice definitely came from the rock. "I am honored to meet the one who has meant so much to her."

Briar thought about it for a moment, then looked at Rosethorn. "You gave me another dose of painkiller potion, didn't you? I'll take willow tea from now on."

Evvy's tale was a long one. The healers fed Briar and changed his bandage as she told it. By the time she was done, Parahan, Souda,

Lango, and Jimut had come to listen, not having heard every detail. If he hadn't been clutching her arm most of the time, Briar would have thought it another mad dream, from her capture to her travels deep in the earth until they had found Sayrugo's army.

Sayrugo had agreed to transport Evvy and Luvo to Melonam, where they were supposed to join the troops led by Captain Lango and his companions. They would have done so, too, but their force had come across Yanjingyi soldiers chasing fifty warriors led by Soudamini. Now the Gyongxin and Realms troops were joined, and Sayrugo was in command.

"If you're up to a wagon ride, we're close to Melonam," Rosethorn told Briar when Evvy had finished. "You'll be more comfortable in a proper bed than here."

"I don't need a wagon," Briar protested, swinging his legs to the side of the cot. "I can sit on a horse." He put his feet down and stood, or tried to. His thigh hurt so much that he bit the inside of his cheek until it bled. He sat down.

"Wagon," Rosethorn said. Jimut nodded and left the tent.

To save his self-respect, Briar looked at Luvo. "If you're a mountain, how did you get so small?"

"Your manners are as dreadful as ever," Rosethorn murmured. She was measuring pain-killing medicine into a cup.

"This part of me is the heart of the mountain, and much of its mind," Luvo explained, turning his head knob so he appeared to look at Briar with the pits that served as his eyes. "I do not think your manners are dreadful. I have only Evumeimei to measure by. Never before did I believe that meat — that humans were worth the trouble to converse with, so I have no standard for their manners."

"Evvy also thinks we humans aren't worth the trouble to talk to." Briar looked at Rosethorn. "Rosethorn, I thought we agreed, no more of that stuff."

"We have to lift you into the wagon, my dear."

Oh, this was very bad. The cut must be deeper than he realized, if she was not blistering him for being rude to Luvo, or telling him to be silent and take his medicine. He watched while she dropped another liquid into the cup.

"Don't worry," she said, and smiled. "This will make it taste so bad you won't care about the rest."

Evvy, sitting quietly by Luvo, actually giggled.

Briar gulped the potion. It was even viler than Rosethorn had hinted it would be. He struggled until he was sure he wouldn't bring it back up again. As his head spun, he mumbled, "Rosethorn, take my seed bombs."

"I already have," she told him as she beckoned to Jimut and another helper. They did their best to lift Briar gently, but he still screamed once before he fainted.

A crimson naga pecked his forehead like a bird, one head after another. Briar tried to tell her that snakes don't peck, but she ignored him. He woke in a jolting, bumping wagon. His leg ached. He wanted to throw up. He wanted to dig a hole in Gyongxe all the way to the world's molten heart and bury Weishu and his mages there, where they would never smell another rose.

"Does it hurt so much?" asked a very deep voice by his elbow. "Even when Evumeimei wept in her sleep her face did not make that shape."

Briar turned his head. The day was too bright; he shaded his eyes so he could see the talking rock. "I wasn't thinking of pain," he mumbled. "I was thinking of revenge."

"I think about revenge, too," Evvy said. She was on Briar's other side, leaning against his packs. "I want to dump a few Drimbakangs on Weishu, but Luvo says the mountains won't let me."

"I don't blame you," Briar said. "If they hurt me like that, I'd want to drop mountains on them, too."

"Yes, but I'm over the hurt. It could have been worse. They *wanted* to do worse. See, I'm fine." Evvy stripped off one of the overlarge slippers someone had given her and the heavy sock she wore underneath it. Gripping her ankle, she raised her foot until Briar could see its sole. "Not too bad, right?"

Briar swallowed. Evvy's feet were normally brown and callused from years of running on rock and dirt with no shoes at all. Now her sole was puffed and pink, with horizontal scars across it.

"It's tender yet. I can't walk too far, but it's not raw, and the wool doesn't hurt it," Evvy said, turning her sole to give it a critical look. "I can even pick up Luvo and carry him and it doesn't hurt my feet. I just have to remember that my bones are made of granite so his weight doesn't bother me. How's your wound?" She let go of her ankle and put her sock back on.

"Fine," Briar said, ashamed for whimpering. He was still somewhat muzzy, but the pain wasn't what it had been. He smiled at Evvy. "I think my revenge could be easier to get than yours. He just made me mad. I'll be happy if we send him running back to Dohan."

She looked away. "*That's* what hurts. They took all I had. I can't ever get justice for that. My feet would heal no matter what. But everything that was mine is gone, even my alphabet that you gave me. Even . . ." She folded herself over, burying her face on her knees.

Briar wriggled to sit up, not caring if his leg hurt. This was one thing he could do for her, after he had left her behind for the torturers. "Evvy. Evvy, give me that pack. The one with the embroidered lucky ball on the left strap!"

She groped and handed it to him without raising her face from her knees. Briar fumbled with the straps. "Look here. See what some Yanjingyi *kaq* had when our fellows raided their camp!"

He pulled out her alphabet. Since she still hadn't unfolded, he placed the rolled bundle on the tops of her slippered feet.

Evvy parted her knees to peek. Then she whispered, "No . . ."

"Yes," Briar said.

She pushed her legs out flat and reached for the heavy roll of cloth. Her fingers trembled as she undid the ties that held it shut. There were more than twenty-six pockets in the cloth, since jasper, obsidian, jade, sapphire, moonstone, opal, and quartz came in many varieties. Evvy stroked each and every sample, tears on her cheeks.

"Evumeimei?" Luvo asked. "Why do streams run down your face?"

"She has her alphabet back," Briar replied for Evvy, who was too overcome to speak. Then he had to explain what an alphabet was, and what writing was. By the time he was done, Evvy's crying was over and the army had reached the walled town of Melonam.

They waited in the sun for a short time before Jimut rode back to find them. "They want to leave the wounded here and press on," he told Briar. "Rosethorn said to give you this." He handed over a small vial.

Briar knew the medicine as soon as he smelled it. It was one of the quick-heal potions they used only when things were desperate.

If they're going to leave me here with the rest of them that are hurt, that's pretty desperate, he thought. And I don't want to be left!

Before he could lose his nerve — there was a reason these medicines were seldom used — he slit the wax on the cork, yanked it free, and swallowed the contents of the vial. For a moment he felt nothing. Then the flames came roaring up his throat to set his teeth, tongue, eyeballs, and nose on fire. He stuffed one arm into his mouth to keep from screeching and forced himself to stare at Melonam's walls. That was a mistake. The stone walls were painted with four-headed orange gods with boars' tusks. In their hands they gripped spears tipped with jawbones. Looking at Briar, they stuck out their tongues and waved their weapons.

Briar covered his eyes with his free arm.

"Briar?" Luvo asked. "Why do those gods of the plain wave to you?"

"I don't know what you're talking about," Briar mumbled. Then he realized what the rock had said. He uncovered his watering eyes and blinked at Luvo. "You can see them? You can see them *moving*?"

"Why would I not see the gods?" Luvo inquired. If Evvy heard their conversation, she gave no sign of it. She had moved down to the tail of the wagon, where she sat with her alphabet. She was taking each stone from its pocket and pressing it first to her lips, then to her forehead, before she put it back.

"I thought I was just imagining things," Briar mumbled. Then he had to explain what "imagining" meant, though he wasn't certain, in the end, that he got his meaning across.

"Gods are too important to be left to the imagination of meat — humans," Luvo observed. "These paintings are a door to the local gods' homes. For some reason they believe that you can see them, so they mock you."

"I understood the mockery part," Briar admitted. "What is that thing you keep saying and correcting? Meat what? Is it an insult? I suppose it is, or you wouldn't keep changing to 'humans.'"

"Formerly I thought of animals, birds, insects, and humans as 'meat creatures,'" Luvo explained patiently. "It distresses Evumeimei. She asked me to use the word *humans* for those of you who waste two of your limbs and put all of your weight on the other two."

Despite the pain in his throat, Briar sighed. "We don't *waste* what we do with our hands. You think your orange gods over there would be so bright if they didn't get their colors touched up now and then by painters? Those are humans who spread color at the end of little stick tools they hold in their hands," he said hurriedly, before Luvo could ask what a painter was. "We couldn't fight the emperor's soldiers if we didn't have hands and weapons we made with them."

"Neither could he fight you," Luvo said.

Briar made a face. "True enough. But Rosethorn and I make medicines with our hands that help the wounded to heal. We also help plants to grow with them." The medicine's fire died away and, with it, the pain in his leg.

Jimut, who had left Briar to drink his medicine, now returned at the trot, leading Briar's riding horse. The gelding was saddled and ready.

"Forgive me," he said, "but General Sayrugo says those who cannot ride will be left here. We are two days from the capital. It is under siege by the imperial army. And Princess Soudamini says that Evvy must stay here, too. A battleground is no place for a child. She said that, not me," he said hurriedly after a look at Evvy.

Evvy jumped down from the wagon. "Oh, no," she snapped. "I'm not getting left behind. Not after what they did to me. Jimut, where is she?"

Jimut whistled to a passing soldier. "Take Evvy to Her Highness, will you?" he asked the man.

"Evumeimei?" Luvo called. "Shall I go with you?"

Evvy shook her head and let the rider swing her up behind him. "I try to behave myself in front of you, Luvo," she explained. "I don't want you confusing me just now."

As her soldier carried her to the princess, Briar stood in the wagon's bed. "I'll ride or I'll bust," he told his companions. They would not leave *him* behind, either. Jimut nudged the horse closer, until Briar could grab the saddle horn and swing his weak leg over the animal's back. After that it was easy enough to place his good foot in the stirrup.

Evvy soon returned on a horse of her own. Her smile was grim, but pleased.

"Were you rude?" Briar asked sternly.

"Not exactly," she replied. "I said I've been fighting in this war ever since Snow Serpent Pass, and they can't call me a child when I can make horses and men fall. And Rosethorn said that if we lost, Melonam would be the emperor's next conquest. So here I am. Children fight all over the world, and Her Highness wanted to keep me safe!"

"She knows His Highness and Rosethorn and Briar all care about you," Jimut said with reproach.

Evvy rolled her eyes. "I know *that*. But nobody's let me be a child since my mother sold me. Can we just drop it?"

Briar hid a grin behind his hand. The only time anyone got to protect Evvy was when Evvy wanted protection; he knew it very well. Once she got her hackles up, it was best to stay out of her way.

One of Jimut's friends arrived with a packhorse whose saddle had been arranged to carry Luvo as well as belongings. Evvy tucked Luvo into the open seat on the saddle, then helped Jimut arrange packs around him. As soon as their wagon was emptied of everything but bedding, the driver headed toward the rear of the supply train. Jimut closed in on Briar's left, Evvy on his right. Together, with Luvo on Evvy's free side, they trotted up the road to find Rosethorn.

Briar glanced back at Melonam. The four-headed god to the north side of the gate had turned around to show Briar a naked green bum with four cheeks. The god was bending over to ensure that Briar got the message.

"Do you see that?" Briar demanded of Jimut, pointing to the god.

Jimut looked. "The walls? Those are paintings of the god Shidong, king of the winds and doors and patron of the town. Surely you have seen him before."

Briar said nothing. He doubted that Luvo would think the god's behind was unusual in any way. He wondered if Rosethorn could see it. He wasn't about to ask her, that was certain. He would not risk being tied once more to a sickbed while his friends risked their lives against Yanjing.

"Good, you're still with us," Rosethorn said when they reached her. "I was worried that medicine wouldn't work and we'd have to leave you."

"As if you could," Briar retorted.

Parahan, just ahead of them, looked around. "You have something that heals faster than ordinary medicines?" he demanded, scowling. "Why has it not been used on the wounded we left back there? We'll turn around right now!"

Souda put her hand on her brother's arm. "Perhaps Rosethorn has a reason," she said quietly.

Rosethorn met Parahan's glare. "Do you truly think I would not have used it if I'd had enough of it? The ingredients are rare. I don't have enough to heal a hundred wounded. I must use it sparingly. If Briar stays with us, he can keep plenty of mages and warriors alive with his own medicines and knowledge. Ask your healers if they can do better!"

Souda kicked her brother. "Go scouting if you have forgotten these realities, my dear," she counseled. "Have a gallop. Ride with the general for a while. Soon enough you'll have plenty of things to occupy you."

Parahan growled under his breath and rode off. Souda sighed. "He always gets silly before a major battle, Rosethorn."

Briar looked to the west, where hills rose a mile or so off. Those were the leading edges of the Drimbakang Zugu, whose white-capped peaks gleamed in the distance. To the right the grassland was striped with charcoal streaks where it had been burned. Buzzards rose from the carcasses of horses and humans alike. Among the bodies and the burns he saw blast craters, the marks of the Yanjing empire's *zayao*.

The smell was unspeakable. From the condition of the dead, Briar guessed they had lain in the open for at least five days. The cool nights would slow the decay, but the sun and the scavenger animals would speed it up again. He noticed that Rosethorn was holding a handkerchief to her nose.

They soon left the scene of the fighting that had taken place here and rode steadily all day, stopping only to rest the horses and to grab cold meals. The road moved deeper into the hill country as they drew closer to the Drimbakang Zugu and Garmashing. Twice they passed massive temple fortresses. Their gates were closed and barred. The general sent messengers to speak with the temples' commanders, but the army itself continued north.

They halted ten miles from Garmashing. General Sayrugo called the commanders and the chief healers, including Rosethorn, to a meeting in her tent, along with the leaders from the eastern and western tribes and temples. The rest of their army camped on a hillside that overlooked the road. Sentries were posted everywhere around the camp, together with mages who could sense the presence of spells.

Evvy stuck by Briar as he brewed their supper tea. Jimut, who was keeping an eye on them, brought a pot of noodle-and-dumpling soup for all of them to share. He joined them, but he was the only one. Evvy heard him tell Briar that he didn't mind not having more company. Everyone could see that Evvy needed quiet.

She did, too. She had gotten used to the emptiness of the tunnels under Gyongxe where she and Luvo and Big Milk had traveled. She wished she could talk Briar and Rosethorn into going back into the tunnels with her, where they would be safe. They would never listen; she knew that.

Before she conferred with the general, Souda had told them to go to bed early, saying, "We'll be fighting the emperor's main army in a day or two. You need rest."

The thought gave Evvy the crawls. How could she rest? She and Rosethorn and Briar and Parahan were the only ones who really knew what they faced. They would be in battle against the imperial army, its ranks full of men like Musheng and Dawei. There would be mages who wielded battle-magic spells similar to the ones placed on General Hengkai's beads. Cruel spells. None of the people who had come north with them had seen the emperor show off hundreds of thousands of archers and soldiers on his birthday, so many that acres of land were covered with them. There would be catapults to fling *zayao* bombs into the middle of General Sayrugo's army. Everyone she knew would die or be taken off and tortured. She would have to stay with them, and risk the emperor's wrath all over again.

How did Parahan stand it? She had seen him joking with some of his soldiers earlier. He knew what they faced even better than Evvy, and yet he could grin and tease and even steal a kiss from Rosethorn in the shadow of a tent when they thought no one was looking.

Evvy got to her feet. She wasn't strong like Parahan. "I'm tired," she said abruptly. "Luvo, are you coming?"

"I wish to remain here for a time more," Luvo replied. "You do not need to be concerned for my well-being, Evumeimei."

She nodded and retired to the tent she now shared with Rosethorn. Whoever had put up the tent had also laid out her bedroll, which was a kind thing to do. She lay down on it without removing her clothes. It was hard to undress, even to change to clean clothes or a nightdress now. She was terrified someone might come in and see her naked. Luvo didn't count, but a strange man . . . She didn't think she could endure being seen unclothed by strangers again.

She lay in the dark, listening to camp noises. Playing with the stones of her alphabet helped a little. Their textures against her fingers calmed her. Still, they weren't calming enough to make her sleep, and they weren't the textures of the alphabet she had been making on her own. They weren't the textures of her quartz and flint disks, with the different kinds of magic she had been learning to place on them. They weren't the textures of the flint arrow and dagger blades she had made herself, after months of study in the art of knapping.

The more she thought about what she had lost, the angrier — and the more awake — she became. She got out of bed.

"Evumeimei?" Luvo stood at the opening of the tent, like a sentry, as he had every night since they had begun living among humans.

"I'm just going out to think. I won't leave the camp," she whispered. She opened the ties and slipped out the back of the tent, grateful that Rosethorn had yet to come in. Quietly she made her way through the rows of tents. Most of the fires were now banked for the night. Just enough torches burned to light the main paths. Heading uphill, Evvy kept to the shadows. She did make certain that the sentries noticed her, though they didn't stop her. There was no point in getting shot by a nervous warrior because she wanted a quiet walk. In any case, she stayed inside their lines.

She made her way to the hilltop where a broad slab of slate thrust out over the northern slope like a shelf. Sentries were posted on the ground below, their eyes to the north, and on the western edge of the ridge, but they were nice enough to let Evvy have the stone to herself. She sat with her knees up, arms wrapped around them, staring at the road they would take in the morning.

A sliver of moon shone down on everything, turning it the color of ghosts. She wondered how many human ghosts might be walking on that landscape soon. Would she be one of them?

She would not let the enemy take her again. She promised herself that. Rather than fall into the torturers' hands a second time, she would turn herself into stone all the way. There would be no little piece of Evvy left behind to wake up to agony. She would join the rocks of Gyongxe forever.

She was so absorbed in her thoughts that she did not hear anything until Briar lay on the stone beside her. He said nothing, only crossed his arms under his head and regarded the sky. Evvy found she couldn't think of dying in his presence. Instead she let herself trickle through the slate under them and on down through the hillside rocks, naming them to herself. Before long Rosethorn and Parahan silently joined them. Both chose to sit cross-legged on the slate, their eyes on the silvery northern view.

Souda was the last to reach them. She carried a silk quilt in her arms and shared it with Evvy, who was shivering. Eventually Briar squirmed under a corner of it, too. Except for that, none of them moved until Parahan began to snore. That startled laughs out of the women, Briar, and Evvy. Without discussion they woke him and returned to their tents for what remained of the night.

CHAPTER
TWENTY

Evvy and Luvo were seated by the morning campfire when Rosethorn and Briar emerged from Souda's tent. Both of them wore armor.

"You," Rosethorn said, pointing to Evvy. "Armor. Now. We're battle mages today and for the duration. We're under strict orders to stay away from the healers and save our strength for fighting."

Briar wandered over to Evvy and Luvo as Rosethorn returned to Souda's tent. "Not that General Sayrugo's happy about it."

Evvy frowned. "Why not?"

"No matter what Parahan and Captain Rana told her about what we did back in Snow Serpent Pass, she doesn't see how plant mages can be of use on a battlefield. That goes a hundred times extra for somebody who isn't even a certified stone mage." Briar reached out to tweak her nose, but Evvy was having none of that.

"*I* don't know what good I'll be with a whole army. I just want to try."

"Probably no good with a whole army," Briar said. "But if you make the horses of a line of archers skid and skitter because the stones under their feet are moving, you can probably keep them from shooting plenty of us."

"Oh," Evvy said, realizing he was teasing her. "Oh, right."

"Armor," Briar said, and pushed her toward her tent.

She was struggling with the ties of her cuirass when Briar came in with a plate of *momos* and a pot of butter tea. Luvo followed him. Evvy happily ate while Briar checked the ties on her armor and did the cuirass up.

"What about you, Luvo?" he asked. "Are you going with us, or are you riding in a wagon?"

"I will stay with Evumeimei," the stone creature replied. "Between us we will not be heavier than an adult of your kind. A horse should carry us both easily. What else will you bring today, Evumeimei?"

"Only my alphabet," she replied. She looked at the packs that had been found for her among the extra supplies. They held the clothing and odds and ends supplied by Sayrugo's people and the clothes Luvo had given to her. "I don't know what to do with those. They'll just get in the way if I'm fighting."

"Her things can go with mine and Rosethorn's, please," Briar told the soldiers who had come to pack up the tent. Evvy grabbed the shoulder bag with her stone alphabet and the rocks she had collected recently and slung it over one arm. Briar lifted some silk scarves that had been offerings from an open pack and held them close to his eyes. "Look at these, Evvy. Someone gave you doubled silk. One of the village weavers I talked to on the road says this kind of cloth is a way to send messages. The arrangement of these slubs — these bumps — in the weave, that's code. They aren't mistakes at all."

She thought he'd lost his mind. "We're going to war and you want to talk about *weaving*?" If the scarves were temple offerings, I guess the message got sent, she realized. "I'll take those now," she said, holding out her hand. Briar passed them to her and watched as she slung them around her neck.

Then he pulled her over and kissed the top of her head. "Lakik and Heibei turn their faces against Weishu and all his mages," he murmured. Evvy rested her face on his shoulder and nodded. "I wish we could call on that ancient sea that used to be here to swallow his whole army." He was trembling. Evvy wanted to comfort him, but she didn't know how.

"I will help you," Luvo said from the ground beside them. "Together Evumeimei and I will teach these lowlanders a thing or two about the stones of Gyongxe."

Briar looked over as Evvy picked up Luvo. "Good. Weishu in particular needs the lesson." He slid his hands around Evvy's and attempted to lift Luvo from her hold, only to find the rock creature was far heavier than he looked. "I don't understand! How does Evvy carry you?"

Evvy resettled Luvo, balancing her friend on her hip. "We worked out a thing in my magic," she explained. "I imagine my bones are granite, and it's easy. He's really not that heavy, now. He's at his lightest."

"His lightest is fifty pounds if it's an ounce!" Briar cried, laughing.

"I can be far heavier," Luvo said.

Briar took a breath. "Let's go. Jimut's waiting with our horses by now."

Rosethorn was waiting with Jimut and the horses as well. "There you are. Luvo, you're riding with us?"

"I am going to help Evumeimei," Luvo said.

Rosethorn raised an eyebrow, but she made no remark.

Jimut handed the reins of Briar's horse to him and Rosethorn's to her. Evvy looked around for someone to hold Luvo.

"I'll take him," Jimut said as he passed the reins of her mount over. Here." He held out his hands.

"He's heavy," Evvy warned. She passed Luvo to Jimut, who staggered.

"She warned you," Briar said.

"You did warn me," Jimut acknowledged as he regained his balance. "How will you keep him in the saddle with you?"

Evvy mounted her horse. Once settled, she knotted the scarves she'd put around her neck and passed them over her head, shoulders, and arms. When they were around her waist, she held her hands out for Luvo. Jimut passed him over. Evvy quickly twisted both scarves around her friend several times, encasing him up to his head knob. When she was done, Luvo was snug in his cocoon and the scarves were tight around Evvy. He would remain where he was unless Evvy fell from the saddle.

"Nice," Briar said with approval. "But you know, if Luvo stays with us much longer, we should work something out that's more permanent."

"Do not concern yourself," Luvo said comfortably. "I am certain I will return to my mountain soon."

Evvy looked down at him, feeling a pain around her heart. She didn't want Luvo to go. She liked him. She felt safe with him. If anything could withstand the emperor, surely it would be a mountain. Yet what could a street rat like her offer him? He had gods for friends, not to mention the inhuman curiosities that were his friends underground, and all of the Drimbakang Lho for his home.

She glanced at Jimut, who was astride his own horse. Today he was serving as an archer. He had two quivers full of crossbow bolts attached to his saddle before his shins and a crossbow across his lap.

Beyond him Evvy saw the gathered mages. They were a mixed lot. Most were shamans, used to working in groups among their tribes and in the performance of great magics, like calling statues out of cliffs. Today they wore cloth jackets embroidered with symbols and pictures of powerful animals. Their necks, wrists, and ears dripped gold, jade, and ivory jewelry that was useful to their work. They carried small gongs, bells, drums, and a variety of rattles. Riverdancer was with them, as was her translator. Evvy didn't think Riverdancer needed the other woman when she worked with the shamans. Perhaps she kept the translator close in case she had to join the healers later.

Tired of waiting, Evvy nudged her horse up to the nearby hilltop. General Sayrugo's troops were spread across the open ground below. Evvy recognized the general's battle flags at the head of the army, together with the vivid colors worn by the eastern shamans who used their magic to protect Sayrugo and her soldiers.

"Evvy," Briar called. "Back here."

As she rejoined her friends, Souda and Parahan rode through the ranks of mages and turned to face them.

"Riverdancer's group of mages, follow us," Parahan shouted. "We're right behind the general. The rest of you mages, your leaders will tell you where to join the order of march with the troops you will defend. They will give you orders in battle. May the gods give us victory this day!"

As those around them cheered, the twins rode down the slope, along with their flag bearers, their personal guard, and their messengers. Riverdancer followed them with a group of western shamans. Rosethorn told Evvy, Briar, and Jimut, "You come with me. We're to stay close to Souda."

"Why aren't we with the other mages?" Briar asked.

Rosethorn looked at him with a crooked smile. "Because General Sayrugo doesn't know what to do with us. We'll have to figure out how to fight, ask permission to do it if we can, and then do it."

Evvy and Briar looked at each other. Evvy wasn't sure — was this the way mages normally fought wars?

Briar answered that question when he asked, "Sayrugo is joking, right?"

"No," Rosethorn said, and sighed. "Souda and Parahan say to just do what we think is useful and try not to let the Yanjingyi mages kill us."

"Well, that's better, anyway," Briar muttered.

They took their places behind Souda and her personal guard. Almost as soon as they had done so, the trumpeters who rode with the general sounded a loud, bellowing horn salute. The army set forth at a walk, which gradually sped up to a trot. Evvy glanced back and saw long, snake-like columns of riders falling into place on the road, four in a row with officers on both sides and scouts spreading out over the uneven ground. The foot soldiers weren't even in view yet. They were guarding the healers and supplies in the rear.

She turned to look forward again, scanning the horizon. There was a hill to come, and more on either side. Was the emperor behind those? She tried to swallow, but her mouth and throat were paper dry with fear. Then she thought of Mystery, shy gray-and-orange Mystery, who loved to run in open grass like this, and Evvy's heart turned into a knot of hate. Mystery had never harmed Weishu or any of his people, but they had murdered her. They had murdered all of Evvy's cats. Behind their armies, they had left Kanzan alone knew how many dead animals who had never harmed them at all. The hate flooded through her veins. Yes, she was scared, scared so bad it made her quiver. But she was burning with rage, too.

Someone had fixed a flask to her saddle. When she unhooked it and sniffed the contents, she discovered it was filled with tea. She took a small sip, just enough to wet her mouth. She would need the rest of the tea later.

Nobody talked. It was hard to do at a trot, and they were too nervous when they stopped to give the horses a rest. Even Briar spoke very little, mostly to check that Evvy and Rosethorn were all right.

Since they had stopped, Evvy eased into the ground and discovered it was full of quartzite stones. Perfect! she thought. Quartzite was regular in its makeup, filled with quartz crystals that would move her power along. She spilled threads of it into the rocks and let it race ahead of the army, feeling for strange magic.

"Evumeimei?" she dimly heard Luvo ask. "Briar, why has she sent her magic ahead of us?"

"She's scouting," she heard Briar say. "The rocks ahead will tell her things, like plants tell Rosethorn and me."

Something flooded over her stones on the far side of the hill ahead, something dark and nasty.

"Rosethorn!" she made her body shout. "Briar! Magic coming!"

Over the hill ahead rose a giant tiger. It was bigger than three elephants standing one on top of the other, with red flames for eyes and claws. With it appeared a more fantastic creature of identical size, a winged lion with a horn on its forehead. The lion had a mane made of gold flames and claws like black sickles. Tiger and lion opened their mouths and roared loud enough to flatten the standing grass between them and the army. Flames spurted where they stepped.

Some horses panicked and reared; others sidled and backed. Souda and Parahan were able to hold their mounts steady. Rosethorn's horse did not even move. Jimut gripped the reins on Briar's horse while another soldier held Evvy's.

"They don't smell them!" Briar called to Parahan. "The horses behind us, they're calm — they can't see them, hear them, can't smell them! Cover your horses' eyes!"

Evvy ignored everything after that. Using the quartzite stones, she flowed under the two monsters. They pressed on her power, making her feel dirty and small. She wriggled deeper in the earth and sped up. She wanted to see what was on the far side of the hill. Was it the imperial army, or just some mages trying to keep the Gyongxin forces here?

The ground over her head shook as the tiger and the horned lion jumped onto the road. They roared again, setting more grass ablaze. Some of her stones blackened and cracked. She passed under the hill's crest and on to the flatlands past it. Weight pressed down on her, rock-crushing weight, as far ahead and to either side as she could sense with her power. It shifted slightly, back and forth. Some moved over Evvy as if it traveled toward the hill.

Swiftly she fled to her body, pulling her magic from the quartzite. Up she popped to resume her normal place within her skin. All around her the air boomed in her human ears with the gongs, the bells, and the deep, buzzing voices of Gyongxin mages. She opened her eyes. General Sayrugo's eastern shamans now faced the horned lion and the giant tiger. Forming a line, they shuffled to and fro, striking gongs or bells and chanting. The noise made Evvy's teeth hurt. It reminded her of the day other shamans had called two stone skeletons out of the cliff behind Garmashing. She wished those skeletons were here now.

The lion and tiger opened their mouths. They seemed to roar, but Evvy heard nothing. They were fading. Then they were gone.

Evvy's head spun. She closed her eyes and breathed slowly through her nose. The weight on the far side of the hill — she had to tell someone about it. Only her stomach was angry, because of all the weight stamping on the stones as she had run her power through them. She opened her eyes and slid from the saddle, almost falling as Luvo's weight dragged her down.

Rosethorn dismounted from her horse and ran to her. "Are you all right?" she asked. Swiftly she cut the silks that held Luvo's sling to Evvy's chest with her belt knife.

Evvy shook her head and turned aside so she wouldn't splatter anyone. Then she vomited the little food and liquid she had swallowed that morning.

Rosethorn passed her a flask.

Evvy tipped her head back and poured a little bit of water into her mouth, rinsed, then spat. She wiped her mouth on her sleeve, then drank. "Sorry," she told Rosethorn when she was sure she was done vomiting. "Sorry, Luvo. Rosethorn, we've reached the imperial army. They weigh *tons*. They're crushing my stones over on the other side of the hill."

Rosethorn reached over and patted her arm. "It could have been so much worse," she said in an overly sympathetic way. "We could have made the wrong turn and fetched up in Namorn. Yes, we knew. The scouts brought the happy word to us."

"I hate it when everything's about to go to pieces and you're all calm," Evvy told her.

Rosethorn raised an eyebrow. "Would you like it better if things were about to go all to pieces and I turned into a ball of panic?"

Evvy wanted to tell Rosethorn she loved her, but she couldn't, not among so many people. She stuck her tongue out at her instead.

The general beckoned for Rosethorn to come forward. Shamans from the western tribes joined the easterners ahead of even the flag bearers to form a line in front of the Gyongxin army. As Evvy watched, the shamans removed their shoes. Their helpers passed them flasks of tea. The shamans kept the flasks, tucking them into the front of their coats as the helpers sat cross-legged on the ground. From their packs they pulled out small drums or flutes.

Rosethorn came back at a trot. "The shamans say they will make it easier for us to survive going over the crest of that hill," she explained as a helper began to strike a drum in a slow, rhythmic pattern. Other drummers and two flute players joined in, weaving their music with his. Rosethorn continued, "It's something we can't do, I assume, or they'd have asked us to assist. The general says we may be a little startled, but try not to make any sound."

Evvy drew her amethyst from her alphabet. It was a good stone for calm. She turned the rough-cut crystal around in her fingers, drawing on the spells she had placed in the stone. Even with that magic, her hands shook.

The shamans bent to place sticks of incense in the ground in front of them. Thin trails of smoke rose through the air. Now the shamans danced, their feet shuffling in the dirt of the road. They dipped and turned, their movements snake-like and alien.

"Watch, Evvy," Rosethorn whispered. "We may never see anything like this again. Lark is always telling me shamans can do things that mages can't."

Evvy clutched her amethyst so hard her fingers cramped. Shapes were forming in front of the mages. At first they were thin and almost see-through, like fine gray silk. Bit by bit they filled in. She saw a curved section of orange skin that slid around. There was a dark fang. When she saw hair like black flames, she covered her face. Rosethorn jabbed her with a sharp elbow, and Evvy dared to look again.

She wished she had not. Creatures not quite as gigantic as the tiger and the horned lion stood before them, but there were more of these. She recognized the four orange beings, with their flaming hair and ivory teeth and claws, from temple paintings. They each had six arms and hands in which they clutched weapons. With them stood six blue-skinned creatures with long, flowing, scarlet locks. They had long yellow claws on their hands and feet and full green lips. Each of them had four arms.

"I don't see what good these things will do if the emperor's mages can make bigger ones," Evvy said as the creatures turned and glided up the hill. She glanced at Briar. He had turned the color of cheese as he stared at the shamans' creations.

"The emperor's spell monsters are built of wind, smoke, fear, and illusion," Luvo told her as the many-limbed newcomers topped the crest. "Our friends are lesser gods, guardians from temple fortresses in western and southern Gyongxe. They carry the power of those places with them."

Suddenly the great brutes let out shrieks that sent many of the soldiers behind them to their knees as they covered their ears. Evvy was proud that Briar hardly flinched. Perhaps she was too used to strange things by now, because she only took another gulp from her flask. The temple gods plunged down over the hill. The shamans and their helpers moved forward, up to the hilltop, still dancing and playing their music.

General Sayrugo gave the command to advance. Rosethorn and Briar helped Evvy wrap Luvo in scarves from her pack and tie him to her chest, then boosted the girl and her friend into the saddle before they mounted their own horses. Together with the army they rode on, keeping a watchful eye on the clouds as black and crimson lightnings flickered overhead.

As they crested the hill, round balls struck the ground and exploded with a roar: The enemy was using catapults to throw *zayao* bombs at the Gyongxin army. Evvy's mare reared. Jimut rode between Evvy and Briar to grab the mare's bridle and draw her back down to all four feet.

"I know it's hard," he told Evvy and Briar, "but these horses are used to *zayao* explosions. That's why they were given to you. Now, ease your grip on the reins, Evvy. That makes her more nervous than anything else right now. Loosen your knees, too, before she bolts."

"Sorry," Evvy whispered. "I wish someone would loosen *my* knees." She forced herself to relax.

She felt a vibration and realized that Luvo had begun a soft, inaudible hum. She was about to tell him she wasn't a baby who needed to be sung to if she was going to relax, and changed her mind. It did help her manage the horse after all, and her mind was still alert.

"Thanks," she told him instead.

They crested the hill.

Spread across the plain for as far north as she could see and for a painful distance east was the imperial army: a huge number of soldiers centered on a massive, stepped platform that had to be Weishu's lookout tower and the place where he kept his best mages. Brigades of cavalry were lined up on the east and west flanks, prepared to force their attackers in to the soldiers at their center. Not only did brigades of infantry wait for the Gyongxin army there, but Evvy could see great crossbows and the kind of catapult that threw giant rocks and *zayao* bombs. Next to them, at the heart of the army, were archers, their crossbows raised.

Evvy fumbled through her alphabet and pulled out her clear quartz crystal. Holding it against her forehead, she used the spells she had placed on it to help her see flares of red where mages stood in the ranks. Each of the catapults had one, while the emperor's platform blazed with them.

She continued to inspect the battlefield, trying to find some good news, some weakness. Where the army's lines ended to the east, its horse camp began. She had never seen so many horses in her life. Her courage was shrinking by the moment.

She looked west. There at last was the great fortress city of Garmashing, safe for the moment behind its thick stone walls. Its temples, palaces, markets, homes, and plazas rose in level after level on its steep hillside, as if it boasted to would-be conquerors that here were treasures they could not touch. Its jagged walls climbed the rising landscape, concealing roads and gardens as they protected the buildings inside. With her crystal against her forehead, she could see the tops of those walls burning red with the presence of mages and the walls themselves red-streaked with magic. After spending her winter there, she had come to love it. The best part was the myriad tunnels that people used when the snows piled to the second story aboveground: It reminded Evvy of her old cave home in Chammur. She hoped the people who couldn't fight were tucked safely away in those tunnels, out of reach of the *zayao* bombs and catapult stones.

Crowning the city's hill was the God-King's palace, its many gold turrets glinting in the sun. Behind it all soared the white-capped peaks of the Drimbakang Zugu. She knew the apparent closeness of the mountains was an illusion: The Tom Sho gorge with its limestone walls provided steep walls at the city's rear.

The mountains themselves were cruel guardians with their trackless cliffs and canyons. Wolves, bears, and snow cats roamed freely on the slopes, together with antelope, sheep, and yaks. There were rumors of worse things. After what she had seen under Luvo's care, Evvy knew they were not rumors. She was wishing for some of those creatures now, not just as magics conjured by mages who would get tired eventually. She wished all of the stone statues born in the gorge would come home to defend their birthplace.

Messengers galloped back down the line of the Gyongxin army, relaying orders to the soldiers behind the mages. Everyone advanced at a trot down the slope, spreading out as they went. They formed on either side of the still-dancing shamans, General Sayrugo, the twins, and their guards, arranging themselves in battle formation. Companies of archers placed themselves on either side of the general and her companions as *zayao* bombs struck the hillside. Mages among the Realms and Gyongxin soldiers began to work their own magic, shielding their soldiers against the deadly explosives.

Evvy was fixed on the sight of the lesser gods as they collided with the emperor's soldiers. Bursts of red flared as imperial mages attacked the lesser gods; foot soldiers flew through the air as the Gyongxin creatures picked them up and flung them among their allies.

Suddenly Evvy heard the whicker of arrows in flight. She looked up, almost dropping her crystal. The imperial archers had loosed a deadly rain straight at the Gyongxin leaders.

Rosethorn and Briar also looked up. They did not so much as stretch out their hands. Suddenly crossbow bolts, sprouting twigs and leaves that slowed their flight, tumbled to the open ground between the armies.

The snap of ropes pulled Evvy's eyes to boulders that arched into the air. She grabbed Luvo. "Can we do something? Please?" There was nothing she could do about the *zayao* balls, but the boulders were different.

Come with me. His voice boomed inside her skull.

She twined with him inside his magic. They rose above their bodies into the unpleasant, thin air. Evvy glanced down. Everyone seemed to be frozen. Even the green-leafed crossbow bolts had stopped where they fell. Five stone balls were above the Yanjingyi army; three were unmoving. Evvy and Luvo spread themselves wide to cover those, sinking deep into the limestone that made them.

Evvy knew a thing or two about limestone. While Luvo did something that made the stones tremble, she sorted through the bits of lesser material that formed them. She couldn't touch the bits of coral. Coral wasn't a true stone, but the remains of an animal, and immune to her magic. There were other minuscule sea animals that had gone hard like the coral. She ignored all of them. With each non-stone thing she thrust aside, the limestone cracked. Luvo's trembling magic made the cracks grow and spread. Evvy made piles of bits of flint, jasper, and chalcedony, leaving gaps behind as she shifted each piece. Abruptly her body down below sneezed. She lost her concentration and separated from Luvo. She was back in her physical shell.

Small pebbles rattled as they bounced off the soldiers' helms. Luvo was covered with gritty dust. So was she. Nearby she heard screams — human and horse. "What did we do?" she asked him.

"We broke three boulders in midair," Luvo said. He sounded very satisfied with himself. "I wish we could have caught the other two. They damaged our army, but two stones did less harm than five would have done."

"Luvo, can we take rocks apart before they throw them?" Evvy whispered.

"Put your hands on me," he said quietly. "It works better with both of us."

Evvy obeyed and left her body again.

The stones of the plain raced under them as Luvo drew her along, bound for the biggest rocks in one Yanjingyi catapult. It went quicker this time. They did not have to work inside moving boulders. Evvy simply ignored the fossil coral and bone, plucking the stones she recognized out of the limestone.

Luvo pulled water from someplace and turned it to ice in the cracks Evvy made. Evvy didn't know where he got it until they rose above the heap of gravel that was the remains of the boulders ready for the catapult. Only then did she see shriveled bodies on the ground through Luvo's vision. They wore the colors of Yanjingyi soldiers and, in the case of two of them, the black tunics and bead strings of mages. Luvo had taken the water from their flesh.

Serves them right, she thought savagely. They're the enemy. I bet they would have tortured us if they could. I'm glad they're dead.

There are other catapults here, Luvo said. *Shall we deal with them? If we reduce the stones to nothing, these humans will have to go far to get others.*

Yes, Evvy told him. *Let's do that.* She was careful not to think about the people ready to load the massive stones into the catapult slings at their officers' commands. She simply followed Luvo into the stones, removing the grains that held the boulder together so he could freeze water in the cracks she left behind. Everywhere around them soldiers and mages gasped for water and died without any idea of what killed them. Evvy did her best to ignore them. Each time she felt her hate weaken, she remembered the heap of cold dead outside Fort Sambachu. Now their ghosts had company. Wasn't that a good thing?

TWENTY-ONE

In the front of the Gyongxin and Yanjingyi battle lines sergeants bellowed for archers to shoot. Just ahead, boulders smashed the Gyongxin army in two places, killing the horses and men that hadn't been able to flee. Briar watched for imperial arrows; he knew Rosethorn did, too. He took a quick glance at Evvy. Seated on horseback, she clung to Luvo, her eyes closed. The youth trotted over and pinched her gently, with no response. He cursed softly, but there was nothing he could do, or dared to do.

"Luvo?" he whispered. "Luvo!"

The rock didn't answer, nor did it look at him, if "look" it could be called when the creature had no eyes that could be seen. Briar thought Luvo turned his head knob just to make people feel better, not because he really needed to do so. Now Briar prodded Luvo, without effect.

Blasted bleat-brain, he scolded himself. You should have told them to do nothing without checking with you or Rosethorn! He took a breath, wondering if he should talk with Rosethorn or keep quiet, and coughed. His mouth tasted as if he'd walked through a dust cloud. Dust lay on his armor, too. He spat and drank from his flask.

Rosethorn was coughing. He ran to her and thrust his flask into her hand, watching anxiously as she drank.

"What targets should we go after when the enemy isn't shooting?" he asked when she returned the flask to him.

"The catapults," Rosethorn said firmly. "Plant them deep and grow them as high as you can."

A soldier nearby heard. "They'll be magicked," he warned. "Written over with spells to prevent other mages from interfering."

Rosethorn smiled at him. "But they won't be spelled against us. We become part of the wood; we don't try to work spells on it."

"As you say," the soldier answered, clearly not believing her. "I'm just here to run errands for you."

"We could use more water," Briar said. The man nodded and left. To Rosethorn, Briar said, "Will you handle catapults and I'll take care of arrows?"

He did not have to ask her twice. She sat and placed her palms flat on the earth on either side of her. Briar sat cross-legged next to her and kept his eyes on the imperial forces. He could not hear their officers' cries, but he saw the next volley of crossbow bolts arch into the air. He reached for them, tapping the memory of their lives as trees deep in the wood. He called those lives out, encouraging the bolts to sprout and leaf. They fought the metal arrow tip and thrust roots past the fletching, slowing the bolts' flight and draining their deadly power as they dropped to the ground. He couldn't reach all of them, but he reached a great many.

He was so fixed on that flight of arrows, and the next, and the next, that he did not hear the groans of the catapults as Rosethorn called upon their own memories as trees. They sprouted roots, splitting their metal fixtures and joins. The catapults exploded into pieces as the wooden towers and throwing arms burst free of their constraints, sank roots, and put out branches. Once a newborn tree was fixed in its bed, Rosethorn moved on to the next.

Briar kept track of her work through occasional touches as he rested between flights of arrows. A glimpse of Evvy as she drooped over Luvo and her horse's neck told him that they had finished whatever they'd been doing.

A roar from a large number of human throats drew Briar's attention to the battlefield. General Sayrugo's trumpets were sounding the attack. On their left, cavalry riders on both sides battled with spears and halberds. On the right, a pit opened under the Yanjingyi cavalry. They were trying to climb out, but the earth was dry. It slid under the feet of horses and fighters, dropping them back on top of those who were lower down.

Whose work? Briar wondered. He looked at the different groups of shamans. One of them sat on the ground, resting. The others were chanting, dancing, or standing with hands joined. He felt magic roll off them in waves. He made a silent vow never to vex the shamans.

A shout drew Briar's attention upward. Twenty or more *zayao* globes fell toward their forces. Lighter than the boulders, they had been thrown by Yanjingyi mages, not catapults. His belly rolled and cramped. He reached with his power but knew the attempt was useless. The charcoal in *zayao* was dead wood, untouchable by Rosethorn and him; sulfur was metal somehow, immune to plant and stone magic. Saltpeter, the third ingredient, was outside all three of them. He had tried to tell Evvy it was part stone, but she did not believe him.

The bombs fell, exploding throughout their army. Horses and soldiers shrieked. Riders and foot soldiers raced to fill gaps in the front and shift the screaming wounded and the dead. Clouds of stinking smoke rolled over the field.

Briar tried not to listen to the cries for help as he reached underground with his power, seeking roots. He groped in his jacket with one hand until he found a vial of strengthening oil. The enemy's cavalry was charging. If he rubbed the oil on his hands to strengthen his power, he could get a wide swathe of grasses to trip the horses. . . .

He was loosening the wax around the vial's cork when fire, or a pain like burning, raced over his skin. A mage had singled him out for attack. He cried out and reached for Rosethorn. She lay on the ground, doubled over on herself. With a gasp she smacked his hand away. "Don't touch me! I'm burning up!" she shouted, though he saw no blisters on her pale skin.

He fumbled to put the vial back in his pocket. He felt more invisible flames spill over him and swore he would have the Yanjingyi mage's teeth out in revenge. He didn't see fire, but he heard it crackle; his nose was filled with the stink of cooking flesh. Tears of pain streamed down his face.

Rosethorn cried out again. He fell to his knees and began to crawl to her, shouting for Evvy and Luvo.

He stopped at a pair of splayed brown feet. Knotted brown hands yanked him up as Riverdancer shouted into his face. More heat engulfed him. Briar shoved the older woman away to keep her from being burned, but he still couldn't see the fire that crack-led so convincingly on his own skin.

Riverdancer grabbed him again. This time her translator stood beside her. "She says, the Yanjingyi, did they get a chance to collect your hair or your fingernails?" the translator bellowed in *tiyon*. "Did they take clothes with your sweat on them?"

He stared at the two Gyongxin women. They had tried to be careful back in the Winter Palace, using their magic to remove all trace of themselves from the guest pavilion, but they could do little about the cushions and drying cloths they had used during all those meals with the nobles and the emperor. A very good mage might have drawn enough of their essence from those to do them harm now. Briar had learned all about sympathetic magic and the uses of all things that were once part of a person on their journey east. He was trying to remember if they had forgotten anything important, like nail clippings or hair, when the pain swept over him and Rosethorn *screamed*.

Riverdancer released him. Briar fell to the ground beside his teacher as the shaman began to dance, one foot up, one foot down. Had he known Riverdancer wore tiny bells in her clothes? One foot up, one foot down in a strange, turning step. She danced around Rosethorn and Briar, her bells singing. Fine white crystals spilled from Riverdancer's fingers. She sang, too. Briar could see her words in the air. They spoke of the strength of the mountains and the power of eagles, about the roots of the glaciers and rivers of Gyongxe. Even though he didn't know the language she used — it wasn't *tiyon* — he saw and understood everything.

As she danced and sang, her white crystals formed a solid, unbroken line. In it tiny shamans danced and twirled like she did.

They made swirls in the white stuff without disturbing the evenness of the white line. The more Riverdancer and the small shamans danced, the more his pain eased. When she closed the circle, the fiery agony stopped. The tiny shamans waved to Briar and vanished.

Rosethorn sat up. "Thank you," she whispered. "That was — horrible. They would have killed us."

Riverdancer grinned and made a remark.

"Now *they* will burn, the Yanjingyi," her translator said. "We will take the power they threw at you and return their curses to them."

"Can you stop them?" Briar asked as Rosethorn leaned against him. "You don't even know who has our sweat or whatever it is."

The translator smiled. "You would be surprised by the things Riverdancer can do on her own."

Rosethorn leaned against Briar. She was reaching for more of the catapults. Briar put an arm around her and watched the shamans. Several of them had come to make a shielding line in front of Briar, Rosethorn, Evvy, and Luvo. They began to chant softly. Now and then they stamped, or rang tiny bells. Their voices soaked into Briar's bones, drifting down through them like silt.

Movement in the air caught his attention. From the walls of Garmashing, arrows and big stones took flight, then dropped down into the ranks of the emperor's army. Again and again the city's defenders shot, hammering the Yanjingyi enemy on the western side.

Briar let his own magic seep into the hillside. His body was weary; he felt battered after the mage assault. But it was spring:

Everything in the southern Gnam Runga Plain was growing. Briar drew only a small part of that strength into his veins, just as he knew Rosethorn drew on part of it. As soon as he was ready, he sped through the interwoven grass roots down the rise and into the flat plain.

Horses thundered over his head. Next came the remains of the catapults Rosethorn had changed to form the trees above him: They hummed with her power. Beyond those lay the weight of more catapults that were in the process of becoming trees once more, stabbing new roots down into the earth. Above the ground he sensed thousands of crossbows and bolts carried by the archers who stood in their ranks around the imperial platform.

Briar was not searching for catapults or archers. He sought the white blaze of magic laid on the cool touch of willow, oak, and gingko.

The mages were bunched in small groups protected by archers, many of them arranged in steps on the great observation platform. To his magical senses they floated at different levels in the air depending on where they stood on the platform. Each mage appeared in his magical vision as a series of bead groups; these glittered with an overlay of Yanjingyi magic. He felt the clash between the magic and the wood's own power: Didn't the Yanjingyi mages understand how much more powerful their spells would be if they worked *with* their materials?

He picked at the alien spells for a moment, curious, then gave up. Whatever they did, it was dedicated to the destruction of the Gyongxin army and the kind of pain that had made Rosethorn scream. He was going to do his best to do some damage to them and to the mages who wielded them.

Briar gave one set of beads a mage's tap. It released the magic that had been forced on them: The wood was already dry and brittle from lack of care. The beads shattered; the oak ones spraying splinters into the mage's face, the tough gingko beads cutting the string on which they were threaded. Briar searched for the next cluster of beads, creaking under their magical burden, and tapped them until they broke. When he found a mage who had strung his beads on cotton or linen, he coaxed the fibers to part and gave the beads enough strength to roll out of all reach. Each time he parted a mage from his beads, Briar immediately turned his attention to the next one, hoping to stop any of them from making Rosethorn suffer again.

Briar was deep in a mage trance at her side when Rosethorn sat up with a moan. Riverdancer and her fellow shamans sat close by, sharing dumplings.

"The work here continues," the translator said, motioning to a group of shamans who danced at the front of the army. Mages in the robes of different temples were nearby, also busy with spell signs and gestures. "There were more of the *zayao* bombs, one batch over our eastern flank and one over the road behind us. The shamans called up a very strong wind high in the air. It blew half of the *zayao* balls aimed at our eastern flank onto open ground." She touched her clasped hands to her head and lips in a prayerful gesture. "The general ordered our people off the road, thinking the enemy might strike there, so the bombs did not kill as many as they could have done. Now they have stopped the *zayao* bombs, because someone put too many trees in the way."

Rosethorn cursed bombs and the enemy under her breath. On the slopes below she could see screaming horses and the slumped bodies of soldiers. How many of the wounded and dead were men and women she had joked with, or healed, before? And when would she be able to help the healers again? She felt wrung out. The wind blew the stench of scorched meat and the dark, bleak scent of black powder into her face. Her stomach rolled.

She looked up, and her blood quickened. There was something . . . *off* . . . about the gigantic observation platform that had been at the heart of the imperial army. She got to her feet, shielding her eyes from the sun. Sections of the steps on the platform had collapsed, as if worms had eaten the wood. She could not see well enough to tell if there were bodies on them or not. And part of the entire platform listed sharply to the east. It looked as though a hole had appeared there, knocking the whole monstrous structure off balance.

To the west, on the open field, the city gates opened. Warriors dashed from Garmashing to attack the Yanjingyi army's western flank; Gyongxin and Kombanpur troops charged past the resting shamans to fight on its southern front. Arrows flew in three directions. The translator was right: So many trees now grew between the observation platform and the Gyongxin army that it was impossible to target it with boulders or *zayao* bombs. The trees obstructed all vision for the remaining, more distant catapult engineers. They had as much chance of dropping a bomb or boulder on their own troops. Now the battle was down to archers and warriors. Everything was shrieking, bloody chaos, with no way to tell who was winning.

She took a breath and entered her mage's trance. She would look for wood beads among the enemy's mages, and see if she could turn them on their masters.

Evvy and Luvo had run out of catapult stones to turn to gravel. Evvy wasn't tired in the least. Working with Luvo seemed to keep her strong. She wanted to do as much harm as she could. Turning her attention to the land, she filled as many middle-sized stones with power as she could and shook her magic. The stones were loose on the ground, having been stepped on by humans and horses and rolled over by carts and wagons. They moved easily at Evvy's urging. Warriors and horses alike lost their footing. They backed up, crowding those behind them. Some fell as they discovered the ground in back of them or to the side was no more stable than that on which they stood.

Evvy heard screaming. She opened her eyes, back in her body again. A reddish cloud rolled toward them from the imperial lines.

"What is *that*?" she whispered.

It swept over part of Sayrugo's troops as they fought a Yanjingyi company. When it cleared, the group of warriors — Yanjingyi and Gyongxin, as well as their horses — lay on the ground, their bodies twisted in agony. Evvy whimpered.

The shamans and their guards ran into the clear space in the middle of Sayrugo's, Parahan's, and Souda's troops. Those with gongs rattled them all at once. As they did, the shamans spun counterclockwise. They then came together in a circle and turned counterclockwise again, chanting an eerie, deep-toned spell. They halted; those with gongs pounded them. The shamans whirled. Then they entered their circle and turned counterclockwise, chanting. With each repetition the earth boomed and the air shivered.

With the fourth repetition the red cloud stopped in its advance. It, too, began to spin counterclockwise, pulling in on itself and rising. Slowly, so slowly at first that she couldn't be sure, the funnel retreated, or advanced on its own army. It had become a tornado.

The Yanjingyi soldiers directly in front of it panicked. They ran, fighting with fellow soldiers who were in the way. Some of the officers, mounted on horses, rode them down, lashing them with whips. Others galloped out of the tornado's path. The cavalry farthest from the panic charged forward.

Taking advantage of the enemy's confusion, Parahan led a charge of horsemen at the imperial lines. Evvy threw herself into the stones underground and raced ahead to help. She grabbed for sandstone: There was much more of it under the flat plain than in the hills. Finding pieces of it, she called the quartz crystals in it to her. They popped free of the other minerals and followed her as stone after stone went to pieces. Suddenly the Yanjingyi cavalry horses were charging in sand.

Evvy was dizzy. She left her crystals and returned to her body. She was aware enough to do that. There she made the discovery that she was too weak to move or call for help. She squinted down at the field. Sayrugo's and Parahan's soldiers were cutting a huge gap in the Yanjingyi lines. On her left, soldiers were pouring out of Garmashing. They smashed into the imperial army. Everything on that side was a mess. The Yanjingyi warriors were retreating if they could. The tornado was chopping the side of the imperial army on her right to pieces. Now it was shrinking, too. Dead soldiers and horses lay everywhere.

Where was Luvo in her magic? She groped with her power and found a rope that seemed to lead to him. It took her to a side of the observer's platform that was falling into a hole in the ground. Since she hadn't caused that, and his rope led her there, she wondered if Luvo was responsible. The Yanjingyi soldiers wouldn't like seeing their generals tilting sideways.

The thought made her giggle.

As far as she could see, trees grew everywhere, though the plain had been treeless. They had sprung from the remains of catapults. Had Rosethorn and Briar done all that? She had known them for only two years. They had done interesting things before, but never so much. . . .

Her mind was wandering. She wished she had something to drink, or something to eat, or a bed. She was very tired, but she wanted to see how the battle came out. Surely the emperor had more soldiers than this.

She had the sense to dismount from her horse. She almost stepped on Luvo, who had somehow gotten out of his scarf-sling on her chest. His spirit was not in the stone body she thought of as Luvo, she discovered when she tried to apologize. She gave up and let her horse's reins trail on the ground. "Don't go away," she told him. Then she sat down.

Riverdancer found her and took charge of her. She made Evvy sit with her and her group of shamans, bundling her up in blankets and scolding until Evvy drank tea. Evvy tried to explain that normally she wasn't so tired after a little bit of magic, except she had been breaking catapult stones and sandstone and limestone when she wasn't shaking rocks under people's feet. The explanation seemed far more complicated than it should have been, particularly when Riverdancer kept patting her on the shoulder, as if to say, "It's all right."

Evvy awoke on a saddle. She lolled against someone who gripped her tight with one arm while he managed his horse with another. She looked up and back. Jimut smiled down at her. "Are you alive, brave girl?" he asked.

"I'm not brave," she said blearily. "I'm hungry. I was with Riverdancer."

"There will be food when you're settled at First Circle," he said. "I have tea."

"Tea's good," she said, and fell asleep again.

The next time she opened her eyes, Jimut was carrying her through a plaster-walled corridor. "Rosethorn? Briar? Luvo?" she asked.

Someone poked the back of her head. "Nice of you to ask." Briar was being helped along by one of Jimut's friends. He was ashen under the deeper bronze tan he had picked up during their travels. "Where did you go to?"

"I was working on stones," Evvy said. "Rosethorn and Luvo?"

"Luvo's coming." Jimut carried her into a room. Rosethorn sat on a bed large enough for all three of them. There was another bed behind a screen. Briar's companion helped him to that.

"Healing," Rosethorn mumbled. "The wounded . . ."

"The city is full of healers. Most are in better shape than you, and you made the choice to be a battle mage," Jimut said. He set

Evvy on her side of the bed she would share with Rosethorn. Nearby was a small table with bowls of barley flour mixed with butter tea and dried cheese. He handed a bowl and spoon to Evvy. She began to eat, looking at Rosethorn with silent apology for not waiting. To her shock Rosethorn reached over and rubbed the top of her head.

"You're sure we aren't needed?" Briar asked as Jimut carried a bowl over to him. He pointed to Rosethorn. "She'll fuss and fret even if she isn't strong enough to crawl." He ate a spoonful, then set his bowl on the floor, put the spoon in it, and curled up on the bed. He was asleep instantly. Jimut began to remove his boots and armor.

Rosethorn struggled to stand.

Jimut shook his head. "I don't mind taking care of him," he said, and flicked his fingers at the door in a beckoning gesture. A girl who wore the undyed robe of a novice in the eastern Circle temples came in and bowed very low to Rosethorn. She placed her hands on the shoulder ties of Rosethorn's armor, checked that Rosethorn did not object, and began to undo them. "Gods all bless me," Jimut continued as he worked on Briar, "how many of my friends have you and Briar cared for all this time? You saved my prince's life, too. I think you have earned some rest, and you can't even stand up, any of you. What you did out there today — I have never seen anything like that, ever. None of us have." He laid the armor on the floor of Briar's side of the room so the sweaty parts could dry.

A Gyongxin man staggered through the door carrying Luvo. "Where — where will you go, old one?" he panted.

"He stays with me," Evvy said.

Jimut put another of the small tables that littered the room by Evvy's side of the bed. "What took you so long?" he asked the newcomer.

"The stone god weighs more than he looks," retorted the man. "And there are many steps from the horse level to this one. All of them are clogged with people who wanted to see him."

"It is perfectly understandable," Luvo said. "They have not seen the heart of a mountain before. I only wish that they would have waited until I had made certain that Evumeimei is well."

"I'm tired," Evvy said. She set her bowl on the floor, just as Briar had done, and fumbled at the ties of her armor. Her fingers were strangely clumsy. She gave up and lay on the mattress with her head close to Luvo. "Did we catch the emperor?" she asked him.

"Soudamini and the Garmashing soldiers are chasing him," he said. It was the last thing she heard him say.

When Briar awoke, the shutters were open. He stumbled over to look outside. If he judged correctly, it was well past noon. Rosethorn and Evvy still slept. Luvo was nowhere in sight.

He stood for a long time, eyeing the view. Their room was on the southern side of the temple, with half of Garmashing spread out below. The city he remembered had been hammered. Everywhere he saw blackened pits where bombs and fires had destroyed homes, temples, and public buildings. Holes had been blown in roads and parks. The air smelled of burning and death. People labored to drag war's debris into piles, except for the dead people and animals. There the scavengers were having a feast.

The vultures were so bold they didn't even flinch away from the humans.

Briar turned away from the sight. He'd found a lot to admire in Gyongxe, but sky burial still unnerved him.

A look at his hands showed him that he was utterly filthy. He opened the door and peered out.

A novice sat there reading a scroll. "Sir?" he asked. "How may I assist?"

Soon Briar was soaking in a huge tub full of hot water. He got out only when he started to sleep and slipped under the surface. *Back to bed for me*, he thought, once he stopped choking. He was drying off when Parahan arrived.

The man wasted no time in stripping off his clothes. "Bliss," he announced as he settled into the bath. He looked exhausted. "Souda and Sayrugo are back," he told Briar. "They chased the imperial army as far as they dared, but the enemy got away. We'll see if they return."

"You think they will?" Briar asked. He put on the narrow breeches and long tunic that someone had left for him.

"The emperor isn't nearly beaten enough. He'll get more troops and mages and he'll come back. We'll be waiting, too. Actually, I don't think the emperor was with this army. He might be in the north or northwest — those troops haven't arrived, which has the God-King worried. Weishu knows he has to take Garmashing, though, to hold Gyongxe. I'm not sure he can."

"Why not?"

"The shamans were always going to be a problem, even more than the tribes themselves," Parahan explained. "Half of battle magic is knowing what the other side will use. Weishu's famous mages don't know how to fight shamans, because the shamans don't work alone. The mages cannot direct their power at one person. Shaman magic is based on the combination of five or six different people with different strengths and skills. They practice weaving those things together all their lives. And if any of the court mages have ventured out to learn the shaman music and dances, I, for one, will be much surprised. Do you scrub feet?"

"No," Briar replied, thinking over what the prince had said. "Do your mages in Kombanpur study the shaman dances?"

"No," Parahan told him comfortably, "but we have never been stupid enough to attack Gyongxe. There are easier places to attack on our side of the Drimbakang Lho."

Several novices entered in a rush to open the taps on another big tub. Steaming water rushed into it as the novices placed soap and scrubbing sponges on one of the benches within reach. Briar was about to leave and Parahan was sinking into his bathwater when Rosethorn, Evvy, and Souda came in, all dressed in bathing robes.

"Do any of you ladies scrub feet?" Parahan asked as Rosethorn stripped off her robe and stepped down into the water.

"Scrub your own feet, you lazy oaf," she advised him.

Evvy stood there, trembling. Parahan covered his eyes and Briar looked away. It was Souda who said, "It's safe, lads." She and Evvy were tucked into the rising water. The novices closed the taps when the water reached a couple of inches from the rim of the tub.

Briar silently cursed himself for missing a glimpse of Souda, but he knew he wouldn't have felt right. Bathing wasn't for ogling women; it was for getting clean. It worried him that Evvy was so clearly frightened of being bare when she had taken baths in groups all of her life. She had sunk down in the shared tub until her chin rested on the top of the water.

"So can the shamans drive the emperor out of Gyongxe?" Briar asked, returning to his conversation with Parahan.

Their friend shook his head. "If the three of you were to stay, perhaps we could come up with something that would kill Weishu," he said. "That would force Yanjing out. It's his ambition that brings him here, and greed. Without him, his generals would retreat to fight over the rest of the empire. His sons would fight, too. That would keep all of them busy."

"I hate to agree with my brother on politics, but for once he's right," Souda remarked.

"I will have you know that in the years I trailed the emperor like a chained monkey, I received a very good education in politics," Parahan retorted. "You can't ask for a better teacher than Weishu. That's how I know Gyongxe doesn't have enough soldiers to send against him. That's not even counting devices of war. We fight him with no catapults, no *zayao* bombs. We didn't have any pitch, for that matter. Without Briar, Rosethorn, Evvy, and Luvo to work on them, those catapults would have been the end of us. I would do anything to get my hands on the *zayao* formula. It's death for anyone in the empire to sell it."

"You don't need to buy it," Rosethorn said with a yawn. "It's evil stuff, but if you truly need the formula, Briar and I both know how to make *zayao*."

Souda and Parahan stared at her.

"Do you know how much my uncle paid the empire for sixty kegs of it last year?" Souda whispered.

"We'll teach you how to make it for free if we leave you to face him," Rosethorn announced. "But it's evil. Once you have it, you guarantee your enemies will get their hands on it so they can use it against you."

"Let's not get carried away with this 'for free' stuff," Briar said quickly. "If Gyongxe can pay there's nothing wrong with that. We have a long journey to reach our ship."

Now the twins were staring at him.

"So you mean to leave us," Parahan said.

Briar shrugged. "We're supposed to be on our way home now," he reminded their friend. "If we don't catch our ship when it makes port in the southernmost Realm of the Sun, we risk getting caught in your monsoons. We have family at home we won't have seen for three years if we have to wait."

"You could make the difference between victory and slavery if you stayed," Souda explained.

"You know Weishu," Parahan added. "He destroys what he cannot keep."

Briar glanced at Evvy, who had sunk almost to her nose. She was weeping silently. The others saw him looking at the girl.

Souda reached out and stroked Evvy's hair. "What is it?" she asked gently.

Evvy sat up enough to clear her mouth of the water. "He'll torture us," she whispered. "He'll whip our feet till we can't walk and he'll murder our friends. His people killed my cats because they were in the way. They killed the villagers and Captain Rana's soldiers for the same reason. They don't care about anyone." She was shivering so hard her teeth chattered. "I want you to kill me. Don't let him get me."

"No one will let —" Rosethorn began, putting an arm around Evvy.

She got no farther. The door blew off its hinges and fell onto the floor. A deep, powerful voice boomed, "Why does Evumeimei weep? Who has terrified her so much that her bones shudder?"

Luvo stood at the door. For someone that's a chunk of crystal, he looks seriously angry, Briar thought. "We were just talking, Luvo."

"Your talk has meddled with the healing I did with her," Luvo said. He waddled into the bathing room. Several novices peered through the open doorway, but they did not seem to want to come in. "Much rockfall singing, much time spent with Big Milk, yet now Evumeimei is as frightened as she was when I called her to me. Why? She was good when she had slept and eaten. You are her friends. What have you said to do this to her?"

"Luvo, it's all right, I'm fine," Evvy said. She wiped an arm across her eyes, but the tears kept coming. "We were just talking about staying for a while because maybe Gyongxe needs us, that's all. I'm being silly."

Briar realized this might take some time. With a grunt he lifted the rock creature up onto the bench where the women had placed their robes. When he leaned the fallen door back over the opening in the wall, he wasn't surprised to find it weighed less than Evvy's friend.

"Evumeimei," Luvo said slowly, "you wish to leave here? I can find you small furry creatures. There are many of them here."

"No!" Evvy shouted, standing up. "I don't want any more cats! I don't want anything that can get killed! Look at Briar, he got wounded, he could have *died*. . . ." She looked down and realized she was naked. Climbing from the tub, she dragged her robe over herself and squeezed through the opening between the leaning door and the frame.

They heard a novice outside ask if she could help. Evvy shouted, "Get away from me!"

Luvo turned his head knob toward the others. "She wishes to leave this land."

"She's afraid to stay," Briar said quietly. "She's afraid the emperor will get her and torture her — or us. You did a splendid job of putting her back together after what those monsters did, Luvo." He had to stop talking then. He was afraid he might weep.

"Only time heals such deep wounds," Rosethorn continued. "Briar, perhaps you should take Evvy home. The First Circle Temple is the home of my religion. The obligation is mine."

"Why don't you take Evvy home and I stay?" Briar asked sharply, the idea of leaving Rosethorn here cutting into his heart like a dagger. "You've got a cool head for a long journey, and Lark is waiting for you."

"We are all tired and hungry still, and truly, I did not mean to start a quarrel when you have helped us so much already," Parahan said. "Come. Let us set this aside for later. Souda and I have warriors to see to."

Briar and Rosethorn exchanged looks. "We should look in on the healers," Rosethorn said.

"*No*," Souda told them flatly. "If the enemy returns while you are still here, you are battle mages. Do what you can to restore your strength, but do not heal, *please*."

"I will speak with Evvy and sing to her," Luvo said. "If it is for the best, of course she must go home. I had only hoped to show her all of my mountain."

Parahan climbed out of the bath and lifted the crystal creature down to the floor. "Welcome to the human world, my friend," he said quietly. "We all have those we wish to show our favorite treasures, if only there was enough time."

TWENTY~TWO

FIRST CIRCLE TEMPLE

GARMASHING, CAPITAL OF GYONGXE

Evvy didn't stay in the room once she had dressed. The others would be asking her questions and trying to understand her when she didn't even understand herself. Instead she fled the Living Circle temple to wander Garmashing.

There were people in the streets, all busy. Most were hauling debris out of the yards of houses and temples. The imperial army had rained stones and *zayao* bombs on the city for days before General Sayrugo came to distract the soldiers. Now even the smallest children helped to clean up, dumping little baskets of trash into wheelbarrows and carts. Evvy felt guilty to be loafing, but her power was still not what it had been a week ago. Even her body was exhausted: Her arms and shoulders felt like overcooked noodles when she tried to use them for lifting.

She had not considered that people might care that she was Yanjingyi now. It was hard to keep her temper when someone did and spat on the ground at her feet. Luckily this did not happen often. When Evvy saw others with Yanjingyi blood, she nodded, and they nodded back. They knew what it was like to have the enemy's face, even if they had lived here all their lives. Evvy had seen a couple of *baita* temples here when they lived in the city that winter. They were built for the worship of Kanzan, the goddess of mercy and healing, and for Tuyan, the god who was heaven itself. It made sense that there would be some Yanjingyi people in Garmashing, with so many foreign temples in this country. Had they been watched, or even locked up, during the siege?

Briefly she considered going to a *baita*, but she changed her mind. She didn't know how long she could wander before she got too tired and had to hitch a wagon ride back to the Living Circle temple. She did mean to walk as far as she could, though it was sad to see all the damage done to the vividly painted homes and temples. At least they had put a stop to that, she and her friends.

She stopped to stare at one untouched temple wall. It was illustrated with a number of Gyongxin figures. Since her time underground with Luvo, it seemed that every painted image she saw was moving. These had decided to rejoice in the siegeless day. An ice lion danced with a snow leopard, then leaped across it to chase a large yak. The snow leopard chose to keep dancing with a spider the size of the leopard itself, while several of a naga's heads read a scroll and the other heads looked bored.

"Sometimes I throw pine nuts over their heads," the God-King said, "and they get angry because they can't catch them."

Evvy looked him, startled. "Should you be wandering around by yourself?" she asked. "What if there are spies in the city and they grab you, or —" She blinked at what she was thinking, and her voice shook. The thought in her head was too awful: The

God-King strapped up like she had been, lashed like she had been. "There are bad people in the world."

He slung an arm around her shoulders as she began to cry. "Come here," he said, and led her to a bench against an unpainted portion of the wall. He sat with her there, her head on his shoulder, letting her cry out the tension and fear that had swamped her. "I am protected," he said. "You would be surprised how protected I am." He looked at the wall paintings, which had come to stare at Evvy and pat her head and back. "Evvy, you're worrying them."

"I'm sorry," she said, wiping her face on her sleeve. Rosethorn could not seem to break her of the habit. "I'm just tired." She frowned at the God-King. "And it doesn't seem very god-like, or king-like, to tease paintings with pine nuts," she told him sternly. The images halted their previous occupations to make faces at the God-King.

"They tease me right back," he told Evvy, nodding at the grimacing creatures. "They come into my throne room when I'm hearing complaints and make rude gestures while people speak to me. They know I don't dare laugh, or people will think I don't take their problems seriously." He looked like the farm boy he had once been, except for his braid rings and earrings.

"*These* paintings come into your throne room?"

"Not exactly. There are paintings like them in the room," he replied. "Paintings from all over the city, for that matter. I think they trade turns tweaking me." He offered her some of his pine nuts. "It must be your exposure to Luvo that allows you to see them in motion now. You never said you could see them when you were here before."

"You talked with Luvo?" The nuts were nice and sweet. She had forgotten the world had good things like pine nuts.

"You three were asleep for a while," the God-King said. "It was Luvo who told me what happened to you." He looked away, his face shadowed. "I am so sorry, Evvy. You did nothing more than travel here to learn and to share your wonderful magic."

Evvy suddenly had another horrible image in her head: The God-King, chained as Parahan had been chained, at the foot of Weishu's throne. He said all she had ever done was visit Gyongxe, but all he had ever done was spend long days on his uncomfortable-looking throne, listening to people complain, or at meetings with adults who talked at him, not to him, or reading messages. Did he ever get to run and play as boys did? She felt a hand squeeze her heart.

"Has the emperor gone home?"

The God-King shook his head. "He has only retreated, and not far. He is resting and summoning his northern troops. We can only be grateful that he is also giving us time to rest and wait for more of our allies to come."

"Will they be enough?" The war was almost a more comfortable subject than anything that had happened to her in Gyongxe.

"It is our land. Things happen in Gyongxe that can happen nowhere else," he replied. "We must pray that is enough."

A man had come to speak with him. Evvy watched, thinking, I can't take Rosethorn and Briar from him. If I go, I bet Luvo will return to his mountain, so I can't take Luvo, either — if he'll stay for me, anyway. But I can't leave and turn a whole country over to Weishu. Not without trying to help.

I just can't let them get me again, that's all.

Rosethorn went in search of First Dedicate Dokyi when they returned from their bath. Briar envied her energy, but he was still tired and his leg pained him. He apologized to Luvo for being poor company and went back to sleep.

The Snow Serpent River glittered in the sunlight. He sat on the bank, fishing. In the dream he knew that he rarely fished, but he was doing it here, and the crystal waters had produced a bite. He wrestled his fish up onto the riverbank. He had landed a body, that of an old woman. He looked at the river. It ran with the bodies of the dead: men, women, children, animals. They bristled with arrows or showed gaping wounds as the river turned them over and over in the rapids.

For some dream reason he put his hook and line into the water again. The next body he pulled onto the bank was Evvy. Her feet streamed blood.

He sat up in bed, gasping.

No more of that, he told himself. No more of that at *all*. He found a cloth and dumped some water on it from a pitcher beside his bed, then used it to wipe the sweat from his face and neck. Rather than try to sleep again, he would make himself useful, tired as he was. He collected a pack with his medicines and found his way to one of the infirmaries where the wounded were kept.

Much to his surprise, his work as a healer was not wanted, though the medicines were. It was true: Gyongxe had plenty of healer mages. He did find that his friends among the wounded soldiers wanted to see him. They were eager to introduce him to their friends. Briar did the rounds, sitting with each of them and joking, fighting to keep a cheerful face no matter how upset he might be at the extent of a soldier's wounds. Many of them had mage fire burns, a sight that deepened Briar's hate for Weishu. Why couldn't the man be happy with what he had?

He was almost finished in the main infirmary when he saw Rosethorn, Evvy, and Luvo were also visiting the wounded. When he was done, Briar joined Evvy. Everyone wanted to meet the girl and the heart of the mountain. He helped those who could to sit up so they might talk with the odd pair. Evvy, so shaky in the bath and in their room, was endlessly patient as she lifted the crystal bear for those who could not sit. Briar realized that Luvo was giving out a soft hum, one so deep that he felt it in the soles of his feet as much as he heard it. It seemed to leave the wounded stronger.

They might have been there all night, except the healer in charge shooed them away so her staff could feed everyone and change bandages. A messenger found them with an invitation to join First Dedicate Dokyi for supper.

Rosethorn and Evvy were glad to see Dokyi. The old man was leaner than he had been when they saw him last, but his gaze was no less sharp as he looked each of them over. He clasped hands with Briar and bowed to Luvo, but he embraced first Evvy, who had been his winter student, and then Rosethorn. "You did well," he told the woman quietly. "*Very* well."

"Thank my horse," she said wryly, her voice just as soft. "He took me there and back. And if we did so well, why do I still see moving paintings? My errand is over, yes?"

Dokyi smiled. "That effect may remain while you are in Gyongxe, where we sit between the divine and the earthly."

"Paintings didn't dance and cavort this last winter," Rosethorn told him.

"Carrying the burden changed your ability to see the portals. That is what the paintings are." Dokyi looked at Briar, who was chatting with the temple's other supper guests, the God-King, Parahan, Sayrugo, and Soudamini. "Though I have yet to explain what happened to Briar."

"He touched the pack that I carried my burden in," Rosethorn explained. "We had to tie him to his horse for half a day. He wouldn't sleep in the temple fortresses after that, though he didn't tell me why."

Dokyi grinned. "Ah. That explains why he jumps so. Like you, he now sees the little gods as they really are on the walls, alive in their doors to our world."

"Are you two going to eat?" called the God-King. "Or do we have to finish all this ourselves?"

Rosethorn had needed a meal like this with friends and very little talk of the war. It was understood by the adults, she was certain, that they would be working on strategies soon enough. Evvy was quiet, not sulky. Something she told the God-King struck him as quite funny; he nearly choked, he laughed so hard. They broke up in a good mood and went to bed early.

In the morning, Briar and Rosethorn found a workroom in the part of the Living Circle temple given over to the use of the Earth temple. There, with pots and earth from the temple supplies, they began to replenish their thorny seed balls. Evvy helped, carrying in jars of water and filling the pots with enough earth to take the seed.

"I do not understand," Luvo said as he watched them work. "Surely this emperor will go home now that he has lost so many of his people to the fighters of Gyongxe."

"That is exactly why he *won't* stop until we find a way to beat him like a drum," Briar said bitterly. "He could lose three times as many people as he did and still have plenty more to throw against us. He wants this place. He wants the temples and the God-King's palace and all their treasures. He wants a hold on all the religions that have temples here. And he won't take no for an answer. He's the kind of fellow who will burn a whole garden because one plant is sick."

"I do not understand," Luvo replied again.

Briar had just finished the tale of Rosethorn's attempt to save the rose garden when Jimut arrived carrying two small wooden kegs.

"What are these for?" Rosethorn asked when he set them on the table.

"Well, a slinger who's a long way off might not get one of your cloth seed balls very close to the enemy," he said cheerfully. "That's why I had to go back to my old way of fighting when we twisted the emperor's tail."

"It doesn't seem to have hurt you," Rosethorn replied with a smile.

"Yes, but I felt bad," he told her. "Most of my friends never got to see what happens when one of your little balls explodes. And I was, well, I was exploring hereabouts, feeling like I have nothing to do. I just happened to find the wine cellars. . . ."

Briar began to laugh.

Jimut said loftily, "*And* they have all these empty kegs waiting for transport to the Yanjingyi wine makers, except there's a war. So I got an idea. What if you put one or two cloth balls in an empty keg and load *that* into a catapult? A small catapult, maybe, like the ones they have on the rooftops here? The keg will pop when it hits the ground, and your seeds will scatter and grow."

Rosethorn clapped his shoulder. "That's a *very* good idea. Now, go find the First Dedicate of the Water temple and ask her to her kegs. I'm certain she will be pleased to do so."

Jimut stared at her. "I thought you might handle that part."

Rosethorn sighed in mock regret. "I would, but I am growing thistles so they will give us more seed. Tell her I'm sorry I couldn't come myself."

Jimut looked at Briar, who shrugged. "I'm doing the same thing," Briar explained.

"I'll come," Evvy volunteered, "if you think it would help."

Jimut sighed. "No offense, Evumeimei, but you are not always careful about what you say. I will be in enough trouble when she hears I was prowling in her wine cellar." He wandered off.

Rosethorn watched him go. "I hope Parahan and Souda appreciate that fellow," she said, thinking aloud. "He's clever, he thinks fast, and he doesn't frighten easily. And he's loyal. They should promote him." She turned it over in her mind as she settled seed after seed in the earth and called to the growth in them. Up sprouted the plants, to bloom and go to seed. It was work she would set a novice to at home, or several novices. It was pleasant to greet the plants — their thorns were as long as her forearm once they were more than two feet tall, though they were sweet-natured to the gardener who appreciated them — but she wanted to do more.

She *could* do more. For all the harm she had done, she was not a battle mage; she was a medicine mage, a planting mage. Rose Moon was nearly over; winter came early here. How much of the fields had the imperial armies destroyed already? "Evvy, you are now a thorn seed harvester," she announced, moving her sprouting plants to Briar's side of the room.

"I am?" the girl asked, though not irritably. She had been dozing on a heap of sacks.

"Evumeimei's power is not with green things," Luvo said from his spot of observation near Briar.

Briar started to explain how he could keep the plants growing as Evvy watched and harvested. Rosethorn hurried down the hall, searching for Dokyi.

"I did understand correctly?" she asked the First Dedicate when she found him. "Barley is the most popular grain crop in Gyongxe?"

"It is the hardiest of the grains," he said. "Others do not fare as well. Why do you ask?"

"I know a way to replace some of the grain that's been lost to Weishu's army."

Dokyi's face lit. "That would be an incredible blessing to our people if you can manage it. Do you need anything from me?"

She nodded and began to explain. The First Dedicate listened to her idea, thought it over, and led her to a storeroom. He helped her carry a number of flat, shallow planting boxes back to the workroom, and appointed two strong young novices to haul in more sacks of earth.

She set out a row of the planting boxes and dug her hands into a bag of soil, feeling better than she had in days. *This* was what she needed to do, not killing. Not seeing visions. Moreover, the strength she still held after her stewardship of the Four Treasures surged forward as she worked, pouring into the dark earth in the boxes and the barley seed that she scattered over it. Of course the Treasures would lend themselves to crops.

She had to grip that power to keep her new plants a simple two feet in height. As it was, a quarter of them was heavy with seed. Swiftly she harvested and planted it all for a new crop. She remembered to teach them only to grow under an open sky when their farmers gave them a particular word. It would do no one any good if the new crop grew only to be trampled by armies again.

She also arranged her magic so the plants would grow to maturity in the field in four weeks. With luck, even if the war ran another couple of months, the people of Gyongxe would still be able to gather at least one crop, perhaps two, from these plants.

Dokyi brought their midday meal. He remained to help Briar, Evvy, and Rosethorn as they packed the seed that was ready to plant and sprouted more. Luvo had gotten bored and wandered off. Jimut and Riverdancer, who came by in the midafternoon, told them he was replacing entire walls by humming at the debris in the street until it rose and packed itself in place where the walls had been.

"He offered to teach some dedicates to do it, but they could not sing so low," Jimut said with a grin.

"I don't think this city is going to recover from Luvo's visit any time soon," Rosethorn observed. She looked at her hands and grimaced. Barley plants and constant hand digging had not been kind to her skin.

"I think it confuses him," Evvy says. "Not all the temples, but why so many people would want to live in such a small place."

Since the God-King had invited them to supper that night, they bathed in the temple's newly repaired bathing room and dressed in clean garments for the evening.

Luvo joined them at the God-King's table, as did Parahan, Souda, Sayrugo, and the First Dedicates of the Fire, Air, Water, and Earth temples of the First Circle. Rosethorn had feared that with so many adults present, Evvy might go quiet or find an excuse to leave. She had not reckoned on the girl's friendship with the God-King. He was even able to startle a laugh out of Evvy. The other First Dedicates, who might have been stiff in such an unconventional group, relaxed considerably when Dokyi told them about the work they had been able to do toward proper barley harvests, war or no. Rosethorn was delighted to see Briar grin at them when he saw how happy they were. He, too, needed something better than combat to take away from his time here.

They had finished their meal and were simply lazing when a Gyongxin man in gold-trimmed armor and one of Sayrugo's soldiers came to see them. Both communicated in whispers, the gold-trimmed man with the God-King. They left as soon as they had delivered their messages. The God-King and Sayrugo frowned as the others continued to talk.

Finally the God-King looked at his companions and smiled, though it was a smaller smile than usual. "There's no reason not to tell you. General Norbu at the Lake of Birds reports that his scouts to the northwest are late to return, that's all."

Sayrugo said, "As are mine to the east."

"We have been preparing for a fresh attack," the God-King said. "The emperor will not catch us unawares. I think we should get a proper night's sleep."

Evvy stood. "We should all stay here in Gyongxe. Me, Rosethorn, and Briar. Till it's over. Till he's beaten." She turned and fled the room.

Rosethorn took a breath. Evvy's courage hurt her heart. "Wait a moment, Briar, Luvo. Don't let her think we're chasing her," she said.

When Parahan spoke, his voice was cracking. "I wish I had the bravery of that little girl."

Souda rose. "We will find such bravery for our own, or not, God-King, but we will fight for you. You will never regret taking us in."

The boy looked up at her. "Make no mistake, Princess, Prince, it was the gods of Gyongxe who wanted you here." He looked closely at each of them, and then at Rosethorn and Briar. "All of you. I am grateful, don't think I am not, but the gods brought you here for a reason. It may take a long time or a short one, but sooner or later the gods of this land always have their way."

When Briar and Rosethorn returned to their room, Evvy had brewed a pot of calming tea and was drinking some. She poured out cups for them. One corner of the room was crowded with the products of their day's work: kegs upon kegs containing one or two thorn balls each, ready for the catapult, and bags of barley seed, ready to sow. Briar was thinking of burying some thorn balls in choice places before the gate as a way to welcome the imperial army when he felt the overwhelming need to sleep. Evvy and Rosethorn were already abed. Rosethorn's light snore sounded from the other side of the barrier that gave them all privacy.

He could barely keep his eyes open. "Luvo, do you sleep?"

"Not as you do," he heard the rock creature say. "Were I to sleep, it would be for centuries, and I would be reluctant to wake."

"Oh. I s'pose this is different." Briar had a jaw-splitting yawn overtake him. He curled up in his blanket. "G'night, Luvo."

He didn't hear Luvo's reply. He slept deeply.

The big cats of the Temple of the Tigers nudged Briar, holding him up as the priestess's cub tried to nibble his hair. He saw Discipline Cottage, his home. Lark was throwing his belongings out into the dirt. Rosethorn and Evvy floated downriver among other bodies, their eyes missing. Briar struggled to wake up, but he couldn't. The emperor's young mage, Jia Jui, stood in the air, a glowing set of beads in her hands. Briar fell, landing in a field full of the dead. Sandry, Tris, and Daja were standing on its edge, but when he pleaded for them to help him find Rosethorn and Evvy, they turned and walked away.

No matter how he struggled to wake, the nightmares went on and on. He called up dream plants and wove them into screens to shut out the view of ugly things, but they withered in his hands or collapsed when he held them up.

Just as he thought he might go mad, a rude hand poked his shoulder. A *real* rude hand. A voice shouted, "Wake up! No tricks! You're a prisoner of our glorious emperor, and if you try anything, we'll cut the girl or the woman!" The same rude hand pulled him from his bed onto the floor.

TWENTY-THREE

THE GOD-KING'S PALACE
GARMASHING, CAPITAL OF GYONGXE

Weishu looked glossy and pleased, seated on the God-King's throne. He did not look like a man who had been fighting for weeks. Briar stared at the flagstones, wondering if there was dirt under them, and plants. Don't try it, he warned himself. You'll get someone killed. The God-King's audience chamber was ringed with Yanjingyi archers, each with a crossbow pointed at a captive. The mages who flanked the throne had beads ready in case their foes among the captives got any ideas.

Like a vision from his ugliest nightmare, he saw that Weishu held a chain with the God-King at the other end. The boy sat on his heels two steps below the throne, his face unreadable. He showed no signs of a beating. Either the kid had gone along peaceably, Briar thought, or Weishu realized that hurting the God-King was a very bad idea.

Briar shook with rage. Parahan, Soudamini, and Sayrugo *were* badly beaten. Rosethorn had a bruise shaped like a hand on one cheek: If Briar had been awake when that happened, the one who dealt it to her would be dead.

"My good friends," Weishu said in *tiyon*. "Did you enjoy your sleep? It lasted for three days. I trust you will forgive me. I had to travel for some time to sit in this splendid chair, and I did not wish you to wake until I could greet you. I hope you are not too stiff."

"Where are my priests and priestesses, please?" the God-King asked. "The heads of the temples should be here."

Dokyi, Briar realized. Is he dead?

"They are locked in their temples and still slumbering, boy," Weishu replied. "I will not have this discussion interrupted with more religious babble than necessary." He raised his right hand and beckoned with his fingers. "Hengkai, get them on their knees," he ordered, his voice no less friendly.

The general walked out of the shadows behind the throne to stand at the emperor's right. He held a rope of mage beads in one hand. He'd lost weight since that breakfast in the oak grove. Briar was interested to see a bright gold band of metal around the man's neck. How could he command an army if he was one of Weishu's slaves?

Hengkai looked over the prisoners assembled in front of the dais. When his eyes lit on Briar, and on Evvy nearby, he spread his mouth in an ugly grin. He rolled a pair of beads between his fingers. They weren't wood: Briar checked them instantly, though he didn't mean to try anything that might vex the emperor.

Suddenly Briar felt pressure — on his shoulders, head, and hips. The pressure grew and grew. He wasn't sure when it got to be too much. One moment he was standing; the next he was on his knees. He looked around in panic. Rosethorn and some of the shamans were still up, including Riverdancer. Then they, too, were forced down. Only the mages had knelt. The guards beside Parahan, Souda, and Sayrugo shoved them or kicked their shins to force them down.

Weishu smiled. "Hengkai does know how to use magic on mages."

Briar yawned. He raised a hand to cover it before Rosethorn tweaked his ear for bad manners, and heard the sound of a blade coming out of its sheath. No hand movements, he thought, and slowly lowered his arm. It was sore. Were we really asleep for three days? he wondered. That's why I feel like I'm made of wood.

He smiled cheerfully at Weishu and Hengkai. Sooner or later they would leave an opening. They might know academic magic, but ambient magic was trickier by far. Briar could pass a river of it through the ground under Garmashing and these people would never feel it. He only needed a plan.

"Much more respectful to have you on your knees," Weishu said as if they were all friends. "What a splendid gathering of talents. Soudamini, it is an honor to meet you at long last. I have heard tales of your beauty, but they were inadequate. You and your brother will make fitting ornaments to my throne." He looked at Parahan. "And this time I will ensure the chains cannot be removed."

Parahan leaned forward and lazily spat on the floor.

"You will give in," Weishu said gently. "Or I will return *you* to your uncle and I will give your sister to my concubines. They can be very jealous, and very good with poisons when they sense a woman does not have my favor." He looked at Rosethorn, Briar, and Evvy. His face darkened with anger. "I show you my hospitality; I welcome you to my palace; I shower you with gifts, and this is how you repay me," he said, his voice expanding to thunder in the chamber. "You side with my enemies. You slaughter my soldiers. You will spend your lives working for me, each of you hostage for the good behavior of the others.

"And *you*," he said, glaring at the God-King as he yanked the chain leash on the boy. "I sent a command of surrender to you and you defied me!"

The God-King stumbled and fell on the throne's steps. There was a rustle and a soft growl from the Gyongxin captives. The Yanjingyi archers and mages went very still, their eyes on the shamans. The archers fingered their crossbows.

"Of course I did. I still defy," the God-King replied, his youthful voice breaking the tension. Everyone watched him. "You are greedy and foolish."

"Stop!" Evvy cried. "Don't make him angry!"

The God-King looked at her. "Don't worry, Evvy. We're having a talk." To Weishu he said, "Shame on you for allowing what was done to her. Shame on you for what you have done to this land. You understand *nothing* about Gyongxe, but you think killing and burning will make it yours." Weishu yanked his leash again, dragging the boy up a step. The God-King continued without stopping. "You will never rule this country. As well ask to rule the desert sands as you grasp them in your fingers. And if you try, your own lands will be deserts in the time of your grandchildren."

"*You* will die horribly, where many of your people can see

it," Weishu said, leaning forward. "That will teach them who rules here."

The God-King chuckled. "*I* don't rule. I only speak for the gods. They will not speak to you."

Briar was so overwhelmed by the boy's courage or folly — he was still trying to decide what it was — that he didn't notice the vibration under his feet until his teeth started to knock together. He glanced at the wall paintings. The people and the creatures in them leaned forward, their eyes fixed on Weishu. The paint actually bowed out from the walls. Most important of all, the large figures — the nagas, the winged lions, the giant spiders, and the huge vultures — were wriggling, as if they meant to peel themselves free.

"Stop it," he mouthed at the walls. Too many guards were ready to kill the prisoners beside them. The paintings stared at him, but they settled down. "I don't understand," Briar said, to distract Weishu and because he really wanted to know. "How did you get here without us knowing?"

The emperor smirked. "For all your intelligence, you thought you couldn't be beaten, is that it? Kings plant traitors in foreign cities like you sow plants abroad. Such traitors may live in a city for decades before their masters call on them. It is then that they drink a certain keep-awake tea so they can open the gates. I would have called on them earlier, but I wanted you five foreigners in Garmashing before I sprang my trap." He smiled. "My mages put the rest of the city to sleep and my traitors let me in."

The ground still trembled. Some of the archers were beginning to notice. Worse, Briar saw movement in the darkness at the top of the hall, on the very high ceiling in the rear. It was strange, disjointed movement.

"Since you are going to kill me," the God-King said, taking a more normal seat on one of the throne's steps, "would you answer a question for me? There are no tricks or mockery in it," he assured Weishu, as if he were the conqueror's elder and Weishu the captive. "It is a straightforward question. I hope you will be able to answer." More than at any time before, Briar thought he did not sound like a boy at all.

"Ask it," Weishu replied, all good humor.

"When you studied this realm before you began your conquest," the God-King asked seriously, "did you wonder why so many religions begin in Gyongxe, and why so many religions have at least one temple here?"

If Briar had not turned his head to look at Rosethorn just then, he might have missed the glint of light on thin, silk-like strands behind the mages and the emperor.

Weishu chuckled. So did a number of his mages.

"Even some Yanjingyi gods have temples here," the God-King went on. "But you don't understand at all, do you?"

"What I understand is that all of these temples will surrender their treasures to me, and I will carry them to my palaces," Weishu replied, still amused. "What do I care if people choose to haul themselves here to knock their heads in your dirt? Temples are places for priests to milk money from worshippers. I am the only god they need to worry about now."

All around him Briar felt Rosethorn working on crossbows, drawing the strength from the wood until it was as dry and brittle as kindling. He quickly helped her, feeling scared. There was something in the air, a feeling like that before a thunder- or sand-storm. Power was building all around them that had nothing to do with the kind of magic he knew. He didn't know what would happen if it got loose.

"I will explain," the God-King was telling the emperor, "though you have said enough that I am fairly certain you will not believe me."

Weishu yanked on the God-King's leash. The metal cracked to pieces and fell on the floor. "People come here to be close to the gods," the boy told the emperor. "Things happen here that happen nowhere else." As the emperor straightened, ready to shout an order, something that looked like a metal snake with a skull for a head slid down the filament over him and dropped to his shoulders. Swiftly it wrapped itself around the emperor's neck.

Rosethorn sighed. "Who let the cave snakes out?" She didn't seem to expect an answer. She also didn't seem surprised.

Guards behind the captives threw the doors open. More Yanjingyi soldiers poured into the throne room, filling the space behind the captives and joining the other soldiers along the walls.

Behind the throne a familiar deep voice boomed, "Try to kill anyone here and your emperor dies."

Hengkai raised his hands. Immediately the filament above him captured them and bound his arms. It whipped like a spinning rope, fashioning a cocoon for him from shoulders to hips. He cursed, furious, then shrieked in terror as giant spiders lowered themselves to the dais on ropes of web, giving every mage who stood there the same treatment. Hengkai croaked something, seemingly the start of a spell, only to have a strand of web fall over his mouth. At last the spiders dropped to the floor behind the imperial mages.

Briar and Rosethorn pulled what life remained from the crossbows and the crossbow bolts of the imperial archers. Already dry and splitting, the weapons broke apart and fell from their holders' grips.

Evvy had not been idle. In the hands of the mages beads made of jade, cinnabar, and quartz split, cutting the strings on which they were hung. The rest of the beads fell to the floor as the spiders bound the mages together in bundles.

Briar looked at the paintings on the walls. "You may as well help," he told them. "You know you've been itching to."

The paintings walked off the walls. The large ones, the gods and goddesses, grabbed those soldiers who ignored Luvo's warning and went for their swords. The painted gods seized the weapons and threw them aside. Unnerved and undone by the sight of a painted, many-armed god or a very tall, red goddess standing over them, the soldiers fell to their knees and pressed their faces against the floor. The little creatures from the borders of the paintings swarmed the soldiers and mages who continued to fight, taking up positions on their ears or faces. Suddenly the humans went quiet, not daring to touch the alien beings perched so close to their eyes or ears. Many of the painted gods bore weapons.

Luvo came forward from the back of the throne room, mounted on the back of a giant peak spider. They climbed the dais until Luvo could step off onto the top. The spider retreated to the foot of the steps and crouched, waiting.

The God-King still sat on the steps by the throne as if this were a normal day in the palace, watching as crossbows and mage beads went to pieces and paintings came to life and battled. Now he stood and bowed to Luvo, the spiders, and the paintings. "I am honored beyond all words by this visit, Great Ones," he said. "I am only sorry that you could not see the capital at its best."

"Do you think you have the upper hand?" Weishu shouted. He had pried the cave snake a couple of inches from his neck so he could speak. "Have you forgotten my army? It will avenge me! Every one of Yanjing's armies will cross your mountains. There will be no Gyongxe when they are done! Those of you who are not Gyongxin, my assassins will hunt you until the end of time! They will kill you, your children, and all you hold —"

By then the cave snake had changed its hold enough to tighten its grip on the emperor's throat again. Briar was close enough to see that its body was in reality all backbone, made of metal and dirt like its skull. He wanted one.

"He has a point." Parahan, Soudamini, and Sayrugo had left their guards to stand with Rosethorn. Briar and Evvy went to join them. "We have the emperor and his mages, but it will do us no good," Parahan continued. "The army is still here. His heirs will want to finish what he began."

Luvo walked closer to the God-King. "Your nearest army has its own problems at this time."

The God-King sat up, eager. "Would you show me?"

The biggest spider of all slid down a flaxen rope to the floor. Everyone stepped back except Evvy, who bowed low and said, "Hello, Diban Kangmo. It's very good to see you again."

The great creature uttered several squeaks and touched Evvy's cheek with the hard edge of one arm. Then she settled back and began to eject fluid from her spinneret. Evvy backed up then, too.

"Who's your friend?" Briar asked Evvy.

"She's Diban Kangmo. I told you about her. She's a peak spider. She and her daughter helped heal me after Luvo brought me into his mountain," Evvy explained. "The peak spiders are the gods of the highest parts of the mountains. I'm not going to look at that," she added, turning away from the pool of spinneret fluid. "I know it's perfectly natural, what they make the webs from and all, but I think that looks nasty."

The milky pool spread over the floor until it was several feet across. Diban Kangmo straightened and stepped away from it. The peak spider that had placed Luvo on the dais now carried him down to the floor and set him at the pool's edge.

As Luvo waited, an image grew in the milky liquid. It was a view of the plain outside the main gate. Briar did his best not to gape. There were creatures out there. Horse-like ones with eagles' heads, thin legs, and metal hooves fought the cavalry, their golden beaks and silvery hooves cutting deadly wounds on horses and riders. Lions that looked, impossibly, as if they were made of ice fought beside snow leopards, cave bears, and nagas, fully fleshed, not painted. Cave snakes shone as they slithered through the ranks of foot soldiers. Peak spiders walked among them, casting webs over several soldiers at a time. Giant vultures attacked from overhead. Whole companies of soldiers were giving the creatures the great bow, their foreheads on the bloody ground.

And it was very bloody, Briar saw. The creatures who fought for Gyongxe could die. The Yanjingyi soldiers were dying, too. The peak spiders had a stinger; it killed. But they were vulnerable to arrows or swords. Many of them lay sprawled in the dirt, their limbs and heads hacked away. The horse-like creatures bled dark blood when they were cut down.

"What are those horse things?" Briar asked, pointing.

"Deep runners," Rosethorn answered, to his surprise. "They live far underground."

"Sometimes my brothers and sisters get bored, and they make things," Luvo said. "Sometimes things make themselves."

There was movement in the pool. A company of soldiers, battered and limping, was struggling away from the field of battle. More turned to follow.

"Cowards!" Weishu shouted. "You will die for this!"

More soldiers saw what was taking place. They abandoned their flags and fled, the strange creatures pursuing them.

"Your army has abandoned you," the God-King said, facing the emperor. "I think that if you want to live, you will have to make some arrangements, don't you? Oh, hello, small one." He reached down and lifted something from his shoe. It was a baby cave snake. The God-King looked at the one around the emperor's neck. "Is this little one yours? I won't hurt it."

Briar could have sworn the skull on the serpent around the imperial throat looked cross. It nodded to the God-King. A moment later small cave snakes were crawling on many of the captive mages. Hengkai in particular was horrified and struggled to get away from the one that was tugging on his mustache. He fell over. Briar was in no way inclined to pick up the general.

"I'd kill him." Souda eyed the emperor with intent. "He's earned it a million times over." She looked over at the mages. "And them."

"But there are so many problems that come from his death," the God-King reminded her. "If you two are to regain your kingdom, you can't worry about imperial assassins, or imperial money going to pay every rebel who ever dreams of raising an army against you."

I will never think of him as a boy again, Briar thought, staring at the God-King. How does he not go mad, with all those gods talking to him and giving him advice? I go crazy with my sisters, or Rosethorn and Evvy, telling me what to do, and none of them are gods.

"I don't believe that." The emperor pointed to the pool, which was vanishing into the cracks between the stone tiles. "Magic. I can buy a thousand illusions like it. Any of these hand wavers could have done the same." His own wave of the hand dismissed the mages bound in spider silk on both sides of him. "I demand to look on the field of battle myself."

The God-King shrugged. "Please yourself. Zochen Brul, would you be so kind?"

That appeared to be the cave snake's name. It unwound from the emperor's neck and slid down the throne to the God-King's side in a clatter.

"I want a guard, as is my due," Weishu said, shaking out his robes as he stood. His eyes glinted with his familiar arrogance.

Briar shook his head with reluctant admiration. It took a great deal to shake Weishu's sense that he was entitled to rule over everything, it seemed. He could never feel that way — his teachers and his girls would never allow it.

"You may have whomever you wish," the God-King said agreeably. Suddenly he looked much less agreeable. "But first, you will order your mage to wake my city. *All* of my city."

"Your monsters hold him," Weishu said, looking down at the cocooned Hengkai. He stared up at his emperor without trying to utter a word past the spider silk that bound his mouth.

"If you would?" the God-King asked the spider that lurked in the shadows behind Hengkai. It reached out a long leg and touched the cocoon. The silk shriveled and fell away from the general. Gingerly Hengkai sat up and looked around himself on the dais. He picked up several beads and held them in one trembling hand.

Parahan turned on the guard closest to him and grabbed his sword from its sheath. The guard didn't try to resist. The big man strode up the steps to the throne and put the tip of the sword to Weishu's throat.

"Call me untrusting, God-King," he said apologetically, without taking his eyes from the emperor, "but in case Hengkai *does* try something, I will take his master's head. He was Weishu's chief general because he can work battle magic very quickly."

"The cave snakes have an eye on Hengkai, Parahan," the God-King assured him. Briar looked at the general. A number of baby cave snakes and two of the larger ones lay at Hengkai's feet, watching him. Perhaps that was why the man trembled so much. Perhaps he was steadfast enough in ordinary battle, but these strange beings were too much for him.

Hengkai handled the beads he'd gathered in a particular order, his lips moving. He passed his free hand over them. That done, he shifted the beads to his free hand and murmured, then passed the other hand over them. Briar felt a pressure on his ears, then a pop.

"Don't you feel better?" the God-King asked Hengkai. "It can't have been easy for you, holding such a vast spell for so long a time."

The general did not answer him. He sank onto the top step by the throne and put his head in his hands.

Weishu did not even ask if he felt unwell. He ducked Parahan's sword and walked down the steps, ignoring the God-King. He brushed past Rosethorn and Sayrugo, pointing to different Yanjingyi soldiers. The others moved out of his way.

"They will leave their weapons here," Sayrugo called as Weishu was about to pass through the open doors.

"Very well," the God-King said. "Weishu, you heard General Sayrugo."

The emperor did not move, but the soldiers he had chosen did. They stripped off their sword belts and even their daggers, leaving them in a heap before they accompanied Weishu out of the throne room. Without discussing it, the God-King, Parahan, Soudamini, Rosethorn, Briar, and Evvy followed.

"Are you coming?" Evvy asked Riverdancer when they passed her.

The shaman shook her head. "I have see too much . . . death," she said haltingly, proving that she spoke a little *tiyon*.

They kept pace with Weishu and his soldiers as they passed

from the God-King's palace onto the wall that encircled the city. From there they followed the wall down, level by level. All the way to the gate they saw that Gyongxe's big and little gods had been fighting here, too. They found Yanjingyi soldiers in smothering bundles of spider silk and others bloated and face-black with poison. More were wounded or hacked apart by sharp edges. On and off Briar looked over the edge of the wall, inside the city and out. Quite a few soldiers had jumped to get away from whatever had attacked them up here.

Weishu pretended to see none of the men and women who had died for him.

At last they came to the main gates and the scene they had viewed in the spinneret pool. No inch of ground on the plain was untouched. The earth was dark from spilled blood. Parts of it moved. The creatures they had seen in the pool — cave snakes, peak spiders, the eagle-headed horses Rosethorn had called "deep runners," nagas, ice lions and lionesses, and mortal snow leopards and cave bears — wandered everywhere, together with huge red, blue, green, and orange many-armed gods. Giant vultures wheeled in the sky together with mortal eagles and ordinary vultures. Some were busy killing those of the enemy who were still alive. The rest were pursuing the fleeing army. And it *was* fleeing.

Any sense of victory Briar felt over Weishu's army vanished. These poor bleaters had no idea of what they might be walking into. They were used to fighting their northern neighbors' armies, horse nomads, and imperial Namorn's trained army in the northwest. The emperor had walked them into a storm of magic and creatures from their nightmares. He wondered if they had even been given a choice about joining the army. Knowing Weishu, probably not.

He glanced at Rosethorn. She was even whiter than usual. Only Evvy looked happy. There was a small, tight smile on her lips. She's entitled, maybe, Briar thought. More than maybe, after what they did to her.

There was no expression on the emperor's face at all.

The God-King had to reach up to put a hand on his enemy's shoulder. "Let's go back inside and talk about a treaty. You won't even think of breaking it when you get back to Yanjing, I know. You can never tell what kind of spies will choose to come back with you."

They turned back toward the palace. Briar chose not to mention the baby cave snake dangling from a silk thread — or a spider thread — on the emperor's robe.

Rosethorn drew a deep breath. "I'm going to get my kit and go down there," she said. "I won't hold it against you if you stay behind."

As if he would let her go alone! Briar looked at Evvy, who was shaking her head. "I'll keep Luvo company," she told them. "There isn't much I could do down there. At least here we can help rebuild."

Rosethorn nodded. She and Briar went in search of their medicines.

GARMASHING, CAPITAL OF GYONGXE

A week later, Riverdancer came to the workroom to tell Rosethorn and Briar that Weishu had left for Yanjing with those healthy soldiers who remained to him. He had needed a cart just for the agreements he had signed with the God-King.

Rosethorn murmured, "Mmhmm." Briar made no sound at all. They had spent most of their time with the Earth temple novices, filling bags with their fast-growing barley. With luck, the Gyongxin farmers might get four short, plentiful harvests before the winter snows.

"Hengkai did not go with him," Riverdancer said through her translator.

That got the attention of the two green mages. They stared at her.

Riverdancer smiled and passed each of them a seed cake.

"Hengkai has entered the temple of the Yanjing goddess Kanzan. He hopes the goddess will forgive him his many killings and keep him safe from cave snakes and peak spiders, he says."

Riverdancer and her translator took stools and nibbled on their own cakes when Rosethorn and Briar relaxed.

"It is too bad, in a way," Riverdancer went on. "If he had gone home to Yanjing, he would have forgotten them, except for some dreams."

Rosethorn looked sharply at her friend. "What?"

The translator nodded. "The gods protect Gyongxe," she said, and translated her words for Riverdancer. The older woman spoke. The translator said, "Surely you have heard no tales about the things you have seen? Nothing about the creatures that showed themselves to you or to the emperor?"

Rosethorn and Briar both nodded. "You're right," said Rosethorn. "Not a word."

"The gods do not want folk from the world over coming to disturb their peace," the shaman said through the translator. "A veil will fall between you and these memories when you leave us. You will remember the humans, but the nagas, the cave snakes, the ice lions?" Riverdancer shook her head. "Only in dreams. They will be rich dreams."

Briar scratched his cheek and heard a rasping noise. He would have to start shaving more often. "I'm surprised the emperor let Hengkai stay."

"The emperor blames his defeat on Hengkai. He took away Hengkai's lands and fortune. He wanted to take Hengkai back to Yanjing a prisoner, but the God-King left him no choice about any of Yanjingyi who wished to remain." Riverdancer smiled. "A number of mages and generals also stayed."

Briar whistled softly. "Weishu won't forgive the God-King any time soon."

"The emperor will have signs to remind him of his fate if he thinks he will take revenge," Riverdancer said, and shrugged. "Maybe he will die of a long illness. I do not think it will be that. Many of his nobles are unhappy with his wars. He will have enough to keep him busy." She tousled Briar's hair. "But you have finished with your seeds, yes? It is time for you three to go home."

"And we'll forget?" Rosethorn asked wistfully.

"You will dream of the nagas, the spiders, the cave snakes," Riverdancer said. "We would be sad indeed if you were to forget those of us among the humans. We will certainly remember you."

TWENTY~FIVE

THE TEMPLE OF THE GODDESS RIVER
KANPOJA PASS

Two weeks later the twins accompanied Rosethorn, Briar, and Evvy to the Kanpoja Pass leading to the Realms of the Sun. Jimut and Luvo came as well. Jimut wanted to pay his respects to the river that was worshipped in Kombanpur as the goddess Kanpoja. Like the twins, who meant to work for the God-King for two more years to earn a nest egg for their coming war against their uncle, Jimut was remaining in Gyongxe.

Luvo had come to say good-bye to Evvy. One of Diban Kangmo's daughters would carry him back to his mountain afterward.

"You're the only thing I'll miss about this place, really," Evvy told him as they watched the river tumble by. It seemed less personal than watching Parahan and Rosethorn. "I mean, I'll miss Parahan and Souda, but they'll be riding all over the country and getting rid of any soldiers left behind. I don't want that. No fighting, no war. I wish I could have stayed with you and learned more."

"I wish you could stay, too," Luvo said. "This traveling is so odd. We mountains never stray. It astounds my kin that I went to Garmashing."

Parahan came over to Evvy and crouched before her. "I owe you everything," he told her quietly. "You know this, don't you?"

Evvy flapped her hand at him, her way of saying, "Forget that."

"I would heap you with jewels were I at home, but here I am only a poor soldier. The God-King hasn't even paid me yet!" Parahan smiled at her. "The gods bless you in your journeying, and give you sweet dreams." He put his palms together before his face and bowed. Evvy hugged him fiercely. She would never get another chance.

When they let each other go, Souda was waiting. She, too, bowed to Evvy, her hands pressed together before her face. "Thank you for helping my brother to escape the emperor," she told Evvy. She looked at Briar, who had come over with Jimut. "Briar, my thanks to you both. If our prayers count for anything, you will reach your home in health and safety."

Rosethorn led her horse over to them. The peak spider followed her.

"Please count my prayers, too," Jimut added. He had splashed river water over his face and head for what seemed like the dozenth time since they had reached the pass. "Because of you I have seen the place where the beautiful river crosses into the Realms of the Sun!" He looked at Parahan and Souda, then grinned at Briar and Evvy. "Don't worry. I will take good care of them."

"Then we should all go," Rosethorn said, swinging into the saddle. Evvy and Briar did the same. "We have a long journey ahead. Emelan is almost half a world away. Luvo, your spider friend is ready to take you home."

Luvo had been rocking back and forth on his stubby feet as everyone talked. Now he turned to the peak spider. "I thank you, but no," he said with his usual courtesy. "You do not need to return me to Kangri Skad Po."

"I beg your pardon?" Rosethorn asked.

Luvo made a humming sound full of rises and falls. The spider crouched low to the ground, then rose to the top of its toes. Luvo hummed louder and deeper, then turned toward Rosethorn. "If you will permit, Rosethorn, I wish to journey to this Emelan with you." He turned his head knob toward the mountains. "No, my brothers and sisters!" His voice thundered against the rocky heights all around them. Everyone covered her or his ears. "That *you* have never gone forth does not mean I should not do it! My mountain is fine! Its waters and plants and creatures will do nicely without me, and I will wander where I choose!"

By the time he had finished, all of those near him but Evvy had moved away and were using their forearms to put as much flesh as they could between their ears and his thundering voice as it echoed in the pass. Evvy was crying. "You don't have to do this," she told the creature who had made her feel safe in those ugly hours after she fled her torturers. "You don't have to leave your only home."

Luvo turned his head knob up to her. "I have seen how your education goes, Evumeimei," he said quietly. "It is well enough, but I can teach you other things. And I do not wish to sleep eternity away. I wish to see more. You and Briar and Rosethorn, and your friends, among you I have felt more awake than I have felt since the first humans came to Gyongxe. I wish to stay awake with you."

"Well, if that's settled, we still need to go." Rosethorn opened a bag on one of the horses and pulled out some of the scarves the God-King had given them. "Will you ride a packhorse or with Evvy?"

"I will ride with Evumeimei for a time," Luvo said.

Rosethorn and Briar quickly wound scarves around Evvy and Luvo until the living stone was tucked and secure in front of the girl.

Jimut handed Evvy the reins. "Give my greetings to the river goddess when you reach Kombanpur," he told Briar. They clasped hands.

"I will," Briar said. He bowed to Parahan and Souda and rode to Rosethorn, taking the lead rein for their string of pack-horses from her.

Evvy waved as the twins and Jimut turned to gallop back to the main road to Garmashing. She waited until they were out of her view before she leaned over and spat on the earth of Gyongxe. "Pass that on to Yanjing, if you'd be so good," she whispered to the gods of the realm. "I know at least a couple of you are listening." She looked ahead. "C'mon, Luvo. Any place that gave us Briar and Rosethorn has to be interesting."

"I look forward to it," the heart of the mountain said.

"I look forward to going *home*," Briar said. "Home! My sisters, and Lark, and a city where winter means rain and wool clothes, not furs!"

"Our garden," Rosethorn added. "Winding Circle temple. The *sea*."

"I have not been near the sea in a long time," Luvo said. "It must have changed very much."

"You will have to tell us," Briar replied. "And the Kanpoja River will take us there."

They set off at a trot, the road clear ahead of them.

The Calendar of Months
for the Circle Universe

January ~ Wolf Moon

February ~ Storm Moon

March ~ Carp Moon

April ~ Seed Moon

May ~ Goose Moon

June ~ Rose Moon

July ~ Mead Moon

August ~ Wort Moon

September ~ Barley Moon

October ~ Blood Moon

November ~ Snow Moon

December ~ Hearth Moon

GLOSSARY

abatis(es) ~ branch(es) or X-shaped log structure(s) set in ditches with sharpened point facing outward; an obstacle

Alion ~ province where Winter Palace is located

bag(s) ~ Briar's slang, moneybag(s)

baita ~ home-away-from-home, a Yanjingyi temple in a foreign land

Banpuri ~ language of Kombanpur and its neighbors

bleat-brain ~ Imperial slang for someone stupid

caravansary ~ an inn with a large courtyard that provides accommodation for caravans

cave snake ~ a creation of the mountains from human bone in the beginning: a skull with a body that is all vertebrae; they now breed on their own

Chammur ~ Evvy's most recent home in eastern Sotat

Chammuri ~ dialect of Chammur

chetu ~ toad spit in *tiyon*

company ~ (of soldiers) 100 fighters

cuirass ~ piece of armor that protects the chest and back

damohi ~ homosexual in Trader-talk

deep runner ~ a creation of the mountains, horse-like, with an eagle's head, golden beak, thin legs, and metal hooves

Drimbakangs ~ tallest mountains in the world

Lho ~ longer arm of Drimbakang mountains south of Gyongxe

Sharlog ~ arm of Drimbakang mountains in southeast of Gyongxe

Zugu ~ "finger" of Drimbakang mountains, reaching from Lho around Garmashing

emchi ~ mage in Gyongxin

flank ~ the right or left side of a military formation

fluorite ~ a transparent crystal that comes in many colors, in this case clear, dark green, and purple

frog ~ braid loop-and-knot fastening

Garmashing ~ capital of Gyongxe

get ~ child

gilav ~ head of Trader caravan

greaves ~ leg armor worn below each knee

halberd ~ long spear with a broad blade that can be used to chop as well as stab

Hanjian ~ port city on Storm Dragons Ocean, southeastern Yanjing

Heibei ~ Yanjingyi god of luck

Imperial ~ language common to the countries around the Pebbled Sea, all part of the Kurchal empire before its fall; home language for Briar and Rosethorn

infantry ~ foot soldiers

Inxia ~ kingdom to immediate north of Yanjing

Kajura ~ nation to south and west of Kombanpur

Kanzan ~ Yanjingyi goddess of healing

kaq ~ Trader-talk slang, someone useless, non-Trader; an obscene term

knap ~ to chip stone with sharp blows, as when shaping flint or obsidian to form an edge

Kombanpur ~ Parahan's home in the Realms of the Sun, to the south and west of Gyongxe and Yanjing

Lailan ~ Chammuran goddess of water, mercy, and healing

Lakik ~ Briar's trickster god

La Ni Ma ~ southern Gyongxe sun goddess

    Ganas Rigyal Po, Snow King (southeast husband)

    Ganas Gazig Rigyal Po, Snow Leopard King (west)

    Kangri Skad Po, Talking Snow Mountain King (middle)

lathe ~ the arch or bow part of a crossbow

Long ~ present ruling dynasty of Yanjing, also Yanjingyi term for dragon

lugshai ~ craftspeople, Trader-talk

mage ~ someone who has received formal training in the use of magic at a school or through a succession of teachers who are trained by schools

midday ~ lunch

Mila ~ Living Circle goddess of the earth and growing things

mimander ~ Trader mage

Mohun ~ Chammuran god of silence, stone, dark and secret places

momo ~ Gyongxin dumpling with various stuffings

nanshur ~ mage in *tiyon*

neb ~ Briar's slang for "nose"

Ningzhou ~ language of Yanjingyi imperial court

numia ~ Banpuri for "little sister"

pahan ~ Chammuri for "teacher," "mage"

palanquin ~ covered and enclosed platform chair with cushions, set on rods front and back, used to carry people

pipa ~ four-stringed musical instrument; strings are plucked with a plectrum, or pick

prebu ~ Banpuri for "master/mage"

puissant ~ powerful, mighty

Qayan ~ kingdom to north of Yanjing

qi ~ (kee) Yanjingyi court dialect for power, magic

qus ~ Zhanzhi (Evvy's birth dialect) for "maggots"

Raiya ~ Kombanpur goddess of mercy and kindness

Realms of the Sun ~ lands, including Kombanpur, south and west of the Drimbakang mountains

regular(s) ~ regular army, professionally trained soldiers, not recent volunteers or those recently drafted to fight

semjen ~ Gyongxin for "animals"

sep(s) ~ Banpuri for "louse (lice)"

Shaihun ~ Chammuran god of desert, winds, sandstorms, serious mischief and destruction

shakkan ~ miniature tree formed like an elongated S pointing to the right of viewer

shaman ~ someone from a tribal society who is a medium between the real world and the spirit world and who also does magic; in the tribes between eastern Sotat and Yanjing, shamans practice magic in groups, often by dancing

Storm Dragons Ocean ~ ocean to the east of Yanjing

takamer ~ Chammuri, rich person

tiyon ~ common language spoken between eastern Laenpa to the Storm Dragons Ocean, and from the Sea of Grass to the southern Realms of the Sun

waigar ~ foreigner in *tiyon*

Yithung ~ kingdom to far northeast of Yanjing

yujinon ~ rotters, lowlifes, incompetents (Chammuri)

zadan ~ bomb

zayao ~ explosive powder

zernamus(es) ~ Chamurri slang: tick-like parasite

Zhanzhi ~ Evvy's home province

Zhanzhou ~ language of Evvy's home province

ACKNOWLEDGMENTS

Thanks to my Scholastic editors Anamika Bhatnagar, who got things rolling, and Kate Egan, who saw it through, and the wonderful Scholastic gang, including the Boss, David Levithan, and Emily Seife, our concertmistress.

Thanks and sorrow to Judy Gerjuoy, who did research on historical China, including menus, for me, and couldn't stick around to read the end result.

To the Sunday night Bollywood gang: Bruce, Kathy, Cynthia, Tim, Craig, Catherine, Julie, and Cara, because of the characters and actors and just plain relaxing fun.

To Bruce Coville, my writing partner, whose patience, good humor, and excellent advice helped keep the story on track and contributed some strong reality testing, and to Bruce and Kathy for admitting me to vacations at the lake, which soothe my brain.

To Cara Coville, Julie Holderman, Tim the Spouse-Creature Liebe, and the fans on my "Dare to Be Stupid" Live Journal, for bailing me out when I get stuck and remembering what I have forgotten. To Andy Samuel, who makes sure I can find things in my office.

And to Tim, who still puts up with me. It's thirty-one years in August, and you haven't come to your senses yet.

Tamora Pierce
March 12, 2013

ABOUT THE AUTHOR

TAMORA PIERCE is the critically acclaimed author of nearly thirty novels, including the Circle of Magic and The Circle Opens quartets; *The Will of the Empress*; *Melting Stones*; and, most recently, the *New York Times* bestselling Beka Cooper trilogy.

In 2013, she was honored with the Margaret A. Edwards Award for her significant and lasting contribution to young adult literature. She lives in Syracuse, New York, with her husband, Tim, her rescued cats, and two parakeets.

Visit her online at www.tamorapierce.com.

Circle of Magic #1: Sandry's Book
Circle of Magic #2: Tris's Book
Circle of Magic #3: Daja's Book
Circle of Magic #4: Briar's Book

The Circle Opens #1: Magic Steps
The Circle Opens #2: Street Magic
The Circle Opens #3: Cold Fire
The Circle Opens #4: Shatterglass

The Will of the Empress

Melting Stones

this is teen

Want the latest updates on YA books and authors, plus the chance to win great books every month?

Join the conversation with This Is Teen!

Visit thisisteen.com to find out how to reach us using your favorite form of social media!

TEEN2